THE SIDEKICKS INITIATIVE

BARRY J. HUTCHISON

Zertex Media Ltd

For Steve Ditko

ALSO BY BARRY J. HUTCHISON

CHAPTER ONE

ALL THOSE WATCHING on television saw the exact moment when Grunk, Warrior King of the Morruks, realized he had made a mistake.

It was not the moment when he first clawed his way out of the wide crack he'd made in a downtown Cityopolis street, leading his small but terrifying army of hard-shelled under-dwellers in an assault on the overworld.

It was not when he laughed off the bullets of the lone police officer who had the misfortune of being first on the scene, or when he ripped the poor cop's arms off and blud-geoned him unconscious with the elbows.

It was not even when the streak of red spandex came rocketing toward him along the canyon of tower blocks, blue cape fluttering in its wake. Although, those looking closely enough might have spotted a flicker of concern playing briefly across the monster's craggy features at this point.

But no.

The moment that Grunk, Warrior King of the Morruks truly realized quite how grave a miscalculation he had made came three-thousandths of a second after that, when a man with the power to push the moon out of orbit kicked him squarely in the balls.

Doc Mighty, defender of the innocent, champion of justice, sworn protector of Cityopolis had arrived. And the crowd, as usual, went wild.

To say he lapped up the adoration would be unfair. He acknowledged it with grace, brevity, and a smile so dazzling it was practically a superpower all of its own, and then he got on with the business of being a hero.

Moments before, the frightened citizens had been fleeing in panic. Now, they stood their ground, watching and cheering, safe in the knowledge that their champion would protect them.

Many of them laughed and pointed at Grunk, Warrior King of the Morruks, who was now several hundred feet in the air and still rising, his mighty slab-like hands clutching his groin. None of the onlookers had Doc Mighty's enhanced hearing, so only he could pick up Grunk's high-pitched whimpers drifting down on the breeze.

The Morruks had all danced this dance before, and very likely knew that the next few moments held pain, humiliation, and not a whole lot else. To their credit, they performed their parts with gusto, several of them charging at Doc Mighty with their armored shells fully deployed, while a few more moved to grab themselves some hostages.

Considering they were all lumbering foot soldiers from a race of underground savages, Doc Mighty appeared almost impressed by this tactical decision. The Morruks were usually villains of the 'Let's all just rush him at once, lads!' variety, so it was refreshing to see them branching out into something less obvious.

Unfortunately for the would-be hostage-takers, by the time they reached their targets, every single one of them had been carried to safety by a streak of red and blue.

The safety in question was a rooftop café several blocks away, where they had been deposited at a table with a pitcher of ice-cold drinks and a note that read: 'This one's on me, citizens. Doc."

That done, he returned to the scene, whisked the fallen cop off to the nearest hospital, tucked him in, brought him some ice water, then rushed back.

The Morruks, who had never been particularly gifted when it came to improvisation, spent the second and a half that Doc Mighty was away sort of standing around in confusion, wondering what they should do.

Luckily, the decision was taken out of their hands upon Mighty's return, when he flew through them like a bowling ball through pins. Or, more accurately, like a *rocket-powered* bowling ball through soft-boiled eggs.

A shocked silence fell over the crowd as several intact Morruks went up... and then several dozen distinct and separate Morruk parts came back down again.

For a moment, the whole of Cityopolis seemed to hold its breath as Doc Mighty alighted amidst the carnage, his cape billowing behind him.

Raising an eyebrow, Mighty regarded the twitching Morruk parts, before giving a satisfied nod. He turned to the silent crowd, a smile tugging at the corner of his mouth.

"Steeeee-rike!" he announced.

There was a scream from behind him as Grunk, Warrior King of the Morruks, smashed into the street like a meteorite.

And with that, the crowd went wild. They whooped and clapped and stamped their feet in approval. The Morruks would pull themselves back together, they knew—they always did. But that didn't matter. The good citizens of Cityopolis were safe. They were *always* safe. Doc Mighty had come from the stars, but he had chosen Cityopolis as his home, and the forces of evil were powerless against him.

In moments, the chant rose up—"Migh*ty*! Migh*ty*! Migh*ty*!"—and the usual scramble of reporters rushed to snatch up any pearls of wisdom that might tumble from the hero's perfect mouth.

"Look out for one another," had been a favorite of late, although he'd also been experimenting with a humble half-smile and a sincere, "Just doing my job."

If they were lucky, they might hear one of his rare warnings to any supervillains watching from their evil lairs, reminding them that Cityopolis was not only under his protection, but the protection of the entire Justice Platoon, and that evildoers should think twice before trying any of their shenanigans in the future.

And yes, he often used the word 'shenanigans,' and not even in an ironic way.

"Doc Mighty! Jodie Malone, Cityopolis News Online," announced a woman in a lime-green suit that she somehow managed to successfully carry off.

Mighty nodded politely and smiled down at her. "I know who you are, Ms. Malone. I'm a fan of your work."

"Thank you, Doc. And I can safely say we're all big fans of yours," the reporter replied, eliciting more cheering from the crowd. "Do you have anything to say to the people at home?"

Doc Mighty, defender of Cityopolis—and the world—smiled sincerely straight down the lens of the camera. "Stay in school, kids," he announced. "And don't do drugs."

≽

Sam Summers flicked his eyes to the wall-mounted TV for only the second or third time since the footage of Doc Mighty's latest city rescue had started to roll.

"Stay in school? Jesus. He's gone back to using that?" Sam muttered. "What is this, the nineties?"

He lowered his gaze to his own screen and resumed typing as the report cut back to the studio. A superimposed box in the top right corner of the TV continued to show the hero repairing the cracks in the street by melting the edges together with his Plasma Vision.

Sam's colleagues—nine of them in all, six of whose names he didn't know—had jumped up from their desks when the report had first started, gawped and cheered as Mighty's heroics played out, and now hurriedly returned to their terminals before Dirk came out of his office and caught them slacking off.

The guys were generally approving of Mighty's performance, discussing it like they might discuss a big football game, suggesting strategies they themselves might have employed had they found themselves in the same situation, and if they'd somehow become the single most powerful entity on the face of the Earth.

The women were more breathless about it all, two of them practically giddy with excitement. Only Stella, the oldest of the team, was critical of Mighty's performance. Not as critical as she'd been of Sam's own performance in the storeroom during the office party a few months back, mind you. He'd had to explain he was still emotionally fragile after the divorce, that he'd had too much to drink, and that, honestly, this had never happened to him before.

After he'd burst into hot, embarrassed tears and projectile vomited down her partially exposed back, they'd both agreed never to speak of it again and, as far as Sam knew, Stella had never uttered a word about it to anyone. Probably for her own sake, as much as his.

"I mean, it was OK," she said, taking her seat two desks along from Sam. She was beside Romesh, whose name Sam had made a point of learning in case not knowing it would one day make him look like a big racist. "I'm not saying there was anything wrong with it, exactly..."

"He saved us from mollusks," said one of the guys who'd made most of the football comparisons Sam hadn't really understood.

"Morruks," Sam corrected, not looking up.

"No, I know he did, and I'm grateful for it, don't get me wrong," said Stella. "Just... where's the *pizazz*, you know?"

One of the other guys whose name Sam didn't recall snorted. He was the youngest of the team, vegan, and cycled everywhere on a folding bike made of bamboo. Sam had felt a near-overwhelming urge to dislike him immediately but had decided to give him the benefit of the doubt.

Which turned out to be the wrong call. He was a dick, there were no two ways about it. Sam suspected he hadn't learned the guy's name almost as a sort of protest against his very existence.

"*Pizazz?*" the unnamed co-worked sneered.

Stella blinked very slowly and deliberately in the guy's direction. "Yes. *Pizazz*. It's a real word, not like your stupid LOLs and Twitterers and *Fo Shizzle*s, or whatever it is you lot say."

"Jesus, how old *are* you?"

Sam flicked his eyes to Stella for a moment, trying to figure out the answer to this question himself. It had kept him wondering for a while now. She'd mentioned kids a couple of times, but in a way that suggested they'd all flown the nest. Forty-five, maybe? Fifty-five? He'd never been good with ages.

Sixty-five? Christ, he hoped not.

"Old enough to give you a clip around the ear," Stella said. "I'd just have liked some more whooshing about. I like it when he whooshes about."

There was a general murmuring of agreement that suggested everyone liked it when Doc Mighty whooshed about.

The conversation clattered to a halt, and everyone got back to typing as the door to the manager's office opened and Dirk emerged. He clutched his *World's Best Boss* mug like it was a cherished and hard-earned award, rather than something he'd bought for himself in a thrift store back when he'd first been promoted.

Dirk had the appearance and demeanor of a boxer a decade past his prime. He was mostly solid, but with a paunch around his belly and some drooping under his jaw. He didn't have a Roman nose so much as a roaming one. It meandered crookedly down his pock-marked face, bent out of shape from a punishing history of hooks and jabs.

Stopping at the end of the row of desks, Dirk pushed out an ear. One of the lower buttons of his shirt had come undone, revealing a diamond of hairy stomach. The stench of his cheap cologne wafted along the row of desks like a creeping fog of cedarwood-scented testosterone.

Dirk closed his eyes and let his head tilt from side to side as if detecting music in the rhythm of everyone's typing. "That's what I like to hear," he said, sniffing deeply. "Everyone hard at work, being productive. Definitely not all gathering around the TV to watch Doc Mighty do his thing on company time. No, sir."

He slurped from his mug and smacked his lips together —*Aaah*. One hundred fingers and thumbs continued to type.

"Good though, wasn't it?" he said, jabbing a thumb in the direction of the TV screen. "You know what I like about him? About Mighty?"

He cast his gaze along the long row of desks, like a teacher deciding which student to pick on today. "Kara?"

Sam followed Dirk's gaze and made a mental note as to

which one Kara was. He was a little dismayed to discover she was the young-ish black woman he'd been calling 'Carol' for the past four months.

"Huh?" said Kara. "I mean... sorry?"

"Do you know what I like about Doc Mighty?" Dirk asked again, speaking slowly as if addressing a child.

"Uh, no. I don't know," she admitted, looking around at her colleagues for help, but finding none forthcoming. "His cape?"

"His...? No, not his cape. Jesus, Kara, do I look like a child?"

Kara gave a nervous chuckle.

Dirk waited.

"Oh, was that an actual...? No. You don't look like a child."

Dirk puffed himself out a little, before continuing. "I like that he's not afraid to take the cheap shots. All the power in the world and he has no qualms about just kicking a guy in the nuts. Just right in Peter Enis and the plums. You gotta respect that. Right, Sammy?"

Sam missed a digit on his keypad and had to backspace to correct it. He thought about correcting Dirk, too, pointing out that he always went by 'Sam,' and never 'Sammy,' but they'd had that conversation four or five times now without anything productive ever coming of it, so he chose to save the energy.

"I guess so," he said, not taking his eyes off the screen.

"Boom!" Dirk proclaimed. Nobody really knew why. "Sammy gets it. Sammy totally gets it." He mimed kicking someone in slow-motion. Presumably in the balls, although it was hard to tell without knowing the height and position of the imaginary recipient.

That done, Dirk took another slurp from his *World's Best*

Boss Mug, told everyone to, "Carry on," then about-turned in the direction of his office.

He clicked his fingers. All along the row, everyone bristled and held their breath.

"Oh! One other thing," he said, turning back. "Stella, I need you to come in tomorrow."

Nine people, including Sam, exhaled with relief. Their fingers continued to *clack* across their keys.

"I can't," said Stella. "My grandson's in a play."

Sam let out an involuntary squeak. *Grandson?!* Jesus.

"What's that got to do with anything?" Dirk asked. "No one's making you go."

"But I want to go," Stella told him.

This proved a difficult concept for Dirk to get his head around. "You *want* to go?"

"Yes."

"To a kids' play?"

"He's hardly a kid. He's twenty-three."

Twenty-three?! Sam grimaced behind his screen and felt his cheeks flush red.

"And yes, I want to go."

"Well, you can't. Sorry. I need you," Dirk told her.

Sam glanced along the row and saw the defeat on Stella's face. He groaned inwardly, knowing he should keep his head down, but also painfully aware he wasn't going to.

"You can't just order her to come in," he piped up.

All around the island of desks, the sound of typing faltered. Dirk's shoes *creaked* as he turned in Sam's direction.

"What was that?"

"No. It's just... Regulations. You know, like employment law? She doesn't have to... I mean, you know? If she doesn't want to," Sam said, his chest tightening with every word. He licked his lips, which were suddenly very dry. "That's all I was saying."

"Oh, that was *all you were saying*, was it?" asked Dirk. He clicked his tongue against the back of his teeth a few times. "Right. I see. Well here's all I'm saying—that big contract came through. The one you and I spoke about? We need someone to do the old..." He mimed typing with one hand. "So, if Stella can't do it, then fine. You can do it, right?"

"What contract? We didn't... I mean, I don't remember..." Sam shook his head, more as an admonishment to himself than as a refusal. "I can't. I have my son tomorrow. It's my weekend."

Dirk's mug froze halfway to his lips. "Sammy. It's the big contract."

"No, I know, it's just... It's my weekend."

"We spoke about it."

Sam didn't think they had spoken about it, in fact, but he didn't really want to go there.

"If it was any other weekend..." he said. He fished in his jacket pocket and pulled out a bright blue soft toy. "I got him this. It's his favorite color."

"What the fuck is that thing?" Dirk asked.

Sam regarded the soft toy. "It's... I think it's a hippo."

"Looks more like an elephant. Maybe an anteater," said Stella, peering at it over the rim of her glasses.

"Isn't it that keyboard player from *Return of the Jedi*?" asked one of the guys whose name Sam didn't know. "From Jabba's palace?"

"I don't give a shit what it is," Dirk snapped.

Sam lowered the toy. "Oh. It's just... you did ask."

"Jesus, Sammy, we spoke about this contract," Dirk insisted. "First you tell me Stella can't do it, and now you're giving me this shit with the elephant, or whatever it is."

"Hippo," Sam said.

"*Or whatever it* is," Dirk reiterated. "You've got me over a barrel here. What do you want me to do?"

Sam slipped the plushie back into his pocket. "It's just... It's my weekend."

Dirk sighed and shot Sam a look that was perfectly balanced on the knife edge between disappointment and contempt. "Fine. Fine. Kara can do it. But you owe her one."

"Wait, what?" asked Kara, looking up from her terminal.

"He'll work your next two weekends for you," Dirk said, pointing to Sam. He shrugged. "Best I can do."

Sam squirmed in his seat. "Next two? How is that...? I don't see how..."

Kara glared along the row at him, then tutted. "Fine."

"Attagirl," said Dirk, winking at her over the rim of his mug.

"Hold on a minute," Sam croaked.

"Say 'thank you' to Kara," Dirk told him.

"What? But I didn't..."

"Jesus, Sammy, is it so hard to just say 'thanks' to your fucking colleague?" He held up a hand in apology. "I mean, pardon my language, I just happen to think that manners matter."

Sam felt everyone else watching him over their screens. He wasn't quite sure how the conversation had taken him to this point and was struggling to see a route back. "No, I mean... *thanks*, Carol, obviously. *Kara*. I meant Kara. Sorry. It's just, I don't really see why it should be down to me to..."

His voice trailed away into an awkward silence under the weight of all those gazes. He cleared his throat and shuffled in his chair again. He could use the overtime, anyway.

Yeah, that's what he'd tell himself.

"No, it's fine. Of course. No problem."

"Good boy, Sammy," said Dirk. He clapped him on the shoulder with one of the fleshy slabs he called hands. "Glad we got all that sorted."

Dirk was halfway to his office when he clicked his fingers

again. There was more bristling and holding of breath, but the others all relaxed when Dirk fixed his gaze on Sam once more.

"But you can give me an extra hour tonight, yeah?"

"Well, I'm supposed to be at the house to pick up my..." He felt the wind go out of his sails. "One hour?"

"One hour. That's all," Dirk promised. He brought his mug to his lips. "Ish."

CHAPTER TWO

"You're two hours late."

Sam conceded the point with a spell of awkward nodding. "Yes. I know. It was a work thing. I tried to call."

Laura, his ex-wife, uncrossed her arms long enough to check her phone screen. "You didn't."

"I called the landline," Sam said.

"We don't have a landline."

Sam blinked. "You don't? Since when?"

"Since Brian pointed out we don't use it," Laura said.

Sam glanced past her into the apartment. "Right. Brian. He's really... He's really making the changes, isn't he?"

"We both are," Laura said. There was a lot of meaning in those three words, Sam knew. He just couldn't quite figure out what it was.

"So, uh, has he had dinner?"

Laura frowned. "Who, Brian?"

"No, Corey."

"Oh. Yes, he was hungry, so we had to make him something."

Sam shuffled on the spot. "Right. Just, I'd kind of promised we'd get a Five Guys."

Laura shrugged. "What do you want me to say, Sam? You're two hours late. He was hungry. We had to make him something. And anyway, we don't like those places. You know that."

He flinched but hid it with a half-hearted smile. There was that word again. She'd used it a lot recently. 'We.' *We* had to make him something. *We* don't like those places. It was as if her new boyfriend hadn't just moved into the apartment, but had somehow bonded with her to such an extent they now formed a single entity.

"We had our first date at one of 'those places,'" Sam reminded her.

"Yeah, and look how that worked out," Laura replied. "We'd just rather keep him off the junk food."

"Was that Brian's idea?"

"Don't be a dick about this, Sam."

Sam sighed and held up his hands in surrender. "OK. OK, that's fair, I guess. I'm sorry."

Laura crossed her arms again. "Thank you," she said, a little sarcastically. Before Sam could say anything more, she half-turned into the apartment. "Core? Your dad's here!" She lowered her voice before adding, "At last."

Sam heard his son's giggle and the day's worries melted away. The heart-swelling sense of euphoria was short-lived, though. It crashed to a halt when Brian appeared in the hallway behind Laura, the giggling Corey dangling upside-down over one of his impressively broad shoulders.

"Hey, you guys seen Core around here anywhere?" Brian asked, turning to look in all directions.

"I'm here! I'm right here!" Corey laughed, his arms flailing as Brian spun in search of the voice.

"Who said that?" Brian demanded. "Corey? Is that you, pal? Where are you?"

"I'm right here!" Corey wheezed, barely able to speak for laughing.

Sam cleared his throat. "So, uh, anyway. We should get going. There's a bus in..." He checked his watch. "...soon. If we move quickly we can catch it."

Brian stopped spinning, and Corey's giggling gradually faded.

"You're right, Sam. Sorry, just messing around," said Brian. "Hold on..." He flipped Corey over his shoulder and deposited him on the ground. "*There* you are!"

"I was there the whole time!" Corey laughed.

Brian jabbed a thumb at his shoulder. "Seriously? The whole time? Babe, did you see him up there?"

"Nope, I did not," Laura smiled.

"Sam?" asked Brian. "How about you?"

"Ahaha. No. Didn't see you, buddy," Sam said, tousling his son's hair.

"Hey, Dad!" Corey chirped. "Look."

He pushed up a lip and pointed to a spot where a tooth had been. "See it?"

"Awesome! It came out," Sam said. "Did you bring it so we can put it under your pillow for the Tooth Fairy?"

"It fell out on Tuesday," said Laura. "Tooth Fairy's been and gone."

"Oh." Sam blinked as he processed this. "Well, we should really get going," he said at last. "The bus."

"I'll go get my bag!" Corey said, darting past Laura and Brian and disappearing into his bedroom.

The three adults stood in uncomfortable silence, waiting for him to return. Sam tried not to notice Brian's hand on Laura's back or the way she leaned her weight into it.

Corey was taking longer than expected, and the sheer density of the silence was starting to feel smothering. Sam rifled through his brain, trying to find something to talk about. Just some amusing little detail about his day he could share to break the tension and, ideally, make him look interesting.

Just one. That was all.

Just one interesting thing.

Just *one*.

...

...

Fuck.

"So, uh, either of you see the game?" he asked.

Laura frowned. Without him even being able to see this, Brian's expression mirrored hers with remarkable accuracy. Maybe they really were becoming the same person.

"What game?" Laura asked.

Sam's shirt stuck to the sweaty pool of his lower back. His lips moved silently, trying to formulate a response that felt just out of reach.

"You know, the..." He gestured vaguely, then leaned into the doorway a little and called past them. "You nearly ready there, buddy? Don't want to miss the bus!"

To Sam's relief—and probably everyone else's, too—Corey emerged from his room, an Oscar the Grouch backpack slung over his shoulders.

"There he is!" Sam announced. "You all ready, sport?"

"Nearly!"

Corey hugged his mom. Sam found himself glancing away when the boy hugged Brian, too.

"See you Sunday, honey," Laura told him. "Be good."

"I will, mom," Corey promised. "I'm always good."

Brian emitted a loud *bzzzzzt* noise that made Sam jump.

"BS Alert! BS Alert!"

Laura nudged him playfully with her elbow and he stopped.

"I mean, *suuuure* you are. Totally," Brian said. He winked and tapped the side of his nose, which set Corey off giggling again.

Pulling his backpack higher on his shoulders, Corey stepped out into the corridor and took his dad's hand. Sam felt the sticky warmth of the boy's much smaller palm against his own, and suddenly everything was alright.

"Ready, Dad," said Corey, showing off the gap in his teeth again.

"OK, then." Sam smiled down at him. "Let's go have some fun!"

Sam hurried through the rain, head down, jacket held open to shelter the boy at his side. They'd made it to the bus stop in the nick of time, but there had been a lot of gang colors sitting in the back, and Sam had decided not to risk it.

The next bus was a forty minute wait, unless they took a crisscrossed network of other routes that Sam could never remember the numbers of.

The tube was out of the question. *At best* it was a panic attack waiting to happen. At worst, it was...

Actually, he didn't want to think about the worst that could happen in the underground system.

The elevated train that ran through and around the city wasn't much better. It was a little safer, sure, with an onboard AI that could lock down individual carriages and summon the police when necessary. But it was also more expensive, and Sam wasn't sure the trade-off was worth it, even if the artificially intelligent seats did politely thank you for sitting on them.

He'd tried to make a game out of them walking the eight blocks to Sam's apartment, but the rain and the growing darkness had turned it into a feat of endurance.

"Dad, I'm cold," Corey said, shouting to be heard over the roaring of the city traffic, and the thundering of the El Train on the tracks overhead. "Can't we get a cab?"

"The cabs are all busy, buddy," Sam lied. The truth was, if he wanted the lights to stay on that month, a cab was out of the question. He'd had to budget tightly to afford the Five Guys visit, and while that had been canceled for tonight, he was planning on surprising Corey with it tomorrow.

"What about that one? That has its light on," said Corey, pointing ahead to where a yellow taxi was prowling for business.

"Which one?" asked Sam.

"There!"

Sam stared blankly in the direction his son had pointed, pretending to only spot the cab when it was too late to flag it down.

"Ack! Sorry. Good spot, though," Sam said. "It's not far now."

Corey groaned. "Is there at least an umbrella store?"

Sam smiled at that. "Maybe!" he said, pulling the boy closer to him and weaving them both through a throng of pedestrians coming in the opposite direction. "You keep a look-out for one, OK?"

"OK, Dad!"

They trudged on for a while longer, through puddles and pools of light that seeped from the windows and open doors of the late-night stores, bars, and restaurants that lined the street.

"We should've asked Brian to drive us. He has a car," Corey said.

"Does he?"

"It's awesome. It's red," Corey gushed. "He chose it because red's my favorite color."

Sam frowned down at him. "I thought blue was your favorite color?"

"It used to be, but now it's red," Corey explained, with a grave sincerity that suggested this change of opinion had required a significant amount of thought and introspection.

"Well, that's good to know," Sam said, feeling the weight of the bright blue cuddly hippo in his jacket pocket. "I'll keep it in mind."

Corey stopped so suddenly Sam almost tripped over him.

"What? What's wrong?" Sam asked, his eyes darting around for danger.

Corey stood sniffing the air, a wistful look on his face. "Mmm. Hot dogs."

Sam searched around again, this time looking less for danger and more for sausage-shaped pork products. The smell came wafting out of a convenience store that appeared to be *just* on the right side of skanky not to be closed down for public health violations.

"You want one?" Sam asked.

The torment was written all over Corey's face as he reluctantly shook his head. "Brian says I shouldn't eat that stuff. He says it's all eyeballs and asunes."

Sam's lips moved as he figured this out. "Do you mean anuses?"

"Oh. Yeah. Eyeballs and anuses. That's it," Corey said. He gazed up at Sam with wide-eyed sincerity. "So, I probably shouldn't, should I?"

Sam hesitated, but only for a moment. "Brian isn't here," he pointed out. "And anyway, I'm your dad, so I outrank him. You want a hot dog? Let's get a hot dog."

"Al*right!*" Corey whooped, and Sam felt like he was walking on clouds as he led the boy into the store.

Inside was pretty much what he'd expected. Two surly-looking clerks stood behind a long counter that was laden with candy, pre-packaged cakes, and other junk food. The hot dogs were shriveling under heat lamps, displayed behind glass like some weird alien specimens.

The rest of the store was the usual mix of overpriced groceries and slushy machines, with everything worth stealing —cigarettes, alcohol, and anything even remotely resembling medication—kept in a locked cage behind the counter.

A couple of dead-eyed customers shuffled along the narrow aisles, their faces washed out by the stark fluorescent light strips on the uneven ceiling.

"Can I help you?" groaned an overweight white woman behind the counter, clearly grudging every word. Her nostrils were flared like someone had taken a dump on her top lip and her nose was doing its best to get away.

"Uh, yeah. We'd like a hot dog, please," Sam said.

The woman's over-plucked eyebrows raised briefly in surprise and horror, then she shrugged and reached for a bag of buns. "Just one?"

"Aren't you going to have one, Dad?" asked Sam.

Sam thought of the contents of his wallet and the looming Five Guys bill.

Mind you, they *had* saved on bus fare...

"Sure. Make that *two* hot dogs," he told the woman.

The clerk's eyes went all the way wide this time. "Oh, shit!"

"Is that a problem?" asked Sam.

"Open the register and put the money in the bag," barked a voice from behind him. The world ground into slow-motion when Sam heard the unmistakable *clack* of a bullet entering a chamber.

"Oh no. Oh God, no," he whispered, pulling Corey in tight against him.

"Dad?"

"You listening to me? Open the register or I will shoot you in your fat fucking face!"

"It's OK, Corey, it's OK," Sam assured the boy, not daring to turn. He shuffled them sideways until a hissed command from the robber stopped him.

"You! Don't move. Stay right where you are while this tubby bitch gets me my money."

Sam raised one hand while keeping the other around Corey's shaking shoulders. Neither of the clerks had made a move to open their registers yet. Idiots.

"Just do what he says," Sam pleaded. "Just give him the money."

"What was that, man?" the robber demanded. He caught Sam by the shoulder and turned him. Sam caught a glimpse of gang colors and wide, frantic eyes before diverting his attention fully to the gun that was now pointed at his face. "You getting all up in my business?"

"N-no," Sam said. "I was just... I was trying to help."

"I look like I need your help?"

"No. No, you don't. Sorry. I'm sorry," Sam said.

"Maybe I'll blow your brains out. Maybe that'll make Tons o' Fun here move her lardy ass," the gunman sneered. He couldn't be much older than seventeen, Sam thought. The gun trembled in his hand through fear, or adrenaline, or whatever new designer drug was doing the rounds.

"Please, I just wanted to buy my son a hot dog," Sam said.

"From this place?" the gunman sneered. "You're the worst father in the world. You know what goes into those things?"

He kept the gun on Sam, but twisted his head to the clerks. "I don't hear those fucking registers opening! You want me to shoot this guy?"

Sam felt a hollow void opening in his chest as the gun swung down to point at Corey.

"You want me to kill this little kid?"

"Jesus, Clarice, open the register," the second clerk said. "You've got the code."

"Dad!" Corey whimpered.

"Stop it! Stop pointing that gun at my son!" said Sam, the words ejecting from him as a series of throaty sobs.

"I'm not *fat*, OK?" said the doughy-faced woman behind the counter. "It's genetic."

"I don't give a shit! Open the register!"

"Point it at me!" Sam pleaded. "At me, not at him."

The gunman eyeballed him, his voice like cold gravel. "I'll point it where I fucking choose to point it," he warned, bringing the muzzle closer to Corey's forehead.

"Cops are on the way," said Clarice. "You should run."

The gunman's face twisted into a snarl. "You hit the alarm? Aw, you dumb... You got five seconds to empty the money into the bag, or I kill this kid, then I kill his dad, then I kill everyone else in this shithole store. Five."

"Please! No, please!" Sam whimpered.

"Daddy?"

"Four."

Behind the counter, Clarice rolled her eyes. "Fine."

"Three. Better hurry the fuck up, Lady Godzilla."

There were a series of bleeps as Clarice keyed in a code. The register remained resolutely shut.

"Oh shit," she groaned.

"Two!"

"Open the register! Give him the money!" Sam yelped.

"Once the alarm's been tripped, the registers go on lockdown," Clarice explained. "I can't!"

"Bullshit. *One!*"

Sam heard Corey cry. It cut through all other sound, silencing the world. He felt it, then, something he hadn't felt in years. Something he'd kept locked up deep down. A slithering, like snakes moving through his brain. His dirty secret.

"Leave my son alone!"

"Zero!"

The robber's finger tightened on the trigger. The weapon squished wetly, then slipped from his grip. It landed on the floor with a *splurt*, the gray metal now a yellow semi-solid on the dirty floor.

For a while, everyone stared at it, nobody saying anything. The sunshine-colored sludge was still vaguely gun-shaped, although around half of it had spattered across the scuffed lino when it had hit.

It was Clarice who eventually broke the silence. "Dude, was your gun made of butter?"

The robber raised his eyes from the firearm-turned-dairy product, his expression alternating between amazement and terror. Stepping back, he raised a finger to his ear.

"He's active," he whispered, and then the doors flew open, the front window smashed, and a SWAT team was suddenly swarming up the aisles.

Sam sobbed with relief, pulling Corey in close. "It's OK, Core. It's OK. It's over. Nobody's going to hurt us. We're safe. We're OK."

He stared defiantly at the robber, wanting to see the moment the bastard was brought to justice. To Sam's surprise, the man stepped aside, making room for a couple of the SWAT guys to sweep past him, their guns trained on Sam.

"Down on the floor! Hands where we can see them!"

Sam frowned. "Huh? No, it wasn't... I'm not..."

"Down, down, down!" roared one of the SWAT guys, so aggressively that Sam instinctively dropped to one knee.

"Daddy? What's happening?" Corey squeaked.

"It's OK, Core. It's just a misunderstanding. That's all.

These are the good guys. They're here to help us, OK? They just made a mistake. There's nothing to worry..."

And then something sharp stabbed into the side of Sam's neck. He felt a rush of cold fire fill his throat and flood his brain, and then the floor came up to meet him, and the fluorescent glow of the store became an inky well of darkness.

And the only sound was the frantic screaming of his five-year-old son growing steadily fainter and more distant.

CHAPTER THREE

EIGHTY-ONE HOURS EARLIER...

Absorbo had never been one of the team's big hitters. Not really. Sure, he could take one hell of a beating, and then return it with interest in the form of kinetic energy blasts, but he'd never been up there with the greats.

That didn't matter now. Nothing mattered now. Not his reputation, not his pride, not even his life.

Especially not that last one.

The station's integrity was holding, but the screeching alarms and the groans from the Durium hull told him this wouldn't be the case for long. It was supposed to be the strongest metal in the multiverse—essentially unbreakable—and the bulkheads had been constructed from it in the Hellfire forges of Lady Demonstrous herself.

And yet, the station was on the brink of collapsing. The unbreachable walls were about to give way, and no amount of absorption ability would save him from the cold yawning chasm of space.

Absorbo ran. There was nothing else for it. He barreled through the station's labyrinth of corridors, past smoke-spewing engine rooms and armories containing some of the most powerful weapons in existence.

He didn't bother to collect any. There were no guns or blades or energy whips that could save him now. There was nothing that could stop what was about to happen. All he could hope for was to get out a warning. To send a message to the unsuspecting world below. Apologize for failing them. Urge them to hold their loved ones close while they waited for their horrible, inevitable end.

His breath came in heavy, heaving gasps. Prior to a full rebranding by a very persuasive PR company, he'd been known as 'The Chunk,' and considered one of North America's lesser heroes.

He'd shaved off some weight since the makeover—a couple of hundred pounds or so—but he was still so far away from athletic he wasn't even in the same hemisphere. He'd never been able to run very fast or very far, but the devil was chomping at his heels now, and no force on Earth or off it was going to stop him reaching the communications station.

With the sirens screaming and the indestructible walls collapsing behind him, Absorbo, last survivor of a once-great alien race, ran for his life, and for the lives of the seven billion people far, far below.

CHAPTER FOUR

SAM JERKED AWAKE. The sudden movement made him roll sideways off the narrow bed he found himself lying on. He tried to throw his hands out to break his fall, but they were cuffed behind him. For the second time in recent memory, his face hit the floor.

With some difficulty, he twisted himself into a vaguely upright position, his legs spread out in front of him, his back propped up against the sturdy steel bed frame. A single metal door stood across from where he sat, surrounded on both sides by whitewashed walls made of heavy cinder blocks.

"Hello?" he called. The effort of it made his head spin, although the falling onto his face thing probably had some part to play in that, too. "Is anyone there?"

A sudden thought cut through the fuzziness. "Where's my son? Where's Corey?"

"Your son is fine," a voice told him, hissing faintly with speaker static. It was a man's voice. New York accent. Brooklyn-ish, Sam thought, although this was a complete guess based on nothing whatsoever, as he'd never been to New York in his life.

"He's with his mother and step-father," the man assured him.

"They're not married," Sam caught himself saying. He admonished himself with a tut and a scowl. "I mean... How do I know you're telling the truth?"

"She told me to say, 'We're not happy about the hot dogs,'" the voice continued. It was followed by a series of light crunches, like the person speaking was eating something. Sure enough, when he continued, his voice was a little muffled by whatever he had crammed in there. "Asked me to really stress the 'we.' That mean anything?"

Sam nodded slowly. "Eyeballs and anuses," he muttered.

"Excuse me?"

"Yes. No. I mean... I believe you," Sam said. He looked around the cell and spotted a small black device, not much larger than a pen, fixed into a corner near the ceiling. A camera, he assumed. He shot it a pleading look. "You've got the wrong guy. There's been a mistake."

More crunching. More chewing.

"There's no mistake, Sam."

Sam stiffened. "How do you know my name?" he whispered.

"Well, it was on your driver's license for one thing."

Sam relaxed. "Oh. Yeah. That makes sense."

"Also, we've been tracking you for the past twenty years."

It took a moment for what the man had said to fully register.

"Wait, what?"

"We know all there is to know about you, Sam. Everything. Hell, we know things even you don't know."

"What are you talking about?" Sam asked. A hazy memory of every TV cop show he'd ever seen wafted into his head. "I want a lawyer. And a phone call. I want to phone my lawyer."

The voice laughed. "Sorry, pal. This isn't that kind of place," it said.

Sam tried to stand, using the bed to support himself, but his legs and arms were heavy. So heavy. And the door was so far away, and getting further by the second.

"Night night, Sam," the walls whispered. "See you on the other side."

⸎

Sam blinked.

Technically, he winked, as both eyes moved independently, closing and opening again in sequence rather than both at the same time, but he was in no condition to split hairs.

"Huh?"

His voice caught him off guard. He jumped a little in his plastic chair and craned his neck to see who had spoken. When he saw no one, he blinked sequentially again, frowned for several seconds at a spot on the wall that appeared to be identical to all the others, then nodded a little drunkenly.

He could, if he tried hard enough, remember entering the room through the single door on the otherwise featureless wall. He had been carried by those things. You know the ones.

He clicked his fingers a few times, searching for the right word.

"Legs," he said aloud.

This took him by surprise, and he began the process of searching for whoever had spoken again, once more to no avail.

The blinking thing was bothering him. It should probably, given the circumstances, have been near the bottom of his list of priorities, but the way his eyes were refusing to fall into step annoyed him greatly. He muttered uncomplimentary things about them and then spent a good three or four minutes forcing them to behave themselves.

By the time he'd broken them in, the lightheaded drunkenness had become a heavy-handed throbbing pain at the base of his skull. In hindsight, he preferred the first one.

Now that he was starting to think more clearly, he was able to take in his surroundings in a bit more detail. Or, he would have been, were his surroundings not utterly lacking in any sort of detail whatsoever.

The room he was in was stark and clinical, with walls that were mostly featureless, a ceiling devoid of anything interesting, and a floor that was utterly nondescript in every possible way. He was sitting at a round table just large enough for the four chairs positioned around it, three of which were empty. The chairs and table were all made of the same firm but flexible plastic, like whoever was supposed to be sitting in them was a suicide risk who couldn't be trusted with anything hard or sharp.

In fact, the whole room had that sort of 'institutional' feel about it. It was a room designed to be as unstimulating and unthreatening as possible which, of course, only served to make it all the more so.

Sam's seat was positioned so his back was to the room's only door. He dimly recalled shuffling toward one of the other chairs, but someone had quite forcibly directed him to this one. A man, he thought. Maybe a woman. He closed his eyes and tried to concentrate, but only saw arms and legs and a general surliness, which didn't help narrow those choices down any.

He didn't like having his back to the door, but didn't feel comfortable with just changing seats at this stage. Evidently, he was supposed to be sitting here for a reason, and until he knew more, it probably wasn't wise to go messing around with the seating plan.

Turning his chair to give him a better view of the door proved to be impossible, as the plastic legs were affixed to the floor by hard plastic rivets. He probably could've broken them off if he'd put his back into it, but that felt like even more of a liberty than swapping seats would have been, so he settled for twisting his body around and shooting anxious glances in the door's direction every few seconds.

"Hello?" he said, after a few silent and breathless false starts. His voice sounded reedy and thin. He cleared his throat, mentally gave himself a good talking to, and tried again. "Hello? Is anyone there?"

Silence.

Apparently, there wasn't.

"Great."

Sam looked around the room a few more times, searching for a camera, but finding none. In a way, the idea that nobody was watching made him more nervous than the thought that somebody was.

It was then that he realized his hands were no longer cuffed. There were red welts around his wrists from where they had been, but he was no longer shackled and was now free to do whatever he liked.

He chose to sit quietly and wait.

Sam was still wearing his work clothes—cheap white shirt, nylon blue tie, and pants that charged up with static electricity whenever his thighs rubbed together. Which was whenever he walked any distance greater than six feet or climbed more than two steps in a row.

The clothes were crumpled and creased now, suggesting he'd slept in them. He wasn't normally the type to loosen his tie or undo his top button, but given the circumstances, he decided to do both. It made him feel less relaxed, rather than more, and so he tightened them both back up again.

He watched the door. No one was coming. As far as he could tell, no one was watching. Even if they were, what right did they have to hold him like this, anyway? He'd done nothing wrong.

Sam winced a little at that. No, not 'wrong' exactly, but he *had* done something, hadn't he? Something he hadn't done in more than two decades.

But still, that didn't give anyone the right to lock him up. He hadn't had his phone call. He was supposed to get a phone call. Everyone knew that.

He had a good mind to complain. There had to be someone in charge he could talk to, probably right outside that door. Well, he'd go out and talk to them. He'd go out there and let them know that Sam Summers wasn't the type of guy who would just let himself be pushed around. No siree.

Sam stood up.

"Sit down," commanded a voice from nowhere.

Sam sat down.

"Hello?" he said.

The voice that had spoken had been the same one he'd heard back in the cell, he thought, although it was hard to be sure, what with the shortness of the sentence, the different acoustics, and the impending panic attack Sam was currently hovering on the brink of.

The voice didn't answer. Instead, the door opened, and Sam yelped in fright as he spun toward it, almost bending the legs of his plastic chair.

A red-haired woman in a green dress trudged in, clutching her head with one hand while carrying a single high-heeled red shoe in the other. She had a general air of dishevelment about her, from the creases and, if Sam was not mistaken, vomit stain on her dress, to the way her hair appeared to have been styled with some sort of whisk implement.

"Shit," she spat, blinking in the room's fluorescent glare. She battered the shoe a few times roughly in the area where someone might reasonably expect a light switch to be positioned.

She gave up after six good *thwacks*, groaned in annoyance, then spotted Sam for the first time. For a while, she just scowled at him, although she'd been scowling already, so he didn't think it was anything personal. He gave her a smile and a little wave, but didn't stand up in case the nameless voice shouted at him to sit down again.

"Who are you?" she asked. Quite accusingly, he thought, as if she had already decided that she wouldn't like the answer.

"Uh, I'm—"

"Where are we? Are we in jail?" she asked, squinting around at the room. She glared at him again, her anger growing. "Did you do this? Was this you? Where the fuck are we? Who are you, exactly?"

Sam shook his head. "What? No. No, it wasn't... I don't know where this is. I'm—"

She flopped down into the chair across from him and groaned with something that was either satisfaction or the exact opposite. "You sure?" she demanded.

Sam hesitated. "Am I sure of what?"

"That you didn't do this. That you didn't spike my drink and take me back here to your creepy evil lair so you could have your way with me?"

There was something about the way she said 'have your way with me' that suggested she wasn't being completely serious. To avoid any confusion or risk of future legal proceedings, though, Sam answered with complete sincerity.

"No! No, definitely not. I mean, I wouldn't."

"You wouldn't what?" the woman asked, narrowing her eyes and leaning closer. She reeked of alcohol, perfume, and just the faintest whiff of vomit.

"Drug you and have sex with you," Sam blurted.

Her eyes narrowed further. "Why not?"

This caught Sam off guard. "Well, because it's wrong. It's... you know. It's..."

"It's what?"

Sam lowered his voice to a conspiratorial whisper. "Rape."

The woman's scowl deepened. She stared at him for several long seconds.

"Jesus," she muttered. "That's one heavy first conversation to have with someone you've just met. I mean... rape? Wow. Where do you go from there? The Rwandan genocide?"

"What? No!" Sam replied. "Anyway, you were the one who started talking about... You know? And I don't think there was a Rwandan genocide."

"You sure about that?" the woman asked, fixing him with a look so utterly and unshakably confident that Sam had to admit that no, he wasn't.

There was something about the woman that set his nerves on high alert. She seemed wild and unpredictable—two things he wasn't—but there was something else, too. A familiarity, almost. A sense that he knew this woman, and that it wasn't wise to be this close.

"You smoke?" she asked.

Sam shook his head. "No. Sorry."

"You're sorry you don't smoke?"

"No, I mean I'm sorry I don't have any cigarettes to give you."

"Who says I wanted a cigarette?" she asked.

"I just thought..."

"Did you just touch my leg?"

Sam looked down at the table as if he'd find the answer written there. "No."

"Who are you, anyway?" the woman demanded. She held her shoe up like a weapon, heel pointing vaguely in Sam's direction. "Did you do this? Did you bring me here?"

Sam was starting to feel like they were stuck in some sort of loop. "No, I didn't bring you here. I didn't even bring myself here. I don't know where we are. My name's..."

The shoe banged down on the table, making Sam jump. He tried to push backward but only succeeded in temporarily bending the plastic legs of his chair. They made a rubbery *boing* sound as they pushed him forward again.

"Holy shit! Wait a minute! I know you!" the woman said, and as her eyes widened in wonder, he recognized her, too.

Oh God. Oh God, no.

She made two circles with both forefingers and thumbs, then pressed the joins together until they made a sideways figure-eight shape. She raised them up in front of Sam's face, positioning them so that when she squinted, they looked like they were covering his eyes.

The sharp, sudden intake of breath she gave seemed to cut through her half-drunk hangover. Sam jumped to his feet, the worry about what the voice might say now a secondary consideration to what this woman was about to.

"You're—"

"Sam. Sam Summers," he said, thrusting his hand toward her. He smiled. Desperately. Hopefully. Pleading with his eyes. "Call me Sam. *Just* Sam. Please."

She studied his face, her mouth hanging open. He nodded encouragingly at his hand, his forced smile tightening into a grimace of fear.

"Uh, Anna," she said, taking his hand and shaking it. His skin prickled a little at her touch, and any doubt that might remain about her identity evaporated. "Anna Allen."

She pulled him toward her a little and lowered her voice to a whisper. "What the hell is this about?"

"I don't know," Sam mouthed, then he extracted his hand from hers and waited until he was sitting down again before subtly rubbing his palm on his thigh in an attempt to quiet the itch.

Now that he'd recognized her, he wondered why it had taken him so long. For the most part, she looked exactly like she used to. Same red hair, same withering expression, same sprinkling of freckles across her nose that she'd always had.

She was a little taller and not as painfully skinny as she used to be. Not fat by any means, just not as wiry and elf-like as before.

And she was older too, of course. Twenty years, give or take.

"Are they watching?" she whispered, holding his gaze.

"Is who watching?"

"Them. They. Whoever," Anna said, barely moving her lips. Sam felt her nudge his foot under the table. "Is *someone* watching?"

Sam nodded.

"Shit." She picked up her shoe and hefted it from hand to hand. "Can you still do your thing?"

Sam's voice came out as a squeak of terror. "What? No! I can't."

"Can't or won't?" she asked.

"Both!"

She tossed him the shoe. "Then take this."

Sam caught the shoe and clutched it in his non-itchy hand. "Thanks," he said. Then, after some consideration: "What am I supposed to do with it?"

"Hit people," Anna said. She mimed battering someone over the head with the shoe. "Like that."

"OK," said Sam. He looked down at the shiny red material and the pointy heel, then back to Anna. "Who?"

"Next person that walks through that door," she said. "You club them, and I'll do my thing."

Sam's eyebrows raised in surprise. "You can still do your thing?"

"Yeah, I can do my thing. I assumed we could all still do our thing." She glared at him and lowered her voice further. "You sure you can't do *your* thing? Because your thing would be pretty handy right about now."

"I can't do my thing," said Sam. "I don't have a thing. I lost my thing."

A smirk tugged at the corner of Anna's mouth. "So many jokes, but now isn't the time. Let's put a pin in them and revisit it at a later date."

She shrugged. "Fine. Then shoe it is," she said, standing. "You whack, I'll—"

"That won't be necessary," said a voice from over on the left. Or the right, depending whose point of view you were going by. It was the same voice Sam had heard earlier, only this time it was different. This time, it was coming to them live from within the room.

They both turned—Anna left, Sam right—to find what looked to be a shaved Yeti leaning against the wall, his arms folded across his superhumanly broad chest. He was dressed for a funeral—Sam hoped it wasn't going to be his—and wore a pair of mirrored sunglasses that reflected the table and its two occupants.

Sam regarded the behemoth for a moment, easily six and a half feet tall while slouching against the wall.

He considered the weight of the shoe in his hand.

Slowly, and very deliberately, he slid it back across the table to Anna.

"Yeah," she said with a resigned little shrug. "I guess I

can't really argue with your decision-making process on that one."

The gorilla in the dinner jacket fished a handful of pistachio nuts from his pocket and tossed a few into his mouth, shell included. He crunched for a while, rubbed his slab of a hand across a head of silver stubble, then nodded in Sam and Anna's direction. It was a testament to the size of his skull that he was able to indicate both of them with the same nodding gesture.

"I'm guessing you have questions," he said. "No doubt you're wondering why I brought the three of you here."

"You're damn right, buster," Anna slurred, wagging a finger. Sam wasn't sure if she'd relapsed into drunkenness again, or if this was an act for the big guy's benefit. "I've been arrested on... Well, let's just say 'several occasions' and I've never been..."

The rest of the sentence stumbled into silence as the second part of what the behemoth had said sunk in. Sam beat her to the question.

"Wait. What do you mean the *three* of us?"

"Aha!" cried a voice from under the table. It was followed immediately by the sudden *thump* of something hitting the underside. This, in turn, was followed by a muttered, "Fuck," and a slower, more deliberate series of movements as a bearded man in a red satin cape and flying goggles clambered out.

He sprang to his feet with a flurry of arm movements and karate chops that almost saw him throttle himself with his cape.

Once he'd successfully untangled the cape from around his neck, he placed both hands on his hips and puffed out his scrawny chest, showing off the symmetrical symbol printed on his shabby-looking t-shirt.

Sam and Anna's jaws dropped open. For a moment,

neither of them knew quite what to say. It was Anna who eventually made the call.

"Ho. Lee. Shit."

Sam swallowed. "Funny," he croaked, looking the newcomer up and down. "That's exactly what I was about to say."

CHAPTER FIVE

"Well, well, well," said the man in the cape, ejecting the words as a raspy, menacing, Batman-like snarl. "We meet again, we three harbingers of *justice!*"

"What's wrong with your voice?" asked Sam.

"More importantly," said Anna, indicating with a look that Sam should shut up. She tapped the table. "Were you under there the whole time?"

"Like a shadow," the man in the ill-fitting cape growled. "No. Like a *shadow* of a shadow."

"He didn't always sound like that, did he?" Sam asked. "I mean, I can barely understand what he's saying."

"No, wait. Like the *dream* of a shadow of a shadow. Lurking silently, undetected by—"

"You kept touching my leg," said Anna. "That was you, wasn't it? I thought it was him being a sleaze, but it was you."

"I guess we'll never know," the man replied, holding one edge of his cape in front of his face so only the lenses of his goggles and the top of his leather flying hat were visible.

He yelped in surprise when Anna caught him by the neck, twisted his arm, then slammed him face-first onto the table.

"OK, OK, it was me! It was me!"

"Let him go," said the behemoth in the suit.

Anna gave another twist, eliciting a strangled sob of pain before she released her grip. The goggle-guy jumped up, brushed himself down, then shot her a pitying look.

"You know I let you do that, don't you?" he growled. With a nod, he indicated the shaved Yeti. "Chuck there begged me not to hurt you two. Which is real lucky for you, Red."

"Don't call me 'Red,'" Anna told him.

Ignoring her, he continued: "But I'm going to say this, and I'm only going to say it once..."

"Then can you say it more clearly?" asked Sam. He pointed to an ear. "It's just... I'm having trouble with the voice. I'm really having to concentrate to make out what you're saying."

Goggle-guy squared up to Anna and jabbed a finger right up in her face. "Touch me again and you're opening a doorway to a whole world of pain and—"

His head *whanged* off the table with enough force to dent the plastic. Anna released him immediately and stepped back, raising her hands in a deeply sarcastic gesture of surrender.

"Sorry, that was an accident."

"Argh! My face!"

"I was just making a downward motion with my hands, and he got in the way."

"You broke my whole face!"

"Nobody broke nothing," said the man named Chuck. He pushed his sunglasses up onto his forehead, revealing two piercing blue eyes and a look of mild exasperation. "If you want that state of affairs to continue, I suggest you all sit down."

Goggle-guy dabbed his cape under his nose, checking for blood, then ejected another series of guttural snarls. "I don't sit. I lurk. Like the night itself. Like a half-forgotten nightmare of a dark void in the heart of a..." He struggled a bit while he grasped for the end of the simile. "...forest," was the best he could come up with, and even he looked a little disappointed by it. "We've discussed this, Chuck. Come on!"

"Yeah, well, today you sit," Chuck told him, in a tone that suggested there was no further discussion to be had on the subject. "You can lurk on your own time."

Holding Chuck's gaze, the man in the cape slowly lowered himself into the third chair. Anna slumped down into hers again, then crossed her arms over her chest in something not unlike a sulk.

"What's this all about?" asked Sam. "Are we under arrest? Because I haven't done anything."

"Come on. You know why you're here," Chuck replied.

Sam shook his head. "No," he said, although this was only half true. He didn't know specifically why they were here, but he'd been living in fear of this day for his entire adult life. "I was in a store, there was a robbery..."

"Yeah. That was us," said Chuck.

Sam looked blankly back at him. "Sorry?"

"The robbery. The hold-up. That was us."

Sam's blank expression tipped over into confusion. "What was you?"

Chuck tutted. "The hold-up. The gunman. He was one of ours."

"The gunman?" said Sam. "What do you mean?"

Across the table, Anna sighed. "Jesus. I wasn't there and even I follow what he's saying."

"It's not hard," growled the guy with the cape. "It's pretty self-explanatory."

Sam shook his head. "Jesus. You just went full Christian Bale there. I got, like, three words."

He turned his attention back to Chuck. "So, you're saying the gunman was one of your guys?"

"Bingo. You got it," said Chuck.

"But he pointed a gun at my son!" Sam said, his voice rising an octave. "At *my son!*"

"You have a kid?" said Anna. "Wow. Didn't think you had it in you."

"He didn't," said goggle-guy. "That's not how babies work. It's the mom who has it in—"

"It wasn't loaded," said Chuck, interrupting. "Well, no, obviously it was loaded, but he wasn't going to shoot him. We just wanted to see if you were still active. It seemed like the easiest way."

"The *easiest way?!*" Sam spluttered. "You pointed a gun at my son, then tackled me to the ground! How was that the easiest way?"

Chuck's eyes were glassy and cold. "Would you have preferred we'd done it the hard way?" he asked.

Sam's expression revealed that he almost certainly would not have.

"No? Then shut the hell up," Chuck told him.

Sam moved petulantly in his seat. "You could've just asked," he muttered.

Anna peered at Sam through her tangled fringe. "You're active? I thought you said you couldn't do your thing?"

"I can't. Not really," Sam insisted.

"Bullshit. He can do his thing," Chuck said.

Sam sighed, exasperated. "OK. Yes. Fine. But I can't control my thing."

"I can control *my* thing just fine," said goggle-guy. He glanced between Sam and Anna, then shrugged. "Just saying. Also, I'm not referring to my penis. Because it may have sounded like it. That would've been inappropriate."

Chuck squeezed the bridge of his ample nose, muttered something below his breath, then straightened up and began to pace. "For the benefit of the recording, let's make some introductions."

"What recording?" asked Anna, looking around them. "Are you filming this? You need our permission to film us."

"I don't need your permission to do shit," Chuck retorted. He eyeballed her for a while, trying to force her to look away. Instead, she uncrossed her arms, gave him the finger, then crossed them again.

Chuck cleared his throat. "Anna Allen, aged thirty-five, formerly known as Allergy Girl. Ex-sidekick to Memetzo, Mandroid Master of the Mystic Arts and co-founder of the Justice Platoon."

Goggle-guy reacted with a growl of surprise. "What? You co-founded the Justice Platoon?"

"No, Memetzo co-founded the Justice Platoon," Anna said.

"Are you sure that's what he's saying? I think he meant you."

"I didn't mean her. I meant Memetzo," said Chuck.

"Oh. It's just, the way you phrased it..."

"Shut the hell up, Randy," Chuck told him.

Sam frowned. "Randy?" he said. "Huh. I just realized I never knew your real name."

"Randy Rabble, age unknown," continued Chuck. "Formerly known as Butterfly Kid, now going by the name..." He sighed, almost imperceptibly, "... Butterfly King."

"*The* Butterfly King," Randy corrected, before reconsidering. "No. Wait. Just Butterfly King."

"Ex-sidekick to Su Man Chu, Bolderface, and the Great Gassby."

Anna snorted. "Who's the Great Gassby? Aside from the recipient of the Worst Name in Human History award?"

"He's the third goddam greatest hero I've ever had the

honor to fight alongside," Randy snarled. "Fourth, if I count myself. Chuck, can I count myself?"

"I don't give a shit," Chuck told him.

"I'll count myself. He's the fourth goddam greatest hero I've ever had the honor of fighting alongside. Sworn guardian of north-west Minnesota. Really underrated. And he picked *me* to be his right-hand man. The guy who had his back!"

Randy rocked back in his chair, his chest swelling with pride.

"And where is he now?" Anna asked.

"He's dead," said Chuck.

"Stabbed in the back, ironically," Randy added.

"How do you stab someone ironically?" asked Sam.

Randy shook his head. "No, I mean... given what I just said about me having his back, it was ironic that he was stabbed in it."

"Six hundred times," Chuck added.

"Jesus," said Anna.

"Then set on fire," Randy concluded. He stared wistfully off into the middle distance and shook his head. "Damn shame. A real loss to the hero community."

Chuck clicked his tongue against the roof of his mouth. "Aaanyway. That brings us to you," he said, turning to Sam.

"It's fine. You don't have to do me. Please."

"Sam Summers, age thirty-four," said Chuck, ignoring Sam's protests. "Formerly known as Kid Random, sworn sidekick of Doc Mighty, Earth's greatest hero."

"Come on, he's no Bolderface..." Randy muttered.

Sam shook his head. "No, that's... You've made a mistake. I don't know what you're talking about."

Anna rolled her eyes. "Dude, seriously? The game's up. He knows who we are."

She stood up and threw Chuck a suspicious look.

"Which is more than we can say for you, 'Chuck,'" she said. "Exactly who are you?"

"I was just getting to that," Chuck told her.

Anna deflated a little. "Oh. Well... good."

She sat down again and coughed quietly.

"Continue."

"They call me Chuck. Nothing else, just Chuck," he explained.

"Like Cher," said Randy. "Or Madonna."

"Yes, thank you."

"Or Adele."

"Exactly."

"Or Prince."

Chuck remained tight-lipped for a few moments until he was sure Randy had finished.

"I head up a... let's call it a *project* for the United States government," he continued. "We call it the Sidekicks Initiative. And you three, God help us, are the stars of the show."

"The Sidekicks Initiative?" said Sam. He looked around at the others. "What's that?"

"It's a contingency plan. It's one of those *just in case* strategies we put in place in the hope we'd never have to use it."

Anna uncrossed her arms. "And yet, here we are."

"And yet, here you are," said Chuck. "I know you guys have been out of the business for awhile..."

"I'm not out of the business," Randy pointed out. "I live the business. I *am* the business."

Chuck tried very hard to pretend he hadn't been annoyed by this latest interruption, but the slight flaring of his nostrils gave him away. "I know *most* of you guys are out of the business, but times have changed. Circumstances beyond our control mean we've got no choice but to pull you back in."

Sam leaned forward. "Wait, what? No. How? What? You're not serious?" he babbled. "In? Like... *in* in?"

"Like all the way in," Chuck confirmed.

Sam let out a shrill giggle of panic. "No. That's not... That's ridiculous. I have a job. A life. A family."

"Your kid comes to stay with you a couple of nights a month. Let's not oversell it," said Chuck.

"That's still a family!" Sam insisted. "It's still my life."

Chuck cracked his neck. He looked to a spot on the wall as if seeking confirmation from someone hidden there. If he was, then he got what he was looking for.

"We've found ourselves in a situation," he said. "A grave one."

"Sorry to hear that. Honestly," said Sam. "But I'm sure the Justice Platoon can deal with it. You said it yourself—Doc Mighty, greatest hero on Earth. Give him a call, tell him what's what, he'll have you fixed up by lunchtime."

He frowned as a thought occurred. "Actually, what time even is it? Is it still Friday?"

"It's the same time it always is," Randy growled, slamming a fist down on the tabletop. "Time for *justice*."

He looked at his watch.

"And also just after ten-thirty."

"Friday night?" asked Anna.

Randy studied the watch again. "I don't know. It doesn't tell me that. That's not how watches work."

"Yeah, I'm pretty sure some of them do," Anna pointed out.

"Saturday morning," said Chuck. "You slept through the night."

"Not me. I never sleep," Randy growled.

Anna flicked her gaze his way. "Jesus. Is that healthy?"

"It increases my risk of certain cancers," Randy admitted. "But that's a small price to pay for crushing injustice."

"Whatever," said Sam, leaning forward to physically cut off their conversation. "The point is, whatever your situation,

Doc Mighty, or Su Man Chu, or Brown Thunder, or one of those guys will be able to help you. We don't have to get involved. I'm *not* getting involved."

He stood, nodding to Anna and Randy as he extracted himself from between the chair and table. "Uh, nice to see you both again. Let's do it again sometime. But, like, a long way off in the future. Like, *waaaay* down the line," he said. "If you'll excuse me, I'm going to head back to reality and try to salvage the rest of the weekend with my son."

Chuck watched him head for the door. "Sam," he said, but he made no move to block his path.

"Seriously, it's been great, but I'm leaving now," Sam insisted, his heart buzzing in his chest as he hurried for the exit. "Good luck with everything. If you could just let me out..."

Chuck shrugged. "It isn't locked," he said, making no attempt to hide his disappointment.

"Great!" said Sam. "That's... unexpected, but great."

There was a bar across the door like the handle of a fire escape. He pushed down on it and the door swung open.

A howling vortex of ice and snow raged against him, soaking his shirt, freezing his eyebrows, and turning his nipples diamond-hard. The force of the wind shoved him back into the room, but not before he caught a glimpse of a brooding purple sky filled with ribbons of rippling green light.

Sam staggered backward, his whole body vibrating from the sudden cold. His lungs burned. The lids of one eye had frozen together. He was suddenly filled with a desperate, near-overwhelming urge to urinate.

"What the hell is...? Where are we?" he managed to wheeze between body-wracking shudders.

Chuck leaned outside and pulled the door over. The howling wind was suddenly silenced, although the floor around the doorway remained carpeted with fluffy white flakes of snow.

"We're somewhere north of the Arctic Circle," Chuck explained, dusting some snowflakes off the front of his suit. "Near Doc Mighty's *Sanctuary of Me-Time*."

Sam prised his frozen eyelids apart, swiveled his eyes around to check if they were both still working, then finally processed what Chuck had said.

"What? No. The Sanctuary's in the Caribbean."

"Not anymore. Some developer built a hotel right next door a few years back, so he moved it."

"To the Arctic?" said Anna. "That seems kind of..."

"Hardcore!" said Randy.

"I was going to say 'stupid.' I mean, the Arctic? That's insane."

Chuck shrugged, still working to fasten the door. "What can I say? The man liked his *me time*."

Still shivering, Sam returned to his seat. He appeared to be nodding, although that might just have been the convulsions. "Th-that's true," he said, through chattering teeth. His brow furrowed, making tiny ice crystals fall from his eyebrows. "Wait. 'Liked?' What do you mean, 'he liked' it?"

There was a *clunk* as Chuck finally managed to seal the door. He inhaled slowly, still facing away from the table. When he finally did turn, his expression made fear coil like a snake in Sam's gut.

"What I am about to show you is so far above Top Secret it's practically in orbit," he said. "There are three people who have seen the footage you are about to see. Me, the communications operative who first received the transmission, and the President."

"The President of what?" Randy asked.

Chuck's eyes closed for a fraction of a second longer than a standard blink. "Of the United States."

"Thought so. Makes sense," said Randy, nodding sagely. "But it's always best to check."

"What footage?" asked Sam.

Chuck gestured to one of the featureless white walls. It illuminated with a faint glow as if being lit from behind. "See for yourself," he said. He straddled the one remaining chair and leaned his arms across the back of it. The light from the wall-screen reflected in his icy blue eyes. "But you might want to go ahead and brace yourselves."

CHAPTER SIX

"THIS IS ... *tsskt* ... bsorbo, aboard the Justice Platoon's ... *fzzzrk* ... ttle station."

Only the top half of Absorbo's head was visible down near the bottom of the screen, rotated at an angle that suggested either he or the camera had been knocked off-kilter. A chunk of debris around the size of a grapefruit drifted lazily behind him, and those seeing the footage for the first time realized the station's artificial gravity must have been compromised.

"We are under attack. We don't know how, but ... *tssshkt* ... from nowhere ... *brssst* ... more powerful than anything we've ever ..."

Interference flickered across the image, painting it with a zig-zag of jagged lines and pixels, and turning the audio into a series of squeals and static hisses.

When the image cleared again, several other items had drifted into shot behind Absorbo. One of them made Sam, Anna, and Randy gasp, swear loudly, and dramatically punch a fist into the opposite palm respectively.

It was Doc Mighty. Specifically, it was the dead body of

Doc Mighty, drifting limply across the background like a discarded rag doll.

It took Sam a few seconds to conclude for sure that this was, in fact, Doc Mighty. He wasn't used to seeing his former mentor's face like that—eyes wide in horror, mouth twisted into a grimace of pain. His deadness was quicker to establish. Even Earth's mightiest champion couldn't come back from the gaping hole that had been burned all the way through his invulnerable torso.

Or his *once-thought* invulnerable torso, Sam supposed, because current evidence quite firmly suggested otherwise.

"Is that...?" asked Anna.

"I'm afraid so," Chuck confirmed.

Anna's mouth tried out a few different responses, before settling on the simple, elegant, "Oh fuck."

Sam realized he'd been so fixated on Doc Mighty that he'd stopped listening to Absorbo. He could still only see the top half of the superhero's face, but even that small section was a portrait of absolute terror.

"...coming. We couldn't stop him," he babbled, tears filling his eyes. "We couldn't..."

From somewhere off-screen there came the sound of rending metal. Absorbo's head snapped in the direction of the noise, giving those watching a view right up his nose.

Randy whistled quietly below his breath. "He is Blair Witching the shit out of this thing," he remarked.

Absorbo's voice became a rising squeal of panic. "No, no, no, no, please! Please!"

He turned back to the camera. "I'm sorry! I'm sor—"

There was a flurry of movement, too fast for the camera to capture anything but the vaguest blur. What they could see of Absorbo's face took on an expression that bordered on indignant, then the top of his head drifted upward, filling the screen. The bottom of his head did not. Sam's stomach tightened and he had to swallow down the rising nausea as Absorbo's eyeballs, sinuses, and brain all flopped out of his cranium and floated off to join the rest of the station's debris.

For just the briefest moment, a shadow passed across the camera. The screen turned dark, then became nothing but a faintly glowing wall again.

Nobody said a word. Not at first. There were no words, Sam thought. None that could accurately describe the enormity of what they'd just witnessed.

"Wow," said Randy. "That was some full-on crazy shit. Good thing it's not real."

"It's real," said Chuck.

Randy pointed to the wall where the images had just been displayed. "What is? That?" he asked. "That was real?"

Chuck nodded.

"That was real? What we just watched? With Absorbo? That wasn't a movie? It was real?" asked Randy. "That's what you're telling me right now?"

"Yes!" Sam snapped. "That's what he's telling you! It's real! Absorbo was just murdered. Doc Mighty is..."

The word wouldn't come. It couldn't. It was too ridiculous an idea. Too unbelievable. Doc Mighty was invincible. Immortal.

"Dead," said Chuck, and the enormity of the word seemed to expand to fill the room. "He's dead. They're all dead. The whole Justice Platoon."

"When?" asked Anna. "When was this sent?"

"Four days ago," said Chuck. "Came through on a secure encrypted channel only the Platoon has access to. *Had* access to."

Sam shook his head. "Wait, wait. Four days ago? Then it can't be real. I saw Doc Mighty on TV yesterday. He was fighting Morruks."

"That was us," said Chuck.

"What do you mean?" asked Sam.

"I mean we staged it. That was us."

"Jesus, is there anyone who's *not* you?" asked Anna. "Why would you stage it?"

Chuck shrugged. "To avoid panic. To stop all those asshole would-be supervillains out there getting ideas. We used some old footage, some CGI, a couple of actors, spliced it together and gave it to the media. Malone—the reporter— she owed us one, so we brought her in, too. Told her the Justice Platoon were off somewhere on a mission, and this was just to head-off any panic."

"*Stay in school*," Sam muttered. "I knew that was old."

Chuck nodded. "One of the benefits of having a super-hero who doesn't age, we've got a lot of archive footage to work with."

"But they'll figure it out," said Anna. "People aren't idiots. They'll figure out that something's wrong."

"You have a higher opinion of people than I do," said Chuck. "But yes, ultimately we can't keep it up forever. Luckily, we don't have to."

Sam and Anna exchanged puzzled looks. "Why not?" Sam asked.

"We tracked whatever it was that took out the Platoon's space station. We didn't get a lot of readings from it, but those we did get suggest it's more powerful than almost anything we've encountered before," Chuck said.

"Great, so it's going to wipe out the planet before anyone notices the Justice Platoon are all dead?" said Anna. "I'm not sure that qualifies for a 'luckily.'"

"That's not the lucky part," Chuck told her. "After it killed the Justice Platoon, the... space entity vanished. We've got no readings of it anywhere. Far as we can tell, it's gone. That thing, whatever it was, isn't our problem."

"It killed Doc Mighty," Sam pointed out. "That feels like a problem."

Chuck conceded the point with a nod of his enormous head. "It's not our *immediate* problem," he corrected. "Once the Platoon's rogues gallery of villains gets wind of this—and they will, if they haven't already—then they're going to start slicing up the world however they see fit. We'll be knee deep in killer robots, fish-men, and Christ knows what else before we can find our own asses."

He straightened and fixed each of them with a solemn look in turn. "Which is where you come in."

"Al*right*! Butterfly King is *all the way in!*" announced Randy in his guttural rumble. He pushed his goggles up onto his forehead and narrowed his eyes. "Although, quick question. In what?"

"The Sidekicks Initiative was set up in case of this exact scenario," said Chuck. He looked up to the ceiling for a moment, like he was recalling some long-forgotten memory. "We feared there might come a day when the whole world was in danger and we found ourselves all out of superheroes. The Justice Platoon were the best we had. The best there's ever been. The strongest, the smartest, the fastest..."

"The most absorbent..." added Anna.

Chuck fixed her with a glare. "He was a good man. He died trying to warn us."

Anna shifted awkwardly in her seat. "Sorry," she mumbled. "Force of habit."

"With the Platoon out there doing their thing, the other heroes kind of faded away. Retired, mostly, although a few got sloppy while trying to prove something to themselves and ended up worm food."

"Worm Master!" spat Randy, banging a fist on the table. "That twisted fiend!"

Chuck sighed. "It's a figure of speech. I meant they got

themselves killed and we buried their dead bodies in the ground," he explained. "Also, who the fuck is Worm Master?"

Randy shrugged. "I don't know. I just assumed when you said... I mean, there's probably a Worm Master, right? That sounds like a thing someone might be."

"Says the Butterfly Kid," Anna replied.

"Butterfly *King*," Randy snarled.

"Right. Is that, like, a purely ceremonial title, or do you have royal duties you have to fulfill?" probed Anna. "Asking for a friend."

She looked at Chuck. "Also, any chance that this place has a mini-bar? This hangover is really starting to kick my ass, and I'd like to head it off if, if that's OK with everyone?"

"Guys. Please," said Sam. "I'm trying to listen here."

"You ass-kissing son of a bitch," Randy growled.

Sam shot him a look of annoyance but said nothing.

"So, when the chips are down and the world's all out of heroes, who do we turn to?" Chuck asked.

"Villains!" guessed Randy.

"No, Randy. That would be insanity. We want to stop the villains. That's literally the whole point of the conversation we're having right now," said Chuck. "No, we turn to the sidekicks. You guys."

Randy let out a long, protracted gasp of excitement as he got to his feet. "At last, the apprentice has become the master!" he growled. "Finally! I've been waiting for this moment my whole life!"

Anna puffed out her cheeks. She also stood, then jabbed a thumb in the direction of the door. "I think I'll take my chances outside. Which way's civilization? I'm guessing south?"

"I'm with her," Sam said. Everyone else was on their feet, so he felt like he probably should be, too. "We're not heroes. We're not anything."

"Speak for yourself," Randy hissed. "Butterfly King is someone—he's *Butterfly King!*"

"Great, now he's talking about himself in third person," said Anna. "That's definitely my cue to leave."

Chuck's broad forehead pulled into a scowl of annoyance. "Did you listen to anything I said? Did you see that footage?"

"We saw it," said Sam. "And we—I mean, I can't speak for both of us—but I appreciate you thinking of us. That's a vote of confidence I really needed right now." He shook his head and smiled ruefully. "But I can't help you."

Chuck exhaled slowly through his nose, deliberately ignoring the hand Sam had held out for him to shake. "You used to stand for something, kid."

"We were a fad," Sam said. "We were a gimmick designed to sell more comics and merchandise, that's all."

"Bullshit," Randy spat. "We were an integral part of the whole hero industry. Our mentors trusted us with their very lives!"

"We were a sales tool," Sam told him. "I mean, the world's greatest heroes all taking orphans into their care and training them to fight criminals? Back then, that was PR gold."

"Nowadays, they'd be looking at a custodial sentence for reckless endangerment of a minor," said Anna. "And rightly so, I might add."

Chuck blocked the door, although they had made no serious move toward it yet. "So, what? The world can just go to Hell, is that what you're saying? You'll just stand aside and let an army of supervillains do what they want? Take what they want? *Hurt* who they want? You'd be happy with that, would you?"

"No, of course we wouldn't be happy," Sam protested. "But there's a big difference between being unhappy about something and being able to do something about it! What about the police? The military? Call those guys."

"Pah!" spat Randy. "How can some poor hick cop hope to stop someone like Worm Master?"

Chuck sighed. "There is no Worm Master, Randy. Let it go."

"I meant metaphorically. I was using him as an example, that's all. I didn't mean they'd be standing up against an *actual* Worm Master," Randy clarified. His eyes narrowed into angry slits as his voice became a rasping whisper. "That son of a bitch is mine."

"I hate to say it, but Randy's right," Chuck said. "Cops and the military aren't trained to take on superpowered criminals. You three are."

"Were," Sam corrected. "We *were*. A long time ago. And even then, we didn't really do any of the dirty work."

"Hell, I was a glorified human shield," said Anna. "I've still got the scar where the Gunslinging Gal shot me that time."

"I thought she shot Calcu-Lass?" said Sam.

Anna shrugged. "I think she shot a lot of people. It was kind of her whole M.O."

"Actually, what happened to Calcu-Lass?" Sam asked, turning to Chuck. "Or the other guy. What was his name? The fire one."

"Jim Flammable," said Chuck. He shrugged. "We don't know. We lost track of them both."

"Shame. That whole 'master of fire' thing could've come in handy with your current predicament," said Anna.

"Meh. Not really. He could generate fire, but his skin wasn't actually fire*proof*. Every time he used his powers he almost burned his own hands off."

Sam and Anna both blinked in unison.

"Jesus," Sam muttered.

"It was a last resort kind of thing," Chuck explained.

"Sounds like it," Anna agreed.

They fell silent for a moment. Sam thought back twenty years. Jim Flammable had seemed like a nice kid. A little shy and reserved, but then he'd been a couple of years younger than the others, and rumor was that he'd come from a pretty rough background. He'd worn heavy leather gloves, which Sam had thought at the time was just part of his costume, but now realized must have been hiding his burned and blackened hands.

"Poor guy," he said, then he gave himself a shake as if chasing the image away. "But that's exactly my point. We were never heroes. Some of us didn't even have powers," he added, shooting Randy the briefest of pointed looks.

"That better not have been aimed at me," Randy spat. "I have powers. I have all the powers and abilities of the noble butterfly."

"What, like flying?" asked Anna, crossing her arms and slinking her weight onto one hip.

"Except flying, obviously," Randy hissed. "All their abilities except flying."

"Or—"

"Or being small, yes, OK. All their powers except flying or being small." He looked Anna up and down. "Anyway, what about you, *Allergy Girl?* What was so great about you?"

Anna shrugged. "Nothing. You're right. There was, and there still is absolutely nothing great about me. Hence why I'm not interested in..." She waved her hands vaguely around the room. "Whatever all this is."

"Same here," Sam agreed. "I can't get involved. Not again."

"We need you," Chuck told them. "Everyone needs you."

"Why us?" Sam cried. "What can we do? *He* talks to butterflies, *she* breaks people out in spots, and I..." His brief explosion of anger faltered, becoming a damp squib. "I can't do anything."

Chuck shook his head and stepped in closer. Sam tried to retreat, but the bigger man's hands caught him by the upper arms and held him firmly in place. Sam got the impression those hands could crush his bones to dust, and wondered if Chuck packed some superpowers of his own.

"Listen to me, Sam. That's not true, we both know it."

"It is true," Sam insisted. "Honestly. I can't help, even if I wanted to."

Chuck's voice became low and intense, almost like a conspiratorial whisper. For a moment, Sam forgot the other two were even in the room.

"I said earlier that whoever that space bastard who killed the Platoon was, its readings suggested it's more powerful than almost anything we've ever encountered. Keyword 'almost.' There's someone even more powerful, Sam."

"Doc Mighty," Sam guessed, but Chuck dismissed the suggestion with a shake of his head.

"You, Sam. It's you."

Sam snorted. "Me?"

Randy snorted even more loudly. "*Him?* Sure you don't mean me?"

"He definitely doesn't mean you," said Anna.

"He might mean me," Randy countered. "Chuck, do you mean me?"

"You talk to butterflies, Randy. Clearly, I don't mean you," Chuck said, without looking at him.

Anna sized Sam up, looking for some clue that would either back-up or contradict what Chuck was saying. She remembered Kid Random from back in the nineties. They'd fought side by side against Thrumduk the World Slayer, and he hadn't demonstrated any great power then. He had seemed much more able, willing, and generally *gung-ho* than this older version, but then it was hard not to get swept away by the thrill of it all at the time. She was also well aware of how much she herself had changed since her teenage years, and the lengths she'd gone to leave those days behind.

He'd been fun to hang out with. They'd even flirted a little, although her multitude of spots, rashes, and other skin complaints had probably thwarted any chance of actual romance. Besides, the Platoon actively discouraged any inter-team relationships, even among the thirteen-year-olds.

Especially among the thirteen-year-olds, in fact. Which was why the team's kindly old butler, Albert, had been quietly retired, Anna seemed to recall.

Did Sam have a certain *something* about him back in the day? Yeah. She had to admit that he had. But superpowers greater than those of Doc Mighty himself? No, she was pretty sure she'd have noticed.

"No," said Sam. "No, there's been a mistake. I mean..." He gestured down at himself, like this would somehow demonstrate just how wrong Chuck was. "Look at me. I'm not powerful."

"You turned a Glock 17 into butter without even thinking about it," Chuck pointed out. "If that isn't power, I don't know what is."

"He... He had a gun to my son's head," said Sam, wringing his hands together. "That wasn't... I didn't mean to..."

Sam straightened suddenly and fixed Chuck with the sternest glare he could muster up. "I'm sorry. You've wasted your time. I'd like to leave now."

Anna shrugged. "Well, if he's our big hitter and he's leaving, I'm out of here, too," she said. "So, if you have, like, a coat or some gloves or whatever, and can point us in the right direction, we'll be on our way."

Chuck looked between them for several seconds. The intensity of his blue-eyed glare almost made Sam chuckle, but the presence of Anna behind him helped him stand his ground.

"Fine."

Sam leaned back a little in surprise. "Fine? So, what? We can go?"

"You're not prisoners," Chuck said. "You heard me out. I can't force you to do the right thing."

Sam winced a little at that.

"Mreow," said Anna, curving her fingers into cat-like claws. "Trying to guilt trip us into a suicide mission. Smooth."

"If you want to leave, you can leave," said Chuck.

"Like the filthy cowards you are!" said Randy. He'd pulled his goggles back down over his eyes and spat out the words in his best Batman-like growl.

"Yeah. Good to see you, too, Randy," Sam said. "Good luck with..." He looked Randy up and down, taking in the flying hat and goggles, scruffy t-shirt, and ill-fitting cape. "...everything."

Chuck stepped aside and pushed down the bar of the door. Sam wrapped his arms around himself, bracing against a blast of cold air that didn't come.

Instead of the Arctic wilderness, the door opened onto a basketball court.

"What the hell is this?" asked Sam.

"It's the way out."

"I thought we were somewhere up north?"

"We were," Chuck confirmed. "Now we're not. You leaving, or what?"

Sam leaned through the doorway and examined the room beyond. A few racks of tall metal shelves had been positioned around the court, each one laden with what looked like random pieces of junk.

A baseball bat lay beside two plastic hubcap covers. Two fire extinguishers stood guard either side of a stack of cooking pots and a child's kite.

And so it went on. The shelves groaned under the weight

of diving equipment, broken toys, musical instruments, and dozens of other items too diverse to accurately catalog. There was no apparent logic to any of it, and Sam's first instinct was to give the shelves a good tidy, possibly involving some light alphabetization.

"Where the hell are we now?" Anna asked. "And what's with the junk?"

"The way out's that way," said Chuck, ushering Sam and Anna through the door.

"That's it?" said Sam. "We can just go? Just like that?"

"Just like that," said Chuck. He began pulling the door closed behind them, then paused with it half open. "Oh, but one thing. Those guys are going to try to stop you."

"What? What guys?" Sam spluttered, but then he saw them. They stepped out from behind one of the shelving units at the far end of the court, all snarls and skinheads and matching orange jumpsuits.

"Who are these clowns?" Anna asked.

Chuck shrugged. "Just some assorted henchmen types. Thugs for hire. Nothing you guys can't handle," he said. "You want out? You go through them."

Sam gawped at him in horror. "No! That's not... You can't do that!"

"I can, and I am," Chuck told him.

"Stand aside, good citizen! Butterfly King is totally getting in on this!" Randy announced, sidling past Chuck and onto the basketball court. He pointed dramatically in the direction of the henchmen. "Evildoers, prepare to meet your fate!"

"We won't fight them," Sam told Chuck, ignoring Randy completely. "We just... We won't fight them."

"Fair enough. That's completely your choice," Chuck replied. "But FYI, these people will kill you. Also, bonus fun fact, one of them's a necrophiliac. I'll let you figure out which one. But I'll give you a hint—it's the one with 'Imma fuck your dead body,' tattooed on his face."

Chuck winked and smiled at Sam. "See you around, kid," he said.

And with that, he closed the door.

CHAPTER SEVEN

RANDY STEPPED in front of Sam and Anna, clutching his fists down near his hips and thrusting out his chest.

"Sidekicks!" he barked, his voice echoing around the basketball court. "Let's kick some *side*!"

Anna shot him a sideways look. "What's that supposed to mean?"

"I just thought it was a thing we could say," Randy explained. "You know, like 'Avengers Assemble!' or 'Platoon Commune!'"

"What's 'Platoon Commune'?" Anna asked. "The Justice Platoon never said that."

"Well, no, but they totally should have," Randy said.

Anna rolled her eyes. "God. OK, let's just get this over with."

Sam looked along the court to where the henchmen were gathered. They had spread out a little to search the closest shelves. He was a little concerned to note that one had picked up what looked to be a meat cleaver, and was now *swishing* it around in the air, getting a feel for it.

"We're not actually going to fight those guys!" Sam hissed.

"I mean, I don't want to," said Anna. "But I also don't want to get corpse-raped, so I'm kind of..." She made a weighing motion with her hands. "You know?"

Sam shook his head. "We're not in High School here. I'm sure we can just talk to them. They probably don't want to do this anymore than we do," he said. Raising a hand, he hailed the henchmen. "Hello there!"

There was a roar of gunfire and the contents of the shelf closest to Sam disintegrated. Sam and Anna threw themselves to the ground, covering their heads with their hands as the *brrrrrrrp* of machine-gun fire continued to reverberate around the hall. Randy, meanwhile, cartwheeled clumsily toward another of the shelves, lost his balance, and crashed onto the polished wooden floor.

"They've got guns!" Sam screeched. "How come they have guns? Why don't we have guns?"

"Because we're heroes, dammit!" Randy spat. He was squatting behind one of the shelving racks, his back pressed up against it. "Heroes don't use guns!"

"What about Crime Killer?" Anna yelped. "He has hundreds of guns!"

"Or Blastatron the Living Gun?" Sam added. "He literally *is* a gun!"

"OK, but technically, those guys are more like anti-heroes," Randy explained. "So, they don't really count."

The gunfire stopped, leaving only a fading echo to bounce around the court. Sam and Anna slowly raised their heads just as something around the size of a grapefruit rolled to a stop between them. It *ticked* faintly.

"Hey, they've got grenades, too," Randy pointed out.

"Jesus *Christ*!" Sam yelped. He jumped up and tried to kick the grenade back the way it had come, but it sliced sideways off his foot and *clonked* the still prostrate Anna on the forehead.

"Ow! Shit! Watch what you're doing!" she spat, clutching where the grenade had hit her just above her right eye.

Sam pointed frantically to the explosive. "Grenade!" was all he could think to shout. "There's a grenade!"

Anna threw out an arm, sweeping the explosive across the floor. It skittered back down the court and wedged under a shelf roughly halfway between the Sidekicks and the Henchmen.

At both ends of the hall, everyone who wasn't already ducking ducked.

Nothing happened.

"A dud. Of course it is!" said Randy, stepping out of cover. "These idiots wouldn't know a real hand grenade if they—"

The grenade exploded, filling the air with smoke and fire and bits of flying shelf. Sam shoulder-barged Randy and they both clattered to the ground just as chunks of debris came whistling through the air above them.

"I totally would've dodged that on my own," Randy insisted, but all Sam could hear was a high-pitched ringing in his ears, and a tiny voice in his head telling him that he was almost certainly about to die.

The whole middle section of the room was filled with thick black smoke, from the polished floor up to the high ceiling. Through the black cloud, Sam could hear the henchmen coughing and spluttering.

"We should hit them before they pull themselves together," Anna suggested.

Sam's voice came as a high-pitched squeak. "You're not still planning to fight them? They've got a gun!"

"Kind of struggling to see how we've got a lot of choice," said Anna. She fished in a pocket of her dress, retrieved a grubby elastic band, and scooped her unruly hair back into a ponytail. "Did anyone see how many of them there were?" she asked. "Because I'm still a little drunk, and I may well be seeing double."

"I made six," Randy told her.

Anna winced. "Shit. Not seeing double. That's disappointing. So, two each."

"No, not two each!" Sam protested. "Not anything each. I'm not a superhero, I'm a data entry clerk. I don't fight crime, I type numbers into boxes. That's it. That's my whole skillset. I can't get involved in this." He crossed his arms for emphasis. "I won't!"

Anna made no effort to hide her disappointment. "Huh," she said, then she shrugged. "Fine. Whatever. Three each, then."

"I prefer those odds, actually," growled Randy. "In fact, you take one and I'll take the other five."

"Are you nuts?" Sam snapped. "This isn't like the comics, Randy. You can't take on five guys on your own."

Randy smirked behind his scruffy beard. "Who says I'll be on my own?" he asked, then he whipped his hands around in a series of complex, yet ultimately quite clumsy-looking gestures. With that out of the way, he pressed the first two fingers of his right hand to his temple and bellowed: "Come to me, my butterfly brethren!"

For a moment, nothing happened.

Then, for a longer moment, nothing continued to happen.

"Give it a minute," Randy muttered, still holding the pose.

"We don't have a minute!" Sam hissed. "They could start shooting again any second."

Randy snorted. "Oh, I don't think so. See, I counted how many bullets they fired, and by my calculations, those scumbags are all out of—"

BRRRRRRRRAP!

Flashes of machine-gun fire illuminated the cloud of smoke, as lumps of hot lead came screaming along the court.

Sam and Anna both ducked again, but the shots were too high and sailed harmlessly above their heads before peppering the plaster of the wall behind them.

The roaring of gunfire became a definitive *click*.

"My bad. My bad. Completely miscounted," admitted Randy. He cocked his head, listening. "*Now* they're out. I guarantee it. Unless they've got more bullets, obviously. Or another gun."

"Let's not find out," said Anna, flexing her fingers and taking a series of deep breaths. "I'm ending this." She cricked her neck a couple of times. "Come on, Anna. You've still got it. You can still do this."

She brought her hands close to her chest, then pushed them forward, fingers splayed outward. "Anaphylactic Shockwave," she said, faltering a little as she uttered the words.

Sam looked toward the smoke, where they could just make out a few hints of orange jumpsuits. Anna's display didn't seem to have achieved much of anything.

"Wait. I think I did it wrong," she said.

"It's fine. I got this," Randy hissed through gritted teeth. He had the first two fingers of both hands pressed against his temples now, and was going vaguely purple around the cheeks through sheer force of concentration. "Come to me. Come... to... your *king*!"

"No, I know what I did wrong. I've got it this time," said Anna, spreading her feet further apart and adopting something resembling a fighting stance.

Sam, meanwhile, shifted his weight from foot to foot, convinced that fiery hot lumps of lead were going to tear through them all at any moment. The smoke was beginning to clear, and so the henchmen would soon have much easier targets to aim for.

"Anaphylactic *Shockwave!*" Anna cried, putting some enthusiasm into it this time.

The forward thrust of her arms coincided with the arrival of a dozen or so butterflies, apparently from nowhere. They fluttered around her head, startling her and throwing her aim off. Something rippled through the air from her hands. Sam clutched at his throat, wheezed loudly, then fell over.

"My *thung!*" he sobbed, his tongue flopping out between his rapidly swelling lips. It was substantially fatter than it had been and covered in hundreds of tiny white blisters. "My thucking thung!"

Anna bit her lip. She looked partly apologetic, and partly like she really wanted to giggle. "Shit. I am *so* sorry," she said, her nostrils flaring with the effort of not laughing. "Although, I have to say, it was kind of the butterflies' fault."

"Don't listen to her, guys," Randy told the small cloud of colorful insects that danced in the air around him. He pointed along the court, to where several orange-clad shapes were appearing through the smoke cloud, clubs, axes and other weapons raised. "Now go, my Rhopaloceran warriors. Fly like the wings of justice!"

The butterflies meandered gently toward the smoke. They were just about to vanish into the cloud when a jet of flame erupted from within it, instantly incinerating them.

"Oh, sweet mother of God," Randy whispered, his eyes widening behind his goggles.

The first of the henchmen appeared through the smoke, clutching a deodorant can in one hand and a Zippo lighter in the other. He sprayed and flicked, propelling another burst of flame in the sidekicks' direction.

Randy launched himself toward the henchman, ducking the flame and driving a shoulder into the guy's stomach. They went down together with a *thud*, sending the deodorant can skidding across the floor before they were lost to the smoke.

"Well, well, look what we got here," sneered another of

the thugs-for-hire. Sam and Anna heard him, but couldn't see him through the smoke.

"Lay a hand on me, and I'll kill you," Randy barked back. Sam and Anna heard that, too. There was a moment of silence. No, not quite silence. It was filled with the sound of something heavy hitting something soft. Randy's voice, when it came, sounded strained. "OK, lay *another* hand on me, and I'll kill you."

There was a series of *thuds* and *oofs* that suggested the henchmen hadn't taken the threat well.

Sam and Anna exchanged resigned looks.

"Aw, thuck it," said Sam, still struggling with his swollen tongue and fish-lips. These had now been joined by an itchy red rash that spread up both sides of his neck and across his cheeks.

He grabbed for the closest weapon he could find. It turned out to be an egg whisk, so he grabbed for the *second* closest weapon he could find—a cast iron frying pan—and shuffled nervously into the smoke.

Anna strode past him, and for a moment he was almost shamed into hurrying up. Instead, he grabbed for her, catching her by the arm and slowing her down. He tried to put a finger to his lips to warn her to be quiet, but his lips were enormous and he was carrying a frying pan, so the gesture was confusing at best.

Pulling herself free, Anna pressed on, and Sam had no choice but to hurry out of the smoke after her, pan raised to head level, ready to strike. To his surprise, he found two of the henchmen lying unconscious on the floor, and a third on his knees with Randy standing behind him. Randy had one hand under the henchman's chin, and the other on the top of his head. He glowered furiously at the three remaining men, his glare practically burning through the lenses of his goggles.

"Take another step and I snap his neck!" Randy warned.

Each of the three upright henchmen looked at the others a little awkwardly, then shrugged. "So? Go ahead," said one. "He's one of the Golden Skull's boys. We ain't got no loyalty to him."

"We barely even know the bloke," said another henchman.

"I'll do it! I mean it! I'll snap this guy's neck like a twig!" Randy insisted.

"Don't do it, Randy," said Anna. "We don't kill. That's, like, the number one rule."

"This subhuman scum doesn't deserve to live. He killed my butterflies!" Randy snarled. "Are you saying you think a human life is more important than a butterfly life?"

"Well, yes. Obviously," said Anna. "I mean, who doesn't think that?" She looked to Sam for confirmation. "You think that, right?"

"Yeth," Sam confirmed. He clutched the handle of his frying pan and eyed the three still-standing henchmen. "Look, guyth, we thould thtop fighghting and dicuth thith like... *thuck*! My thucking thung!"

"What the hell's wrong with him?" demanded one of the thugs.

"Ith wath her fault," Sam explained.

"Everyone *shut up*!" roared Randy. "And say goodbye to this piece of criminal filth!"

"Randy, don't!" Anna yelped, but it was too late. Randy pushed and pulled simultaneously, wrenching the henchman's head around with all his might.

"Ow! Shit! What are you doing?" the henchman hissed. "Like, seriously, dude. That hurts. Stop it! Cut that shit out!"

Randy gritted his teeth and twisted. "Hnnng!"

"You're pulling my hair! Ow! *Ow!* Jesus. *OK, that's it!*"

Grabbing Randy's arms, the henchman bent forward sharply. Randy's cape flapped behind him as he was flipped over the villain's head and landed flat on his back on the floor.

The henchman stood up, cracking his neck and gingerly rubbing the top of his head. He drove a kick into Randy's ribs with jackhammer force.

"Ain't so tough now, are you?" he spat.

"Ha! That's what you think. You just fell right into my trap," Randy wheezed. "This is exactly what I wanted you to do."

"Then you're in luck," said the henchman, driving another boot into his ribs. He patted another of the henchmen on his broad chest, before gesturing to Sam and Anna. "Now, let's kill these fucks."

Sam shot the villain closest to him an anxious grin, then swung with his frying pan. The henchman blocked the attack, closed the gap between them quickly, and brought up a fist.

A sound filled Sam's head. It was somewhere between a *crunch* and a *thwack*, and seemed to come from somewhere inside his skull, rather than outside.

Pain flooded his body and clouded all his senses. His legs became soft and pliable like warm toffee. He looked for the frying pan, but it was no longer in his hands. Instead, all he found there was a smear of blood across his fingers. There were a growing number of red spots on the floor at his feet, too. He watched them appearing for a moment, as if by magic.

And then the floor rolled away as if someone had pulled it out from under him, and he sat down with a *thud* and a jolt of pain.

"Get... *off*," hissed Anna, struggling in the grip of a dark-eyed henchman with copper-colored teeth. Her arms were pinned to her side, trapped by the villain's bearhug. He sniffed her hair, most of which had shaken loose from the ponytail, and his expression became one of gleeful arousal.

Randy was still down, but trying to get up. Whenever he made it as far as his knees and elbows, the Golden Skull's henchman drove another boot into his ribs, knocking him down again. Still, he persisted. The guy was a trier, if nothing else.

"Thtop. Pleathe," Sam pleaded, gagging on his own blood. "Why are you doing thith?"

The henchman who had floored him sneered down. To Sam's dismay, he realized the guy really did have a 'Imma fuck your dead body,' written on his face. This dismay was added to by the fact that it wasn't tattooed, exactly, and more sort of carved into his forehead. Also, he'd missed the 'a' in 'dead' and used the wrong version of 'your'.

Through his haze of pain, swelling, and hot, itchy rashes Sam briefly lamented the state of the education system today, before his eyes fell on the meat cleaver in the henchman's hand. The blade was lightly pitted with spots of rust. It looked more heavy than sharp, and Sam couldn't decide if this was a good thing or a bad one.

Bad, probably, given the way his day was going.

The henchman holding Anna let out a low, sickening laugh. Sam heard the *crunch* of a boot in Randy's ribs, and a quiet, "I have you now, evildoer," that was less of a growl and more of a whimper.

Sam's eyes followed the cleaver as the henchman raised it. He thought of his son, and something stirred at the back of his head.

And then Chuck was there, and the movement in Sam's brain faltered as he watched the man in the suit demolish the henchmen with brutal, ruthless efficiency.

He was fast for his size. Graceful, too. He moved through the villains like a ballet dancer, albeit one who punctuated each plié and pirouette with a punch to the nearest throat, or a knee to the closest available balls.

Sam let himself sink back onto the floor. The blood from his nose ran back into his constricted throat, making him gag, so he turned his head to the side. The wooden floor was soothing and cool against the rash on his cheek.

He lay there for a while, listening to the *thwacking*, yelping, and the various other sounds of violence until they eventually fell silent.

"Thanks," said Anna.

"No problem," Chuck grunted.

"You idiot," Randy seethed. His voice was slurred, and each word was accompanied by a tiny gasp of pain. "I had them right where I wanted them."

"Sure you did," said Chuck.

Sam's eyes were closed, but he felt the shadow pass across him. With an effort bordering on Herculean, he managed to turn his head and squint up at the outline of Chuck that loomed above him, silhouetted by an overhead light.

"Well, this was disappointing," Chuck sighed.

Sam tucked his chin into his chest. It was the closest he could get to a nod. "Told you," he croaked.

"But with some training..."

Sam managed an approximation of a laugh. It hurt considerably in a number of places.

"It's pointleth," he said. "Jutht let uth go. Pleathe."

Chuck turned his head away. For a while, he just stared along the basketball court at nothing in particular. Finally, he nodded.

"OK. Maybe this was a bad idea," he admitted. With a sigh of resignation, he held a hand out to Sam. "Come on. I guess we should get you all out of here."

CHAPTER EIGHT

FOLLOWING SOME URGENT MEDICAL ATTENTION, a good wash, and a terse apology, Sam and the others were led through a warren of mostly identical corridors, before emerging into what appeared to be an office reception area.

The reception was made up of a single desk, six plastic chairs, and a little coffee table covered with magazines that all looked too pristine to have ever been read. There was no one sitting behind the desk, but a sign on the wall announced the place as 'Bland, Inc.'

"It's a cover story," Chuck said, catching Sam reading the sign. "Far as anyone knows, this place makes... Actually, I can't remember what it's supposed to make. Some kind of paper fastener. Nothing anyone would be interested in, anyway."

"Right," said Sam. Sure enough, he wasn't interested in the slightest. He *was* intrigued as to how the room they'd been in could be in the Arctic one minute, then somewhere else the next, but they were so close to freedom now that he didn't want to risk getting sucked back in, so he elected to leave it a mystery.

They stopped at the door. It was mostly glass, and Sam could see traffic moving on the street beyond. It was moving reasonably fast, rather than crawling at a near-stand-still, so he guessed they had to be near the outskirts of the city.

Damn. The bus fare was going to kill him.

Zipping up his jacket, Sam slipped his hand into a pocket. There was a lump in his throat when he felt the hippo or elephant or whatever the hell it was. He'd phone Laura as soon as he was out of here, make sure Corey was OK. Hopefully, she'd let Sam see him.

"Remember what I told you," said Chuck.

Anna rolled her eyes. "Yeah, yeah. Don't say a word to anyone. We get it. We might not be a well-oiled fighting force, but one thing we do know how to do is keep a secret."

She waved her red stiletto vaguely in Chuck's direction. "And, you know, if the other one of these turns up... In fact, no. You have it," she said, handing him the shoe. She gestured to his shirt collar. "It matches the blood stains."

Chuck hooked the shoe onto a rack displaying various types of paper, then leaned forward and opened the door. The sound of Cityopolis rushed in to fill the reception area, and those familiar, everyday city sounds came as some comfort to Sam as he stepped out onto the sidewalk.

The others bundled out behind him. Sam turned to say a final goodbye to Chuck, but the door closed in his face, and a blind with 'Closed' marked on it was pulled down behind the glass.

"Right. Well... I guess that's that," said Sam. "This was..."

"Weird and awkward?" Anna guessed.

"Uh, yeah. Pretty much," Sam agreed.

"Sorry about the whole fat tongue thing," Anna said. "The rash is really fading now. This time tomorrow, it'll all be cleared up."

"Well, that's reassuring," Sam said. "Totally an accident. No one's fault."

"We had a chance to make a difference, and you two blew it!" Randy spat. He was still wearing his homemade outfit, but had pushed the goggles up onto his forehead. There were two red rings around his eyes marking where the lenses had been. "But it's fine. I work better alone. So now I'll melt into the shadows, becoming the dark fabric of the city itself."

The other two watched as he stood there, looking a little awkward.

"Go for it," said Anna.

Sam gave him a little wave. "See you around, Randy."

"Look! Over there!" Randy cried, pointing past them. "Whoa! That's so awesome! I've never seen one of those before!"

"Do you want us to turn around?" Anna asked him.

Randy shrugged with practiced nonchalance. "I mean, only if you want," he said. "If you don't want to see the amazing thing behind you, I don't care. It's totally up to you."

Anna met Sam's gaze and rolled her eyes. They both turned in the direction Randy had been pointing.

"Oh, hey, what could possibly be over in this direction?" Anna asked. "Sam, can you see anything?"

"No," said Sam, not really getting into the spirit of it.

They turned back. Randy, to no one's surprise, was gone.

"How *does* he do that?" Anna wondered, making a point of saying it quite loudly.

Sam, meanwhile, was looking along the street in both directions, searching for some sort of landmark that might tell him which part of the city they were in. There was nothing that set this street apart from any other, though.

"Where are we?" he asked.

Anna lifted her head and sniffed deeply. "Corner of Eighty-third and Ditko," she declared.

Sam was impressed. "You can work that out from smell?"

"Totally," said Anna. "Also, it's on the street sign over there."

"Oh. OK, yeah, that makes more sense," Sam said. He smiled awkwardly while calculating how long it would take him to walk from Eighty-Third all the way home to Seventeenth. Too long. He'd have to set off now if he hoped to get there before it got dark.

He extended a hand in Anna's direction. "Well, it's been—"

"Do you want to get a drink?" Anna asked him. "Because I don't know about you, but I could do with one. And by 'one' I mean 'as many as it takes until I can't see.'"

Sam looked along the street in the direction of home. To his surprise, he found himself considering it.

"I don't have much money with me," he said. "Maybe another time."

"Screw that, I'll cover the tab," Anna told him. She maneuvered herself in front of him, and there was something pleading in her eyes. "Come on. I don't like to drink alone. But I will if I have to, and that'll just be a mess. Help a girl out here."

Sam smiled unconvincingly. "OK. No, it'll be... nice. But just one."

"That's a start," said Anna, clapping a hand on his back. She jabbed a thumb behind them. "What about him?"

Sam closed his eyes for a second, then shrugged. "Randy? We're going for a drink. You coming?"

For a moment, nothing happened. Then Randy stood up from behind a parked car, adjusted his cape, then drew himself up to his full height. "OK," he growled. "I'm in."

Sam leaned an elbow on the table. His finger swayed drunkenly as he pointed across the booth to where Randy sat. All three of them had consumed... Sam tried to count the empty glasses, but they kept moving, so he settled on 'a lot of drinks,' and left it at that.

"My point is," he said, trying to recall what his point was. "My point is... What were we talking about?"

"Su Man Chu," said Anna, knocking back another shot of clear-colored liquid. Her voice was a little slurred, although Sam thought that might well have been the fault of his ears. Only Randy looked fully sober, although the fact he hadn't drunk any alcohol and had instead lapped at a single glass of water with his tongue for the past two hours probably helped a lot.

"Yes!" Sam announced, slapping a hand on the table. "Su Man Chu!"

"My old mentor," said Randy, with a wistful sort of snarl.

"My point is, my point is... My point is—she's racist. Her whole thing. It's racist."

"*Was* racist," Anna corrected.

Sam raised one eyebrow and lowered the other at the same time. "She stopped being racist?"

"Mm. No," said Anna, sipping a different drink from another glass. "Stopped being alive. She's dead, remember? They're all dead."

"Shh," said Sam, putting a finger to his lips. "We're not supposed to talk about that." He tried to tap himself on the nose, but missed.

Across the table, Randy's face was a mask of dark fury. "You take that back," he spat. "Su Man Chu wasn't racist."

"Come on, she wore a cymbal!" Sam argued.

"They were goddam heroes. They all wore symbols!" Randy said, jabbing at the butterfly emblem on his chest.

"No, like a musical cymbal. From a drum kit. On her head," said Sam. "And she said 'Ah-so!' a lot."

Randy snorted. "That's not racist. Chinamen say 'Ah-so!' That's not racist, that's just a fact."

"They don't!" insisted Sam. "And you can't call them 'Chinamen' these days."

"Why not? They're men from China."

"And women," Anna pointed out.

"*China*women," Randy corrected.

Sam waved his hands vaguely in front of him like he could somehow swat away Randy's objections. "You just can't call them that."

"Well, what should I call them?"

"I don't know, I'm not the... naming police. Asian Americans."

"Su Man Chu wasn't American," Randy pointed out.

"Oh..."

"Or Asian."

"See?!" Sam exclaimed. "Racist!"

Randy pulled his goggles down over his eyes. "Take. That. Back," he warned.

Sam looked to Anna for support, but she was fumbling with a pack of peanuts and didn't notice. He shrugged. He'd had enough fighting for one day. One lifetime, in fact.

"Remember, I took out two of those henchmen," growled Randy. "And I would've got the third if his neck hadn't been freakishly strong."

Sam held up his hands in surrender.

"Fine. I take it back. She's not racist," he said. He nudged Anna. "Aren't you allergic to peanuts?"

"Meh. I'm allergic to most things," she replied. The bag tore open in her hands, launching the nuts everywhere. She sighed and swore quietly below her breath.

"Thank you," said Randy, raising his goggles back onto his

head again.

Sam squinted. His brain whirred, trying to remember what he'd been talking about. "For what?"

"For acknowledging that Su Man Chu wasn't racist," Randy replied.

"Oh. Right. But what she did *was* cultural appropriation."

"I don't know what that means, so I'm going to let it go," Randy told him. He lowered his tongue into his glass and lapped up some more of his water.

Sam had never really been sure about Butterfly Kid, even back in the day. Randy had never really spoken to the other sidekicks then, tending to stick close to Su Man Chu. Sam had read his origin story comic, detailing how Randy's parents had died in a plane crash in the Canadian Rockies, and how their baby son had been raised by a troop of butterflies. The comics had tended to take some pretty huge liberties with the truth, though, so Sam had no idea how much of that was accurate, and he hadn't really liked to ask.

He was almost certainly an orphan, though. They all were. Sam didn't know if it was in the rules somewhere, or if his own orphan status had simply started a trend among the other heroes. Sam had become the first sidekick after Doc Mighty had saved him from a burning children's home. Sam had been the only survivor, and the sounds of those screams had haunted him most nights since.

"I want to make a toast," said Anna. She searched through the sea of glasses until she found one that still had liquid in it, and raised it into the air. "To the Justice Platoon. Yes, they were a bunch of self-serving assholes who exploited us for their own commercial gain, but... *but...*"

She closed one eye and concentrated for a moment, then clicked her tongue against the back of her teeth. "Actually, I can't think of a 'but' right now." She raised both the glass and her voice. "To the Justice Platoon!"

"Damn right!" cheered a guy in a checkered shirt and baseball cap, raising his own glass as he passed the table. "Those guys are *heroes!*"

"Right?" Anna laughed. She punched the air a few times, then dropped her voice to a whisper once the man was out of earshot. "Wow, is *he* going to be disappointed when he hears about the whole..."

She drew a thumb across her throat and mimed being dead.

"I gotta go for a pee," Sam announced. He hadn't actually meant to say it aloud, but his inner monologue had taken it upon itself to become an outer one. He leaned on the table and spent a few seconds trying to extricate one of his legs from the other.

With this difficult mission eventually accomplished, he stumbled away from the table, stopped, then wandered in the opposite direction.

"You love him, don't you?" said Randy.

Anna spluttered into her drink, spraying it up her nose. "Shit! *What?*" she spat, wiping her face on her arm. "Why would you say that? No!"

"You've always loved him," Randy said. He licked his own drink, holding her gaze.

"No, I... Will you stop doing that? It's fucking weird. Drink it normally."

"I am drinking it normally," Randy insisted. He lapped at it again.

"That's not how normal people drink."

"It's how normal butterflies drink."

"Well, I hate to break it to you, but you're not a butterfly," Anna pointed out.

"I'm the King of Butterflies," Randy countered.

"Still not a butterfly," Anna said. She gestured to him. "What's with the get-up?"

"It's my costume," Randy said in his now-trademark growl. "Some of us didn't turn our back on our duty."

Anna blinked. "Our doody?"

"Duty!" Randy barked.

Anna shook her head. "I'm still hearing 'doody,'" she said. "It's hard with the whole Batman voice you do."

"Du-ty."

"How are you spelling it?" Anna asked him, staring intently at his mouth.

"D-U— Forget it! Doesn't matter," Randy hissed. "Some of us didn't turn our back on *the mission*."

Anna nodded slowly and drained the dregs from one of her many glasses. "So, what? You're, like, a full-time super-hero these days?"

"Yeah. I am," Randy confirmed. "Pretty much. I was practically a member of the Justice Platoon."

"You were?" Anna gasped.

"Practically," Randy confirmed. He lapped his drink again and peered at her over the rim. "Nice change of subject, by the way. Anyone else wouldn't have noticed. But I did."

"Well, good job," said Anna, giving him a thumbs-up. "Now, if you'll excuse me, I'm going to get some more alcohol. A lot more alcohol."

She hesitated halfway to her feet. "And no, of course I don't love him. Eurgh. As if."

A few minutes later, Sam stumbled from the restrooms, still struggling with the fly of his work pants. The bottom of his shirt had gotten partially stuck in the zipper, and this was making fastening it much more difficult. He hadn't wanted to stand there in the middle of the restroom fiddling with the front of his pants, although he couldn't quite figure out why he'd thought it would be better to do so in full view of everyone in the bar.

He was so focused on the task at hand that he didn't

notice Anna until he bumped into her.

"Sorry," he said, then she came into focus and he smiled. "Hey!"

"Hey," she replied. Her eyes flitted down for a moment. "Problems?"

Sam blew out his lips. "Where do you want me to start? My job sucks. My wife left me. I—"

"I meant with your pants," Anna said. She held up an empty glass, trying to catch the attention of the bartender. He was fixated on the TV screen mounted on the wall behind him, though, and didn't notice.

"Oh! Yeah. It's fine. It's just the zip," Sam said. He did a little jump and yanked harder on the zipper as he was coming down, in the hope that gravity helped him out. It didn't.

Anna *clonked* her glass on the bar a couple of times. "Barkeep!" she said. "More drinks, my good man."

"I think it's broken," Sam said. He sniggered. "I broke my pants."

He had a very hazy thought about bank balances and price tags, but it felt like a distant worry that he could come back to at a later date.

"Jesus, what does a girl have to do to get some service around here?" Anna demanded.

Sam looked over at the bartender. The guy was well within earshot, so he must've heard Anna's increasingly emphatic demands. Damn, that was rude.

Through the blur of all that alcohol, Sam noticed that everyone else at the bar was staring in the same direction as the bartender. He followed their gaze until he found the television.

It took a moment. Several of them in fact. A full twenty or thirty seconds passed before Sam successfully processed what he was seeing.

The giddy, lightheaded happiness drained out of his body

and seeped into the floor. He leaned on the bar to support himself, not because he was drunk, but because he was suddenly sober. Perhaps more sober than he'd ever been before.

A female newsreader stood on-screen. Behind her, several paramedics walked around, examining several fallen... What were those things? They had been people at some point, Sam thought, but now they were gristly lumps of meat, their outsides and insides having been swapped around.

There was blood on the street. So much blood. In the background, the front window of a branch of Cityopolis Central Bank had been smashed open. Another of the mutilated people was impaled on the broken glass. Part of a uniform could just be made out among the shape's twisted innards-turned-outtards. It had been a cop.

Had been.

"We're dying of thirst over here!" Anna announced.

"Anna," Sam said, and the urgency of it cut through Anna's own drunken haze. He nodded to the screen, and she frowned as she stared up at it.

"What am I looking at?" she asked.

As if in answer to her question, the newsreader was replaced by some amateur footage taken from just outside the bank. A towering figure wearing a horned animal skull on his head and an armor of leather and bone splashed through the blood puddles. He held a squirming female bank teller in one hand, hefting her into the air by her throat.

She kicked and thrashed in his grip for a few moments, before something exploded simultaneously through her back and front. Her stomach, Sam guessed, from the way her intestines spilled out through the holes. The guy with the skull helmet tossed her lifeless body aside, then turned his attention to the person filming. The footage froze as he closed in, giving a blurry close-up of his leering face.

"Who the hell is that guy?" Anna muttered.

"He calls himself the Beef Chief," said Randy, appearing between them in a genuinely impressive display of stealth. "Absorbo had some run-ins with him a few times a couple of years back. Big hitter. Far as anyone has been able to figure out, his powers grant him mental command over meat."

"*Meat?*" said Anna.

"M-E-A-T," said Randy, bypassing any confusion.

"How the hell does that work?" Anna wondered.

"Those people," Sam whispered. "Look what he did to those people."

The amateur footage cut out and was replaced by some lingering and lurid high-definition close-ups of blood pools. A scattering of hundred dollar bills floated atop one of them, suggesting this had been a robbery gone wrong. Or gone right, depending on who you were.

It was the next puddle that made Sam's chest go tight, though. A child's soft toy lay there, partially submerged. One glassy eye was above the surface. It stared blankly at the camera, and Sam couldn't shake the feeling that it was staring directly at him.

"My God," Sam wheezed, turning away from the screen. "What did he do? What the hell did that guy do?"

"He made a bunch of people's guts explode," Randy explained. "And then partially turned them inside-out."

"What? No, I know, I just... I mean..."

His legs gave way. He sat heavily on the floor. Nobody at the bar noticed.

"Those people," he whispered. "All those people."

"Why didn't the cops do something?" Anna demanded.

A man at the bar answered. "You kidding me? They tried to. He killed eight of them. Split them right open. This was after he'd taken out maybe a dozen people in the bank. Kids, too."

"Jesus," Anna whispered.

"Where was Doc Mighty? That's what I want to know," said another man a little further along. "Where were the Justice Platoon? Ain't they supposed to protect us from guys like this?"

Sam clutched his head in his hands and rocked back and forth. The eye of that soft toy seemed to accuse him from the puddle on the screen. *This is your fault*, it told him. *This is on you.*

He thought back to the other soft toy in his jacket pocket.

He thought of his child, and of those children who would now never be returning home.

The rest was easy.

Chuck crossed the reception area, his hand going to the gun tucked into the back of his pants, more through force of habit than anything else.

He paused at the door, took cover beside it, and then rolled up the blind. "Huh," he said, peering through the glass.

The door creaked a little as he pulled it open.

Sam stood outside on the street. He was swaying slightly, looked like he'd been crying, and part of his white shirt poked out through the zipper of his pants like some weird fabric penis.

Anna stood a few steps behind him, her face pale behind her freckles. Randy was beside her, his cape pulled up over his face in a pose that was presumably meant to be mysterious.

"So," said Chuck. "You saw?"

Sam swallowed, then nodded. "We saw."

"Well, OK," said Chuck. He stepped aside and opened the door all the way. "Then I guess we'd best get started."

CHAPTER NINE

CHUCK STOOD by the sliding doors of a wide elevator, but hadn't yet pushed the call button. He regarded the trio standing before him, two of them gently swaying, one hiding his face with a bright red child's cape.

Anyone looking closely at Chuck's face would have seen that his current expression was the visual equivalent of a lengthy sigh. Fortunately, Sam and Anna were too inebriated to notice this, and the change of humidity between outside and inside had made Randy's goggles steam up to the point he could barely see a thing.

"And you're sure about this?" Chuck asked.

"We're sure," said Sam.

"Ish," Anna added.

"Oh. Yeah. We're sure-ish. But, like, mostly sure and just a tiny bit *ish*."

Anna frowned at him. After a brief spell of near-sobriety, she had returned to a rubbery-faced level of drunkenness which made her look a bit like a cartoon character.

"Maybe not a *tiny* bit. Let's say a bit. We're a bit *ish*."

"I'm not any *ish*," Randy said. "I've never been more sure of anything in my whole damn life!"

Chuck clicked his fingers a couple of times. "Uh, Randy? We're over here."

"Oh." Randy rotated himself thirty degrees in the direction of Chuck's voice. "I've never been more sure of anything in my whole damn life!" he repeated, lowering his cape and punching a fist into the opposite palm for emphasis. "Nobody turns the good citizens of Cityopolis inside out. Not on my watch."

Chuck puffed out his cheeks and looked between them all again. "OK. OK. But this is your last chance to back out. Once you're in, you're all the way in. Your lives? They're not just lives anymore. They're secret identities. If you do this, everything changes. Everything."

Sam raised a hand.

"You don't have to put your hand up. What's the question?"

"Can I still see my son?"

"Of course," said Chuck. "We're not monsters. But make no mistake—if anyone finds out who you are, they could go after him. Your very existence will put him in danger."

Sam pictured that soft toy lying in the blood pool. He felt the other one tucked up in his pocket. "Way I see it, he's already in danger," Sam said. "At least this way maybe we can protect him. All of them."

"And everyone's agreed?" Chuck asked.

"You're goddamn right!" Randy spat.

"Yeah. You know, *ish*," said Anna. She pinched her forefinger and thumb close together and held them up. "Can we get on with it? I'm this close to throwing up."

"OK, then if everyone's in, let's do this," Chuck said. He tapped the only button on the wall by the elevator door. The door slid aside smoothly, revealing the starkly lit elevator car beyond. It was large enough to accommodate twenty or more people, or roughly five Chucks.

After ushering the others inside, Chuck stepped in. The weight of him made the elevator cable squeak, and Sam was relieved that he was too drunk to really dwell on what would happen if the cable snapped.

They started moving without Chuck having to press anything. A tiny jerk and a microsecond moment of weightlessness told them they were traveling downward, descending into some underground lair built deep below the city.

"Only a handful of people alive know about this place's existence," Chuck told them. "Even fewer have ever seen it. Until you are ready, this will be your home."

The elevator glided to a stop. Chuck straightened the lapels of his jacket and adjusted his tie.

"Lady. Gentlemen. Welcome to the Sidekicks Initiative."

Sam's eyes twinkled with anticipation and wonder as the door slid open.

They immediately stopped twinkling when a small, cluttered storeroom was revealed. Battered cardboard boxes had been stacked haphazardly against every wall, and a layer of dust had accumulated across pretty much every surface.

The only dust-free exception was a table near the center of the room. It was the kind of thing you might find in a staff canteen—thin Formica top and black metal legs. A stack of newspapers sat on top, alongside a dirty mug with a fork in it.

"Sweet," said Anna. "Justice Platoon, eat your heart out."

"Yeah, we had some budget cuts a few years back," Chuck admitted, scratching the back of his head in a subconscious attempt to hide his embarrassment. "This isn't all of it, we just moved a lot of stuff in here so we didn't have to heat the rest of the place."

Sam noticed a fold-down camp bed in the corner of the

room, half-hidden by towers of boxes. He chose not to comment on it. Hell, his own apartment wasn't much better.

"Mari's powering everything up, so we'll be good to go in a few hours," Chuck explained.

"Who's Mari?" Randy demanded. "And why haven't you mentioned her before now?"

"Because it was none of your damn business until now," Chuck replied. "She helps me run the project. She handles a lot of the tech stuff."

"So... she's your assistant?" asked Randy.

"No. And I wouldn't let her hear you calling her that," Chuck said. "She's my partner."

"Your sexual partner?" Randy demanded.

"What does that have to do with anything?" asked Sam.

"Because relationships between co-workers can get messy," Randy growled. "If those two are..." He made a circle with finger and thumb and poked the opposite pointer finger through it, sliding it back and forth and whistling in time with each thrust. "... then they could be putting this whole thing in jeopardy."

"OK, one, that's none of your damn business," Chuck told him. "And two, absolutely not. We work together, that's all."

Randy's eyes narrowed to slits. "Good. Then I suggest you keep it that way. For all our sakes."

"Thanks. I'll keep that in mind," Chuck told him.

Sam took another look around the place. He'd been expecting some vast underground complex with computers lining the walls and probably some sort of moving walkway. To say this was underwhelming would be quite the understatement.

"So, what happens now?" asked Sam, a little afraid of what the answer might be. "Do we go after this Beef Chief guy?"

Chuck snorted and smirked. Several moments passed like that, before he realized Sam wasn't joking.

"Oh, you're being serious? No. The Beef Chief is a Level Six supervillain. Maybe even Level Seven, we don't know enough yet to make that call. He's way out of your league for now."

Sam's eyes widened. "What? So, we're just letting him get away with what he did?"

"No. Not permanently," Chuck countered. "But for now, until we've got you trained up, yes."

"Well that's bullshit," said Anna.

Chuck turned on her. "No. It isn't. Those guys you fought earlier? The ones that handed you your asses? You want to guess what their supervillain level is?"

It quickly became clear that no, she didn't want to guess. Sam took a stab on her behalf. "Three?"

"Zero," said Chuck. "Because they weren't supervillains. They were nobodies. And yet they took you all down."

"They had guns!" Sam protested.

"*Of course* they had guns! What, you think the ones out in the real world won't? Guns are easy. You did just see the Beef Chief turn those people inside-out, yes? You did watch that?" asked Chuck. "I ain't ever seen a gun that can do that."

"Well, yes..." Sam began. The way he said it suggested it should've been followed up with a 'but,' only he couldn't think of one.

"Randy took out two of them," Anna said. "The henchmen, I mean. That's not bad."

"Took them out my ass," said Chuck. "They collided in the smoke and knocked each other out."

Sam and Anna both turned to Randy. "You said you knocked them out," said Sam.

"I did. In a sense," Randy argued.

"Was it a made-up sense?" asked Anna.

There was a loud *buzzing* from the other end of the store-room that made Sam jump and also dropped some subtle hints about the severity of the hangover he could look forward to later.

"Relax, dude," Anna told him. "It's just a... Actually, what was that?"

"Security door," Chuck explained. "Mari's back. Want to meet her?"

There was a vague rumble of apathy from Anna, some sounds of polite agreement from Sam, and a growled, "Not really," from Randy.

"Tough shit. It wasn't really a question. You're going to meet her," said Chuck. He gestured to a door that was half-hidden behind a stack of boxes just as it slid open. "Here she comes now."

It was safe to say that Mari was not what Sam had expected. She was shorter for one thing, barely clearing five feet. She was unusually proportioned, with an egg-shaped torso, stumpy legs, and arms so long her knuckles brushed against the floor.

She was also made entirely of metal, and had a circular screen for a head, on which an animation of some cartoon-like facial features were being displayed.

"Mobile Armored Roving Interface," Chuck announced. A flicker of doubt crossed his face. "Or Mobile Artificial Robot Intelligence. Or mobile something. I just call her Mari."

"She's a goddam robot!" Randy barked.

Anna raised her eyebrows. "So?"

Randy shrugged. "Nothing. I was just pointing it out."

"She clanks when she walks and has a TV for a face," said Anna. "We didn't need it pointed out."

"Oh, my dears, let's get a look at you!" said Mari. Her voice was what Sam would describe as 'grandmotherly.' There was a hint of artificiality about some of the words, but overall Mari had the air of a kindly old relative about her, albeit one housed entirely inside a metal exoskeleton.

"You must be Sam. Goodness, how you've grown. I remember you when you were way down here," she said, holding a hand up to indicate a height just a few inches shorter than herself.

"Uh, hi," said Sam. "What do you...? Do you mean we've met before?"

"Not officially," said Mari. The features on her face showed a dazzling digital smile that suggested a face much younger than the accompanying voice. "But you know how it is."

Sam didn't have time to point out that no, he didn't know how it was, before Mari clanked across to Anna.

"Ms. Allen," she said, bowing her flat screen head a little. "So good to see you. Have you been taking care of yourself, dear? You're looking a little worse for wear?"

Anna self-consciously touched her hair, then crossed one arm across her body, catching the other arm by the elbow. "Jesus, what are you, my mother?"

"No, dear. You're an orphan, remember?" said Mari, that animated smile still fixed in place. "It's quite clearly marked in your biographical information."

"Figure of speech," Anna replied.

"Oh. My apologies. That is not one I have come across before. May I have your permission to store it in my databanks?"

Anna shrugged. "Do what you like."

"Thank you!" said Mari. Her eyes blinked, becoming two black lines on the pale pink background of her face. "Done. I am very sorry if I caused any offense."

She waddled around on her stubby legs. "Randy Rabble, as I live and breathe!"

"You don't live or breathe," Randy pointed out.

"Hmm. Not breathe, maybe," Mari admitted. "But I like to think I'm alive in my own way."

"But you aren't," Randy countered.

"In my own way."

"Which isn't a real way," insisted Randy.

"It is. In my own way," said Mari. To her credit, she didn't seem to be getting the slightest bit annoyed, and remained as cheerful as ever.

"But that's meaningless," Randy growled. "I could say I'm a bunch of bananas *in my own way*. Doesn't mean I am."

"Yeah. I'm actually pretty sure you might be," Anna told him. She smiled at Mari. "Ignore him. He's... Actually, you don't need an excuse. Just ignore him in general."

Chuck stepped forward and patted Mari on her rounded shoulders. "Mari here is going to help with your training. She's also responsible for the outfits you'll be wearing."

Anna's eyes widened in horror. "Wait. What? What outfits?"

"Our costumes," said Randy, practically frothing at the mouth with excitement. "How can we be heroes without costumes?"

"It will be a cold day in Hell before anyone gets me in spandex," said Anna. "Seriously, I'm all for saving the world, defeating villainy, all that jazz, but if it involves squeezing my thighs into a spandex jumpsuit, I am out the door."

"There's no spandex, dear, I promise," said Mari. "This isn't the nineties. They're much more practical these days."

Anna still looked a little doubtful.

"Also, they have built-in exoskeleton technology which will enhance your strength, speed, stamina, and reaction times."

Anna looked a little less doubtful. Sam was positively beaming.

"That sounds useful," he said.

"I don't need that stuff," said Randy. "I'm already good to go."

Chuck looked him up and down. "Well, guess we'll find out. You're all booked in for a test in five minutes so we can assess your current level of fitness."

Sam's face fell. His hangover had been creeping up on him. He could feel it thumping at the base of his skull, and yet he was still drunk enough for the room to be gently spinning. Neither of these helped get him excited for a fitness test.

"Can't it wait a few hours?" he asked. "Or until tomorrow, maybe?"

"No," said Chuck.

"I just think, if we have a good night's sleep, and maybe some Advil..."

Mari's face became a garish shade of red. Her features twisted into a furious scowl. "Get going, you pathetic, sub-human filth!" she roared in a voice that ramped Sam's headache up to full volume. One of her long arms extended toward the door. "Hup, hup, hup. Move out, move out!"

"OK! Wow," Sam protested. "Calm down."

"Don't you back sass me, you worthless little asshole!" Mari boomed. "Move, move, move! Go, go, go! Or so help me, I will kick your skinny behind all the way there."

"I'm going!" Sam yelped, hurrying in the direction of the door.

"Thank you, dear," said Mari, calming down instantly. Her face returned to its usual soothing shade of pink. "I appreciate your cooperation, I really do. This way."

"You gonna let a robot talk to you like that?" Randy asked.

"Yes. Yes, I am," said Sam, following Mari toward the door.

Randy nodded slowly and made a drawn out, "Uh-huh," sound under his breath, like he was making a mental note of this.

Sam could feel the back of his shirt sticking to him with

sweat. His breathing was shallow, and the drum solo headache had now become a full marching band.

"Hey, relax," said Anna, spotting his look of terror. She gave him a playful nudge. "We used to train every day with the damn Justice Platoon. How hard can this be?"

CHAPTER TEN

"KILL ME," Anna wheezed. "Please God, someone kill me."

Despite her protests, and the rictus of pain and horror that currently made up her face, her legs continued to move as the treadmill belt trundled by beneath her. She gripped the rails of the machine with both hands, which allowed her to occasionally lift both feet off the belt, to rest, before Mari would scream at her to, "Cut that shit out!" in a high-pitched, inhuman squeal.

She wore baggy shorts and an oversized gray t-shirt, both of which Chuck had provided. She'd been offered running shoes, too, but had chosen to run barefoot for the first few minutes, until the belt had torn a layer of skin off both her soles, and she'd taken up the offer of shoes.

Sam ran on the machine on her left, dressed pretty much identically. He stared down at the display on the treadmill, rather than at the mirror that ran the length of the wall ahead of them. He didn't like watching the way he jiggled beneath his t-shirt, felt awkward looking at Anna, and was slightly creeped out by the way Randy stared back at him from his own machine on Anna's right side.

The first few minutes had been hell. There were no two ways about it. His legs had quickly begun to ache, his headache had gone from 'marching band' to 'the New York Philharmonic Orchestra', and his chest had tightened to the point where he was convinced he was having several simultaneous heart attacks.

Since then, though, things had improved. It was still far from being an enjoyable experience, but it wasn't as body and soul-destroying as he'd been expecting. His legs still ached, but it was more of a vague '*this is doing us good,*' sort of dull throb, rather than the urgent '*call us an ambulance!*' burn of previously.

His headache had retreated back to being a lurking grumble, and while his bladder situation was on the brink of becoming a pressing issue, he was generally feeling not-too-terrible.

"How are you doing this?" Anna wheezed. Her face was a shade of scarlet that absorbed all her freckles, making them disappear. Several long strands of hair were plastered to her forehead with sweat, and she was breathing like a racehorse having a panic attack.

"I walk a lot," Sam said, meeting her gaze in the mirror. This was, he supposed, the truth, although he left out the bit about it being a way of saving on bus fares, and the fact that he speed-walked everywhere in the hope of avoiding confrontation.

He looked further along the mirrored wall to where Randy continued to glare at him. He had turned down the offer of running gear and was still kitted out in his cap, cape, and jeans combo. His boots were heavy, workmanlike things, and thudded heavily on the treadmill belt with each increasingly unsteady step.

"You OK there, Randy?" he asked.

"Just... fine," Randy replied, although the three-second

pause between each word suggested he was struggling more than he was letting on. "This is... a walk..."

He wheezed through his nose several times, still holding Sam's gaze.

"... in... the park."

"OK, good," said Sam. "I just thought you looked like you were struggling a little."

"Struggling?" Randy said. He tried to laugh, but it came out as a series of hissing gasps. Sweat ran down from beneath his leather cap and into his darkening beard. "I think... we should go... faster."

"Fuck off!" Anna spat.

"Yeah, I'm not sure that's a good idea," Sam told him.

"What's the matter?" Randy coughed. "Chicken?"

Sam shook his head. "No, I just..."

Randy's hand went to the lever controlling the treadmill's speed. He squinted at Sam as he nudged the yellow plastic handle forward a few notches. The thumping of his feet increased in both volume and frequency.

"Please return your treadmill to the previous speed," said Mari.

"Oh, I think..." Randy began, but the rest of the sentence became just a series of breathless whispers. His cape flopped up and down with each frantic step, as every footfall brought him closer to the end of the treadmill belt.

"Randy, slow down," Sam said. "It's great. We're all impressed, now slow down."

Randy composed himself enough to spit out a full sentence in one breath. "I'm just getting started!" he growled, jamming the treadmill up a gear.

Everyone watching knew, of course, what was going to happen. It was the speed at which it happened that caught them off guard.

The moment he lifted his hand from the speed control

lever, Randy lost his footing on the treadmill. His legs were whipped out behind him until he was horizontal in mid-air. His hands frantically grabbed for the treadmill's controls, fell short, and then his upper half landed heavily on the belt.

The belt, now a whirring blur of speed, clearly resented his presence and catapulted him off, flipping his legs backward over his head. To his credit, Randy made not a sound as he was launched across the room, his face dragging on the rough carpet tiles. He hit the wall knees first, his momentum such that he left two rounded dents in the plaster, then another where his head hit a split-second later.

"I'm OK. I'm OK. Totally meant that," he announced, jumping up.

Sam and Anna both dismounted their own treadmills, ignoring Mari's barked protests.

One of the lenses of Randy's goggles had been cracked, and there was a red mark running the whole length of his nose, presumably from where his face had been dragged along the carpet.

Blood seeped through his jeans at both knees, and the palms of his hands were shiny, not with sweat, but from where the top few layers of skin had been worn down.

"You sure you're OK?" Anna asked, bending over with her hands on her thighs as she gulped in sweet, sweet air.

"Couldn't be better," Randy said. He took a step toward them. His eyes widened in pain, and a strange, high-pitched babble burst from his lips.

A moment later, he hit the floor.

"OK, so maybe I could be a *little* better," he admitted.

✈

"We brought you some grapes," said Anna. She *clonked* the half-empty wine bottle on the bedside table. "Kind of."

Sam leaned on the railing at the foot of Randy's hospital-style bed. He wasn't sure whether to be worried or relieved that the complex came complete with its own state-of-the-art medical facilities. The fact they'd passed a door marked 'Morgue' on the way in was definitely giving him cause for concern, though.

"Feeling better?" he asked.

"I feel great," said Randy, although the low moan he punctuated the sentence with didn't help convince them. "I don't know why they've put me in here. I broke some ribs, that's all. It's nothing serious."

"That's pretty serious," said Sam. He shook his head when Anna offered him a glass of wine.

"Ha!" Randy snorted. "You think that's bad? Check this out."

He threw back his covers to reveal that he was naked from the waist up. His left side was a collage of purples and blacks, but it was the rest of his torso that really took the breath away.

His chest was a checkerboard of scar tissue, some of it recent, but most of it old. It started with a jagged scar across the base of his throat and concluded with a series of slash marks just above his solar plexus.

His chest wasn't the only part of him to have suffered. The skin was puckered around two round craters in his upper abdomen—gunshot entry wounds which hadn't healed well, Sam guessed.

Despite being tall and skinny, Randy had the beginnings of a slight podge around his middle. Hair grew unevenly from it, mostly thanks to a couple of burn marks that rippled the skin to the right of his belly button, and which were completely bald.

"My God. What happened?" asked Sam.

Anna winced at the sight of the damage, then took a

good-sized glug of wine to help take her mind off it.

"A lifetime of crime-fighting, that's what happened," Randy growled. He pointed to a gouge-mark on his shoulder. "That was Millennium Bug," he said. "Got his suckers into me real good back in ninety-nine."

"Wow," said Anna.

"It was New Year's Eve," Randy said. "Had to burn him off with a dessert sparkler."

"Jesus," Sam muttered.

"That's nothing," said Randy. He pointed to the gunshot wounds. "Sniper fire from an international assassin sent to kill the president."

"The US President?" asked Anna, her wine glass almost to her lips.

"President of the Denver Horticultural Society," said Randy.

"Oh. So next best thing," said Anna.

Randy nodded, apparently missing the sarcasm. "You'd be amazed how seriously those guys take what they do."

"So it seems," Sam conceded.

"This was Burn Baby. That little bastard," Randy spat, continuing the tour of his torso. "And you see these bite marks?"

"They're pretty hard to miss," said Sam.

Randy nodded. "You know Pat Sharky? The gangster?"

Sam wracked his brains. "No..."

"Based in Vegas?" Randy explained. "Has a sister who married a cop? Caused all kinds of friction in the family back in the day."

"Um... It's not ringing any bells," Sam was forced to admit.

"Drives an old Pontiac Firebird? Muscles in on a few casinos, but makes most of his money from drugs and people trafficking? Brings them in from Eastern Europe?"

"Which ones, the drugs or the people?" Anna asked.

"Both. Usually one inside the other," Randy growled. "And not in the order you probably think."

Sam puffed out his cheeks. "No. Can't say I know him."

"He walks with a cane? Always has a handkerchief in the top pocket of his suit, a different color for every day of the week?"

Sam gave a vague shrug of his shoulders. "No..."

"Has the head of a shark?" Randy said.

"Oh, *Pat* Sharky," said Anna. "The shark head guy? Gotcha." She pointed to the bite marks. "Was that him?"

"You bet your ass it was," Randy growled. "Well, someone pretending to be him, anyway. Which is pretty much the same."

"Loosely," said Anna.

"More or less the same," Randy insisted.

"Yeah, but more less than more," said Anna. She topped up her glass. She had so far not offered any of the wine to Randy, mostly because she didn't want to have to watch him lapping it up.

There was something bothering Sam about Randy's torso. The scars and bruising were the big headline events, obviously, but there was something else he couldn't quite put his finger on. Something not quite right.

"Nipples!" he cried, when the realization finally hit him.

Randy regarded his chest. "Oh. Those. The Flesh Collector took them."

Anna snorted into her glass, inhaling wine through her mouth before immediately exhaling it through both nostrils. "*Who?*" she wheezed.

"The Flesh Collector."

"Who the fuck is the Flesh Collector?" Anna demanded.

"He was one of the Great Gassby's big villains. Took both my nipples for his collection."

"Jesus. For his collection of what?" Sam asked.

"Nipples, presumably," said Anna. She looked to Randy for confirmation. "Right?"

"Well, just body parts in general," Randy replied. "He took both nipples, one of my earlobes, and a three-inch square section of my left butt-cheek."

"But... why?" asked Sam. "I mean that is..."

"Totally fucking *bananas*," Anna concluded. "Can I assume he's safely locked up forever in a psychiatric hospital somewhere?"

"He *was* in the Cityopolis Asylum," growled Randy. "But he escaped. Just like they always do."

"You know, I always wondered about that," said Sam. "I mean, the Justice Platoon spent... what? Ten billion dollars on a space station? They couldn't have helped pay for better locks for the asylum? I swear to God that place has a revolving front door."

Anna topped up her glass again. "Speaking of crazy..." She gestured to Randy's ruined torso. "How come you kept doing that stuff to yourself?"

"I didn't," said Randy. "Those villainous scumbags did. You think I cut off my own nipples?"

"Well, no, but—"

"Carved a chunk out of my own ass? Shot myself? Stabbed myself? Vigorously sandpapered my own scrotum?"

"No—also, ew, too much information—but what I'm saying is, you didn't have to get involved in any of that stuff. You could've just walked away."

Randy looked blankly back at her. "Walked away?" he said, speaking the words slowly as if trying them out for the first time. "When the world was in danger? How could I walk away?"

"Easy," said Anna. She used two fingers to mime a walking action. "Like that. The Justice Platoon and all those other guys could've taken care of it, I'm sure."

Randy appeared to consider this. He pulled his covers back up, hiding his scars. "I was given great power," he said.

Sam and Anna both opened their mouths to dispute this, but the look of sincerity on his face stopped them both.

"With that great power..."

"Comes great responsibility," said Sam.

"Came *awesome opportunities*," Randy corrected. "To kick villains in the balls. And occasionally the vagina. And also to make the world a safer place for those less capable, less able to defend themselves."

Sam thought about pointing out that Randy's own inability to defend himself had led to him having both nipples and part of his ass removed, but the poor guy's day had been rough enough without him being hit by that particular dose of home truthage.

"Maybe you two felt comfortable turning your back on the world, but not me," Randy spat. "You may have quit being soldiers, but for Butterfly King the war never stopped."

"OK, well... good for you, I guess," said Anna. Both her bottle and glass were now empty, which seemed to be her cue to leave. She collected both, caught Sam's eye, and motioned with her head toward the door.

"We'd better let you rest," said Sam. "Chuck tells me we have a big day tomorrow."

"I don't need rest," said Randy, but the way he stifled a yawn suggested this wasn't entirely true. "But you two go. Do what you have to."

"OK," said Sam.

"Just don't have sex with each other."

Sam's cheeks tingled. He glanced at Anna and gave a derisive laugh. "Ha! What? As if! No. I wouldn't! Nuh-uh. No, way."

"Thanks for the confidence boost there, Sam," Anna replied. "Appreciate it."

Sam's cheeks stung hotter. "Well, I mean... We... You wouldn't. We wouldn't. That's just... Haha! No. Right?"

"Depends how much wine Chuck's got stashed away," she said, looking him up and down. "I mean, it'd have to be a lot..."

"Don't do it," Randy warned. "We all know what happened with Wildebeest and Lady Magma, right?"

"No," Sam admitted.

"They started a relationship, and when it all went wrong they couldn't work together. Their whole team collapsed. And all because Lady Magma couldn't keep it in her pants."

"Couldn't keep *what* in her...?" Anna began to ask, before deciding that she didn't really want to know. She bustled Sam toward the door. "Doesn't matter. We'll keep it in mind and try not to have sex with each other."

"Promise me," said Randy. "Swear it—in the name of justice!"

"Cross my heart, hope to, you know, whatever," said Anna. She waved an empty glass vaguely in his direction. "Get some rest. See you tomorrow!"

"Take care, Randy," Sam called, but he was bundled out into the corridor before he could catch the reply.

A few moments of uncomfortable not-quite-silence followed, as Sam tried to find the right words to say, but found only 'ums' and 'ahs' and other vague vocalizations.

"So..." was pretty much the pinnacle of it. He followed that up with a few sporadic clicks of his fingers, some uncomfortable shuffling, and a nod toward Randy's door.

"You see all those scars?" he eventually asked. "Wow."

"Right?" said Anna. "Crazy."

"Cra-zee," Sam agreed.

"Remind me never to cross swords with the Flesh Collector," said Anna.

Sam laughed, a little too loudly. "Ha! We don't want you

losing your nipples, too!"

Shit. Why had he mentioned her nipples?

He realized he was staring at them.

Double shit!

"Or anything else!" he quickly added. "I wouldn't want to see any part of you being cut off. Or carved out. Or otherwise removed."

"Aww. That's so sweet of you," Anna said. "I mean, I think."

Sam could feel himself becoming a babbling mess. He was uncomfortably out of his depth here and sinking fast.

"No, I just meant... I mean..."

"It's fine. I get it," said Anna. "Relax." She jabbed a thumb along the corridor behind them. "I'm going to find some more wine. You coming?"

Sam's jaw flapped open and closed a few times. He pointed in the opposite direction, toward a door. "Actually, I think I'm going to go get some rest, too." He yawned theatrically. "I am beat. It's been a long day."

"It's three-thirty in the afternoon," Anna pointed out.

"Loooong day," Sam reiterated. He stretched, yawned again, then gave Anna a sheepish wave as he made for the door. "So, uh, I'll see you tomorrow."

"See you tomorrow, then," said Anna. She watched him open the door. He stared into it in silence, not quite sure what to do. "You do know that's a closet, right?"

"Hmm?" said Sam. "Oh! Yes. Yes, I know," he said. Then, with a final smile and an awkward nod, he stepped inside, turned around, and quietly closed the door.

Anna waited.

The door opened. Sam stepped out.

"Yep. That's... Everything seems..." He gestured the other way along the corridor. "So... this way?"

"This way," Anna confirmed. "Come on, I'll walk you out."

CHAPTER ELEVEN

SAM'S NIGHT was a restless one, plagued by nightmares when he could sleep, and worry when he couldn't.

He'd been allowed to phone Laura to check how Corey was after his ordeal, but Brian had answered. Brian had told him that Laura didn't want to speak to him, then had spent a good eight or nine minutes admonishing him, as if it had somehow been his fault that Corey had been put at risk.

In hindsight, of course, it sort of was, but he was damned if he was going to tell Brian that.

"Here's the thing, Sam," he'd said. "Laura has moved on, as you know. She's with me now, we're very happy."

"And I'm very happy for you," Sam had lied.

"Thank you. That's good to know," Brian had replied, but in the tones of someone who knew bullshit when they heard it.

It was at this point that he'd caught Sam off guard.

"Here's the other thing, though—Corey, he hasn't moved on. He'll never move on. I might be living in the house, driving him to school, having regular athletic sex with his smoking hot mom..."

There was a *thwack* sound, and Sam could picture Laura slapping him on the arm.

"But you're his dad. Always will be, Sam," Brian continued. "The kid's nuts about you. Talks about you all the time. You're his hero."

Sam had felt his heart surge at that. So much so, in fact, that it had blocked anything coherent coming out of his mouth. "Uh, well... That's..."

"But you can't go putting him at risk like that," Brian continued. "You want to play the hero? You do it on your own time, not when you've got Corey with you."

"The guy had a gun pointed at Corey's head," Sam had protested. "What was I supposed to do, let him shoot him? I did the right thing. I'm not the bad guy in this situation, Brian!"

"Oh? Then how come you're the one who ended up in jail?" Brian had asked.

The conversation had ended very soon after. Sam had hung up the handset eight or nine times, each one more violently than the time before, then found Mari and asked her to take him to his quarters.

His quarters, it turned out, were so cramped they were more like eighths. The room was barely large enough to contain the set of bunk beds and small sink that made up the entirety of its furnishings.

At first, Sam had worried that they were all going to be sharing accommodation, but when midnight came and went, and there was no sign of anyone else, he began to relax a little.

By 3am, he'd never felt more lonely in his life.

Next morning, Sam stood in a line between Anna and a

surprisingly mobile Randy, listening to Chuck. He was complaining about their performance so far, which came as no surprise to Sam or Anna, but seemed to be a personal affront to Randy.

"Fitness test results were disappointing," he said. "We all saw what happened to Randy. Anna, I'm pretty sure you clinically died at least twice..."

Anna nodded, almost proudly. "Right on."

"And Sam, yours was just generally something of a letdown."

Sam took issue with that. "I thought I did OK. I hit a pretty steady jog."

Chuck peered at him as if over the rim of a pair of invisible glasses. "And you think that's going to take down a supervillain, do you? A 'steady jog'?"

"Well, no. But..."

Chuck folded his hands behind his back and resumed pacing before Sam could offer any sort of counter-argument.

"Mari and I reviewed the footage of your fight with the henchmen yesterday. Some of the moves we saw there were surprisingly effective."

Sam and Anna exchanged looks of pleasant surprise. Randy rocked back on his heels a little with satisfaction.

"Sadly, they were all moves made by the other guys. You three were terrible."

"*Two*," Randy corrected.

"Say what?" Chuck asked.

Randy gestured down the line. "Those *two* were terrible."

"No. No, it was all three of you," Chuck insisted.

Randy smirked. "Oh, I don't think so."

"Well... I know so."

"Sure," said Randy, winking behind his goggles. "You keep telling yourself that. We both know the truth."

"One of us knows the truth," said Chuck. "And that's me."

"Gotcha," said Randy. He tapped himself on the side of the nose and winked again.

Chuck sighed, spent a long time just standing there shaking his head, then moved back to loom in front of Sam. Placing his hands on his hips, he addressed all three of them.

"Turning you into a cohesive and organized team of crime-fighters is going to be more of a challenge than I thought," he said.

"I've said that from the start," said Sam. "Maybe we should forget the whole idea. I mean, I know we have to stop the Beef Chief, but maybe we could act as, like, advisors or something, you know? Rather than actually go do the fighting stuff."

"I'd be up for that," said Anna.

"Run from the mission? I'd rather be impaled through both thighs by a rusty metal spike," Randy growled. "Again."

"Again?!" said Anna, leaning past Sam.

"Spike Master," Randy said, like that explained everything.

"Everyone shut up," Chuck barked. He turned to the door of the briefing room, where Mari stood waiting. "Can you go bring him in?"

"Sure thing!" Mari chirped. Her various parts spun as she turned herself toward the door. It slid open at her approach, then closed behind her as she left.

"Are we getting someone new to play with?" asked Anna.

Chuck nodded. "I'm bringing in a mentor. Someone with experience of running a superteam," he said, fumbling in his pocket. Sam expected the agent to produce a business card or something else that would reveal the mentor's identity, but instead, he took out a crumpled pack of cigarettes.

"Who?" Sam asked again. He was pretty up to speed on the Justice Platoon, but hadn't kept track of the smaller teams that had sprung up across the country over the years, let alone who had led any of them. "Red Dervish?"

Chuck drew a single cigarette from the pack and clamped it between his lips. "Red Dervish died in oh-four."

"No, I meant the other Red Dervish," said Sam. "The new guy."

"Oh, that one. Died in oh-five."

"Wow."

"Bomb up the ass," Randy added.

"Jesus."

Sam looked to the others for suggestions while Chuck lit up his smoke.

"Power Rod?" Anna guessed.

"Dead," said Chuck, inhaling slowly.

"Brasshands?" Sam suggested. "I think he led the West Coast Protectors for a while."

Two plumes of white smoke drifted from Chuck's nostrils. "Did he?"

"For a while. I think," Sam said.

"It's not him. And he's also dead."

Sam blinked. "Wasn't he invulnerable? Or was that just his hands?"

"Just his hands. They're still fine."

"Oh. Well, I guess that's something." He puffed out his cheeks. "So, who? If it wasn't one of those guys, then who..."

"Wait. Not Magic Circle?" Randy snarled.

"Christ, no," said Chuck, coughing out a lungful of smoke. "Last I heard he was in some fucking... I don't know. Shadow realm. With any luck he'll stay there."

Everyone nodded in agreement at this.

"Who, then?" Sam asked.

Chuck looked away, rubbing his chin. There was a shadow of stubble there that suggested his night had been almost as long as Sam's had.

"Kapitän Nazi," Chuck muttered.

"What?!" Sam yelped. "Kapitän ...? But he's a bad guy!"

"He's not *that* bad."

"Not that...? He was one of Doc Mighty's old regulars. His name's Kapitän Nazi for Christ's sake! He led a team of villains called *The Bastard Squad*. The second-in-command of which was called Face Cannibal. Which means he was one *worse* than that guy!"

"Calm down before you give yourself a heart attack," Chuck told him. "Kapitän Nazi was just his schtick. It was a persona. A performance. You know that. Under the armor and, you know, the Swastika face tattoos, he's just a regular Joe, like you and me."

"He has Swastika tattoos on his face?" said Anna. "Wait, what am I saying? Of course he does."

Chuck dropped his half-smoked cigarette on the floor and ground it under his heel. "Look, the point is, he's on our side now. You don't have to like it, but he wants to help. And you don't have to call him Kapitän Nazi. In fact, he's specifically requested that we don't. He's asked us to use his real name. John."

"John?" Sam frowned. "That's it? Kapitän Nazi's real name is John?"

"His real name is John," Chuck confirmed. He straightened up, adjusted his tie, and lowered his voice to a barely audible mumble. "John Hitler."

Anna coughed. "Wait, what?"

The door opened then, stopping the conversation dead. Mari entered first, her digital smile bobbing gently on her face screen. A tall, athletic-looking man with a sensible haircut that was graying at the temples entered behind her, a duffel bag slung over one shoulder.

Sam bristled at the sight of him. Or rather, the long-dormant Kid Random bristled at the sight of him, as the memories of countless frantic battles and evil schemes came rushing back.

Kapitän Nazi had been one of the most persistent thorns in Doc Mighty's side back in the day, as he attempted to establish his 'Fourth Reich' with the help of his army of Robo-Fascists.

His powerset was ridiculously impressive. He had been the prototype *Gottmensch*—which literally translated as 'God man'—created by the Nazis using a combination of early gene therapy, unstable chemical treatments, and some good old-fashioned robotic implants, all under the watchful gaze of Adolf Hitler himself.

A fortuitously timed Allied attack had collapsed the bunker where the Gottmensch was being worked on, killing the scientists responsible, and burying him alive for almost half a century.

When he eventually clawed his way free, the Second World War was long over. For Kapitän Nazi, though, the battle was just beginning.

His experimental heritage granted him great strength, speed, agility, and stamina. None of these on their own came close to Doc Mighty levels, but his devious, diabolical mind made him a force to be reckoned with. The ten-thousand strong army of Nazi robots helped, too, although quite where he sourced these from, nobody knew. There were rumors that some wealthy Cityopolis businessman had helped fund and create the robots, but Doc Mighty was never able to find proof.

Kapitän Nazi had almost brought Cityopolis to its knees a dozen times. He had killed, maimed, and tortured heroes and civilians alike. He'd even briefly stripped Doc Mighty of his powers, before breaking his back on live TV. It would almost certainly have been the end for Mighty, had it not been for the intervention of Memetzo, Mandroid Master of the Mystic Arts; an advanced alien healing pod from the Doc's home planet; and the three best chiropractors in town.

And now, here the bastard was, standing in front of them and smiling. *Smiling.*

"Hi there," he said, in an accent that was far removed from his familiar German screech. It was mostly a Mid-Western drawl, with just a hint of something European coloring the edges. His complexion was ruddy and tanned, and while there were no Swastika tattoos to be seen, some heavy scarring on both cheeks and the middle of his forehead indicated where they must once have been.

He held a hand out to Sam. "I'm John."

The hand hung there in the air, waiting.

Sam let him wait.

Kapitän Nazi's face had always been hidden by his mask, but Sam had seen those eyes up close often enough. Too often.

Too close.

"I know who you are," Sam said, still ignoring the hand. He felt something moving at the base of his brain again, like a terrifying sea monster stirring in the depths. For once, he was almost tempted to let the Kraken awaken.

Almost.

Kapitän Nazi lowered his hand. "OK, well... I get it. I do. You have reservations, and that's understandable. We don't have to be friends."

"*Friends*?!" Sam spat.

"But we *do* have to work together," Nazi continued.

"Do we, though?" asked Anna. She looked to Chuck, raising her eyebrows. "You seriously think this is a good idea? After the stuff he did?"

"Everyone deserves a second chance," Chuck said.

"Not everyone," Randy growled.

Chuck sighed. "Look, I'm not saying he didn't make mistakes..."

"I did not make mistakes," the Kapitän corrected. "Far from it."

"Are you listening to this son of a bitch?" Sam gasped. "He's still standing by the things he——"

"I was an abomination. What I did went far beyond being 'mistakes,'" Nazi continued. "I was a monster. I killed without remorse. I hurt people—good people—and I laughed while I did it."

"Really hoping there's a 'but' coming," said Anna.

"I wasn't in my right mind," Kapitän Nazi explained. His eyes had taken on a dazed look, like a boxer who'd recently taken one too many punches to the head. His voice became softer, as if speaking too loudly might startle the memories and drive them away. "When they made me, they didn't just shape my body, they shaped my mind. They twisted it. Warped it. Turned me into a champion for a cause I had never believed in."

He inhaled slowly. His fingertips traced the shiny scars on his face. "I had spoken out about their regime. I had defied them. And for that, I had to be punished."

"They made him one of them," Chuck explained.

"The greatest of them all," whispered Nazi. "And the worst."

"We helped him break his programming," said Chuck. "He's on our side now."

Anna puffed out her cheeks. "Well, I'm convinced. Don't know about you guys."

Sam turned to her, his eyes widening in surprise. "That's it? Just like that?"

"Pretty much." Anna shrugged. "See, I had an epiphany last night. While drunk." She held her arms out, gesturing to the briefing room in general. "This doesn't matter. None of it matters."

Chuck's eyes narrowed. "Oh yeah? And what makes you say that?"

"Because think about it—since when did superheroes ever stay dead?" she said. "There's always some, I don't know, birthing matrix, or space god or something that steps in to bring them back. Or we find out they were never really dead in the first place, and it was all an illusion."

"Or robots," said Randy. "Sometimes it's robots."

"Exactly! Yes. Or sometimes it's robots." Anna rocked back on her heels. "None of this matters because the Justice Platoon will be back. So, sure, let's team up with a super-strong Nazi from the 40s. Fuck it. Why not? Everything'll have worked itself out before we ever have to lift a finger, anyway."

"I don't think they're coming back this time," said Chuck. "We've been scanning for life signs up there, and we've come up with nothing."

Anna waved her hand, dismissing this. "Yeah, but that's all part of the drama. They'll come back. Their types always do."

Despite the presence of one of the most evil individuals he'd ever encountered, Sam felt a surge of hope. Anna was right, superheroes never died. Not really. Just because they'd seen Doc Mighty's body on the screen didn't mean it wasn't in the process of healing now. Or that it had even really been him.

The real Justice Platoon was probably trapped in some splinter universe, fighting to get back. Or shrunk to the size of atoms. Or hurled backward and/or forward in time. One of those, anyway, Sam was suddenly sure of it.

It was all going to be OK. He almost laughed. Everything was going to be OK.

Chuck approached and stood beside Kapitän Nazi. "Well,

I hope you're right, Anna. I do. But in the meantime, we press on as planned, and John here is a part of that plan, like it or not. He's paying his dues. And he can help. He knows how to lead a team of superpowered individuals."

"How *is* Face Cannibal these days?" asked Sam.

"Dead," replied the Kapitän.

"John tracked him down a few years back. Found him with six teenage girls, plus the remains of several more. You know, *sans face*s. John took him out. Saved those girls, single-handedly."

"Well... whoop-de-doo," said Sam, although even he felt it was a pretty lame response as responses went. "That doesn't excuse all the other things he did."

"Nothing ever will," Nazi agreed. "But that won't stop me trying."

He held Sam's gaze, smiling grimly, then looked around at Chuck. "So. Who do we have?"

"Mari, lights," said Chuck. The briefing room plunged into near-darkness. "Show him," Chuck ordered.

Nothing happened. Chuck sighed. "Please."

"That wasn't too difficult, was it?" Mari said. Her face seemed to detach itself from her screen, growing larger as it became a hologram in the air in front of her. Her features vanished, then were replaced by an image of a teenage girl in a tight-fitting costume. Fiery acne stained both her cheeks, while her bare arms were a mess of rashes and boils.

"Oh, Jesus," Anna muttered. "Did you have to? Would you look at my skin?"

"Good legs, though," said Randy.

"You know I'm like twelve in that picture, yes?"

"Good crime-fighting legs, I meant," Randy replied. "You know, for kicking and... Well, mostly just kicking."

"Allergy Girl," Chuck announced, gesturing to both Anna and the image that was now being projected into the air in front of her. He took a touchscreen tablet from Mari and scrolled through a few screens of text before stopping at the relevant section. "Her powers grant her the ability to trigger allergic reactions in her enemies, with varying degrees of success."

"Ah. The fat tongue thing," said Nazi, shooting Sam a look that sailed far too close to 'amused' for Sam's liking.

"The exact effects of her powers vary from person to person," Chuck explained. "They include hives; blisters; headache; nausea; constricted throat; sneezing; swelling of the lips, face, and tongue; itching; eye-watering; dizziness; and—occasionally—diarrhea."

"Huh," said Kapitän Nazi, appearing neither impressed nor unimpressed by this.

"And nasal congestion," Anna added, with a confidence that suggested this would be the final detail that tipped the scales.

"I'll keep that in mind," said Nazi.

Chuck guided him along the line, and Sam braced himself. They skipped right past him, though, and stopped in front of Randy, instead. He drew himself up to his full height, his mouth twisted into a snarl, the corners of his cape clutched in each hand.

Mari shuffled along behind them. To Anna's relief, the image of Allergy Girl was replaced by a holographic picture of a scrawny boy in a butterfly costume with brightly patterned wings that were almost as big as he was. The boy had one hand raised, a finger outstretched. A single butterfly was alighting on the fingertip, its wing design a near-perfect match for Randy's childhood costume.

"The Butterfly Kid," Chuck announced. "Now going by Butterfly *King*. Listed powers include 'Kinship with butter-flies,' and, uh..." He consulted the tablet, sliding the on-screen text up, then back down again. "That's it."

"Ha! Like that's not enough," Randy sneered. "Also, let's not overlook these babies."

He threw a few punches at the air before a searing pain in his side forced him to stop.

"You're *welcome*," he finished, somewhat inexplicably.

"Butterflies?" said Kapitän Nazi, who was clearly having some trouble with this concept. "As in..."

"As in the little things that flutter around, yes," Chuck confirmed.

"Oh," said the Kapitän. "And he fights crime with those?"

"You bet your ass I do," Randy seethed. "My butterfly brethren and I fly side by side in the name of justice!"

Nazi's scarred forehead wrinkled as his eyebrows raised. "Aha! You fly?"

"Metaphorically," said Randy, in a way that suggested this was somehow better than actual flying.

"Oh. I see," said Nazi.

"I'm also the night's shadow," Randy declared.

Kapitän Nazi frowned, good-naturedly. "The night's...?"

"Shadow," Randy said. "I'm its dark underside. Its righteous fury."

"Dude, the night doesn't cast a shadow," Anna pointed out. "It's not a tangible thing."

Randy hesitated, but only for a moment. "It does now," he said, in a tone that sat halfway between 'cryptic' and 'deranged'.

"Well... good for you," said Nazi. "I'm sure that's all going to come in very useful."

"You don't *sound* very sure," Randy pointed out. "And that'll be your biggest mistake."

Anna leaned forward so she could see past Sam. "I don't know. I think the whole being a Nazi and killing a bunch of people were bigger mistakes. This feels like it'll be waaaay down near the bottom of his list."

"And that brings us back to you," said the Kapitän, turning his attention to Sam. "You seem kind of familiar, somehow."

"Kid Random," Chuck announced. Mari's projection switched to show a short, skinny kid wearing a red hood and blue spandex outfit, and not wearing any of it particularly well.

He looked anxious and ill-at-ease, like he wasn't completely comfortable with the heroic pose he was striking. The patch of his face that was visible around his mouth was almost the same shade of red as his hood and mask.

"Of course," said Nazi, clicking his tongue against the back of his teeth. "The apprentice to my old nemesis." He bowed his head, just a little. "My apologies for not recognizing you before now."

"*That's* what you're apologizing for?" Sam hissed. "Seriously? After everything you did?"

Chuck intervened before things could escalate. "His powers are... complicated," he said, without consulting his tablet. "From what we can tell—"

"I know what he can do," said the Kapitän, holding Sam's gaze. "I heard much about his powers, although I have to say, I have yet to see them demonstrated first-hand."

Sam swallowed. "Maybe you will," he said, and the thing in his head stirred once again.

"Fingers crossed," Nazi replied. He looked across all three faces, then turned to Chuck. "Is this it? Weren't there others? What about the fire one? Flameboy or whatever he was called."

"Jim Flammable," said Chuck. "No, we lost track of him and the others. This is it."

Kapitän Nazi puffed out his cheeks. "What about the girl with the computer brain?"

"Calcu-Lass," said Chuck. "Again, no. This is all we've got."

"Right. Right," said the Kapitän. He clicked his tongue against the roof of his mouth. "And the Justice Platoon are *definitely* all dead?"

"They're dead," Chuck confirmed. "We had a satellite do a flyby. They're all the way dead."

"Oh. I see. That's disappointing," said Nazi. He shrugged. "Well, I guess these will have to do."

He eyeballed each of the sidekicks in turn as he unbuttoned his shirt sleeves.

"Now," he said, rolling the sleeves up to his elbows in a series of crisp, neat folds. "Shall we begin?"

CHAPTER TWELVE

ANNA VAULTED OVER A TRASH CAN, sprinted flat-out for a stack of boxes, and almost made it into cover before a tennis ball *whanged* her in the face.

"Ow! Son-of-a—" she protested, clutching her forehead and dropping into cover behind the cardboard barricade. Several more balls rattled against the other side of it in rapid succession, and Anna knew she didn't have much time before the boxes gave way.

She was in a long, narrow room that Chuck had referred to as 'the Peril Chamber,' and which he'd claimed was fitted with state-of-the-art training equipment. Anna was pretty sure it was actually just a wider than average corridor with some junk in it, though, and the state-of-the-art equipment appeared to be nothing more than a tennis ball launcher.

Chuck's voice bellowed from the far end of the room/corridor. "Sam. Randy. Make your move."

Randy didn't need telling twice. He sprang up dramatically from behind a wooden crate a dozen feet further back, holding his cape out at both sides. With a roar, he began to run. He made it an impressive six or seven feet before a ball hit him in the throat, then a second followed up to his testicles.

Still he ran, albeit a little more cross-legged than he had been a moment ago. He crashed through the trash cans, stumbling as another volley of balls thudded into various bits of him.

Anna's eyes went wide when she realized what was about to happen. "Randy, no, don't!" she yelped, but it was no use. Off-balance, he fell through the cardboard boxes, crushing them flat and exposing the back of Anna's head to three tennis balls in quick succession.

"Jesus! Will you cut that out?" she cried.

Randy looked up from within the nest of boxes. "Who? Me or him?"

"Both of you!"

"It's all on you, Sam!" Chuck bellowed. "Get moving!"

Beside him, Kapitän Nazi's finger hovered over the trigger of the tennis ball launcher, one eye squinting down the sights. With the other hand, he cranked the machine's power all the way up to maximum and smirked as it *hummed* in his grip.

"Come on, Sam. Don't disappoint me," he whispered.

Down at the far end of the Peril Chamber, Sam sat with his back to another wooden crate, breathing slowly as he tried to compose himself.

"This is ridiculous," he muttered. "What's the point?"

"Go, Sam!" Anna cheered. "Sam, Sam, he's our man, if he can't do it—"

"Randy can," Randy concluded. "But, uh, chose not to on this occasion."

Sam took in another few breaths. "OK. Just run and dodge. You've done this before," he told himself, trying not to dwell on the fact that the last time was twenty years ago, and he wasn't as limber as he used to be.

"Hurry the hell up!" Chuck shouted.

Sam groaned. "Ah... shit," he whispered, then he spun onto his knees and leaped out from cover. A tennis ball immediately *whistled* past his head, a blur of spinning yellow speed.

Whoa. That would've hurt.

He yelped and ducked as another ball rocketed toward him, then jumped in fright at the loud *thwack* it made as it slammed into the wall far behind him.

Frantically, Sam began to zigzag, chanting, "Ohshitohshitohshit," below his breath. There was another stack of cardboard boxes over on his left. He made for it, only for a spray of tennis balls to tear it to shreds before he got there.

Sam gave a little *cheep* of panic that he hoped nobody else had heard, but knew in his heart that they had, then danced to his right as another of the fast-moving projectiles *whooshed* past him.

The trash cans were just ahead, but they had been knocked over and scattered, so offered nothing useful in the way of protection.

Or did they?

Sam spotted one of the lids lying on the floor ahead, the handle pointing upward. Ducking, he raced for it and emitted a little sob of triumph as he snatched it up.

He'd barely raised it in front of his face when a ball *clanged* against it. The impact almost wrenched the lid from his hand, but he kept his grip and pulled it in close to his chest, jamming his other forearm against it to give it some support.

"Yes!" Anna cheered. "Captain America the shit out of this thing!"

Sam raced on, only his eyes visible above the top of the trash can lid, only his lower abdomen, groin, legs, and both feet visible below it.

Damn. Maybe he should've grabbed the second lid.

Another ball hurtled toward him. He deflected it and felt

a little flutter of excitement as he charged past Anna and Randy. Anna's *woo* bolstered his nerve and he charged onward, barely even bothering to dodge.

Clang! A ball slammed into the center of the shield. This close, the impact was jarring, and his knuckles went white as he tightened his grip.

Wham! A shot came low, and Sam barely managed to bring the trash can lid down in time to protect himself.

BANG! Another ball clipped the edge of the shield, spinning it out of his grip. He scrambled for it, then hissed in pain as another ball hit him in the ribs. A second followed to his thigh. He felt the skin sting and the muscle go dead.

"Ow. Jesus!" Sam protested, turning his back to protect the parts he cared about most.

Balls slammed into both kidneys, forcing him to reconsider this tactic. He bent for the shield, but another ball thundered into his ass, sending him stumbling, face-first, to the floor.

"Stop it!" Sam pleaded, covering his head with his hands and curling into the fetal position. The shape in his brain twisted and screamed. His skin tingled, the hair on his arms standing on end.

Another ball hit him. And another. And another. That bastard was doing this on purpose.

Sam's power surged. He should teach him a lesson. Not just for this, but for everything he'd ever done. It would be easy.

Too easy.

Sam raised his hands. The shape in his head fell still.

"OK. I give up! I give up!" he said.

A final ball bounced off the side of his head, and then the machine *whirred* into silence.

"Well," said Kapitän Nazi. "That was disappointing."

Anna stood up and dusted herself down. "You think *you*

found it disappointing? You weren't the one getting balls slammed into your face."

Randy sniggered.

"Shut up, Randy. You know what I mean," Anna sighed.

Groaning, Sam heaved himself to his feet. Most parts of him stung and those that didn't, ached. He tried not to show it as Kapitän Nazi and Chuck walked over to join them.

"What did you learn?" Nazi asked.

"That you're an asshole," said Anna.

"Already knew that," Sam added.

"I learned that these two can't dodge for shit," Randy growled.

Anna scowled at him. "What? You got hit, too!"

"Or did I?" Randy whispered.

"Yeah," said Chuck. "Yeah, you did. A number of times."

Randy pulled his cape up over his face. "Or *did* I?"

"What was even the point in this?" Sam demanded. "I mean, is there some new tennis-themed supervillain out there we don't know about? Is that what we're preparing for here?"

Kapitän Nazi shook his head. "You know what my old training coach used to say, back in the day?"

"'Heil Hitler'?" Sam guessed.

"Ha. Yes. Well, that, obviously," Nazi admitted. "But he also told me, 'If you can dodge a ball, you can dodge anything.'"

"Oh!" said Anna. "So, he was an idiot or a crazy person? Is that the lesson we've learned here?"

"I thought it was crazy at first, too," Nazi admitted. "But he had a point. The principle is the same. If you can dodge a ball, you can dodge anything. A car. A knife. A bullet."

"A ball," offered Randy, mostly because he felt like he hadn't contributed anything in a while.

Kapitän Nazi side-eyed him for a moment, then shrugged. "Sure. If you can dodge a ball, you can dodge a ball."

"Wise words, Randy," said Anna. "I mean, that's some Dalai Lama shit right there."

"The only difference between a ball and a bullet is how fast you move," Nazi explained.

"That's a pretty big difference," said Sam. "Such a big difference, in fact, that I'd say this whole exercise was completely pointless."

Kapitän Nazi raised an eyebrow. "You would, would you?" He crossed his arms over his broad chest. "Then perhaps you'd prefer something a little more... hands on?"

Sam flew through the (mercifully open) door, landed heavily on the basketball court floor, then rolled, slid and tumbled all the way into the middle with a series of grunts and *oofs*.

"Rule number one," boomed Kapitän Nazi, stalking onto the court and closing the gap on the fallen sidekick. "Take out your most powerful opponent first. Hit them hard and hit them fast. The reason for this is two-fold."

Sam scrambled up onto his knees, only for Nazi to grab him by the hair. With the other hand, the Kapitän caught the front of Sam's t-shirt. There was a grunt, a jerk, and a sudden sensation of weightlessness as Sam sailed several feet across the court, before smacking unceremoniously into a crash mat.

"It removes the biggest threat from the battlefield," said Nazi. "And it gives the less powerful opponents pause to consider if they might be in over their heads."

Randy threw himself at the Kapitän, both fists raised above his head, his cape fluttering out behind him.

"The sensible ones, anyway," Nazi continued.

Spinning, he powered a hammer-strike into Randy's damaged ribs. Randy's face immediately paled. Whether this was due to the pain of the impact, or nausea brought on by the sudden change in trajectory was impossible to tell.

His forward leap became a sideways flip. He hit another crash mat as a ball of arms, legs, snot, and tears, then lay there for a moment as fire consumed his insides and the ceiling spiraled around and around above him.

With Randy out of the way, Kapitän Nazi turned his attention back to Sam. "Rule number two..." he began, curling his fingers into fists as he advanced.

"I got a rule for you, you Nazi bitch!" cried Anna. Her voice echoed around the court. "Duck!"

An empty wine bottle whistled through the air and smashed on the ground a good eight or nine feet away on the Kapitän's left.

Anna's arms flopped to her side. "Well... shit," she said. "That didn't go according to plan at all."

"Why did you get his attention?" Sam wheezed, unsteadily finding his feet. "Why didn't you just hit him with it?"

Anna shrugged. "Well, obviously in hindsight..."

"And why shout 'duck'?" Randy spat, untangling himself from his cape. "I mean, that's literally the one thing you *didn't* want him to do. Not that it mattered, because you throw like a girl."

"Yeah? Well maybe I wasn't trying to hit him," said Anna. "Maybe I was just trying to get his attention. *Get him, Sam!*"

Sam's face froze in a sort of wide-eyed rictus of confusion and fear. "What?"

"Get him, Sam!" Anna repeated. "Use your powers. Take him out!"

"No, but... I can't. It's not that..."

Anna tutted. "Oh, *come on!*"

"You heard her, Sam," said Nazi, turning to face him. "Show us what you've got. Hit me with it."

Sam set his jaw and clenched his fists. He couldn't. It was

too dangerous. And yet...

The Kapitän's face twisted into a grotesque caricature of a sneer. "Vill zis make it easier?" he screeched, reverting to his old accent. His *real* accent, Sam was sure. "Vill zis draw you out, you pathetic, vhining American pig?"

Sam flew at him, roaring, the thing in his head uncoiling. He clenched his jaw, focusing, concentrating hard as he closed the gap on that sneering Nazi bastard, then let fly with a series of punches.

"Vot is this?" the Kapitän demanded, easily deflecting the flurry of blows. "Vot are you doing?"

"Stand still, you piece of—"

The back of an open-hand slap stung Sam's cheek, staggering him and briefly breaking his concentration.

"No, no, no," he whispered, throwing out a leg and driving a kick at Nazi's stomach.

The foot missed the stomach, but found the Kapitän's hip, instead. The villain looked surprised for a moment, but then that leer returned.

Lunging, Nazi caught Sam by the throat. Sam started to raise his fists, but two quick fingertip strikes from the Kapitän hit the nerve clusters above his armpits, and both arms became the heaviest things in the world.

"You cannot defeat me in hand to hand combat, Kid Random," Nazi seethed. Flecks of foam formed at the corners of his mouth as he spoke and those eyes burned into Sam just as they'd done all those years ago. "So, do vot only you can do. Use your power. Unleash it."

"*RAAAAAAAARGH!*"

Randy's shoulder slammed into Kapitän Nazi's lower back. The Kapitän, suffering no obvious ill-effects from this, swung a fist behind him. The blow found Randy's broken ribs and he dropped to the floor again.

Randy coughed a few times, gasped like a fish out of

water, then noisily introduced Kapitän Nazi's shoes to the contents of his stomach.

"Ha!" Randy wheezed, wiping vomit from around his mouth with the edge of his cape. "Check and mate, you villainous fiend!"

The Kapitän took a couple of steps forward, distancing himself from both Randy and the puddle of puke. Sam's arms were still too heavy to lift, so he kicked and stomped at Nazi's shins and feet, but the Kapitän either didn't feel it or didn't care.

"Vot are you vaiting for, Kid Random? Vhy are you holding back?" Nazi hissed. "You alone have ze power to take me out. You alone can stop me!"

"Wouldn't be so sure about that," Anna announced. She thrust both hands toward him. "Anaphylactic Shockwave!"

The air rippled between them. Kapitän Nazi turned sharply, using the limp Sam as a shield. Sam's body vibrated as the invisible energy blast hit him.

"Oh, thor thuck sake," he spat through his rapidly-fattening lips. "Not thith again."

"Sorry, sorry, sorry!" said Anna. "I was trying to hit him!"

"I guethed," Sam slurred.

"To what end?" Nazi sneered. "I vos created to be resistant to illness. I have no allergies."

"Oh, well, that's... disappointing," said Anna. "Not even to *this*?"

She kicked him between the legs with all her might, driving the toe of her trainer right up there. Nazi didn't flinch.

"No. Not even to that."

"Ah, shit," Anna sighed. She looked to the door, where Chuck and Mari both stood watching, and made a T shape with her hands. "Can we get a timeout? I feel like he's just going to kill us otherwise."

"Speak for yourself," wheezed Randy from down at floor level. "I could keep this up all day."

Anna peered down at him. "You know you puked blood, right?"

"Of course I know," said Randy. He tried to laugh, but it came out as a pained grimace. "It's all part of the plan. Lull him into a false sense of security, then—*BAM!*"

"Hit him with the butterflies?" Anna guessed. "And how do we think that would've worked out for you?"

"Thanks to you, we'll never know," Randy growled.

"Meh. Reckon we can take a fairly educated guess," Anna replied.

"Alright, alright," said Chuck, coming over to join them. His broad shoulders were stooped by the disappointment he was making absolutely no effort to hide. It was painted on his face, as well as in his body language, and his choice of words —"Well, that was a big fucking disappointment!"—really helped hammer it home.

Kapitän Nazi's face softened. He released his grip on Sam, then smoothed the front of his t-shirt. "You OK, son?" he asked, his German screech becoming that Mid-Western lilt again. "Sorry if I went a little hard on you there."

"Get oth me," Sam hissed, pulling away. He very deliberately turned away and addressed Chuck. "What wath that? That wathn't thair. We weren't ready. You thould have given uth thome thort of warning."

Chuck was studying his mouth, trying to decipher what Sam had said. "Jesus. Mari, can you...?"

"Of course, dear," said Mari, rumbling over to Sam's side. He yelped as a needle pricked his skin.

"Ow! What the hell?"

"Antihistamine injection," Chuck explained. "It'll counter the effects of Allergy Girl's powers. Although it won't counter the ass-kicking you all just took."

"Just 'Anna' is fine," said Anna. "We don't need to go the whole superhero name route. Also, I'd like to point out that my ass is completely unkicked. No kicking of my ass has taken place."

"Only because you called a timeout," said Chuck. He rubbed a hand across his sandpaper hair. "This isn't working."

"They're just getting started," said Nazi. "It'll take time."

"We don't have time," Chuck replied. "People are already asking questions. They're starting to notice the Justice Platoon isn't around. Pretty soon, every scumbag with a superpower is going to come crawling out of the woodwork, and we need to be ready for them."

"What about the suits you mentioned?" asked Sam. His mouth still tingled, but everything was shrinking back to regular size, and the act of breathing no longer involved forcing air out using all his stomach muscles.

Chuck made a clicking sound at the side of his mouth, considering this. "The suits were supposed to be a reward. You were supposed to prove yourselves without them first. The plan was that you'd become a team, show your potential, and earn them."

There was a loud *rwaaaarrk* noise as Randy threw up again.

"On the other hand..." Chuck sighed. "Mari, let's show them the suits."

Sam, Anna, and Randy stood before three mannequins, studying the outfits the dummies wore.

None of them had been sure what to expect, exactly, although Sam had been quietly fearing some dayglo abomination with knee-high boots and underwear that doubled as overwear.

He was pleasantly surprised to find the outfit was an almost sensible-looking one-piece, with few of the frills and gimmicks he'd been bracing himself for. Even the utility belts around the suits' waists were borderline discreet.

Unlike his previous costume, this one looked as if it had been designed for practicality, rather than as a vehicle for ridicule and shame. The garb he'd worn as Kid Random had been a blend of circus clown and Spanish bull-fighter, with just a suggestion of *moving target* added to help draw both attention and gunfire away from any of the more important hero types.

There was no cape. He was happy with that. Capes only made sense if you could fly, and even then only if you hadn't fully mastered turning at high speed. Some people thought they looked cool, despite—Sam looked along the line to Randy—all evidence to the contrary.

The outfits were all different colors. Sam's was blue, Anna's green, and Randy's a brooding shade of red. They all had a sculpted look to them, suggesting muscles Sam was pretty sure none of them actually had. The closer he looked at his costume's defined six-pack, the larger he could feel his inferiority complex becoming.

Anna gave her outfit a poke. "What's it made of?" she asked. "Is it rubber?"

"It's a lab-grown organic biopolymer," said Chuck. He was standing behind them with Mari, arms folded like he begrudged them every last one of the outfits' stitches.

"It feels like rubber," Anna insisted.

"Well, it isn't," Chuck snapped. "It's an organic biopolymer."

Anna looked back over her shoulder at him, frowning. "Is that better or worse than rubber? I'm worried about thigh rash from chafing. That's my main concern at the moment. Rubber isn't breathable, and if we get sweaty..."

"Then you don't have to worry, because it isn't rubber," Chuck told her.

"No, right. No. But it's *like* rubber," Anna said, giving it another poke as if to demonstrate. "Are you saying it's breathable and that chafing won't be an issue?"

"I'm saying it's a state-of-the-art, multi-million-dollar supersuit developed by our top scientists using materials I'm not even sure originate from this planet," Chuck said. "So yes, I'm guessing they made it breathable."

"You're *guessing*..." said Anna.

"I don't like it," Randy snarled, regarding his outfit with contempt. "Where's the cape? Where's the symbol? Where's the... pizazz?"

Sam raised a hand. "I'm fine without the pizazz," he said. "Just putting that out there on the record."

"It ain't about pizazz. It's about getting the damn job done," said Chuck. "Those outfits will make you all faster, stronger, it'll let you absorb more punishment—hell, it'll even help you heal any damage you *do* take."

"It will also help you focus your abilities," Mari chimed in. "Something you might find particularly useful, Sam."

Sam glanced around at the robot, then turned his attention back to the suit. "I don't need help with that," he said.

Anna snorted. "Yeah, right. I literally haven't seen you do anything yet. What even is your power? I mean, *Kid Random*. I always thought maybe you had, like, gadgets or something? Little tricks, or whatever." Her brow furrowed. "But, come to think about it, I don't think I ever saw you do anything. Power-wise, I mean."

She jabbed a thumb to her right. "Even Randy conjured up some butterflies when we were fighting the henchmen."

"You're damn right I did," Randy hissed. "Wait, what do you mean 'even Randy'?"

"You know what I mean. No offense," said Anna. "You

magicked up a few butterflies. I'm just saying, it was impressive. But not, like, *wow*, you know?"

Randy squared up to her. "I'd like to see you produce an army of butterflies out of thin air," he spat.

"It was, like, eight butterflies," said Anna.

"It was *twelve!* Twelve butterflies! From *nowhere*."

"They were inside your cape," said Chuck.

Randy hesitated. The others looked at him in silence. "Or *were* they?" he whispered, after a while.

"Yes. They were," Chuck confirmed.

Anna and Sam both turned all the way around to face Randy.

"They were in your cape? So... wait. What powers *do* you have, exactly?" Anna demanded. "Or am I the only one here who can actually do anything?"

"I have all the skills and abilities of the noble butterfly!" Randy hissed, bubbles of spit forming between his teeth. "Apart from the flying or being small, as I previously explained."

"Right—"

"Or the stuff about caterpillars," Randy added.

"So, what does that leave?" asked Sam.

Randy didn't answer right away. Not out loud, anyway, although the way his lips moved suggested he was running through some options.

"Confidence," he said, in his usual growl.

"Confidence isn't a superpower," Anna pointed out.

"It's kind of a superpower."

"Nah. It isn't," Anna insisted.

"Oh! Wait! I know another one!" Randy yelped. He waved his hands in front of his face in what was presumably meant to be a mysterious manner and side-stepped in closer to his mannequin. "Camouflage," he whispered.

Sam cleared his throat. "We can still see you, Randy."

There was some shuffling.

"How about now?"

"We still see you," Anna said. "I mean, you're standing right there."

Randy tutted and stepped out from behind the mannequin. "Fine," he grunted. There was a *clack* as he untied his belt, then a rustle as his jeans fell down around his ankles. "Give me the damn suit."

Chuck scraped his top teeth across his bottom lip, like he was stopping himself saying something he'd later regret. Instead, he forced something that wasn't quite a smile, but was somewhere in the same ballpark.

"I thought we'd grab lunch first," he said. "Those things cost millions. I don't want you spilling tuna salad down the front on the first day."

"Great! I am *starving*," said Anna. "There'll be wine, right? Can't be lunchtime without wine."

"There's *kind of* wine," Chuck said, as he and Mari led the way toward the door. "It's non-alcoholic."

"It's what? What does that even mean? 'Non-alcoholic'?" Anna demanded, hurrying after them. "Is that an actual thing? That can't be an actual thing."

Sam didn't follow right away. Instead, he ran his fingers across the chest of his outfit, and felt his skin tingle where they touched.

"Can I let you in on a secret?" Randy whispered.

Sam blinked, as if being awoken from a dream. "Huh? Oh. Yeah, go for it."

Randy leaned in closer, staring into Sam's eyes with a fiery intensity. "I hate tuna salad," he said.

He eyeballed Sam for a moment, really driving his point home. Then, after bending to pull up his pants, Randy headed off after the others.

"Yeah," said Sam, giving the suit one last look. "Me, too."

CHAPTER THIRTEEN

THE WIND WHISPERED between the shining glass towers of Cityopolis and whistled around the four figures perched on the roof of an old brownstone near the heart of the downtown district.

"I don't think this is a good idea," said Sam, tugging on the crotch of his costume in an attempt to stop it cutting him in two. "We're not ready for this."

Kapitän Nazi stood at the head of the group, one foot on the small raised wall running around the roof's edge. He leaned forward, giving him a clear view of the alleys and streets below. One good push would be enough to send him over the drop, Sam thought. That was all it would take.

Of course, there was no saying it would actually hurt him, but it would at least give Sam a fleeting moment of satisfaction as he watched the bastard fall.

"This will make you ready," said Nazi, not looking back.

One push. Just one.

"Hey, wait a minute!" said Anna, her voice rising to an indignant yelp. "Why is my suit the only one with nipples?"

"Huh?" said Sam, turning to look. He felt himself blush

behind his mask. Unfortunately, as the mask covered nothing but his eyes, this was clear for everyone to see. "Oh, um. Uh."

"Your suit doesn't have nipples. Randy's suit doesn't have nipples!"

"To be fair, Randy doesn't have nipples either," Sam pointed out.

"I don't want nipples!" Anna protested. "What am I going to be doing, *breastfeeding* criminals into submission?"

"I highly doubt that'd be effective," Randy growled. He studied her breasts. "If it's any consolation, those are some nice nipples."

"That's not any consolation, no. That's the opposite of consolation," Anna told him. "You've just made it creepy and weird."

Sam tried not to look. "Do they... I don't know, do they maybe do something?"

"Do my nipples *do something?*" Anna scoffed. She twiddled them both in turn. Despite his best efforts, Sam found his eyes drawn to this, so he forced himself to turn away. "No. They don't seem to be doing anything special. They're just big old rubber nipples!"

Randy shook his head. "Big old *organic biopolymer* nipples," he corrected.

"Shut the fuck up, Randy," Anna muttered, almost absent-mindedly.

After they'd suited up, Sam had been expecting another session in the training room. He'd almost been looking forward to taking another crack at Kapitän Nazi, in the hope of maybe kicking the crap out of the guy this time, or at least getting in a couple of solid punches.

Instead, Nazi had suggested accelerating their training by taking them out into the city. Chuck had seemed reluctant at first, but for a mass-murdering super powered fascist, the Kapitän could be pretty persuasive when he wanted to be.

And so now here they were, hanging around on a rooftop, waiting for trouble. Chuck had given clear instructions that they had to avoid any interactions with supervillains, so the trouble they were waiting on was of the low-level variety. Sam took a little comfort from that.

Not a lot, but a little.

"Any sign of anything happening?" asked Anna, stepping closer to the edge and looking down at the street below. It was a narrow side-street, with scuffed and dented ten-year-old cars parked along the whole length of it on one side. The shining towers of uptown cast the whole place into gloomy shadow, and in that shadow, crime could always be found.

Or almost always. Today, it seemed, crime was taking a vacation.

"We've been up here for over two hours," Sam complained. He adjusted the crotch of his suit again and shook the tingling out of his legs.

"Told you, you should've ditched the underwear," Randy said. He squatted a couple of times, demonstrating the freedom of movement he enjoyed around his own groin area.

"I'm not going commando," Sam said.

"You don't know what you're missing," Randy said. He cupped a hand to his ear. "Hear that? That's the sound of my balls breathing."

Sam turned his attention back to the city. He shuffled a little closer to the edge of the roof, but stopped at what he felt was a safe distance from it. "Can you see anything yet?" he asked.

Kapitän Nazi shook his head. "Not yet. Give it time."

"We've given it time," Sam pointed out. "A lot of time. Too much time, if anything."

Randy stepped past him and jumped right up onto the ledge. He stopped with his toes sticking out over the drop, and Sam felt his heart leap into his mouth just at the thought of it.

"Jesus, Randy, what are you doing? Get down!" Sam yelped.

"God, you're so uptight. Just like your balls in that suit. I have an idea," Randy growled. He placed his fingers to his temples. "Butterfly King's subjects will be our eyes. I'll link up with every butterfly in the city. I'll see what they see, know what they know. If there's trouble afoot, we'll find it."

Anna looked almost impressed. "You can do that?"

"You bet I can, Nips," Randy replied. He had forgone his suit's mask in favor of his leather flying hat, and gave Anna a wink through the goggles.

"Did he... Did you just call me 'Nips'?"

"Silence!" Randy barked, closing his eyes. "I'm concentrating."

Randy stood there for several seconds, the cape he had insisted on safety-pinning onto his outfit fluttering gently in the wind.

"Aha!" he cried.

"Get something?" asked Sam.

"Shh. Concentrating."

Several more seconds passed, during which Randy made a few further announcements, including a "Well, well, well" two, "What have we here's?" and one pretty definitive, "Gotcha!"

At last, he opened his eyes and jumped back down onto the rooftop proper, grinning from ear to ear.

"Well?" asked Nazi.

"Hmm? Oh. No, I got nothing," said Randy.

Sam and Anna exchanged looks. "Nothing?" asked Sam.

"Then what was all that 'Aha!' and 'Ooh!' stuff about?" Anna demanded.

Randy shrugged. "I mean there was nothing going on *crime-wise*. But I saw some pretty interesting stuff."

"Like what?" Anna asked, intrigued despite herself.

"Like people walking," Randy said. "Cars. A woman with a dog."

Anna sighed. "That's it?"

"There are only, like, three butterflies in the whole city," Randy explained. "To be honest, it's not really their natural environment."

Not for the first time, Sam was about to suggest they pack up and go back to base, when Kapitän Nazi raised a clenched fist above his head, calling for silence.

"What is it? You see something?" Anna whispered.

Nazi nodded. "Down there. By the garage door," he said.

Anna and Randy rushed back to the edge and followed the Kapitän's gaze. Sam hung back a little, standing on his tiptoes to try to see over them.

"What is it?" he asked. "What's happening?"

"Looks like a good old-fashioned granny mugging," Randy spat. He punched a fist into the opposite palm. "I make two guys!"

Anna side-eyed him. "Well, there's four of them, so..."

"Where?" Randy demanded.

Anna pointed.

"Hmm?" Randy frowned. "Oh. Yeah. There's four. I thought those other two were reflections in that mirror."

"Why would they be...? What mirror?" Anna asked. She shook her head, dismissing the questions before any answers could be given. "Forget it, I don't care. What do we do?"

"I know what I'm going to do," Randy announced. He stepped up onto the ledge again and held his cape out behind him. "I'm going in for the superhero landing."

"We're four floors up," Anna pointed out. "You'll shatter

your spine. Like that other guy did. Back in the day. What was his name?"

"Powerfist."

"No, afterward," said Anna. "He changed it."

"Oh. Wheeled Warrior."

"Right! That was him," said Anna. "Thanks, that would've bugged me for the rest of the day."

Kapitän Nazi gave a shake of his head. "The suit will protect him and prevent him breaking anything. He should be fine."

"Of course he won't be *fine*!" Sam protested. "Suit or no suit, that's too long a drop. Even if he doesn't cripple himself he'll hurt his knees."

"I'm doing it. For *justice*!" Randy announced. He lifted a foot and looked around to Sam as he stepped off into thin air. "Fuck my knees!"

There came four seconds of silence, broken eventually by a *thump*.

"Fuck!" came a strangled cry from below. "My knees!"

"I told him. I told him that would happen," Sam said. "Never do the superhero landing. It's asking for trouble."

Anna winced. "Ooh. Looks like those guys have seen him. They're coming over. He's going to need help."

She and Sam both looked to Kapitän Nazi. It took him a moment to realize. "What are you staring at me for?" he asked. "I'm not the one in the supersuit. This is the whole point of us being out here. Go."

Sam wrung his gloved hands. "Shit. Shit, shit, shit," he muttered, then he drew in a sharp breath and nodded. "How do we get down?"

"Jump," Nazi suggested.

"Fuck off! '*Jump*,'" Anna yelped. "We just saw what happened when he jumped."

"He didn't bend his knees when he landed," Nazi

explained. "You have to bend your knees properly. Don't do the superhero landing thing. It looks impressive, but it's murder on the joints."

Anna shot him a scowl, then hurried for the corner of the building. "Drainpipe," she announced. "We'll take that."

"OK! OK! You do that," said Sam, backing toward the rooftop's only door. "I'll take the stairs and surprise them by coming out through the front door."

Anna paused. "How will that surprise them?"

"I'll, uh, I'll jump out. Like—wargh!" Sam said.

"Oh yeah, that'll do it," Anna conceded, although there was a very real possibility that she did so sarcastically. "They won't see that coming."

If she said more, Sam didn't hear it. Pulling open the unlocked rooftop door, he plunged down the narrow staircase beyond, then raced onto a wider but more dilapidated-looking second staircase that wound down the center of the apartment block in a series of right turns.

Two floors down, Sam considered dropping through the stairwell gap, but the ground still seemed too far away, so he pressed on running and settled for jumping the two steps at the bottom of each set, instead.

At last, he reached the bottom. Lining himself up with the door, he took a few seconds to compose himself. This largely involved him trembling from head to toe and groaning, "What the hell am I doing?" a few times.

After concluding that he didn't really know what he was doing, but that he was going to do it anyway, Sam charged for the door. He emerged with a surprising, "Wargh!" just as planned, only to find an empty street waiting for him. There was no sign of Randy or the muggers anywhere.

It was around this point that Sam realized he'd come out through the wrong door. Turning, he raced back through the graffiti-stained lobby, raised his fists, then barreled out through the other exit.

He smacked straight into the broad back of a shockingly large man wearing gang colors. Sam wasn't sure which gang the colors represented, but he was pretty certain it didn't matter. It wasn't like there was a friendly, considerate gang going around helping people out. Whatever street tribe these colors represented, it was bad news.

The man-mountain turned. This took some time. Sam was dismayed to see the guy held a long piece of jagged metal in one of his enormous bear paw-like hands.

"Dafuq you supposed to be?" the giant demanded. His face was pitted with old acne scars that creased together when he scowled.

Randy was on the ground just on the other side of the big guy, two other men and one heavyset woman all looming over him.

"You shouldn't have come. I've totally got this," Randy wheezed, but the way the bottom half of his left leg was pointing in a completely different direction to the top suggested to Sam that this probably wasn't the case.

Sam took a deep breath. The squirming shape in his head didn't so much as flicker.

"Back away you, uh, punks," he warned.

The three other gang members exchanged puzzled looks. The largest of the four bared his yellow and gold teeth. "What did you say?"

"You heard me," said Sam, hoping they didn't pick up on the croak in his voice. "Back off. Leave him alone."

"We ain't done nothin' to him," spat the woman.

Jesus. *Was* it a woman? Sam couldn't decide. Her voice was like the distant rumbling of thunder. It was a sound that suggested that no matter how good your day had been until that point, it was about to be ruined.

"Dude just fell from the sky, man."

"Like an avenging angel of justice!" Randy added, before yelping loudly and sobbing for several seconds.

"Nice outfits," said the big guy. "Reckon one of them'd look good on me. What do you say, boys?"

"Here, let me," giggled one of the other two (possibly three) men. He was smaller and more wiry than the others, and moved like some kind of rodent.

He was beside Sam before Sam knew what was happening. The rodent's hand came up sharply, and Sam caught a glimpse of a claw hammer as it swung at him, pointy-end first.

Sam recalled all those days of martial arts training, and all those nights spent fighting at Doc Mighty's side, learning how to deal with opponents of every shape and size. He then ignored all that completely in favor of shutting his eyes and screaming, "No, don't!" in a panicky voice.

His hand came up as if working independently from the rest of him. He felt his fingers wrap around the rodent's wrist, heard the *crack* of breaking bone and the clatter of the hammer hitting the ground.

Sam opened his eyes just as the rodent screamed, his hand flopping loosely atop his broken wrist.

The other guy lunged for Sam, thrusting forward with a homemade shiv. Sam drove an open-handed palm strike into the center of the man's chest. The impact rattled Sam's arm all the way up to the shoulder, but this was nothing compared to the effect it had on his attacker.

The guy rocketed backward, both feet off the ground, his eyes and mouth forming three matching circles of surprise. He hit the wall a moment later, then slid onto the sidewalk, unconscious.

Possibly dead, although Sam really hoped not.

"You sonuvabitch!" roared the most-likely female gang member. She—arguably *he*—brought up a snub-nosed pistol and fired two shots directly at the center of Sam's chest before he could get out another piercing squeal of panic.

Sam stumbled back, releasing his grip on the first attacker and accepting that, yep, he was almost certainly about to die. He was very probably dead already, in fact, and these were just the final fleeting moments as his brain shut down and the life ebbed from...

The suit made a couple of soft *popping* sounds. Two bullets *chinked* onto the ground.

Sam patted his chest and let out an involuntary little giggle of relief. There was a dull ache there, but no searing pain, and—more importantly—no bloody holes in his flesh.

"Dafuq?" whispered the big guy.

The one that was *very tenuously female* raised the gun another couple of inches, and Sam's urge to laugh quickly died away as he realized his face was almost completely uncovered.

"Wait, don't shoot!" Sam pleaded.

Before the probable woman could fire, there was a scream from above. Everyone raised their eyes just as Anna lost her grip on the drainpipe. She landed, butt-first, on the gun-wielder. They went down hard, and only one of them got back up again.

"Jesus, that was terrifying," Anna whispered. Her face was pale behind the green figure-eight of her mask. "It was higher than it looked and really hard to get a grip on. The gloves are too slippy."

She leaned back and waved both hands up in the direction of the roof. "The gloves are too slippy!" she shouted.

"Dafuq are you? Dafuq you talking to?" demanded the now sole-remaining gang member.

"Oh, just this Nazi we know," Anna said. She put her hands on her hips, adopting what she dimly recalled was a suitably superhero-ish pose. It was only then that she noticed where the thug's eyes were pointing.

"Hey. Hey! Eyes off the nipples, Tony Soprano," Anna warned. "My face is up here."

Sam frowned. "Tony Soprano?"

"It's the only criminal I could think of," Anna admitted. "It was that or Bluto out of Popeye, and I figured that was probably before his time."

The man-mountain growled, his hand tightening around his shiv. Anna drove the point of her elbow into the end of his nose. Judging by the expression that flitted across her face, she took immense satisfaction from the *crunch* it made, and even more so from the spluttering and squealing that followed.

As he stumbled backward, the gang leader tripped over Randy. He flailed his arms for a moment, before toppling over like a felled great oak and cracking his head on the sidewalk.

"Relax, guys. I got him," Randy crowed. "Thanks for the assist."

"Assist? What do you mean *assist*?" Anna said. Her face lit up as she had a thought. "Wait! We should do a witty quip!"

Sam groaned. "Really? Don't you think that's a little, you know, corny?"

"Something about elbows, maybe?" Anna said. She clicked her fingers a few times. "Shit. We should've workshopped something up on the roof while we were waiting."

"Elbow face!" Randy piped up.

Anna and Sam both looked down at him. "What's that supposed to mean?"

Randy tried again. "Elbow *in* face!"

"Now you're just describing what happened," said Anna.

"I'm making a quip," Randy insisted.

"That's not a quip," said Sam. "A quip is like..."

He looked down at the sobbing, blubbering gangbanger

and thought for a moment. "He *nose* not to mess with us again."

"Ha! Yes!" said Anna. "Genius. Because of his nose."

"That's lame," said Randy. "That's not a quip. It's a pun."

"Most quips are puns," Sam pointed out.

"Face..." Randy's mouth contorted in concentration. "...elbow."

Anna sighed. "Now you're just saying the same thing as earlier, but the other way around. Let's go with the nose thing. It makes sense, it's funny-ish, and *holy shit, look at your leg!*"

"Huh? Oh, this? It's nothing," Randy said, sitting up and placing both hands on his shin. "I'll just take care of it with a..."

There was a *crack* as he twisted the lower half of his leg. Sam and Anna both recoiled in horror at the sound.

"Got it," said Randy.

Everyone stared at it for a few shell-shocked moments.

Sam swallowed. "Should your foot be facing that way?" he asked.

"Which way?"

"Back that way," said Anna. "The opposite way to that one."

"Oh."

Randy looked from one foot to the other. Several times.

"Now you come to mention it, that could be a problem," he began.

Then, his upper half flopped back onto the sidewalk, his head *clonked* against the ground, and his brain dragged him into unconsciousness before the screaming could start.

CHAPTER FOURTEEN

"IT WAS ACTUALLY—I hate to say it—but it was actually pretty awesome," Sam gushed. "I mean, she shot me. She *shot me*, and I didn't die!"

"Wait, that was a woman?" asked Anna. "Are you sure?"

"Well, I'm not a hundred percent, but I think so, yeah. But my point is, *she shot me*." He lifted his t-shirt, showing his bare chest. It looked nowhere near as impressive as his supersuit had suggested. "Nothing. Look. Not even a bruise. And you fell...?"

"Off a drainpipe," said Anna.

"No, I meant distance."

"Oh. Like, two stories."

"And you're fine, too!" Sam said. "We took out a whole gang of bad guys, and we didn't even get hurt."

"Except Randy," Anna pointed out.

"Obviously. Except Randy. But that was his own fault," Sam said. He looked across the counter to Mari. "How is he, by the way?"

Anna held out her tray and Mari deposited a scoop of some sort of congealed pasta dish into the offered bowl. The complex's dining area was small and basic, with three folding tables, a dozen plastic chairs, and a lingering smell that Sam hadn't quite been able to place.

"Randy is doing well, dear, thanks for asking," said Mari, her digital lips moving in approximate sync with her voice. "His leg has been corrected. He'll be joining us shortly."

Sam shuddered a little at the use of the word 'corrected.'

"That's good," he said. "Guess he won't be doing the superhero landing again in a hurry."

"You know he will," said Anna.

Sam held his tray out to receive his dollop of pasta. "Yeah. Yeah, you're probably right," he said.

Chuck was already sitting at the head of one of the three tables, his own tray in front of him. He beckoned them over, gesturing to the seats on either side of him.

"I hear you guys did OK," he said, once they'd joined him at the table.

"Yeah! We did good," Sam confirmed.

Chuck waved his plastic fork vaguely. "I heard 'OK,'" he said. "What did you think of the suits?"

"They were awesome," said Sam.

"I'm not sold on the nipples," Anna added. "But other than that, pretty cool."

Chuck pronged a rubbery pasta shell with his fork. "You still didn't use your powers," he said, eyeing Sam.

Sam shifted uneasily on the hard plastic chair. "No. I didn't need to. We took them down without any of us having to use our abilities."

Chuck chewed on his pasta, nodding slowly. "Not really the point, though," he said, once he'd swallowed. "I mean, we could've given the suits to anyone. We chose you because of your powers. That's why you're here."

"I'm just... It's not that simple," said Sam.

"The suit should help you focus," Chuck continued. "It should make it easier to do... your thing."

Anna reached for a wine bottle sitting in the middle of the table, then sighed heavily when she read the '0% Alcohol' label.

"Why?" she demanded, waving the bottle in Chuck's direction. "Just... why?"

"We did our research," Chuck explained. "Alcohol dulls your allergy powers."

"I know! That's why I drink so much of it! That's literally the entire point."

"Does it dull all our powers?" Sam wondered.

"No. Just hers."

"You still haven't explained what your powers even are," Anna said, shooting Sam a probing look as she poured herself a glass of the stupid and pointless fake wine. "So, spill."

Sam shook his head. "No, it's not easy to... I mean, they're not... It's hard to explain."

"No, it isn't. It's simple."

They all turned to find Kapitän Nazi standing by the table's remaining empty chair, a tray in his hands.

"That seat's taken," said Sam. "It's for Randy. He's coming down."

"Oh," said the Kapitän. He looked across to one of the other tables, but Anna gestured to the chair he was looming next to.

"It's fine. We can pull up another one when he arrives."

Sam glowered at her, but she flashed him a smile in return, before diverting her attention back to the Kapitän. "So, you know what his powers are?"

"Yes. I do," Nazi confirmed, sliding onto the plastic chair. He flicked his gaze across at Sam while unwrapping some disposable cutlery from its sterile packaging. "But it's not fair for me to tell you without his permission."

"Oh, come on!" Anna protested. "We're supposed to be a team. How can we be if we don't know what everyone can do? We know I can do the allergy stuff, Randy can do... well, fuck all, it seems. But Mystery Man here...? I'm drawing a blank."

"Woman's got a point," Chuck agreed.

Kapitän Nazi rubbed his plastic knife and fork together as if sharpening them. "May I?" he asked, raising his eyebrows at Sam.

Sam ground his back teeth together in time with Nazi's cutlery rubbing. He grunted out something vaguely affirmative-sounding. "Fine. Whatever."

"Alright!" said Anna, shuffling her chair in closer to the table. "Here we go. Spill."

"He is... How can I put this?" Nazi said. He subjected himself to a mouthful of the pasta and chewed it thoughtfully. "He is a god."

Anna snorted. "Ha!" she said, her eyes flicking from the Kapitän to Sam and back again. "Wait... what do you mean? Are you serious?"

"No, he isn't," said Sam.

Nazi nodded slowly. "I am. He is. Basically. His powers border on being unlimited. Truly unlimited. He can manipulate matter with a thought. He can create physical objects from thin air, turn people into memories, alter the very fabric of reality itself. Properly focused, there is nothing he cannot do."

Throughout this, Anna's gaze had drifted back to Sam and stayed there. He kept his head down, poking around in his pasta like he might find buried treasure in there somewhere.

"Bullshit," she said. "That would make him..."

"The most powerful being on the face of the planet," said Chuck. "Yeah. That's about the size of it."

Anna knocked back her wine, remembered it was of the non-alcoholic variety, and shuddered with distaste.

"But... I mean... Then why are you so—and no offense here—why are you so hopeless?" she asked.

"I'm not hopeless!" Sam protested. "I helped fight off those guys."

"No, but you could've just blinked them out of existence," Anna said. "Or, I don't know, magicked them into jail, or whatever. Why didn't you do that?"

"Because I can't," Sam explained.

Anna's hand crossed over as she pointed to both Chuck and Kapitän Nazi at the same time. "But they said..."

"I know what they said, and they're *technically* right," Sam said. "But I can't control it. If I use my powers, I don't actually know what'll happen. Sure, I might stop a bad guy, but I might paint the city bright orange, instead. Or turn every car in the country into rubber. Or make every dog within eight blocks catch fire. It's too risky."

"Especially if you're a dog, I guess," said Anna. She whistled quietly through her teeth. "Jesus. Guess we know where the 'Random' part comes from, huh?"

"You see why I'd prefer to avoid using it?" asked Sam. "It's too dangerous."

"Maybe if you concentrated..." Chuck began, but a dry, mirthless laugh from Sam cut him off.

"I've been concentrating every day since I was eight," he said. "I've got the whole concentration thing pretty much nailed down, thanks."

"I can help, Sam," said Kapitän Nazi. "If you'll let me."

"Can we not do this?" Sam snapped, throwing his fork and knife down onto the table. This would've been more dramatic had they not been made from flimsy plastic. "I don't need your help. I don't want your help. I know what you are. I know what you've done. I don't even want to look at you."

"He's not the same," Chuck insisted. "He's changed."

"Oh, well that's fine, then!" cried Sam, his voice taking on a slightly hysterical edge. "He's *different*. He's *changed*. Then let's just overlook the people he killed. The lives he ruined. Will we? Will we do that?"

Sam's face twisted in contempt. "He hasn't changed. It's an act. It's always an act."

"It's no act," said the Kapitän. "I assure you."

"Bullshit!"

"I know it's difficult. I know I'm asking a lot, but you have to trust me."

"*Trust you?*" Sam hissed. "You're out of your mind."

Anna shrugged. "I don't know, Sam. I mean, I get that he did a lot of bad things, but maybe he is different. Maybe he deserves a second chance?"

"What he deserves is to be rotting in a cell somewhere," Sam spat. "Or, better yet, buried in the ground."

"Harsh," said Anna.

Sam's eyes widened. His fists clenched. "Harsh? *Harsh?* You want to know what's harsh, Anna? Hmm? You want to know what's really harsh? Torturing a ten-year-old! That's *harsh!*" he roared, jumping to his feet. "Taking him and drugging him and hurting him for days on end. *Days.*"

Anna's face turned ash-gray. "Jesus. I didn't... I mean..."

"Easy, Sam," said Chuck, reaching a hand out.

"DON'T TOUCH ME!" Sam roared, wrenching his arm away. His breath came in big gulps, hot tears filling his eyes. "OK?" he said, more quietly. "Just don't touch me."

"OK, OK, you got it," said Chuck, keeping both hands where Sam could see them. "Just... Just calm down."

"Hol-ee shit," Anna whispered. She was looking past Sam, her face a mix of wonder and horror.

Sam turned to see the room's other two tables hovering in the air behind him, their legs and tops twisted into impossible shapes that looped and interlocked in ways that hurt the brain and made the stomach flip.

He let out an animal sob of frustration, pain, sorrow, guilt, and a dozen more flavors in between. The tables hit the floor with a *splat*, and collapsed into a goo that fizzled and bubbled for a few seconds, before dissolving into nothing.

"I have to go," Sam muttered. "I can't be here."

He charged for the door without looking back, danced on the spot for a moment while he waited for it to slide open, then hurried through.

Anna stared at the blotchy stains on the dining room floor indicating where the tables had been, then looked to the door just as it slid closed again.

"Well," growled a voice from under the table. "That was awkward."

"Randy?" Anna said. She kicked out a few times until her foot eventually found something solid. "What are you doing? I thought you were still getting fixed up?"

Randy's head popped up from the other side of the table, where Sam had been sitting. "That's what I wanted you to think," he said, before adding, "The night's shadow," in a slightly breathless whisper.

Anna rolled her eyes, then looked back to the door. "I should go talk to him," she said.

Kapitän Nazi stood up. "No. Please, let me," he said. "It should be me."

"You sure that's a good idea, John?" Chuck asked, flicking his eyes to where the tables used to be. "He was pretty upset. He could hurt you."

Nazi gave a nod, then a vague, empty sort of smile. "And he'd be well within his rights to."

After some wandering, interspersed with a few bursts of stressed-out high-speed sprinting, Sam found himself in a part of the complex he'd never been in before. A series of lights *clunked* on as he entered, revealing a room that looked like some sort of museum, complete with glass display cases, framed photographs, and several person-sized lumps with white dust sheets draped protectively over them.

A fanfare blared out from some concealed speakers—the familiar opening refrain of Doc Mighty's theme tune from the blockbuster movie series based on his adventures.

"Oh, great," Sam muttered. He was partly annoyed because the movies had glamorized Mighty to a ludicrous degree while painting Sam himself as a buffoonish comic relief, before eventually killing him off in the third installment.

Mostly, though, he was annoyed because he knew the tune would be stuck in his head for the rest of the day. He caught himself humming along to it, even now, and had to make a conscious effort to stop.

The glass display cases each contained some slice of superhero history. Over there was Su Man Chu's old utility belt. Fastened to the wall was the broken power staff of Thragulos, the Dark Sorceress who Memetzo, Mandroid Master of the Mystic Arts had defeated in magical combat on the peak of Mount... Somewhere or Other. It had been before any of the Platoon had taken on sidekicks, so Sam's memory of it was based on old comic books and half-remembered stories told in the heat of battle.

Sam had never understood Doc Mighty's habit of mono-loguing during his battles. He'd loved nothing more than to wax lyrical while battling giant bog monsters, wrestling energy beings, or rescuing children from burning buildings. It had seemed to Sam that the Doc's mind had always seemed wrapped up in past adventures, rather than on the one he was having right then.

During these moments, Sam's own internal monologue

was usually saying nothing but, "*Ohshitohshitohshitohshit!*" and so he was hazy on some of the details of Mighty's tales.

He stopped at another display case. It contained two metal bracelets, and while he could dimly recall someone wearing them, he couldn't quite place who it had been.

"Mr. Atomic," said Kapitän Nazi, appearing behind him.

Sam didn't turn or acknowledge that he'd even heard.

"Battled the Justice Platoon with his radioactive powers," Nazi continued. "He died in a hospice a few years back. All those battles and turns out the only thing he was truly wreaking havoc on was his own prostate."

The Kapitän shoved his hands down deep in the pocket of his hoodie and looked forlornly at the exhibits around them. "It all seems so silly now."

"Tell that to the people you killed," Sam spat.

Nazi nodded slowly. "Would but I could," he said. He drew in a steadying breath. "I don't remember. What I did to you, I mean. I don't remember."

"I remember," said Sam. "Every second of it."

"I'm sure you do. I am told I was exceptionally gifted when it came to... that sort of thing."

Sam's hands shook. He clasped them together. "I can vouch for that."

Kapitän Nazi opened his mouth to reply, then closed it again. He looked down for a while, carefully formulating his response.

"We were both sidekicks, in a way," he said. "My mentor was not as... celebrated as yours. Not in the end, anyway. And rightly so. But he shaped me in his likeness. Instilled in me his beliefs. When I resisted, he forced them upon me. Bent me to his will."

"Oh, boo-hoo," said Sam, although there was a flicker of something like guilt as the words left his mouth.

"I'm not asking for sympathy, Sam. I haven't earned it,

and I don't deserve it," Nazi continued. "I'm just saying... It took me awhile, but I eventually worked out that I didn't have to be who he wanted me to be. Whatever lessons he taught me, ultimately I could choose not to heed them."

"Great. Good for you," said Sam. "Now, if you don't mind..."

He walked on to the next display, wanting to ask why the hell they'd built a secret superhero museum down here, but not wanting to ask *him*.

One of the dust sheet-covered shapes stood before him. He pulled the sheet aside, then groaned at what he found beneath it. There were two mannequins, one adult-sized, one smaller. The larger of the two wore a replica of Doc Mighty's costume. The smaller wore Sam's own Kid Random costume from back in the day.

Jesus, it looked ridiculous. He felt his cheeks sting with embarrassment even just looking at it, and so he turned his attention to the larger mannequin, instead. It was the old, traditional Doc Mighty costume, from back before his many rebranding exercises and the revamped outfits they inevitably brought with them.

With its blue spandex and red cape, this costume had come to represent the Doc's 'Classic Era.' Ask anyone over twenty to describe Doc Mighty, and the flowing crimson cape would almost certainly be the first thing they mentioned. Ask anyone younger, though, and the answers would likely differ wildly.

They might describe his 'Living Laser' period, when his powers inexplicably changed, and he adopted a garish electric blue costume with a glowing white mask.

Some of them might refer to the 'Doc Negative' era, when, following a trip to the Negative Zone, he occasionally became a reverse version of himself and, through reasons not fully understood, his own arch-enemy.

Very few would mention the joyless and drab, 'Dark Mighty' period, when he wore a muted version of his classic suit and scowled a lot, because everyone agreed it was probably best forgotten.

"He wore that the first time we fought," Kapitän Nazi said, appearing behind Sam again, much to Sam's annoyance. "I dropped a tank onto a shopping mall and declared Cityopolis was under Nazi rule. Before your time."

Sam said nothing, just clasped his hands together more tightly, trying to resist the urge to turn and strangle the evil bastard. The shape in his head twisted and rolled.

"He came out of nowhere," Nazi continued. "I'd heard rumors of the city's protector, but I had no idea. Not really. I found out later he was in France when the tank fell. All I remember is the impact, then the sound of him crashing through the wall, in that order. The noise trailed behind him. I was fast, but not that fast. *No one* was that fast. No one but him."

Sam turned. "What are you doing?" he demanded. "Why are you telling me this?"

"Eight people died when the tank came down," Nazi said. "Four more in the battle that followed. He went to their funerals, I believe."

"Again, why are you telling me this?" Sam hissed. "You killed people. That's not exactly a secret."

Nazi produced a battered leather notebook from inside his hoodie pocket. He held it between finger and thumb for a moment, as if weighing it, then held it out to Sam.

Sam made no move to take it.

"Please," Nazi urged.

With a sigh, Sam took the book. Opening it, he flicked through the first few pages. "Names. It's... It's names. So what?"

"It's *all* their names," Nazi said, lowering his head. "All of them."

Sam scanned down one of the pages. Dozens of names were written on it in neat, studious block capitals, small enough to fit three on each printed line, one above the other. A couple of the names were vaguely familiar to Sam, but not so much so that he could actually picture any of their faces.

"You killed all these people," Sam realized. "That's what this is."

"It has taken years, but I think that's all of them," Nazi said.

Sam thrust the book back at him. "This is... this is sick. You're worse than I thought!" he spat. "And considering I thought you were a mass-murdering Nazi supervillain who tortured kids, that's *really* saying something."

He turned away and started for the door. One of the other exhibits caught his eye, though. It was a long wooden display case, featuring an assortment of what Sam guessed must be less valuable items, as there was no glass protecting any of them.

Sam stopped at it. His hands shook again.

"You don't understand," said Nazi. "People are not black and white, Sam. We are weighed by the things we did, and the things we didn't. I keep this book as a reminder of what I did. My memories of that time are... vague. Distant. Like horror stories I have been told long ago."

He waved the book. "This. This reminds me that *I* did these things. That *I* killed these people. It reminds me that I *was* the horror story."

Nazi traced his fingers across the worn leather, then slipped the book back in his pocket. "Sometimes, I can convince myself that it wasn't me. Not really. It was my programming. I can make myself believe that my actions were merely a symptom of what they did to my mind. How they broke me."

He looked down again. "But that's a lie, isn't it? It was still me. Still these hands that did those things. Still this body that inflicted all that pain. It wasn't someone else. It was me. Whatever the reason, whatever my excuse, it was me."

Sam stared down into the display case. The shape in his head wriggled and squirmed.

"I can lift a car with one hand," Nazi said. "I can throw a rock from one side of the city to the other. But this book... This book is the heaviest burden I have ever carried."

Snatching one of the items from the display, Sam spun. He thrust forward, and the shiny blade of one of Su Man Chu's old throwing daggers *glinted* in the sterile glow of the overhead lighting.

The tip of the blade stopped just a fraction of an inch from Nazi's throat. He didn't react, other than by freezing.

"You're an evil son-of-a-bitch!" Sam hissed. He pressed with the blade and felt the point dig into the Kapitän's skin. "I should kill you! I should kill you for everything you did!"

"You should," Kapitän Nazi whispered. "You should. But, though I might wish otherwise, you won't. That's not who you are, Sam."

"You think I don't have it in me? Is that it?" Sam spat. "You think I can't?"

"I think you *won't*," the Kapitän said.

"And what would those people want me to do? Huh?" Sam demanded. "Those names in that book. What would they all want me to do?"

Nazi closed his eyes. He breathed deeply, and for a moment Sam thought he could feel him leaning into the knife's point. "The right thing."

Sam's hand trembled on the handle of the blade. He clamped his teeth together, biting back the tears that threatened to come. The shape in his head thrashed. Urgently. Violently.

With a roar, he wrenched his arm away and let fly with the knife. It *whistled* across the room, spinning end over end.

Somewhere along the way, it became a fat and really rather surprised frog. It barely had a moment to pull itself together and wonder how it had suddenly come into existence before it was taken back out of it again by the wall.

The frog exploded with a splat against the paintwork. By the time it hit the floor, it was a knife again. Or bits of one, anyway.

The squirming of the thing in Sam's head became a contented wriggle, then settled into stillness.

None the wiser about what had just happened, Kapitän Nazi opened his eyes, and immediately saw the hatred blazing behind Sam's own.

"Stay away from me," Sam warned. "I don't care what Chuck says. You and me? We are *not* on the same side."

CHAPTER FIFTEEN

"KNOCK KNOCK."

Sam looked up from the bottom bunk to find Anna leaning against his doorframe, two glasses of wine in her hands. The rooms they had been given were small but functional, containing the bunk-beds, a desk, a chair, and not a whole lot else. There was a small TV mounted to the wall just beyond the foot of the bed, but Sam hadn't bothered to switch it on.

"You OK?" Anna asked.

Sam nodded too quickly. "Sure. Fine. Sorry about earlier."

"Ah, shut up," Anna told him. "Did John find you?"

A look of betrayal flashed across Sam's face. "You're calling him John now?"

"Kapitän Nazi just feels like a bit of a mouthful," she said. She held one of the glasses out to him. "Here. I talked Chuck into letting us have some of the real stuff. And when I say I talked him into it, I mean I swiped it from a cabinet when he wasn't looking."

Sam regarded the offered glass for a few moments, then

accepted it. He knocked half the contents back in one gulp. "Thanks."

Anna sipped from her own glass as she looked around the room. "Nice place you got here," she said. "I have one just like it. Although, I'm sure if I look hard enough I'll find out mine has a couple of nipples stashed away somewhere."

She turned the swivel chair away from the desk and took a seat. "I mean, who thought that was a good idea?"

"It wasn't a *terrible* idea," Sam said, but the look on Anna's face forced him to reconsider. "No, you're right. Completely sexist and unacceptable."

"Right? It'd be like giving your suit balls," said Anna. She paused momentarily to picture this, then shuddered at whatever image she settled on. "No. Nobody wants to see that."

Sam's jacket was draped across the back of the chair. Something in the pocket caught Anna's eye, and she fished it out. "Nice elephant," she said. "Yours?"

"I got it for my son," said Sam. "And it's a hippo. It's his favo... It's his *second* favorite color."

Anna shoved the plush toy back into the pocket. "Well, I mean, you don't want to spoil him by getting him his first favorite color, do you?"

"He changed it," said Sam. "His favorite color, I mean. I didn't know until after I'd bought it. He changed it to match the color of his mom's boyfriend's car."

Anna winced. "Ouch."

"Yeah."

"So, you're not together? I mean, I'm assuming. Unless... I don't know how your relationship works, maybe you're both into—"

"We're not together," Sam confirmed. "Corey comes to stay over a couple of times a month. We all get together for his birthday."

Anna nodded slowly and took another sip of her wine.

"Right. Still... You have a kid. Crazy. Last time I saw you we all pretty much *were* kids, and now you've actually gone and made one."

Sam smiled. "Yep. Well, he's adopted, but... Yeah."

"Adopted?"

"An orphan. Like us, I guess," Sam said, scratching his head in a way that suggested he wasn't entirely comfortable talking about it. "I knew what it was like growing up the way I did, and I wanted to make a difference for some other kid, you know?"

Anna raised her glass in salute. "Well, good for you, Sam. That is pretty damn decent of you."

"Also, I didn't want to risk passing on my powers in case he started flying or, you know, shitting bullets, or whatever," Sam said. "So, I got the old..." He mimed snipping something with scissors. "... before Laura and I met, and then I told her I was infertile."

"Wow," Anna said. "And she fell for it?"

"Completely," said Sam. "And then she found out, called me a lying scumbag, and kicked me out of the house."

Anna sucked air in through her teeth. "Shit."

"Yeah."

"Although..."

"It was my own fault, and I completely had it coming. Yes. I do understand that," Sam said. "I just couldn't risk it, you know?"

Anna nodded into her glass as she brought it to her lips.

"What about you?" Sam asked. "Any kids?"

"God, no!" Anna snorted. "I can barely look after myself, let alone another human being."

Sam smiled at her. His face felt a little rubbery, and he realized his glass was empty. "You look like you're doing OK," he told her.

"I did have a cat for a while," Anna said. "No idea where it went."

"Uh... OK. Sorry to hear that."

"Don't be," Anna sniffed. "Judgmental little prick. He's probably off badmouthing me somewhere."

Sam laughed at that. A silence fell after a while. It wasn't quite a comfortable silence, although it wasn't entirely uncomfortable, either.

"Married?" Sam asked.

Anna swirled the dregs of her wine around in her glass. "Yeah."

"Oh? Oh!" said Sam, before following up with as nonchalant a third, "Oh," as he could manage.

"Twice. Briefly," said Anna. She stopped swirling for a moment and peered at the wall. "Wait. No. Three times. But that third time barely even counts."

"Right! Right," said Sam. "Right. Three times? Wow. Right."

He brought the empty glass to his lips and drained a solitary drip from the bottom. "And now...?"

"Now? No. Not now," said Anna. "I am done with marriage. Done."

She set her glass down on the desk, the faint *chink* it made punctuating the sentence. She flicked her eyes in Sam's direction and just held his gaze for a while. The wine had colored her lips a deep crimson, and the way they stood out against her pale, freckled skin drew Sam's gaze.

"So," she said.

Sam's throat felt tight. His voice came out as an anxious squeak. "So."

Anna bit her lip to stop herself grinning. It was, Sam thought, one of the most arousing things he had ever seen, although he'd be the first to admit he'd led a pretty sheltered life romance-wise.

He watched her as she stood up, leaning himself back a little as she crossed to him. She was dressed in the same baggy t-shirt and shorts combo as he was, but there was no denying that she wore it better than he ever could.

His head *whooshed* with a thousand thoughts. Had he had enough wine to do this? Had he had too much? Should they be doing it? Were they even going to do what he thought they were going to do?

"Is this allowed?" he whispered.

Anna giggled. It made Sam's heart pump faster. "Allowed? We're not kids anymore, Sam. Stop being so uptight."

"I'm not uptight, it's just—"

Anna bent down, and suddenly her lips were on his. He tasted her, breathed her in, felt her warmth, her closeness against him.

Sam didn't resist as Anna pushed him back onto the bed. The squirming shape in his head was still and silent, like it couldn't quite believe what was happening right now. Or, more importantly, what was about to happen over the course of the next two-to-five minutes.

A thought suddenly occurred to him. It was so pressing that it leapfrogged over the hundreds of others that currently competed for his attention, and so terrible that to his horror he found himself voicing it aloud.

"Will it get itchy?" he asked, his lips brushing against hers as he spoke.

Anna leaned back a little. "Sorry?"

"Down there," said Sam, the words slipping out before he could stop them. "Will it get itchy? Or, I don't know, burn, or something?"

Anna retreated further. She was still straddling him, but the expression on her face suggested she was no longer sure if she wanted to be.

"What are you saying?"

Sam's eyes went wide. "No! I don't mean... I meant because of your powers. Not because of... I wasn't saying you've got..."

Anna's smile returned. "Relax. I'm messing with you. No, it won't get itchy," she said. She lowered herself so her face was by his again. "Not saying it won't burn a little, though," she whispered.

"Not saying what won't burn?" growled a voice from the door.

Randy.

"Oh my God! Were you two going to have sex?" he demanded. He was standing in the open doorway, a scowl on his face. "After everything I said?"

"What? No! We weren't," Sam said, his cheeks reddening.

"Yes, we were," Anna corrected. "And not even because we wanted to. It's just to annoy you. So, go away, Randy. And shut the door."

"No can do," Randy snarled. "Chuck wants to see you both. Says it's important."

Anna sighed. "Can it wait like..." She looked down at Sam and regarded him with a smirk, before turning back. "...two minutes forty-five seconds?"

It took Sam a moment.

"Hey!" he protested.

"Fat chance," Randy growled. "It's vital that he sees us all. Right now. The fate of the world could depend on it."

Anna groaned. "Fine," she said, dismounting Sam. "Stupid fate of the world."

She rolled her eyes and smiled with exasperation, then held a hand out to help Sam up. "Come on, let's go find out what's so important."

Sam lifted one leg a little, disguising the bulge in his shorts. The redness of his cheeks became full-blown crimson. "I'll, uh, I'll catch up."

"Surprise!"

A single party popper gave a disappointing *paf*, showering the floor in front of Mari with thin paper ribbons, sparkling confetti, and other mess she was all too aware she'd only have to clean up later.

Randy had insisted all three of them go at the same time, so Sam had been forced to waddle some of the way, until things calmed themselves down in the shorts department. Anna had taken great delight in this, and had sniggered gleefully for most of the walk. Randy seemed confused by the laughter at first, then increasingly irate when he couldn't work out what was meant to be so funny.

To Sam's surprise, Randy's own walk was completely limp-free. The shape of his leg earlier had suggested he'd at least need crutches, if not a wheelchair. And yet, here he was, skulking along near the walls without a hint of difficulty.

"Apparently, it's the suit," Anna said, seeing how Sam was studying Randy's legs. "It speeds up recovery. That's why he's still wearing the pants."

And now, a few minutes after all that, here they were back in the dining room, with Mari shooting a party popper at them, and an uncomfortable-looking Chuck bellowing, "Surprise" in their general direction.

Anna frowned and looked around. The dining room looked pretty much exactly as she'd left it ten minutes ago. "What's the surprise?" she asked. "Is it that you brought us back here for no reason?"

Chuck, who had been standing up, sat down. "It was Randy's idea," he said.

"Oh, *was* it?" said Anna, turning to glower at him. "He said it was something important."

"It is important," Randy growled. "It's the most important thing in the world!"

Anna crossed her arms and raised an eyebrow. "Is it?"

"OK, no, it's not *that* important," Randy admitted. "That would be insane. But it's still important. To the team."

"He has a point," said Chuck. "You guys did good today. We should celebrate that."

"We were just about to when Randy walked in," Anna said.

Chuck frowned. "Huh?"

Anna sighed. "Doesn't matter."

Sam's head was still a little light from the wine and the abrupt, unexpected movement of blood around his body. He wasn't quite sure what was happening, exactly, but whatever it was, he was pleased to see Kapitän Nazi didn't seem to be part of it.

"Sit down," Chuck urged, gesturing to the seats at the table around him. "Mari, do me a favor? Grab us the bottle of wine from the cabinet. The real stuff, I mean."

"That won't be necessary," said Anna.

"No, please, I insist," said Chuck. He nodded to Mari, and the robot trundled off. Chuck fixed Anna with a somber look. "Unless you have something to tell me?"

Anna's face became a picture of innocence. "Hmm? No. No, don't think so."

"Like that you broke into the cabinet and already took the bottle," said Chuck. "For example."

Anna clicked her fingers. "Wait. That *is* ringing a bell."

"It was my idea!" Sam blurted.

"No, it wasn't," said Anna.

"No," Chuck agreed. "It wasn't."

Sam seemed to shrink a little. "OK, no, it wasn't."

"Under normal circumstances, I'd be pissed," said Chuck. "But, as Randy pointed out, this is supposed to be a celebration, so I'm going to let you off. Do it again, and you're off the team."

Anna's eyes lit up. "You promise?"

"Does that go for me, too?" asked Sam, rising from his seat. "Because if so..."

"Funny," said Chuck, stony-faced. "Look at me cracking up here."

Mari *whirred* in and deposited a full whiskey bottle on the table with an unceremonious *thunk*. "There was no wine, so I brought that," she said.

"Now you're talking!" said Anna.

"Do you want me to open it for you, too?" Mari asked.

"Would you mind?" said Chuck.

"I was being sarcastic," said Mari. "What am I? Your servant?"

Chuck straightened a little. "Oh. *Oh.* Sorry, I just... Sometimes, it isn't clear. With the voice, I mean."

Mari's digital face became a scowl. Everyone at the table jumped as a blade scythed out from within her metal torso and neatly decapitated the whiskey bottle.

"Fuck!" Anna ejected.

The bottle teetered on the tabletop for a second or two, before righting itself.

"There," Mari said. "Enjoy."

She returned to the site of her party popper launch, and as she rolled herself back and forth across it, the streamers, glitter, and other debris were all quickly vacuumed up.

There were four wine glasses on the table. Chuck opened his mouth to ask Mari for other glasses, but then thought better of it. He glugged a shot into each glass, then slid three of them across the table to Sam, Anna, and Randy. Randy peered down at his like it was an unexploded bomb.

"I don't drink alcohol," he growled. "It poisons the body and clouds mind."

"Yeah, pretty sure that'll be the least of your mind's problems," Anna said.

"What's that supposed to mean?" Randy demanded.

"Seriously, still with the voice?" Sam muttered. "Even now?"

"Nothing," said Anna. "It's not supposed to mean anything. All I'm saying is don't worry about it. When has alcohol ever hurt anyone? Booze is our friend, not our enemy. I think we'd all do well to remember that."

Sam swirled the amber liquid around in his glass, then took a sip. His gums drew back of their own accord, then his whole body gave a shudder. "Nice," he said, his eyes suddenly streaming. He tried very hard not to cough. "Smooth."

Anna sniffed her own glass, then touched the liquid to her lips. She smacked them together a few times, and flicked her tongue lightly across their surface, savoring the taste. "Mmm. Yep," she said, nodding her approval. "It's a good one. You know how you can tell?"

"How?" Sam asked.

"Because they're all good ones. It was a trick question," Anna told him. "Again, booze is not our enemy, it's our friend." She raised a finger, emphasizing the point. "*With benefits.*"

Chuck raised his glass to the center of the table. "I'm going to propose a toast," he announced.

Everyone fell silent and waited.

And waited.

"Are you going to propose it today, or...?" Anna asked.

"I'm just trying to word it properly," Chuck said, punctuating the reply with a *tut* of irritation. "OK. Here's the thing," he said. "When we first started this project, I was right behind it, you know? I was fully committed, and I thought— no, I *knew*—that it was a good idea. I knew that, if the time ever came when we had to activate it, the Sidekicks Initiative was a solid plan."

"Amen!" said Anna, chinking her glass against his.

"And then I met you guys," Chuck continued. "And, I'll be honest, I lost some of that confidence."

"Oh, you're not done," said Anna, lowering her glass again.

"You were not what I expected," said Chuck.

"We were *better* than you expected," said Randy, nodding in agreement.

"No. No, worse. Definitely worse. In every way," Chuck corrected. "When I saw you all fighting those henchmen, I thought, 'Chuck, you have wasted your life. You have just gone and thrown those years away.'"

"Amen!" said Anna again, although she didn't bother to raise her glass this time.

"Twenty years, and what have I got to show for it?" Chuck asked. "A god who won't use his powers, a borderline alcoholic who makes people sneeze, and a guy who—and I'm being generous here—*might* be able to talk to butterflies."

Sam looked around the table at the others. "Uh, are you sure you understand the concept of 'celebration,' Chuck? Because this doesn't feel like one at all."

"I'm getting to my point," Chuck replied.

"Thank God for that," said Anna, staring longingly into her glass.

"My point is, John told me how you guys performed out there today. He told me you delivered the goods. Was your style unorthodox?" Chuck nodded. "Sure. Sounds like it. But you worked together, and you stopped four gangbangers mugging an old lady. Hell, maybe doing a whole lot worse. I had my doubts, but I was wrong. You guys weren't sidekicks today. You were heroes."

Anna shrugged and gestured to the others sitting around

the table. "Well, *he* almost killed himself, *he* got shot in the chest, and I fell off a drainpipe, but... fuck it. I'll take it," she said. "To we three heroes!"

They all clinked glasses together. Even Randy, although he didn't join the others in taking a swig. Instead, he brought the glass to his mouth and tentatively touched his tongue against the surface of the liquid.

His face contorted in displeasure and he shook his head violently, flapping his tongue around in an attempt to rid it of the taste.

"How can you drink that? It's disgusting!"

"It's only disgusting the first, like, twenty to thirty times," Anna told him. "After that, it's tolerable for a while, and then, much later, it's awesome."

"So... what now?" asked Sam.

Chuck peered at him over his glass. "What do you mean?"

"I mean what happens next? We've been out in the field. We did good, you said so yourself. Do we go after the Beef Chief?"

"Shit, no!" Chuck blurted, almost choking on his drink. "Let's not get ahead of ourselves here, Sam. You took down four non-powered, lightly armed individuals. There's a long road ahead before you're ready to take on *any* supervillains, let alone one at Beef Chief's level."

He leaned back in his chair. "In a week or two, maybe —*maybe*—you'll be ready to go after someone like Fiddlesticks or Mister Fister, but there's a whole lot of work to do before then."

Randy had set his glass down on the table. Anna eyed it for a while, then reached over to take it. "Well, if you're too much of a wimp, I'm not letting this go to waste."

"Ha!" Randy spat, snatching the glass up before she could take it. "Butterfly King is no wimp."

He drew the glass to his lips, eyeballed everyone in turn over the rim, then knocked the whole shot back in one go.

For a moment, his expression became a grimace of horror, with just a suggestion of surprise, like he hadn't actually been expecting the booze to enter his body.

Finally, he set the glass down. "See? Easy," he said.

His head fell forward and *thunked* onto the table. Everyone watched him for a while, waiting to see if anything else was going to happen.

Nothing did.

"Well, you broke him," said Sam. "Good job."

"Let's be fair, he was already pretty broken to begin with," said Anna. She lowered her voice and directed it at Chuck. "I mean, seriously. What is with that guy? Where did you dig him up?"

"He's been... around. We've kept an eye on him," Chuck said. "He was the only one of you guys to keep up the whole sidekick thing, then he went solo. We hauled him in a couple of times, trying to dissuade him from getting himself killed, but he insisted he was making a difference."

Chuck shrugged. "And I guess he was. Was it a positive difference? That, I don't know. But he was trying. I thought we should give him a shot."

"OK, but we've just seen what happens when you *actually* give him a shot," said Anna, flicking her gaze to the back of Randy's head. "I mean, I'm not saying I don't like him—I don't really, but that's not what I'm saying. I'm saying... is it wise? Having him tag along, I mean? He could've died jumping off that roof. We could've died helping him."

She tapped her glass and eyed the bottle. Chuck got the hint.

"And then there's the whole butterfly thing," she said. "I'm still not clear on what he can do with them."

"Nor are we," Chuck admitted.

"Exactly my point," said Anna. "I just think... You know, with everything... Is it wise?"

"Probably not," conceded Chuck. "But the alternative is he takes matters into his own hands, goes out there on his own, and gets himself killed."

Anna took a glug of her drink. "If the choices are, 'He gets killed on his own,' or, 'He gets killed along with both of us,' then that's not really a choice at all," she pointed out. She gestured around them. "Can't you keep him here? Isn't there some job you can give him that'll keep him safe and out of our way?"

Chuck looked thoughtful as he topped up his own glass. "Like a desk job?"

"Exactly! Like a desk job. He's in the game, but he's not *in it* in it," Anna said. "Sam? You agree with me, right?"

Sam blinked at the sound of his name. "Huh? Oh. Uh..." He regarded the unconscious Randy as his mind raced to catch up. "I kind of like him. I mean, sure, he's got his issues, but he's been out there fighting the fight for years. And he's still in one piece, so he can't be *that* bad at it."

"You haven't seen his medical records," said Chuck.

"No, but I've seen his scars," said Sam. "To get hurt like that and still want to jump right back into the ring every time? That takes a lot of guts."

"Or a complete lack of common sense," said Anna.

"Or that, yes," Sam admitted. He slid his glass across the table from one hand to the other and back again. "I'm just saying, good luck getting him to take a desk job."

Randy muttered something in his sleep. It was loud, but mostly incomprehensible, and while it sounded like it might have been something about goat cheese, it equally might not have been. Whatever it was, it was enough to steer the conversation away from his shortcomings and onto a different topic.

"What's with the museum?" Sam asked.

Anna raised an eyebrow, and Sam realized he hadn't mentioned it.

"There's a room full of old superhero stuff," he explained. "It's like a little museum or something."

"Oh. That. Yeah," said Chuck. "Been so long since I was in there, I almost forgot we had it. It was Mari's idea, mostly." He pointed to the robot. Her digital expression didn't change. "Because we had space down here on the government's tab, they started sending us some stuff for storage. Junk, mostly, but there were some interesting pieces in there."

"Like what?" Anna asked.

"Bits of costume. Old weapons. Artifacts from various adventures. That kind of thing," Chuck explained. "We didn't know how difficult it might be to convince you guys to get involved with the project, so Mari came up with the idea of making like a... What did you call it again?"

"An inspiration room," said Mari.

"That was it. An *inspiration room*. You know, to inspire your asses," Chuck said, grinning at them. "Turned out, we didn't need it."

Randy sat up suddenly, ejecting a loud, "Buh!" that mostly came out through his nose. His goggles had slipped down over one eye, which seemed to confuse him greatly. Both eyes swiveled madly, trying to figure out what the hell was going on.

"Aaand he's back," said Anna.

"You OK there, Randy?" Sam asked.

"Buh!" Randy exclaimed.

His hands slapped at his face until they found his goggles. He maneuvered them back onto his leather flying helmet with quite a lot of difficulty, then blinked for such a long period of time that everyone started to wonder if he'd fallen asleep again.

"Fine!" he declared in a voice so loud it echoed around the dining room. He immediately winced, pulling his head into his neck and closing his eyes again. "Buh!" he cried again.

"Yep. You definitely broke him," said Sam.

Randy stumbled upright, knocking over his glass and staggering out of his seat. His face was contorted in a grimace of pain, and the way his upper body was stooped suggested his head had become a good fifty pounds heavier.

"Must... go," he wheezed, shambling toward the door. "Must commune with the butterflies..."

They all watched him stagger out into the corridor. Anna took a slow sip of her drink. "So, is that a euphemism, do we think?" She shook her head. "I'm sorry, but we have to get rid of that guy."

Sam shrugged. "Honestly? It's not him I'm worried about."

Anna looked offended. "You're worried about *me*? I can take care of myself."

"No! Not you," said Sam. He lowered his voice to a whisper. "Nazi."

"Oh. OK. Yeah, should've realized," said Anna. "You really don't like the guy, do you?"

"He's a mass-murdering Nazi supervillain who tortured children," Sam hissed.

"One child. That we know of," said Anna. She winced. "That sounded like a stronger defense in my head."

"Yes. One child. Me!" said Sam. "So, given all that? No, I can't say I'm his biggest fan."

Chuck clicked his tongue against the roof of his mouth and nodded slowly. "I get it, Sam. I do. I had more than a few doubts about him, too. But, well..."

He hesitated. "Mari. Is John in his room?"

Mari's screen flickered to black, just for a moment. "John is in the inspiration room," she said.

"OK. OK, good." Chuck knocked back his drink and stood up. "Come with me," he said. "I want to show you both something."

CHAPTER SIXTEEN

SAM STOOD by one of several bookcases, his eyes drifting down the shelves of neatly arranged notebooks. Every book had a label on the spine. A different name was written on each one in a studious, block capitalized handwriting Sam recognized.

"OK, first up, how come the ex-Nazi's got a bigger room than we have?" Anna asked. She'd glugged a double into her glass before they'd left the dining room, and was now teasing out the final few drops for as long as she could. "And second, what's with all the notebooks?"

"He was here first," Chuck said. "And he had more baggage than you guys. Both figuratively and literally."

He took a notebook from one of the bookcases, apparently at random. After quickly flicking through it, he passed it to Sam. "Here."

"What is it?" asked Sam, not yet accepting the book.

"Just take the damn thing and see for yourself," Chuck urged.

Sam resisted for a few seconds, then sighed and took the book. He flicked to the first page. It contained a name—

Martin Carter—and some basic stats, including age, gender, address and date of birth. There was a passport photo, too, neatly taped in place above the writing.

"What's this?" he asked.

"You saw his notebook, right?" Chuck asked. "His list of names?"

Sam nodded and flicked to the next page. It was a double spread, with several other names written in, all joined together with ruler-straight lines. It was a family tree, he realized.

"There's a book for every one of those names," Chuck said. "He found out everything he could about the people he killed. He felt that, since he'd taken their lives, he should do something to mark them. I guess he didn't want to forget them."

"Well, that's fucking creepy," Anna muttered.

"I don't mean in a serial killer kind of way," Chuck said. "I mean, like, a shrine to them, or some shit."

"Still sounds *kind of* serial killery," Anna pointed out.

Chuck sighed. "Maybe I'm not explaining it right. It made sense when he explained it. Weird, obviously, but it made sense."

Sam flicked to another page. More pictures were taped to this one. They were lower quality, like they'd been printed on an inkjet. In one of them, the guy had his face painted like a cat. There was no explanation given.

Anna picked up another of the books and opened it. "Angela Crossley," she read. She squinted at the photograph taped to the page. "Ooh. Nice hat."

She showed the page to Sam. The photo at the bottom was black and white, not a passport picture. Sam had to agree that it was indeed a nice hat.

Anna studied the book again. "Cause of death, devoured by wolves," she said. "Jesus. What happened to your guy?"

Sam frowned and flicked back to the front page of his book. "Speared up the anus," he read.

"Fuck!" Anna exclaimed. "With what?"

"Don't know. Doesn't say."

Anna drained the last of her drink. "Poor Martin," she said, replacing her own book and reaching for another. After reading the name, she went straight for the death details. "Geoff Evans. Prolonged crucifixion." She lowered the book. "*Prolonged* crucifixion. Not just crucifixion. *Prolonged*."

"Dawn Ward was crucified, too," Sam said, consulting another book. "Hers wasn't prolonged, though."

"Well, that seems unfair," Anna remarked. "What did poor Geoff Evans do to deserve having his drawn-out?"

They worked their way through almost a full shelf between them, checking causes of death in each book with increasing fascinated eagerness.

Claudiu Oana was consumed by fire. Allison Aul drowned in toxic waste. Chris Green, Andrew Nicholls, and Julian Cheal all suffocated in the empty vacuum of outer space. Roy, Paul, Christopher, and Robbie Smith were all vaporized. It wasn't clear if they all went together, or individually.

Shirley Taylor was crushed by a tank. Slowly.

"Shit. Listen to this one," said Anna. She cleared her throat. "Wally Will. Choked to death on own genitalia."

"Jesus," Sam muttered. His brow furrowed. "Wait. Wally Will. Why do I know that name?"

"Captain Handstand," said Chuck. "North Dakota Defenders."

Sam clicked his fingers. "That's it. Captain Handstand. He applied for Justice Platoon membership once, I think."

"Did they let him in?" Anna asked.

"He could do handstands," said Sam. "Of course they didn't let him in."

Sam slid the book he was holding back into position and

resisted the urge to pick up another. Anna was right, the whole idea *was* creepy.

And yet... it was something. Weird, definitely. Misjudged? Maybe. But something.

"Doesn't change anything, though," he said, to himself as much as to Chuck.

"No. Doesn't change what he did," Chuck agreed.

He gestured to a chalkboard that hung from the wall above the room's single folding bed. There were a couple of dozen white lines drawn on there in groups of five - four horizontal, then one diagonally through the others.

"What's this?" Sam asked. "Is he counting the days he's been here?"

Chuck shook his head. "He's counting the lives he's saved. These are all since we broke his programming. He doesn't keep any details, just marks it on the board. I guess he's trying to shift the balance."

Sam looked from the twenty-odd marks on the board to the rows and rows of notebooks. "That's going to take some shifting," he said.

"Jackie Skidmore. Head swapped with own dog," Anna read. "Jesus, these things are addictive."

"He knows he'll never tip the scales. Don't matter how many lives he saves," said Chuck. "But he's trying. That's got to count for something, right?"

Sam felt like the alcohol was taking hold. The room spun around him, all those names and lines swirling in a blur around his head. His blood felt hot. It flushed upward into his brain, making his skull feel heavy and full.

"I'm, uh, I'm going to go to my room," he said, suddenly finding himself short of air. "I need to... I'm going to lie down."

Anna slid the book she was holding back into its space on

the shelf. "You OK?" she asked. "Should I...? Want me to come with you?"

"Uh, no. Not right now," said Sam. He tried to flash her a smile, but the sight of those books and those names twisted his stomach and turned the grin into a grimace. "I'll... I have to go."

Sam lay in the dark, curled up on his side, one arm buried under his pillow, the other covering his head.

Kapitän Nazi was a bad guy. He was arguably the *worst* guy, in fact, genetically engineered by Adolf Hitler to be the ultimate weapon of war.

But if that was right—if he was a weapon—then could he really be blamed for the things he'd done? If the hammer-wielding thug had managed to hit Sam earlier, it wouldn't have been the hammer's fault.

"It's not the same," Sam whispered, admonishing himself. "He's a monster. He'll always be a monster."

The bed creaked as he flopped over onto his back. He'd closed the door, but a thin line of light seeped in below it. It wasn't much, but it was enough for him to at least make out where the ceiling was. He stared up at its gray fuzziness, seeing some of the faces from those notebooks in the patterns of the darkness.

He closed his eyes, blocking them out.

An image of the giant gang member leered at him from the void. Sam saw the shiv in his hand and felt his heart race.

Jesus. What had they been thinking? They could've gotten themselves killed.

"Madness," he whispered into the darkness.

And yet, they'd survived. Not only survived, they'd *won*.

Somewhere, an old woman still had her purse because of them. Maybe even still had her life. There was no saying what they'd have done to her. Chuck was right—today, they'd been heroes.

He snuggled deeper into the thin mattress, trying to get comfortable. His mind wandered to later in the day, and to what had happened with Anna. Or what had *almost* happened, at least. That had been unexpected.

Now that he was out of Nazi's room and no longer in danger of a full-blown panic attack, Sam was beginning to regret not letting Anna accompany him back here.

Sleep came upon him slowly, lasted a short time, then ended abruptly.

"Sam!"

"Wurgh?" Sam opened his eyes to find Randy's face mere inches from his own. He tried to pull back, but the pillow behind him stopped him from going anywhere. Randy's beard parted to reveal an expectant grin when he realized Sam was awake.

"Ready for some hardcore action, old chum?" Randy whispered.

Sam blinked. "What?" He gripped the edge of his duvet and pulled it up to his chin. "What do you mean? What is this?"

"You can't tell anyone," Randy warned, his face darkening. "This has got to be between me and you. And Allergy Girl, if she wants to get in on it."

His breath was hot on Sam's face. When Randy spoke, Sam could feel his beard brush lightly across his chin. Anna's room was just a little along the corridor. Maybe, if he shouted loudly enough...

"Look, Randy," he croaked. "I'm flattered. Seriously. I'm just... It's just... I'm not..."

"I've found him," Randy said.

Sam's words caught in his throat. He frowned. "Found who?"

"The Beef Chief. I've had butterflies scouring the city for him, and they just hit the jackpot. He's hiding in an old abandoned meat shop across town."

"What's a meat shop?" Sam whispered. "You mean a deli? Or a butcher's store?"

"I mean a meat shop," Randy insisted. "A shop that sells meat."

"So... like a deli or a butcher's store," said Sam. He tried to sit up, but Randy was still too close. "Could you...?"

"Huh? Oh. OK."

Randy jumped up and retreated into the shadows at the corner of the room. Despite his best efforts, he was still clearly visible. Sam could see he was wearing his bright red supersuit with the cape attached.

"What time is it?" Sam asked, swinging his legs out of bed.

"It's Supervillain Ass-Kicking Time!" Randy announced.

Sam sighed. "OK. Cool. And what's that in regular time?"

"Three-twenty-seven AM."

"Jesus." Sam yawned and rubbed his face, trying to wipe away his exhaustion. "Did you tell Chuck?"

"No! Didn't you hear what I said?" Randy growled. "We can't tell Chuck. He won't let us go. He wants to nanny us. Keep us from getting ourselves killed!"

"Isn't that a good thing?" Sam asked. "It sounds like a good thing."

"Not if it means innocent people dying in our place," Randy spat. "You know what makes us heroes, Sam?"

"Superpowers?" Sam guessed.

"No..."

"The suits? A cool hero name?"

"Obviously, all that stuff's important," Randy reluctantly

conceded. "But what *really* makes us heroes is that we always do the right thing, no matter the cost."

Sam didn't think he did always do the right thing, no matter the cost. He wasn't even sure he *mostly* did the right thing, no matter the cost. At best, he *occasionally* did the right thing, and usually bemoaned the cost afterward to anyone who'd listen.

"I don't know, Randy. That Beef Chief guy looks pretty serious. He killed those people. Chuck's right, he's out of our league. For now, I mean. Maybe in a couple of weeks…"

"And what if he kills more people before then?" Randy snarled. "More innocent men and women. More *kids*. What then, Sam?"

Sam groaned. "We could tell the police. Maybe Chuck could help them out. Hell—and I don't believe I'm saying this —maybe Kapitän Nazi could do something. He's on some big, I don't know, redemption kick. Maybe he can do it."

"Listen to yourself, Sam," Randy spat. There was a *thwack* as he slapped Sam hard across the face.

"Jesus! That hurt! What the hell, man?" Sam protested.

"The guy's a murderer!" seethed Randy.

"Wait… which one are we talking about?" Sam asked.

Randy slapped him again.

"Ow! Quit doing that!"

"Both of them," Randy said. "You don't fight darkness with darkness, Sam. You fight it with light."

He grabbed Sam by the shoulders and kneaded them, as if giving him a massage. "And we *are* the light that fights the darkness, Sam. Me. You. Allergy Girl. In that order. With a big gap between us all. It's like me, then big gap you, then big gap… You get what I'm saying."

Randy ran his tongue across his lips, his eyes narrowing. "I forgot my point."

"We're the light that fights the darkness," Sam said.

Randy's eyes widened in surprise. "That's beautiful," he gasped, like he was hearing it for the first time. "And you're goddamn right we are. So, you in?"

Sam ran his hands through his hair. The idea of going to face a murderous supervillain in the middle of the night was not one that appealed. It probably had once, but that was a long time ago when he'd been young, excitable, and eager to please.

Now, just the idea of leaving his warm bed to go outside in the cold and dark actively repelled him. Never mind the supervillain, what if it was raining? Were the supersuits water-proof? Did they have a hood rolled up in the collar? He doubted it.

Clambering about on rooftops in the daytime was one thing, but it was something else entirely to do it in the middle of the night.

Still, Randy had a point. What if the Beef Chief killed someone else tomorrow? Or the next day? Or the day after that? Every minute he was still out there was another minute that the people of Cityopolis weren't safe.

And what if next time it was someone Sam knew? One of the people from work? Or Laura?

Or Corey?

Sam stood up. "I cannot believe I'm doing this," he muttered. "But fine. Let's go and see if Anna's awake."

"I fucking hate you guys."

Anna plodded along the corridor behind Sam, rubbing her bleary eyes on the forest green sleeves of her costume. Her hair was like an animal's nest that had been messed up by another much larger animal in order to send the first animal a message.

"I mean... it's the middle of the night. You do know that, yes?"

At the front of the line, Randy stopped and raised a fist.

"Stop!" he growled.

"You don't have to say it, Randy. That's the whole point of using hand gestures," Sam whispered.

Randy pointed to his eyes with two fingers, then to the corner ahead of them. "I'm going to take a look over there."

"Again, you don't..." Sam sighed. "Fine. Go take a look."

Anna rubbed her eyes more vigorously, made a sound like a sexually frustrated elk, then finished with a sigh. "God, my head hurts. What time is it?"

"Justice time," Randy growled back as he tiptoed to the corner.

"Which is...?"

"About four AM," Sam told her.

"Urgh! I fucking hate you guys."

Sam nodded. "Yeah. I kind of hate us, too, so I understand where you're coming from."

They watched Randy slide along the corridor wall with his back to it, edging closer to the corner.

"This is suicide," Sam muttered. "I mean... what are we even doing? We're not ready to fight the Beef Chief. Are we?"

"Christ, no," said Anna. "But we won't have to."

Sam turned to her. "What makes you say that? You think he'll give himself up?"

"No. We won't find him."

"But Randy said..."

Sam's voice trailed off.

"Exactly," said Anna. "A butterfly sent him a message *into his mind* that told him where to find the guy. What do you think the chances are of us getting to where we're going and finding out it isn't a secret lair at all, just a regular meat shop?"

"Butcher's store," said Sam. "Or deli. No one calls it a *meat shop*."

He had to admit, she had a point, though. About the Beef Chief, that is, not the 'meat shop' thing. Sam wasn't sure whether to be relieved about this or not. On the one hand, he was going outside in the middle of the night for nothing. On the other hand, it would probably mean not being beaten and killed by a supervillain. On balance then, it was probably a win.

Tired of standing around, Anna plodded over to where Randy was peeking around the corner. "See anything?" she asked.

Randy shook his head. "No," he said, then: "Wait. I mean yes. That infernal robot's right down there!"

"You mean Mari?" asked Sam. He leaned out a little to look.

Sure enough, Mari stood at the end of the adjoining corridor, beside a door that led to the way out. Her screen was mostly dark, aside from two horizontal lines that Sam guessed represented closed eyes.

"I think... I think she's sleeping," he whispered. "But we should probably go back."

"Besides, there are cameras everywhere," said Anna. "It's not like they're not going to know we snuck out."

Randy grinned proudly. "I had one of my butterflies disable the camera feeds."

Anna and Sam both regarded him blankly.

"Oh yeah?" asked Anna. She gestured to a camera fixed to the ceiling above Mari's head. "Then how come the light's still on?"

Randy's grin became an angry scowl. "Duncan, you idiot!" he whisper-snarled. "You had one job."

"Yeah, Duncan. You *dick*!" said Anna, shaking her fist. She lowered it quickly, then shrugged. "Well, I reckon that's that. Back to bed we go."

"Wait, look!" hissed Randy. The light on the camera blinked out. He shook his head admiringly. "Duncan, you're the goddam best. I knew you wouldn't let us down."

"Bullshit a butterfly just did that," said Anna.

"You keep telling yourself that, Nips," Randy hissed.

Anna looked down self-consciously, then crossed her arms over her chest. "I swear, if you call me that one more time, I'm going to make you sneeze yourself inside-out."

"Noted," said Randy. "Now, stay close and stay quiet."

He snuck out into the adjoining corridor, then stood his ground for a moment, waiting to see if Mari would open her digital eyes.

Nothing.

He made a beckoning motion with his right hand. "This means follow," he said.

"We know," Sam whispered back. "Everyone knows that one."

They crept along the corridor, Randy doing an exaggerated tiptoe in front, Sam and Anna sort of shuffling along behind him. Neither of them were quite all the way awake yet, and Sam was secretly hopeful that this all might yet turn out to be a dream.

He pinched himself.

It hurt.

Damn.

"Almost there," Randy whispered.

Sam successfully fought the urge to point out that they could see for themselves how close they were, and there was no 'almost' about it. They were still over half the corridor away from the door, and while Mari hadn't yet woken up and made any move to stop them, he was confident it was only a matter of time.

"What if she, like, vaporizes us?" Anna wondered. "Can she do that?"

"I don't think so," Sam whispered.

"But we don't know," Anna pointed out. "Chuck couldn't remember what her name stood for. For all we know it could be 'Murderous Asshole Robot... Iguana.'"

Sam raised a questioning eyebrow.

"I couldn't think of anything else beginning with I," she whispered. "Except 'igloo,' and that didn't feel any more appropriate."

"I don't think she's going to kill us," Sam said. "At most, she'll tell Chuck on us. Then he'll kill us."

Randy jammed a finger to his lips and glowered at them. "This means 'be quiet,'" he said.

"We know!" Sam whispered.

"Then why are you still talking!" Randy hissed back.

"Why are *you* still talking?"

"Because I'm the front guy. The front guy can talk," Randy insisted.

"But you're closer," Sam pointed out. "It's *worse* if you talk."

"Maybe we should all just be quiet for a while," Anna suggested. "Please. For the love of God."

Randy pressed his finger harder to his lips and glowered at them both through his goggles. Sam opened his mouth to protest, but called it off at the last second.

Once he was sure nobody else was going to say anything, Randy crept on.

They were getting closer to Mari now, and could hear a faint electronic whine coming from somewhere within her metal frame. It grew and faded in volume, without ever becoming more than background noise. It was the sound, Sam realized, of a robot snoring.

Randy tiptoed on, holding his breath as he passed the

dormant Mari. Anna went next, sidling past the robot and stopping at the door behind Randy. Sam hung back, waiting for them to get the door open before making his move.

"It's locked," Randy whispered.

"Of course it's locked," Anna muttered. "You didn't anticipate this?"

Randy shook his head. "No. I anticipated every other possible detail, but not this."

"This should've been the *first* thing you anticipated," Anna hissed.

"Shh!" Sam urged, shooting a worried glance at Mari. Her eyes were still two horizontal lines on an otherwise featureless face, but they had brightened a little, like light was about to burst through them at any moment.

"We're turning around," whispered Anna. "We can't get through."

"No, wait!" Randy spat.

Mari's electronic whining stopped. Everyone froze.

Sam held his breath. His heart thudded against the inside of the suit so loudly he was sure everyone else must be able to hear it.

His eyes met Anna's. She looked more annoyed than frightened, but this hadn't stopped her becoming a statue while they waited to see what Mari was going to do.

The whine returned. Mari's eyes darkened, becoming almost black, and Sam almost sobbed with relief. He wasn't sure why, exactly—he didn't genuinely think either Mari or Chuck would kill them—but defying authority went against his every instinct, and the thought of getting caught was making the back of his supersuit damp with sweat.

Breathable my ass, he thought.

He jabbed a thumb behind him, indicating they should make a retreat, but Randy shook his head and placed his fingers against his temples. "I'll summon a butterfly to help us," he whispered.

"What's it going to do? Bring a key?" Anna asked.

"Shh."

Randy closed his eyes and focused, the pointer and middle fingers of both hands pressed to the sides of his head. His lips moved almost silently, his brow furrowing with the effort of concentration.

"This is stupid," Anna muttered. "Let's go."

"Almost... got it," Randy groaned.

Sam side-eyed Mari. Her eyes were still dark, but he could no longer hear her digital snoring. "Randy..." he mouthed, too quietly for anyone to hear.

He was about to try again when there was a soft *clunk* from the door. It opened, just a crack, and Randy clenched a fist in triumph. "Did it! Ha! I told you!" he quietly proclaimed. "Butterflies. Is there nothing they can't do?"

The door opened further, revealing a dark-clad figure standing just beyond. Sam recognized the Mid-Western accent at once.

"There you are," whispered Kapitän Nazi. "I wondered when you'd come."

He opened the door all the way, beckoning for them to come through. "This way," he urged. "And hurry. The cameras won't stay deactivated for long."

CHAPTER SEVENTEEN

KAPITÄN NAZI LED them through the network of corridors until they finally arrived at an elevator they'd never used before.

"They don't monitor this one," he said. "They won't know you're gone. Not right away, at least."

"So... wait. You're helping us go out there?" said Anna. "Shouldn't you be trying to talk us out of it?"

From the way she said it, it was clear she'd have been quite happy to have been talked out of it, and she could barely hide her disappointment when Nazi shook his head.

"Something's not right," said the Kapitän. "I worked with the Beef Chief a couple of times. The way he killed those people, it suggests he's attained a whole new level of power."

"All the more reason for us *not* to go!" Sam pointed out.

"You mean all the more reason for us *to* go," Randy countered. "If he's stronger then there's no saying who he might kill next."

"Yes, us, probably," Anna said. She turned back to Nazi. "Seriously, dude, you should be talking us out of this."

"Wait," said Sam. "How did you even know where we were going? Have you been spying on us?"

He nudged Anna. "He's been spying on us!"

"I know because I'm the one who told Randy where to find him," said Kapitän Nazi, looking a little confused.

"I thought you said a butterfly told you?" said Sam accusingly.

"A butterfly also told me," Randy insisted. "Two things told me—this ex-Nazi and a butterfly. You know what they say, don't you?"

"Is it something about you needing psychiatric help?" Anna asked.

"Always check your sources," Randy replied. "Kapitän Nazi told me, but I had a butterfly double-check."

"Please, call me John," Kapitän Nazi urged. He pressed the call button on the elevator and gazed anxiously along the corridor as the car began to rumble downward. "Chuck won't be happy, but I'll keep him off your trail for as long as I can."

"Wait, you're not coming?" asked Anna. "Why aren't you coming?"

Kapitän Nazi shook his head. "I can't. This isn't my fight. Besides, Chuck has a tracking implant in my head. He's still worried I'll go rogue."

Sam nodded vaguely, impressed by this. He'd thought Chuck was a fool for trusting Nazi, so it was reassuring to hear he didn't fully.

"If I leave the complex without permission, the best case scenario is it'll trigger the alarm and put the place in lockdown before we can get out," Nazi explained.

"And what's the worst case scenario?" Anna asked.

"My head will explode," the Kapitän said. "And no, before you ask, that isn't a joke."

The elevator door opened. Nazi stepped aside and

gestured for them to pile in. "Go. Go," he told them. "Find out what's going on and put a stop to it."

"We will," Randy growled. "In the name of *justice!*"

Anna rolled her eyes and crossed her arms.

"Good luck," Nazi told them. He jammed his arm into the door just as it started to close, stopping it. "Oh, and when you catch up with the Beef Chief, you might want to activate Battle Mode."

Sam frowned. "Battle Mode?" he said.

The suit shifted as if coming alive. Flexible metal plating unfolded itself from within the fabric, locking in place along the length of all four limbs. The molded muscles of the outfit's chest vanished beneath a layer of glossy blue metal, and Sam gave a little yelp of surprise as an armored jockstrap fastened into position across his groin.

The figure-eight eye mask he wore wrapped around his head, becoming a darkened visor, just as several interlocking plates bloomed up from the throat, forming a layer of protection across most of his face, leaving only enough room for his mouth to move.

A shudder ran the length of Sam's spine as the back of the suit's neck grew up over his head, flattening down his hair as it stretched up and over his crown, then down his forehead, before eventually meeting the top of the eye mask-turned-visor.

"Holy shit!" he blurted.

"Is that Battle Mode?" Randy wondered.

Anna tutted. "I'd say that's a pretty safe bet, Randy."

"It uses a lot of power," said Nazi. "You've got about an hour's worth of charge before the enhancements shut down."

"What then?" asked Anna. She tugged on her own sleeve. "It'll go back to this?"

Kapitän Nazi shook his head. "*All* enhancements will shut

down. It won't augment your strength or speed, and you'll no longer be bulletproof. I'd deactivate it until you need it."

Sam flapped his hands in panic. "Quit Battle Mode," he said, hoping that would do the trick. To his relief, the metal plating folded away and was absorbed back into the fabric of the suit.

In moments, he was dressed identically to the others, albeit in a different color.

"How long did you say we can use it for?" he asked.

"Depends on how much you're doing with it," Nazi said. "You'll get a power display in the visor that'll keep you updated. Heavy use? Maybe thirty minutes."

"*Thirty minutes*?!" Sam yelped.

"Less heavy, over an hour," Nazi continued. "Either way, only use it when you have to, or you could be in trouble."

"Pretty sure we're already in trouble," said Anna, as Nazi withdrew his arm. "But thanks for the advice."

"You can do this," the Kapitän said. "Work together. Watch each other's backs. Use your powers."

He eyed Sam meaningfully at that, as the door slid closed. Sam groaned. "This was a bad idea."

"This is it!" Randy growled, turning his gaze to the ceiling. "Evildoers, here we come!"

They waited, not moving.

Kapitän Nazi's voice came muffled through the door.

"You have to press the button."

Randy looked down. "Oh. Yeah," he grunted, finding the elevator controls. He jabbed the top button. "Going up," he announced. "For *justice*!"

"Oh, God," Anna sighed, as the elevator began to rise. "Is it wrong that I kind of hope this Beef Chief guy kills us?"

Sam and Anna stood beside Randy, both hugging themselves self-consciously and doing their best to ignore the occasional gleeful *honks* of the late-night drivers who spotted the three of them as they drove past the bus stop.

Randy studied the bus stop's faded timetable, hands on his hips, feet wide apart in one of his many practiced super-hero poses. "Uh-huh," he said, nodding. He clicked his tongue against the back of his teeth a few times. "Mm-hm."

Sam peered both ways along the street, convinced one of the city's gangs would come shambling around the corner at any minute, then proceed to kick the shit out of them.

"Aha!" said Randy.

"You found it?" he asked, his voice coming as an urgent whisper.

Randy shook his head and stepped back. "No. I can't actually read," he said in his usual throaty growl.

Sam and Anna both stared at him. For a multitude of reasons.

"OK, OK, first up," said Anna. "Why did you insist on being the one to check the timetable?"

"Well, I'm the leader, so..."

"You're not the leader," said Sam.

"I'm kind of the leader."

"You're not in any way the leader," Anna insisted. "Secondly... what do you mean you can't read? Why can't you read?"

"I was raised in the mountains by butterflies," Randy reminded her. "They're not known for their literature."

Sam and Anna exchanged glances. "Well, no, but you haven't *always* lived with butterflies," Sam pointed out. "Didn't Su Man Chu teach you?"

Randy straightened at the mention of his former mentor's name, almost snapping to attention. "She trained me relentlessly. Honed my skills and sharpened my mind, turning me into a living weapon," he said. "Su Man Chu taught me everything she knew."

"Except how to read," said Anna.

"Except that, yes. That, she left out."

Stepping past Randy, Anna consulted the timetable. "OK, so we want to get to Stanswick and Third, right? That's where the meat shop is?"

"Butcher's store. And yes," Sam confirmed. Another horn blasted. A driver jeered through his car window. Sam tried not to look.

Anna traced the rows of numbers with a finger. "OK. OK. Jesus. So, we'll have to take the twenty-seven for, like, six stops, then get the... wait. What time is it?"

"It's—" Randy began.

"Randy, if you say it's 'Justice Time' again, I'll give you a rash so bad your face falls off," Anna warned.

Randy cleared his throat. "Four-thirty-three," he said.

"Ugh." Anna consulted the board again. "No, we have to cross the street and take the number eleven to West and Ward, then walk a couple of blocks and catch the..."

A bus rumbled to a stop beside them, then hissed as the doors opened. "What number is this one?" Anna asked.

Sam walked to the front. "Eight. It says 'Airport via Romero Drive,' if that means anything to you."

"It means it goes to the airport," Randy explained. "But first it goes via—"

"Right. I got it, Randy, thanks," said Sam.

Anna leaned in the bus's open door. A squat black woman with graying hair regarded her impassively from the driver's seat.

"Uh, hi..." Anna consulted the woman's name badge. "... Shanice. Ignore the costumes, we're with the circus."

Shanice's gaze crept up and down, taking notice of the

outfits for the first time. "Uh-huh," she said in a distinctly non-committal sort of way.

"Do you go anywhere near Stanswick or Third Avenue?" Anna asked.

Shanice sighed. It wasn't an angry or annoyed sort of sigh, more a sort of wheeze of resignation and defeat. "I go to the airport. Via Romero."

"No, I know, but..." Anna shrugged. "Ah, fuck it. We'll figure it out on the way."

Hopping aboard, she fished in her utility belt until she found her credit card. "Three Day City Roamers, please."

"How many?"

"Uh, three," said Anna.

"Three Three-Day City Roamers," said Shanice, keying numbers into her pad.

"No. Three Day City Roamers," Anna corrected.

Shanice raised her eyes and fixed her with a look that was somehow both utterly emotionless and brimming with contempt.

"Say what?"

"I want a Day City Roamer ticket for all three of us," Anna said.

"Oh. So, what you mean is you want three One-Day City Roamers? Why didn't you say?"

"I thought I did."

"Well, you thought wrong, honey," said Shanice. She blinked so slowly Anna thought her eyes might not be going to open again. She started speaking before they did. "Peak or off-peak?"

Anna gestured out into the darkness. "Well, it's the middle of the night, so... off-peak?"

"So, you ain't going to use them in the daytime?" asked Shanice.

"Shit. That's a point."

Anna turned back to Sam and Randy, who both stood on the sidewalk just beyond the open doors. "When will we be coming back?"

"I don't know," Sam admitted.

"Say we take an hour to get there, then... what? Another hour to beat him up, or whatever? That's... what?"

"An hour?" Shanice snorted. "To get to Third? From *here?* Girl, you're out of your mind. Trust me, you're gonna need peak. If you're lucky, you'll get there by ten-thirty."

"That's, like, six hours!" Anna groaned.

"If you're lucky."

Anna chewed on her lip for a moment as she processed this. "Ah, fuck it," she said. She hopped off the bus, placed two fingers in her mouth, and whistled. "Taxi!"

With a final glare from Shanice that suggested she didn't appreciate her time being wasted, the bus's doors hissed closed and it trundled off.

"When does the El start running?" Anna asked.

"The train?" Sam glanced up at the tracks of the elevated railway that ran through the city. "Not sure. Six?"

"Fuck!" Anna spat. She sighed. "Fine. We'll get a taxi. But I'm billing Chuck for expenses."

Sam and Randy stood at the curb, watching as Anna tried to flag down a cab.

"They'll probably cut this scene," Randy said.

Sam frowned. "Huh?"

"When they make the movie of our lives. They'll probably cut this part."

"They're not going to make a movie of our lives," Sam said.

"Hey! Taxi! Over here!" Anna called, waving and clicking her fingers. She muttered darkly as the cab swept past.

"I'm just saying, if they do, they'll cut this scene. It'll go straight from us leaving the base to us outside the Beef Chief's lair," Randy continued. "Mark my words."

"You think?" asked Sam, not really listening.

"Of course. Why would anyone want to see this part? It's pointless. From a story perspective, I mean."

Sam considered his response. "Maybe if it's a comedy..."

"Why would it be a comedy?" Randy snorted. "It'll be a big-budget action blockbuster."

"No, I mean, sure. I'm just saying, if it had *comedy elements* they might show this bit."

"Why? It's not funny," Randy said. "It's just us standing at a bus stop."

Sam clicked his tongue against the roof of his mouth and looked around them. "No, you're right," he conceded. "They'll cut this scene."

"Are we invisible here?" Anna bellowed. She lowered her arm and tutted. "Next time, we're demanding a fucking Batmobile."

CHAPTER EIGHTEEN

ONE TAXI RIDE spent in awkward, uncomfortable silence later, Sam and the others stood across the street from a boarded-up butcher's store. Randy had insisted they all tuck themselves into a shadowy doorway, and Sam was now experiencing the mixed emotions that came with having Anna pressed up against his front, while Randy breathed heavily in his ear.

"So, do we think he's in there?" Anna asked.

Even in the cab, and with light traffic, it had taken the better part of forty minutes to get all the way uptown. The sky was still dark, but it was a blue-gray sort of dark, rather than the oppressive blackness it had been when they'd first set out on the mission.

"I don't know," Sam said.

The place looked like it had been deserted for years. The wooden boards had been marked with graffiti, and weeds grew from cracks in the sidewalk outside. The paint on the sign above the door was faded and cracked. Despite this, and to Sam's great annoyance, it was still possible to make out the words: 'Meat Shop.'

"She didn't ask if he was in there," said Randy, his voice a guttural growl in Sam's ear. "She asked if we *think* he's in there."

He brought his mouth in even closer. Sam shuddered as Randy's bristly beard brushed the back of his neck. "Do you, Kid Random?"

"Call me Sam," Sam replied, shuffling aside to try to make more space between them. Anna deliberately pushed back against him. Even though he could only see the back of her head, he could tell she was grinning.

"We don't use real names when on a mission, Kid Random," Randy insisted. "That's Superhero 101."

"Well, don't call me Kid Random. I'm not a kid anymore," Sam pointed out.

"What should we call you?"

"Sam."

"King Random?" Randy said. "Changing 'kid' to 'king' worked for Butterfly King."

"It really didn't," said Anna. "Anyway, it's OK for me to be Allergy *Girl* but you can't be Kid Random?"

"What? No, I mean... It's not..."

Anna pushed back into him and wriggled her hips a little, really winding Sam up and turning the rest of his sentence into an incomprehensible mush of mutterings.

That done, she stepped out of the doorway and onto the street. "I'm going to go knock."

"What? Wait! No, you can't!" Sam protested, waddling after her to try to disguise the bulge in his suit. "We don't know if he's in there!"

Anna stopped and looked back at him. "That's kind of the whole point of knocking. To find out if he's in there."

Randy shook his head. "Kid Random's right," he said. "It's too dangerous. We need to be subtle. We need to get eyes on the inside."

"Then we're in luck!" said Anna. She nodded up to a nearby street light, and the little fluttering insect silhouetted against its glow. "There's a butterfly. You can send that in to scope the place out for us."

Randy regarded the bug, then shook his head. "That's not a butterfly. It's a moth. I can't commune with moths."

"Oh," said Anna. "Well, is there a Moth King? Can we get his number?"

"Aren't they the same thing?" Sam asked.

Randy snorted. "No. Of course they're not the same thing. Are cows and pigs the same thing?" he demanded. "Snakes and fish? Chickens and hens?"

Sam opened his mouth.

"OK, maybe that last one. But moths and butterflies aren't the same. They're not even similar."

Sam opened his mouth again.

"OK, they're a little similar. But they're not the same. Butterfly King can no more control moths than Duckman can control geese."

Sam and Anna both opened their mouths.

"No, there isn't actually a Duckman. I was just giving an example of..." Randy sighed. "Fine. Know what? Fine. I'll give it a try."

The others waited while he placed his fingers to his temples and glowered up at the moth, his face twisting with the effort of concentration.

For a long time, nothing happened.

For a longer time after that, nothing still happened.

The moth fluttered around the light, occasionally bumping into it, then bouncing off again to resume its haphazard flight.

"OK, so we've established that it doesn't work on moths, then," said Sam.

"Wait..." Randy grimaced. "Almost... got it..."

The moth bumped into the light again, then circled around the lamp's glass casing, lining itself up for another charge.

This time, however, instead of flying toward the glow, it banked off and began a leisurely fluttering in the direction of the meat shop.

"Yes... *Yes*!" Randy whispered.

Anna and Sam both watched in a vague, low-level sort of amazement as the moth jiggled gently through the air toward the—

A bus plowed past in a cloud of dust and fumes, splattering the insect against the windshield.

Randy stared in horror as the bus trundled off, then let his arms fall limply to his sides. He turned to Sam and hissed at him through gritted teeth. "You see what you made me do? That beautiful creature's blood is on your hands, Kid Random! *You* killed that butterfly!"

"Moth," Sam corrected.

Randy blinked. "Huh. Oh. Yeah." He shrugged. "Fuck it, then."

"Was that...? Was that Shanice?" Anna cried, watching the bus pull away along the street. "That lying bitch!"

After flipping the bus the bird, Anna began marching across the street. Sam scurried after her, with Randy skulking along behind, his cape raised to cover his face.

"I really don't think we should just go right up and knock," Sam said. "You saw what he did to those people on the TV. We need to get the jump on this guy."

Anna nodded. "You have a point," she admitted. "We'll sneak round the back and see if there's another door. And you know what else we should do?"

"Call the police?" Sam guessed.

"Workshop some witty quips," Anna said.

Sam frowned. "Uh, I'm not sure that's really vital."

"Sure it is," Anna insisted. They reached the sidewalk a little way along from the meat shop, then headed for the entrance to an alleyway a couple of stores along. "If we're doing this, we should do it properly. So, let's think. Beef Chief. What does that say to you?"

"Twisted criminal madman who I'm taking down!" Randy seethed.

"OK, OK. Right. But maybe more light-hearted?" Anna said. "Like... 'Where's the Beef, Chief?' Only not as outdated a reference."

The alleyway was dark and narrow, but the approaching dawn was enough to help them pick their way along it toward a network of fenced-off yards at the back.

"How about, 'We're going to make mincemeat out of you'?" Sam suggested. "Or is that too on the nose?"

"Ooh, no, I like it," said Anna. "Threatening *and* witty. Ish."

"I got one! I got one!" said Randy. "Sell the sizzle, not the steak!"

Anna and Sam both stopped to look at him. "How is that a quip?" Anna asked.

"You know. Steak. Beef."

He made a hiss through his teeth that suggested a sizzling sound.

Sam shrugged. "I mean, it's a step in the right direction, I guess."

Darting ahead, Randy stopped at the end of the alleyway and held up a hand. "Stop," he urged. "Wait."

Sam lowered his voice to a whisper. "Again, Randy, you don't have to keep explaining. These are basic universal gestures. We understand them."

"Right. Good. Good to know," Randy said. He extended his pinkie finger and thumb, flicked his hand sharply left and right a couple of times, then pointed upward.

That done, he slipped out of the alleyway and vanished around the corner.

"OK, that one I do *not* know," Sam admitted. He looked hopefully to Anna.

"Don't look at me," she said.

They continued to the mouth of the alley and peeked around the corner at the yards and fences. Randy was nowhere to be seen.

"Where did he go?" Anna asked.

"Randy!" Sam hissed. "*Randy?*"

They waited.

"No, he's gone," said Anna. She gave a dismissive wave of her hand. "He'll turn up. Come on."

They spent a couple of minutes clambering over fences and through yards until they found the rear of the meat shop. They'd neglected to count how many doors it was along from the alley, but were able to identify the place thanks to the large rusted dumpster with 'Warning: Contains Animal Parts' painted on the side in faded red lettering.

There were no windows at the back, just crumbling brick-work, a heavy door, and the lingering aroma of death. Sam's pulse quickened as Anna crept toward the door.

"Should we power up the suits?" he whispered. He didn't want to use the words 'Battle Mode' in case that kicked it into life.

"Not yet," Anna replied. "We don't know if he's even in here yet or—"

"Leave me alone!"

The voice rolled out from just the other side of the door, freezing them both in their tracks.

"Is that him?" Anna whispered.

"How should I know?" Sam mouthed back.

Anna cleared her throat. "Hello? We're looking for the Beef Chief."

"I didn't do it! They said I did, but I didn't!" the voice said. "So, go away, leave me alone!"

Anna turned to Sam. "Are we taking that as a 'yes'?" she wondered.

Looking around, she spotted a broken piece of brick in the tangle of weeds. She picked it up and held it behind her back, then winked at Sam. "We just want to talk to you, that's all."

"I don't want to talk! I don't want to talk to anyone! Leave me alone!"

His voice faded a little, like he was moving away from the door. "I'm warning you. You don't want to mess with me!"

Anna widened her eyes at Sam, urging him to contribute.

"Uh, come on out," he said. "Or we'll make mincemeat out of you."

"Seriously? You're doing the quip *now*?" Anna whispered. "We're trying to get him to open the door. You've quipped too soon. That was premature quippage."

"Well I didn't know!" Sam whispered back. "I thought... Wait. What's that?"

They listened. There was a sound from beyond the door. It was a thudding sort of sound. A rubbing, too, like something large moving through a narrow gap.

"What *is* that?" Anna wondered.

She was about to put her ear closer when the door exploded, sending her stumbling back into the tangled jungle of the yards' weeds.

A large black bull was wedged in the doorframe, snorting, and stomping as it struggled to free itself. Judging by the size of it, it had to be some sort of mutant, Sam reckoned. Its head was the size, if not quite the shape, of an oil barrel. It thrashed around, swinging its long curved horns around like sword-blades.

"Jesus Christ!" Sam spluttered.

The bull's baseball-sized eyes bulged in their sockets, showing off its bloodshot whites as it thrust its shoulders forward, splintering the doorframe.

"I warned you!" called a voice from further inside the building. "I told you to leave me alone! Get them, Russel!"

"What do we do?" Sam yelped.

Anna looked at her rock, then at the bull's head.

"God knows," she admitted, letting the stone drop. "Run away?"

"Pah!"

Randy's voice came from behind the animal parts dumpster. He stepped out, swishing his cape dramatically. "Butterfly King isn't running away from some dumb horse."

There was a moment of silence, broken only by the snorting and grunting of the beast in the doorway.

"It's a bull," Sam pointed out. "It's not... That's not a horse."

"It's not?" asked Randy. He leaned left and right, studying it from different angles. "You sure?"

"Pretty sure."

"Wait! I got it!" said Anna. She gestured from the bull to Randy's bright red supersuit. "Ta-daa!"

Randy looked down. "What? What's 'ta-daa'? What do you mean?"

"I mean, this big bastard..." she replied, pointing to the bull. "It's totally going to kill us all, unless you step in and save the day."

Randy straightened, his chest puffing out. "I'll save the day, alright. I'll save the day until its head spins." He raised his fists and lunged. "OK, you vile, filthy beast, let's do this!"

Anna put a hand on his chest, stopping him before he could take a swing. "No. That's not going to work. You need to lead it away."

Randy kept his fists raised, appearing unconvinced. "Away where?"

"Just... I don't know. Anywhere," said Anna. "Somewhere that's not here."

"That sounds like I'm fleeing," Randy pointed out. "Like a filthy coward."

"It isn't," Sam insisted. "You're protecting us. It's what the Justice Platoon would do."

Randy lowered his fists and somehow found the lung capacity to swell his chest even further. "You're goddamn right they would," he said.

There was a definitive *crash* as the doorframe gave way and the bull stumbled out into the yard, eyes bulging, steam snorting from its nostrils.

Anna and Sam both neatly sidestepped out of its line of sight, leaving only Randy standing before it in his red suit and cape.

"You want me, you horsey bastard?" he growled, pulling his goggles down over his eyes. "Come get me!"

Randy turned and bounded clumsily over the fence. The bull sprang after him, horns lowered, smashing through the wood with one thunderous lunge.

Sam and Anna waited for the snorting and crashing to fade, before emerging from cover. "Think he'll be OK?" Sam asked.

Anna puffed out her cheeks. "I don't necessarily think he *won't* be OK," she offered, which Sam agreed was probably the best they could hope for.

They turned to the wrecked doorway, and the dark hallway beyond. "Should we go in?" Anna asked.

"That seems reckless," Sam said. He shuffled from foot to foot, wringing his hands. "Maybe he'll come out."

They waited.

"I don't think he's coming out," Anna said. "Hold up, I've got an idea."

She cupped a hand around her mouth. "Hey! Beef Chief!" she hollered. "Come out."

"No," boomed the voice from within.

Anna tutted. "Well, so much for that."

"That was your plan? Shout 'come out,' at him?" Sam asked.

"Well, I didn't see you coming up with anything better," Anna pointed out. She set off for the door. "Fine. We'll have to go in."

"We can't just go in!" Sam yelped.

"Well, he isn't coming out, so what do you suggest?" she asked. She was looking back at Sam as she reached the door, and so didn't see the shape appearing in the doorway, or the makeshift weapon swinging toward her.

"Look out!" Sam cried, but the warning came too late. The impact was solid, yet oddly moist sounding. It sent Anna hurtling backward through the air, arms and legs flailing.

"Fu—" she managed to eject before she smashed into one of the few remaining sturdy parts of the bull-trampled fence. She slid to the ground, wheezing. Sam stared at her in shock, his mouth hanging open. Anna nodded frantically and pointed to the door.

A giant emerged, ducking through the gap in the wall. He was larger than Sam had been expecting, although this was partly thanks to the bull skull helmet he wore, with its two long horns that stabbed angrily at the sky.

His torso was clad in thick black leather and encaged by armor fashioned from the ribs of a large animal. Over his shoulders was a red leather cape that hung down almost all the way to the floor. Clutched in one hand was a large chunk of raw meat. He held the protruding bone like a handle as he swished it menacingly at his side.

"Dude, did you just hit me with a leg of lamb?" Anna coughed, struggling to her feet.

"I didn't want to do this. I didn't want any of this," the giant insisted. His voice was low and gravelly, but with higher cracks that suggested he was on the brink of breaking down. "I just wanted to put it all behind me. They were even going to let me see her."

"Uh, what's he talking about?" Sam asked.

The villain's face twisted in rage. "And now it's ruined. It's all ruined!" His hand tightened on the lump of meat's bone handle. "I'm sorry. I am. But this isn't my fault. I don't have any choice."

"Don't know. But it doesn't sound good," said Anna.

"I am the Baron of Bovine," the giant muttered. "The Prince of Pork. The Master of Meat."

Sam danced anxiously from foot to foot. "OK, look, let's talk about this."

"I am the Beef Chief!" he roared. His eyes narrowed, becoming slits. His voice came as a menacing whisper. "Hear me moo."

He lunged at Sam, moving surprisingly quickly for a man his size. Sam barely had time to bark out a frantic, "Battle Mode!" before the chunk of meat clipped him on the chin, lifting him off his feet and sending him into a fully unintentional backflip.

His landing left a lot to be desired. His face played more of a role in it than he'd ideally have liked, and had it not been for the suit's Battle Mode functionality cushioning his head, he'd almost certainly have lost several teeth.

Sam lay there for a moment, getting his bearings. He knew which direction *down* was, but the others were currently escaping him.

A hand the size of a whole flank steak caught him by the

back of the neck and helpfully showed him which direction was up.

Sam screamed as he hurtled into the air, spinning and flipping, his arms flapping wildly in the hope the suit would suddenly develop the ability to fly.

It didn't. He drew level with the meat shop's roof before gravity took hold. As he fell, he saw the Beef Chief lining up a swing. He had *exactly* enough time to babble out two different expletives before the lamb leg connected with him, propelling him through the meat shop wall in an explosion of bricks, plaster, and dust.

He hit the wooden floor of a dimly lit room, bounced awkwardly, then slid ass-first into an interior wall, punching two round holes in the plasterboard with the suit's armored butt-cheeks and coming to a sudden, bone-rattling stop.

CHAPTER NINETEEN

SAM LAY MOTIONLESS on the floor, waiting to find out which parts of him hurt. The suit seemed to have protected him from the worst of the damage, but he'd still felt the impact. All the impacts, in fact, starting with the Beef Chief's crunching blow, and ending with the moment his ass cheeks met the wall.

"Shake it off, Sam," he whispered, trying to use the wall to pull himself up. His fingers tore through the plasterboard like it was tissue paper, forcing him to stagger upright without any support. The suit was heavier in this mode, but he could feel its strength surrounding him, making him stronger and more resilient.

"OK. OK. Let's do this," he said, bouncing from foot to foot and psyching himself up. As he did, he briefly regarded the room he'd landed in. There was a blanket in the corner with some empty noodle cups stacked up beside it, a dirty fork poking out of one.

Several bottles of water stood in the corner, half of them empty. Beside them was a framed photograph of a girl, maybe nine or ten years old. She wore a sunhat and was blowing on the white puffball head of a dandelion, sending the seeds scattering into the air.

Sam was in the process of wondering what it all meant when he heard Anna shout to him from out back.

"If you're still alive, will you please hurry up and get out —*Jesus Christ!*"

There was a thunderous crash that shook the whole building. Sam launched himself like a sprinter off the starting blocks. He felt the suit hum with power, and screamed as he was propelled forward at blinding speed with barely enough time to throw his hands in front of his face before his body punched another hole in the brickwork.

He stumbled out into the backyard to find the Beef Chief holding the now partially crumpled dumpster above his head. The villain swung it down at Anna, who dodged aside, narrowly avoiding being pancaked by its weight.

"Stay still!" the Beef Chief commanded. "Stay still so I can squash you!"

"You make it sound so tempting," said Anna. "But, no thanks."

"Raaaaargh!" The villain brought the dumpster up again and lunged toward her.

"Hey! Leave her alone," said a voice.

Sam looked around in surprise, before realizing, to his horror, that the voice had been his.

The Beef Chief spun and tossed the dumpster. It slammed into Sam like a battering ram, driving him through two fences before coming to a stop on top of him.

Its immense weight pressed down on Sam's chest. His breathing came in short. Sharp. Gulps.

Static flickered briefly across the inside of his visor, distorting the battery charge display. Pain surged through... well, everywhere, really.

With a grunt, Sam attempted to push the dumpster off

him. For a moment, it seemed to move, but then it came pressing down harder on him, forcing the last of his breath out in one agonizing gasp.

The Beef Chief loomed over him, leaning a hand on the crumpled metal container and driving it down with his weight.

"I didn't want to do this," the villain said, and something about the way he said it made Sam believe him. "You should've left me alone."

Sam wanted to say he was in full agreement, but he didn't have the air left in him to form the necessary syllables.

The weight and the pain both became immense. An exclamation point flashed up on his visor in one of the more urgent shades of red. The Beef Chief was saying something, but Sam couldn't hear anything but the rushing blood in his ears, and the frantic desperation of his own silent screams.

He saw his life flash before his eyes. It started miserably, became briefly exciting, then crumbled into a sense of lingering disappointment. There was one notable bright spot. The best thing he'd ever done. Perhaps the *only* thing he'd ever done.

Corey.

The highlights showreel spooled into darkness. Sam heard something inside the suit go *crack*. Possibly himself.

And then the pressure on him suddenly eased, and sweet, precious oxygen came freely into his lungs, snapping him back to the here and now.

The Beef Chief clawed at himself through his leather armor, dancing around frantically, his face a grimace of discomfort. Red blotches bloomed up the sides of his neck and up both cheeks. Sam watched as they met across his nose, before continuing up onto his forehead.

Pustules grew like tiny flowers. The Beef Chief tore at

them with his gloved hands, scraping their pus-filled heads off and making them bleed.

"Well, I've heard of pork scratchings, but not *beef* scratchings," said Anna. She had a hand raised in the villain's direction, and the air rippled like a heat haze between them. "Boom! Witty quip!"

With her free hand, she helped Sam heave the dumpster aside. He gasped as it rolled away, then lay still for a moment, terrified he'd discover he was crippled.

He wriggled his toes.

"Oh, thank God," he whispered.

Anna helped him up. "In case you don't know, a pork scratching is a snack they have in England. It's made of crispy fat, or skin, or some shit. I mean, as quips go, it's niche, but it counts."

"Totally counts," Sam grunted. He was bent over, his hands on his thighs as his lungs desperately made up for their recent lack of oxygen.

"You OK?"

Sam nodded. "Surprisingly. Thought I was done for there."

"It'll take more than that to..."

She stopped talking when the Beef Chief's hand clamped over her head, completely encasing it.

"You did this!" he sobbed through lips that were becoming more and more bloated. The whites of his eyes were a fiery red and blurred by tears that streamed down over his pustule-encrusted cheeks.

With a roar, he launched her upward, several times higher and faster than he'd thrown Sam. She sailed up over the top of the meat shop, then was hidden from Sam's view by the angle of the roof. He heard her scream a frantic, "Battle Mode! Battle Mode!" before a thunderous right hook sent him spinning, filling his head with a high-pitched whine, considerable pain, and a sense of impending doom.

The suit shook it off before he did, and Sam found himself twisting, his right hand swinging to deliver a return punch. The movement felt fast. Strong. Excitement churned his stomach.

OK. Let's see how you *like it!*

The Beef Chief's colossal hand caught his fist and held it. The villain regarded Sam like that weird kid in school might regard a fly whose wings he was about to tear off.

"Oh, shi—" Sam started to scream, before a sudden impact to his chest—possibly a punch, possibly a kick, it all happened too quickly for him to be able to tell—launched him backward.

Sam found himself in the meat shop again, albeit quite briefly. It flashed past him as one long blur, punctuated by the occasional *crash* as he hurtled through one of the store's thin interior walls.

"—iiiiit!" he concluded, as he erupted through one of the boarded-up windows, taking the plywood board with him.

The board hit the road first, and Sam went skimming across the asphalt like a stone across a still lake. Horns blared. Brakes squealed. Drivers cursed. Sam clung on, his top half riding the board, his legs trailing out behind him.

The scraping of his boots on the road surface eventually slowed him down. He opened his eyes to see the front wheel of a car thundering straight for his head.

Life did its flashy thing before his eyes again, but was interrupted by the high-pitched protests of the tire as it skidded to a stop with inches to spare.

"You idiot! What are you doing?" screeched the female driver as she jumped out. "You almost wrecked my car!"

"Sorry! Sorry. But you almost wrecked my head," Sam

pointed out, using the vehicle's front bumper to pull himself up.

"What are you doing?" the woman demanded. She was shrill and angry, and dressed for some high-powered office job. A well-paid one, too, judging by the car. "Don't you scratch my paintwork, you asshole!"

Sam raised his hands in surrender. "It's fine. It's fine. I'm not going to hurt your car," he wheezed.

Something heavy smashed into the car's roof, collapsing it and exploding the windows out. Sam and the woman both ducked. One of them screamed, and Sam chose to believe that it wasn't him.

"What the *shit*?" the woman demanded.

Anna lay on her back on the roof of the car, her limbs spread in a sort of deformed X-shape.

"Ow," she mumbled, then she slid off the wreckage and *thumped* onto the road.

"My car! Look at my car!" the woman shrieked. "Look what you did to my—*ATCHOO!*"

The sneeze took her by surprise. The eleven that followed in immediate rapid succession, even more so. Sam saw the air rippling between the woman and Anna, and enjoyed a short but satisfying smile.

"Uh, you should back off, ma'am," said Sam, gesturing over to the sidewalk. "I think we're about to have trouble."

"Oh, you—*ATCHOO!*—already have—*AAATCHOO!*—trouble. Tru—*CHOO!*—st me!"

The door to the meat shop became a cloud of splinters as the Beef Chief shoulder-barged through it.

"Shit. Here he comes," said Anna, dragging herself to her feet. She stared down at her suit, admiring the Battle Mode armor. Or most of it, at least. "Seriously?" she groaned. She pointed to the green metal breastplate. "Still with the nipples?"

"He looks angry," said Sam, as the Beef Chief broke into a lumbering run. He realized, to his horror, that the villain hadn't looked angry until now. Irritated, yes. Disappointed, maybe. But this was the first time his face was quite so twisted up in raw fury. "I think we're in trouble."

A horn blared. The Beef Chief was illuminated up one side by the sudden glare of headlights. His head snapped around just as a large refrigerated cargo truck plowed into him.

"Or maybe not," said Anna.

The truck continued for a few dozen feet before the driver recovered from his shock enough to slam on the brakes. The front wheels skidded. The cargo section of the truck swung around, jackknifing the vehicle, but its momentum carried it on.

There was more honking and squealing, followed immediately by the sound of several decisive and probably quite painful impacts. Cars swerved to avoid the out of control truck. A handful of early morning pedestrians dived for cover as it rumbled by, front wheels weaving, back wheels squealing sideways across the asphalt.

At last, it stopped. Sam and Anna stood at one end of a line of chaos, taking it all in. The jackknifed cargo truck marked the other end of the destruction. Between them and it were half a dozen cars, many of them no longer the shape they had been when they'd set off that morning.

Two street lights had been uprooted. Electricity crackled from their exposed wires and licked the ground around them.

A little farther along the street, a fire hydrant was gushing water into the air like a geyser. Luckily, the water and the electricity were too far apart to cause any problems.

Not that they didn't have their fair share of problems.

"We've completely destroyed this street," Sam whimpered. "We're in so much trouble."

"We didn't destroy anything," Anna said. "It was the Beef Chief."

"What about my car?" demanded the woman in the business suit.

Anna scowled at her and shoved her in the direction of the sidewalk on the far side of the street. "Lady, for your own safety, please go stand over there."

The woman snorted. "My own safety? He's been hit by a truck. He can't hurt me."

"I wasn't talking about him," Anna said, cracking her knuckles for emphasis.

A small semi-circle of early risers was cautiously forming around Sam and Anna. Three of them had their phones out, their cameras capturing events as they unfolded.

"What the hell was that?" someone demanded.

"Are you superheroes?"

"Did you kill that guy?"

"Has anyone called the cops?"

Sam looked to Anna for guidance, but she just shrugged and gestured to the small but vocal crowd. Sam drew himself up to his full height. It was easier to pretend behind the mask, and he could almost convince himself he felt confident as he addressed them.

"Have no fear, uh, good citizens," he said, deepening his voice and channeling his inner Doc Mighty. "The villain has been taken care of. You're safe now. We stopped him." He almost laughed at that. "We stopped him. We actually stopped him! Can you believe that?" he said to Anna. She nodded, then flicked her eyes back to the crowd, instructing him to get on with it.

Sam cleared his throat. "Sorry. But... what was I...? Oh, yes. The Beef Chief is no longer a threat. We have restrained him."

"He got hit by a truck," said one man.

"While racing toward us," said Anna. "So, that kind of counts."

"Are you with the Justice Platoon?" asked a woman with her phone out. Sam sucked in his stomach, suddenly aware that this was the moment that would end up on the news and doing the rounds on social media. This was his moment to make an impact.

"Uh, no," he said. "We're not with the Justice Platoon."

He adopted the best superhero pose he could muster, thrusting out his chest and spreading his feet what felt like a suitably heroic number of inches. "We were their sidekicks!"

There was some murmuring from the group, which quickly rose to become a worried rabble. As one, everyone turned and fled, leaving Sam and Anna alone in the middle of the street.

Anna cupped both hands around her mouth and shouted after the feeling crowd. "Thanks for the vote of confidence!"

She lowered her hands and tutted. "Rude."

"That was weird," said Sam. "I wonder why... Oh, shit!"

Sam spun just as a three-thousand-pound mutant bull bore down on them, horns lowered, breath rolling from its nostrils as clouds of angry steam.

He emitted a panicky squeal he hoped no one would ever mention again. Even with the suit's enhanced reactions, there was no time to get out of the monster's path. No way to possibly get clear before—

The shape in his head flicked. A jolt of power buzzed through him. The bull changed direction and rocketed straight upward for nine or ten feet, then vanished as if swallowed by some invisible hole in reality.

Anna crouched a little, getting ready to leap back as she sidled up to the spot where the bull had vanished and peered up at it. There was no sign of the bull anywhere. There wasn't even any suggestion that a bull had been anywhere in the area, beyond the cracks its hooves had made in the surface of the road, and the grimace of terror still imprinted on Sam's face.

"Where did it go?" Anna asked.

Sam studied the spot in the air, like the answer might be written there somewhere. "I don't... I have no idea," he admitted.

"But you did that, right?"

Sam nodded. Slowly. Dumbly. "Uh, yeah. Yeah, I think... Yeah."

"But you don't know where it went?"

Sam shook his head.

Anna snorted with mirth. "Wouldn't it be hilarious if it appeared in, like, a daycare in France, or somewhere?"

Sam considered this. "Not really."

"No," Anna admitted. Her amusement faded. "No, I guess not."

"It'd actually be pretty horrible," Sam said.

"Yeah. Yeah, you're right," Anna agreed. "All those little kids. Doesn't bear thinking about."

They both gazed up at the spot again. "I'm sure it won't happen," Anna said. "I mean, what are the chances? Right?"

She clicked her tongue against the roof of her mouth and winced, just a little. "Nah. I'm sure it won't."

There was a clatter of footsteps from nearby. Sam and Anna both turned, fists raised, just as a breathless, red-faced Randy clattered to a stop beside them.

"Oh, it's you. Hey," said Anna, lowering her hands.

Randy held up a finger to indicate that he needed a moment. He gulped down great lungfuls of air, rasping and wheezing, his sweat condensing on the inside of his goggles.

"I think... I think I lost it," he finally managed to say. He grimaced in pain and bent double like he might be about to throw up. Somehow, he summoned the strength to hold it in. "Wow. That was... wow. Who knew horses could run fast?"

"OK, *one*, everyone," said Anna, counting on her finger. "And two, not a horse."

Randy put his hands on his hips and looked around. Morning was creeping across the sky above the city's towers. The noise caused by the vehicle pile-up had brought several more onlookers out onto the street. Cars were starting to back-up on either side of the accident, and drivers appeared inquisitively from inside a few.

Horns blasted. Lights flashed. Patience wore thin. The wailing of distant police sirens drew closer.

"Feels like this could be our cue to leave," Sam said.

"What about the Beef Chief? We need to stop him!" Randy reminded them.

"He's pretty definitively stopped," Anna explained.

"Oh. Well... great," growled Randy. "Good job."

He gave Anna a congratulatory thump on the upper arm, then looked back at the meat shop.

"Is he still in there?"

"No, he's under the truck."

Randy looked from the store to the truck. He looked from the truck to Sam and Anna. "You dropped a truck on him?"

"More or less," said Anna. "The important thing is that..."

The sentence fizzled out as, from the corner of her eye, she saw the truck tilt. It tipped sideways, creaking and groaning in protest, before crashing down with a hollow *boom* that echoed along the street and silenced the blaring car horns.

The back doors of the vehicle's cargo trailer fell open, and several boxes tumbled out. For a while, nothing else seemed to happen, but then...

"You have got to be kidding me," Anna muttered.

A figure stood in the spot where the truck's front wheels had been, silhouetted against the vehicle's headlight beams. His cape was ragged and torn at the bottom, and one of his helmet's horns had been snapped off, but there was no mistaking who it was.

"Who's that guy?" Randy asked.

"That's him," replied Sam in a throaty, panicked whisper.

"Oh. Damn!" Randy growled. He nodded continuously for a few seconds, before turning to Sam. "Him who?"

"The Beef Chief!" Anna snapped. "The guy we came here to stop."

"I thought you said you *had* stopped him?"

"Well, now he's unstopped," said Anna.

Randy skipped forward into a run. "He's dazed. We need to strike now. Hard and fast!"

"You might want to activate Battle Mode," Sam called after him.

"I don't think so, Kid Random," Randy snapped back. "I can handle this just fine as I—"

Something small and disk-shaped exploded from inside one of the spilled boxes, whistled through the air, then struck Randy on the forehead. The *clunk* it made could be heard from where Sam and Anna were standing and, judging by the intakes of breath from the regathering crowds, even farther than that.

Randy became horizontal in the air. As his head bent back, his eyes briefly met Sam's. He wore an expression that somehow aimed to suggest, 'I totally meant this,' then he crunched to the ground and lay there, wheezing.

"Totally should've activated Battle Mode," Anna muttered.

"What the hell was that?" Sam wondered.

The cardboard box jumped again, as another of the disks came whizzing out. This one sliced toward Sam, but the suit's reactions moved his hand to intercept. He caught it as if it were a Frisbee and turned it over in his hands as he examined it.

"It's a frozen beef patty," he realized.

"Well, of *course* it is," said Anna.

Another of the patties *clanked* off her armored chest plate, right between the nipples. It didn't hurt her, but was enough to nudge her back a half-step. "This guy just doesn't give up, does he?" she said. "This seems kind of ridiculous, though."

Sam shrugged. "I'd rather he tosses burgers at us than tear our guts out like he did to those people on TV."

"Fair point, well made," Anna conceded. "I'll take 'faintly ridiculous' over 'violently disemboweled' any day."

Both the box with the holes in it and the one beside it were torn apart as a hundred frozen patties took to the air. They hovered just above the ground, the Beef Chief gesturing to them with a hand as if holding them back.

"Oh, give it up, already!" Anna hollered to him. "They don't hurt us."

She glanced at Randy, still lying on the ground.

"Well, they hurt *him*, but not us. You're wasting your time, Beefy. Give it up."

"They don't hurt *you*, maybe," roared the Beef Chief. "But who says they're for you?"

Sam saw the first of the patties swish through the air. He heard the murmuring of the crowd behind him.

"Oh no. No," he groaned.

His feet kicked, propelling him sideways. One arm flew out like a soccer goalkeeper stretching for a ball. With a grunt of effort, he got his fingertips to the flying burger, knocking it off course. The frozen meat disk *whanged* against a mailbox, leaving a deep dent in the blue-painted side.

Sam's outstretched arm came down, found the ground, then flipped him over in a one-handed cartwheel. He landed expertly, to both his surprise and delight. It had mostly been the suit, of course, but some decades-old muscle memory had kicked in there for a moment, too, he was sure.

From behind him came a few gasps and impressed *oohs*. Sam turned, smiled and waved at them, then staggered as a patty cracked him on the back of the head.

"Sam!" Anna yelped.

He turned back to see the burgers start carving their way through the air, one by one. Anna bounded to her right and kicked one of the solid meat disks, stopping its momentum and flopping it to the ground.

Another hurtled toward the crowd of spectators. Sam lunged, bringing up an arm just in time to block its flight. It deflected off his wrist and bounced harmlessly away, flipping like a coin.

"Everyone get down!" Sam warned, as the next few meat missiles were launched toward the crowd. Sam and Anna both dived into action, blocking, catching, punching and kicking as many of the flying patties as they could.

"Ow! Will you *quit it?*" Anna barked, as one of the burgers slammed into her lower back, stinging her even through the suit. Another caught her on the thigh. "Right, fuck this," she hissed. "I'm taking him down."

She broke into a run, ducking and dodging as the frozen projectiles whistled toward her, blocking any she could get a hand to.

"Oh God, what is she doing?" Sam fretted. Groaning, he set off after her, cheered on by a handful of voices in the crowd.

Anna raised her hands as she approached the Beef Chief, unleashing an Anaphylactic Shockwave. With a jerk of a fist, another box ripped open. Several packs of ground beef exploded, sailed through the air toward him, then clumped together, forming a meat shield that absorbed the worst of

Anna's blast. Boils and buboes blemished its fat-marbled surface, then the shield became a beach ball-sized sphere that took off toward Anna at blinding speed.

"Oh shi—" she managed, throwing herself aside just a fraction of a second too late. The beef ball clipped her shoulder, spinning her around like a clumsy ballerina.

The ground-beef changed shape, becoming a multi-limbed mass of meat tentacles that wrapped around her shoulders, arms, and throat. She clamped her mouth shut as the meat fought to find a way in. It pressed insistently against her lips, tightening around her throat in an attempt to force her to open wide.

"Fmmk uff!" she protested, wrenching her head away.

She felt the meat squirm and wriggle as it tried to sneak up inside her suit. She tried to claw it away, but the tenderloin tentacles held her arms pinned and she realized to her dismay that this was it. She was going to be murdered by semi-sentient meat, in full view of the general public and—yes, a news team—while dressed in a costume with artificial nipples.

Well, wasn't this just *perfect?*

CHAPTER TWENTY

CHUCK STOOD IN THE SHOWER, head lowered, letting the hot water cascade over him. He'd hit the gym hard that morning, purging his hangover before it could even begin.

He'd devised a new training regimen for the sidekicks during his workout. They had to start upping their game if the project's funding was going to continue. Getting a few lucky punches in on a couple of gangbangers was one thing. Fighting supervillains was something else.

The suits gave them an edge, of course, but the suits alone weren't enough. If they were, he'd have picked three Special Forces guys and had them play dress-up with the outfits. Maybe kitted them out with some of the weapons and gadgets the government retrieval teams had collected from the sites of all those superhero battles over the years.

He closed his eyes and looked up into the spray. Using Special Forces guys was still an option, of course. It was his contingency plan if the sidekicks didn't work out, but he wanted to give them another week or so before writing them off. He would be surprised if they got it together enough to head into battle, but then he'd been surprised before.

Once. Maybe twice.

His third ever surprise came a moment later when he opened his eyes to find Mari standing on the other side of the shower's glass screen, watching him.

"Jesus, Mari!" he yelped, instinctively shielding his genitals with both hands. "What are you doing? I'm in the shower here."

"I noticed," said Mari. "And relax, Chuck. It's not like I haven't seen you naked before."

"No, I... Wait. You have? When?" Chuck demanded.

"That is unimportant," Mari told him. "Have you seen the news?"

"No. What news?" asked Chuck, suddenly paying attention. "What's happened?"

"You might want to sit down," Mari warned.

"Still in the shower," Chuck pointed out. "Show me."

Mari's screen changed. The face disappeared and was replaced by footage of what looked like some sort of road accident. Chuck wiped condensation off the inside of the glass and peered more closely at the footage.

His eyes widened. His jaw dropped.

"Aw," he groaned, "*shit*."

⇥

The door to Kapitän Nazi's room flew open with a *bang*. Nazi, who sat in the Lotus position on the end of his bed, opened one eye to see a semi-naked Chuck barge in, water *pattering* onto the linoleum tiles beneath him.

"John! Did you know about this?" Chuck demanded.

Kapitän Nazi opened his other eye. "About what?"

Chuck regarded him for a moment, his face darkening. "You know damn well what. You helped them, didn't you? No way they did this on their own. Damn it, John, I *trusted* you."

Nazi unfolded his legs and stood up. "It had to be done, Chuck. He needed to be stopped. More importantly, they needed a win. A real win, I mean." He smiled confidently. "They're ready. To be honest, I think they've always been ready. They just haven't realized."

"Oh, they're ready?" Chuck barked. "Mari!"

Mari trundled into the room, her face-screen showing some shaky hand-held news footage.

"Do they look ready, John?" Chuck asked.

It was hard to tell for sure, but the footage certainly implied that no, they weren't. Randy lay in the middle of the street, arms and legs spread in an X-shape, cape wrapped around his face.

Sam and Anna were wrestling with some kind of creature that had entangled itself around Anna. They heaved on its many tentacles, but the limbs collapsed in their hands before resprouting from another part of the thing's flailing body.

"Is this live?" Nazi asked.

"Yes, it's live. But any minute now, *they* won't be!" Chuck said. He inhaled sharply through his nose, swallowing back his rising temper. "You have no idea what you've done, John. You don't have the first clue how badly you've screwed the pooch on this one."

"We have a problem," Mari chimed.

Chuck scowled. "I think we established that we have a problem, Mari," he spat. "I don't think there's anyone in this room who doesn't now appreciate that a problem is what we have."

"No, not that," said Mari. "I mean, we have another problem."

"Well, I doubt it's as big as this one," Chuck said.

Mari's screen changed. For a moment, Chuck wasn't sure what he was looking at, exactly. Data of some kind. Quite a lot of data.

When it eventually hit him, it did so like a horse-kick to the stomach.

Kapitän Nazi realized at almost the same time Chuck did. "Is that what I think it is?" he asked.

"Oh God," Chuck whispered. "Oh God, no."

CHAPTER TWENTY-ONE

"Look out!"

Anna barely managed to eject the words through a mouthful of minced animal flesh before the Beef Chief's slab of a hand caught Sam by the back of his neck and wrenched him away. Half of what Anna had come to think of as 'the meat squid' was ripped away with him, giving Anna the breathing space she needed to fight back against the remaining tentacles.

Sam's legs bicycled wildly as the Beef Chief hoisted him aloft, one-handed. "Look what you've done," the villain hissed through his still-swollen lips. "Look what you made me do. You've ruined *everything*."

Anna tried to stand, but the meat squid fought back against her, tightening its multitude of grips around her arms, head, and throat. Thinned out as it was, though, she and the suit were quickly able to gain the upper hand. She tore it off in greasy handfuls, which she quickly hurled over the roof of the meat shop, hopefully beyond the reach of the Beef Chief's powers.

The impact of the truck had shattered several of the

bones in the villain's armor. Anna let fly with a flurry of jabs, pounding his leather costume and the Beef Chief's own ribs below.

Hissing in pain, the Beef Chief swung Sam like a bat, smashing him into Anna with explosive force. Both sidekicks went rolling and tumbling across the ground in a tangle of arms, legs, and embarrassment. They flopped to a stop against Randy, who immediately sat up like a vampire rising from its coffin.

Randy swayed slightly as he peered in the Beef Chief's direction. "Wow," he said, his voice slurred from what was almost certainly a full-blown concussion. "Since when were there two of him?"

Untangling themselves, Sam and Anna caught Randy by the arms, dragged him into cover behind an abandoned car, and took stock of the situation.

The front of the buildings were illuminated by flashing blue lights at both ends of the street, and a helicopter *whummed* in the sky overhead. It was too far away to be able to tell if it was a police or a press chopper, the pilot having presumably lived through enough superhero battles to understand the dangers of getting too close to one.

The fingers of daylight were creeping across the sky, casting long shadows across the ground. The city was waking, and the crowd of bystanders was growing by the minute.

"Why are they just standing there?" Anna asked. "Are they nuts? They should be running."

"Why would you run from a bad guy in Cityopolis?" Sam asked. He gestured to the crowd. Most of them were scanning the sky, phones in hand, camera apps active. "They think Doc Mighty is going to swoop in at any second and take this guy down, like he always does. They're so used to being rescued they've stopped noticing when they're even in danger."

"That's some deep shit," said Anna.

"We need to take this scumbag down," Randy growled. "Hard and fast. Ideally painfully."

He placed his fingers to his temples. "Come to me, my butterfly breth—"

Anna pulled his hands away. "Let's not call in the big guns quite yet," she said.

They peeked over the hood of the car. The Beef Chief stood at the back of the toppled truck, surrounded by empty boxes and torn packets. Long strands of ground beef slithered along the road toward him. He rolled his head back in pleasure as the greasy meat-snakes began winding their way up his tree trunk-like legs.

"Looks like he's beefing himself up," said Anna.

"What does that involve?" Sam wondered. "Does he, like, absorb it or something?"

"No idea, but if we're going to take him out, now's the perfect time," Anna said. "Let's think. What do we know about this guy?"

Randy raised a hand.

"You don't have to put your hand up, Randy. Go."

"He's called the Beef Chief," Randy growled.

Anna didn't respond for a moment, then tutted. "OK, *you* do have to put your hand up, I changed my mind. But only you. What else? He's big. He's crazy strong. He's covering himself in meat. It might be a sexual thing."

"God, I hope not," Sam muttered.

"He has a horse," Randy said.

"Hand up, Randy," Anna told him.

Randy raised his hand. Anna ignored it.

"Weaknesses. Come on. There has to be something. What would a meat guy be scared of?"

"Veganism!" said Sam, sounding a little too excited about the suggestion.

"OK. OK, what would that translate to?" Anna asked.

Sam hesitated. "What do you mean?"

"How would we use veganism as a weapon against him?"

"Oh. I have no idea," said Sam.

Anna sighed. "How do you beat meat?" She gasped. "Oh! We could use that in a quip. Something about beating his meat!"

"Let's not," Sam replied.

"I've got it!" Randy growled. "We could eat him."

"Shut the fuck up, Randy," Anna sighed. "Come on. He has to have some weak spot. He keeps saying this is our fault. Why is that?"

"Because he's a lying criminal scumbag," Randy snarled. "They're all the same."

"No, but... Anna's right," Sam realized.

"Allergy Girl," Randy corrected.

"He keeps blaming us. Or blaming someone else, at least. He says he just wanted to be left alone. Why would he say that?"

"Because he's a lying—"

"Apart from that," said Sam. "And what was it he said earlier? Something about how they were even going to let him see her?"

"Her who?" asked Anna.

The truth of it crept up on Sam slowly, like a thief in the night, stealing away the final shreds of his faith in humanity.

"Oh... shit," he whispered. "I think... I think I worked it out."

"Worked what out?" asked Anna.

"How we stop him," said Sam.

"We kick his ass!" Randy growled, punching a fist into the opposite palm.

All three of them screamed in fright as the car was smashed aside, revealing them all crouching in the street. The

Beef Chief towered above them, his hands completely encased in enormous fist-shaped lumps of ground beef.

"Fist meat!" Randy spat. He grinned hopefully at the others.

"Still not a pun," Anna was able to eject before the Beef Chief brought both fists down. The sidekicks scattered. The ground where they had been crouching shattered with the impact of his beef-fists.

Anna was up first. She threw out a hand and a rash tore across the Beef Chief's face before he could get a fist up to block it. He swung a wild haymaker with the other fist, and it was only the enhanced reactions of the supersuit that saved Anna from having her head punched clean off her shoulders.

"Sam, whatever you're going to do, do it quickly," she urged.

"OK. Right," Sam nodded. "Keep him busy."

He spun on his heels and ran away.

"Wait, what?" Anna yelped, but then a giant meat-fist slammed into her lower back. The next second-and-a-half was comprised of pain, movement, then a sudden impact as the punch launched her into the side of the car they'd been hiding behind a few moments ago.

Glass splintered and metal crumpled around her. The battery-level indicator in her visor began to flash on and off as she struggled to extricate herself from the tangle of steel.

"That's not good," she fretted. What was even less good was the shadow she saw falling upon her, and the whiff of raw meat that filled her nostrils as a hand caught her by the back of the neck.

"Hey! Pick on someone your own size!" growled Randy.

Anna didn't need to see him to be able to picture him standing behind the Beef Chief, hands on his hips, cape fluttering in the wind, too stupid or noble or—no, probably just stupid, actually—to go for the cheap shot when the bad guy's back was turned.

The hand released its grip on Anna's neck, and the Beef Chief turned away.

"What did you say?" the villain demanded.

Randy spat the words out in his Batman-like growl again, really ramping it up for the villain's benefit. "I said *pick on someone your own size.*"

A frown troubled the Beef Chief's face. "Something about a disguise?" he guessed. "What are you talking about?"

"What are *you* talking about?" Randy said, the growl becoming so deep it was practically a gargle. "I said you should pick on someone your own size."

Recognition lit up the Beef Chief's face. "Oh, pick on someone my own size?"

"That's what I said, yes," spat Randy.

The Beef Chief looked around them. "I don't see anyone here my own size," he sneered.

"Well, maybe you just aren't looking hard enough," said Randy.

The villain hesitated. "What do you mean?"

"You mean what do *you* mean?"

"Huh?"

Randy's eyes narrowed. "Touché," he said. "Well played."

The Beef Chief towered there, staring down at him for a while. "What are you even talking about?" he demanded, his anger temporarily replaced by a sort of confused exasperation.

Only temporarily, though. It returned in a sudden flash, twisting his features and propelling him into action.

A meaty fist grabbed Randy, completely encasing his head and blocking all his airways. Randy drove a solid uppercut into the ground beef, but his hand sunk into the mass of processed meat and got stuck there.

This didn't stop him trying the same technique with the other fist. Predictably, the result was the same.

Having successfully extracted herself from the wreckage of the car, Anna wrenched one of its buckled doors off. The battery display in her visor dropped another few percent. Whatever Sam was doing, he'd better do it fast.

Anna didn't share Randy's aversion to the cheap shot. It was probably her favorite type of shot, in fact, if you excluded the alcoholic variety. She smashed the door across the Beef Chief's back, staggering him.

"I'm *steaking* out your boundaries, Beef Chief!" she announced. She *whanged* him with the door again. "OK, that was terrible," she admitted. "But it was off the cuff, so—"

The other beef-fist grabbed her. Anna tried to swing the door again, but the grip on her head made it impossible to get enough leverage. She gulped down a last desperate breath before the meat fully covered her face, and her world became one of wet, greasy darkness.

"You made me do this!" the Beef Chief roared. "This isn't my fault. It isn't my fault!"

"I know," said Sam, appearing in front of him. "It isn't."

The Beef Chief glowered down at him through red-ringed eyes. Anna and Randy both struggled in the grip of his mighty meat-fists, but the villain seemed to barely even notice.

"Disengage Battle Mode," said Sam.

The suit slithered and changed, returning to its non-enhanced version and revealing Sam's face, aside from the number-eight-shaped blue eye mask.

"You didn't rob that bank, did you?" Sam said. "You didn't kill those people."

The Beef Chief's Adam's apple bobbed up and down as he swallowed. "It was on the news," he said. "I saw it. But that wasn't me. I just wanted to be left alone. *Why wouldn't they leave me alone?*"

"I know. I know," said Sam, raising a hand in a calming gesture. "You wanted to put everything behind you, didn't you? You wanted to leave all this in the past?"

He produced a framed photo from behind his back. "For her sake."

The Beef Chief's eyes shimmered when he saw the girl in the sun hat. The lower half of his jaw tightened as he fought to keep it from trembling.

"Your... daughter?" Sam guessed.

"Granddaughter," the Beef Chief corrected, his voice barely a whisper. "They said... They said I could see her, if I stopped doing... If I stopped being..."

Sam nodded. "You can still stop," he said. "We can help you."

The Beef Chief's face became harder. From the way Anna and Randy both jerked, his meat-fists tightened their grip. "No! No one will believe me! No one *ever* believes me!"

"I believe you," said Sam. "And we'll make them believe *us*."

He gestured to the watching crowds and cameras. "We'll tell them what happened. In front of the cameras. We'll tell them the truth. We'll tell them it wasn't you. We'll *make* them listen."

He held the photograph out. "For her sake."

A battle raged on the villain's face. The struggle of it filled his eyes with tears and made his impossibly broad shoulders shake.

"Gah!" he barked, and there were gasps from Randy and Anna as they both fell to the ground. The meat fists *plopped* onto the asphalt in greasy blobs as the Beef Chief relinquished his control and snatched the photograph out of Sam's hands.

"Thank you," Sam told him. "I meant what I said. We'll help you."

"*Help him?*" Randy wheezed. "I'm going to snap his spine in six places. Just give me, like, five to eight minutes."

Sam held a hand out to the Beef Chief. "It's OK, guys," he said. "He's not the bad guy."

The Beef Chief regarded Sam's hand with suspicion, then met his eye. "You mean it? You'll really help me?"

"I do," said Sam. "And we will."

Slowly, tentatively, the Beef Chief reached out a hand. Sam tried not to show his terror as fingers that could crush steel wrapped around his own.

"Thank you," the Beef Chief whispered. "I don't... And I'm..." He looked down at his feet, composing himself. "Sorry, I'm not very good at..."

Sam smiled. "It's fine. I get it."

The villain smiled back, relief pushing the final furrows of anger from his face. He pumped Sam's hand enthusiastically, almost wrenching the arm from its socket.

"Thank you," he said again. "Thank you so much. You have no idea how—"

He exploded in a ball of fire and guts. A shockwave of sizzling innards hit Sam in the face, launching him several feet through the air and painting him in shades of purple and red.

Sam blinked through the blood and gore, the sound of the blast still ringing in his ears. It took him a moment to realize he was lying on the ground, and a moment longer to notice that he was still holding the Beef Chief's hand, the arm having been blasted off at the elbow.

"Yeurgh!" he yelped, dropping the smoldering limb. "What the *fuck*? What the hell just happened?!"

"You blew him up!" Randy growled. "You tricked him into shaking your hand, then you blew his ass to pieces."

Randy held up two thumbs. "Great job!"

"No, I... That wasn't me. That wasn't me!" Sam protested.

"Uh, no shit," said Anna. Her neck was craned back, her eyes pointed to the sky as she heaved herself back to her feet. "Call me crazy, but I think it was probably that guy..."

CHAPTER TWENTY-TWO

A DARK-CLAD FIGURE descended slowly from the heavens. The air shimmered beneath him, and spots of dust flared bright and brief as they ignited in the column of heat. The smell of sulfur snagged at the back of Sam's throat and nipped at his eyes.

"Who the hell is this now?" Anna wondered, before the cushion of heat forced her back.

A circle of road surface, just a little wider than the length of a car, became a melting gloopy mass. The flying figure glided above it, then dropped onto the more solid ground just beyond the circle's edge.

He was shorter than he'd looked during his descent, although he made up for the lack of height with an abundance of presence. He imposed himself upon the world around him, like he was the star of the show and everyone else alive merely his background players.

His wardrobe was straight from the Fantasy Dark Lord catalog, all armor plating and spikes, with skull-shaped trimmings on the bulky metal shoulder pads to which his flowing burgundy cape was attached. None of the skulls looked human, but they didn't look like any animal Sam had ever seen, either.

He wore a helmet that had a suggestion of dragons about it, although Sam couldn't quite explain why. It was a flat, matte black headpiece, made up of several interlocking layers that rose in swooping curves to form four rows of three points, spaced evenly from the front of his head to the back.

His hands were uncovered. The skin was a dark red, the fingers lined with irregular spots of browns and blacks. Heat crackled and sparked in the air around him, mingling with the general air of menace that seeped from his every pore.

"Is he on our side?" Randy asked.

"I doubt it," said Anna. "I'm going out on a limb here, but I think this might be *you know who*."

Randy blinked behind his goggles. "Who?"

"You know," Anna said.

"I don't. Who?"

"The guy," Anna hissed. She pointed up. "The space bastard."

Randy clenched both fists. "You mean the guy who killed Doc Mighty and the rest of the Justice Platoon?"

Gasps went up from the gathered crowds. Anna glared at Randy, then gestured to the onlookers with her eyes.

"What? What's wrong with your face?" he asked her. "Why are you looking at me like that?"

"The Justice Platoon is dead?" came a cry from the crowd.

"Did he... Did he say this guy killed Doc Mighty?" yelped another.

"Oh God! Oh God, no!"

Anna and Sam both raised their arms, calling for calm. "It's fine. Relax," said Anna. "Nobody killed anyone."

"He just killed that guy!" said a woman in the crowd,

pointing to the gelatinous stain on the ground that had, until recently, been the Beef Chief.

"OK, yes, he killed him," Anna conceded. "But not the Justice Platoon. He, uh..."

"*Billed* Doc Mighty and the Justice Platoon. He sent them a bill. That's all."

"Jesus," Anna whispered. "Is that the best you could come up with?"

"I was going to say he'd *drilled* them," Sam whispered back. "But thought that might actually sound worse."

"Be quiet."

The voice rolled out of the space bastard in a wave of heat that physically shoved the sidekicks back a few steps. This was the final straw for Anna's suit, and with a disappointing *bleep* it disengaged Battle Armor mode. The faint buzzing Anna only now realized the suit had been emitting since she'd first put it on fell silent, as the costume's enhancements became dormant.

"Your 'Justice Platoon' is dead," the new arrival confirmed. His voice was deep, but his words were slightly slurred, tainted by the faintest suggestion of a lisp. It was as if he had overcome some major speech impediment in the past, but the tiniest hint of it had hung around. "I killed them myself."

Sobs and cries and shouts of, "No!" rose up from the stunned crowd. The space bastard's gaze swept across them all, his bloodshot eyes staring out through the oval holes in his helmet.

"It was quick and painless," he continued. "For the most part. More than they deserved."

"Who are you?" Randy demanded. "What do you want?"

The space bastard turned and regarded Randy for a while. To his credit—or possibly to his detriment—Randy stood his ground, fists clenched, cape lightly fluttering in the rolling waves of heat.

"To help," the new guy replied. He stepped past Randy and raised his voice, addressing the crowd and the watching cameras. The battle with the Beef Chief would've made a pre-recorded segment in the news, Sam knew, but this would almost certainly be going out live.

"You have been exploited for too long," announced the space bastard, and the air around him crackled with heat. "Your 'heroes' took advantage of your weakness. Of your frailty. They used their strengths to further their own ends, not yours. I stopped this, and as such, you may call me... Savior."

"Bullshit!" spat a middle-aged cop with a paunch and a mustache. He stood at the front of the crowd, his sidearm drawn but not yet raised. "They were on our side!"

"How many times did they catch villains, only for them to escape? Fight, capture, escape. Fight, capture, escape. Round and around and around," said Savior. "How many innocent people died in this cycle? How many families grieved? And yet, no one ever stopped to ask themselves... why? Why, with all their power, couldn't your Justice Platoon deal with these criminals properly?"

Sam realized Anna was glaring at him. Her eyes darted to Savior's back, then she gave a faint, almost imperceptible nod of her head. Sam urgently shook his own head, mouthed a definitive, "Don't," then went back to watching the show.

"They let you die so they could look good for the cameras," Savior explained. "How else would they sell their branded clothing, or their energy drinks, or their movies? A hero needs a villain, or the public loses interest, and so they allowed those criminals to escape—facilitated those escapes, perhaps—again and again and again."

There were a few jeers and boos from the crowd. Savior appeared to take note of the people responsible, but otherwise didn't react.

"And you bought into it. All of you. You cheered when they saved you from disasters of their own making. You applauded when they avenged the deaths they themselves had caused. And why? Because you are children. Because you are fools."

His voice became harder. The heat rolling off him became a furnace blast.

"I care nothing for your accolades. I do not want your adoration. I am here to make this world a better place. To cleanse it, if necessary, in fire. I have started with this murderer," he said, gesturing to the puddle of flesh behind him. "And I shall continue with—"

"He wasn't a murderer," said Sam, much to his own surprise.

Savior craned his neck and looked back over his shoulder. He was the same height as Sam, but Sam suddenly felt even smaller and more insignificant than usual.

"I'm sorry?"

Sam's throat was dry from the heat and the terror that was now flooding through his body. He swallowed a couple of times before he was able to reply. "He didn't kill anyone. The Beef Chief. It was... It was a mistake."

"A 'mistake'?"

Sam nodded. "Yeah. I mean, not a mistake exactly, but... It wasn't him. He wasn't a killer."

"Oh."

Savior's eyes went to the puddle for a moment, then flicked back to Sam. It was hard to make them out in the shadows of his mask, but the whites seemed yellow and bloodshot, while the pupils were ringed with red.

"But a criminal, yes?" Savior gestured around them at the wrecked cars, toppled truck, and ruined storefronts. "He was responsible for this?"

"Uh, well, I mean... Kind of," said Sam. "But, I mean, I suppose it wasn't *just* him."

Savior turned. Slowly. Ominously. "Then who else was responsible?" he asked.

The question sounded innocent enough, and Sam almost fell for it. He caught himself just before the, "Us," could leave his lips, and turned it into an, "Uh..." instead. He shrugged. "I, uh, I guess it was just him."

The dragon-like helmet dipped in a nod. "As I thought," he intoned, before turning back to the crowd. "The Justice Platoon were not your protectors," he continued. "They were your exploiters. And yet, they were also your court jesters, performing the same tricks in the same brightly-colored costumes for your entertainment, while ignoring the death and destruction they left in their wake."

He took a step toward the crowd, and the heat made the front row recoil. "This ends now," he announced. "There will be more death, yes. More destruction. But those deaths shall be the right ones. The innocents have suffered long enough. It is the guilty who shall now pay the price. This world—all of you—are under my protection. Embrace that. Go about your lives, and you shall be unharmed."

His voice deepened into a growl. "Defy me. Challenge me. And you shall be destroyed, just like your Justice Platoon."

"Screw you!" bellowed a voice from the crowd. A bottle was launched from somewhere. It spun, end over end, as it sailed through the air toward Savior. He watched it approach, then continued to watch as the heat warped the glass and the whole thing *splatted* to the ground in front of him.

There was silence for a while then. Sam looked to the others, but they were both fixated on Savior and didn't notice. Randy still had his fists raised but seemed to be in no rush to run in swinging.

Savior sighed, and the temperature raised a full degree.

"Very well," he said, his yellow eyes turning on the audience. "I see a demonstration is in order."

He cricked his neck, flexed all his blackened fingers, then shrugged.

"Let us begin."

CHAPTER TWENTY-THREE

SAVIOR CAST his gaze across his audience. Despite the obvious danger, and the best efforts of the cops at either end of the street, the crowd had filled out during Savior's speech, and there were now a hundred people gathered there to watch, plus a couple of news crews who'd be widening the reach to millions more.

His head panned from left to right and back again, searching for one specific face in the crowd. After a few seconds of this, he stopped.

"Garry Forshaw," he said.

The crowd parted, just a little, as it turned in on itself to look at a man in a checked shirt and denim jeans. His dark hair was graying a little, and he rocked an impressive mustache that was almost all the way white.

"Uh, yeah?" he said.

"Repeated public intoxication. Multiple counts of public urination," Savior said. "Your police force may not be aware of your criminal actions, but I am. I know what you've done. I know what you've *all* done."

Garry shifted uncomfortably. "I don't know what you're—"

The flames seemed to consume him from the inside out, leaping from his mouth as he screamed, before burning out through his chest. The crowd scattered, stampeding in panic as he thrashed around in agony.

And then, he was gone. In his place was nothing but a pile of black ash, a half-melted shoe, and a smell that no one present would ever forget.

"Penny Willow," Savior continued. "Disturbing the peace."

A blond-haired woman ignited and the crowd changed direction like a shoal of fish in a shark attack.

"Christina Schneider. Trespassing."

"No, please, n—"

Another woman became a pillar of fire. She zig-zagged frantically for a few seconds, her burning flesh igniting the clothing of those around her.

Sam gaped in horror at the chaos, his whole body rigid with fear. It was Anna's voice that finally snapped him out of it.

"Sam! *Sam!* Do something!"

"Wha—?" Sam blinked. "I don't... I can't..."

Randy roared as he raced at Savior, but a cushion of blisteringly hot air kept him at bay.

"OK, you asked for this," Randy growled. He whipped his arms around in what was presumably meant to be a significant way, then pressed his fingers to his temples. "Come to me, my butterfly brethren!"

He thrust a hand dramatically in Savior's direction, and waited.

And waited.

Another member of the rapidly dispersing crowd erupted in flames.

Randy watched the skies. "Any minute now," he growled.

"Sam! Stop him!" Anna begged, as two of the burning figures became ash piles.

The shape in Sam's head shifted, as if waking from a deep slumber. Sam clenched his fists and concentrated on it, concentrated harder than he'd ever done before as, all around him, people burned.

Mary-Ellen Unan, tax evasion.

Dave DeCamp, petty larceny.

Claire Oxborough. Josh Kolakowski. Hayden Ward.

All burning. All dead.

"Battle Mode!" Sam cried, and his suit's armor activated.

Lowering his head to protect the exposed part of his face, he charged at Savior. The intensity of the heat drained the last of the suit's power almost immediately, and Sam howled in pain as the armor retracted and the costume's punishment-absorbing functionality shut down.

The heat tore at every part of him at once, turning his legs to jelly and his head to mush. The agony of it swelled inside him like a balloon getting ready to burst. He couldn't breathe, couldn't move, couldn't think. He felt the suit ignite, the now dormant material unable to resist the heat.

The shape in his head danced in the fire and the chaos, and Sam felt power surge through him as he—

Something heavy and fast-moving slammed into him, launching him backward out of the heat cloud. Sam hit the ground hard, rolled for several feet in a deeply undignified way, then slid to a stop against the wreckage of a car.

His eyes stung. His lungs ached. Most of the rest of him hurt, too, in fact, but at least he was no longer on fire. That was something. He blinked through the tears to find a scarred face staring down at him, brow furrowed in concern.

"Sam. Are you OK?" asked Kapitän Nazi. "I'm sorry. I'm so sorry. I had no idea."

Sam groaned and tried to shove the Kapitän away, but his arms were too heavy to manage more than a shrug.

"Stay here. All of you, stay here," Nazi said, shooting Anna and Randy warning looks. "If you can get anyone to safety, do it. But leave this guy to me."

"Uh, OK," said Anna. "But be careful."

Either she teleported to Sam's side, or he passed out for a moment, because suddenly she was there beside him, an arm around his shoulder, helping him to sit up. Randy stood a few feet away, eyes turned to the sky.

"Come on," he muttered. "Where are they?"

Kapitän Nazi pointed to the wreckage of the car Sam was propped against. "Mind if I take this?"

"Take what? The car?" said Anna. "Uh, no. Help yourself."

"Thanks."

Nazi ran to the front of the car, hooked his arms underneath it, and raised it a few feet off the ground. There were no war cries or witty quips, just a grunt of effort as he flipped the vehicle. It somersaulted through the air toward Savior, flipping end over end.

"Come on," Nazi muttered, watching its flight. "*Come on.*"

Without turning, Savior reached a hand out behind him. A thin beam of concentrated fire sliced through the flying vehicle, cleaving it neatly in two down the middle. A cloud of heat parted the two halves, and they crashed to the ground on either side of him with a couple of disappointing *clanks*.

Only then, once the car halves had stopped moving, did Savior turn. He regarded the Kapitän quizzically for a moment, before asking, "And you are?"

"You want to deal with criminals?" Nazi asked. He jabbed a thumb into his own chest. "Deal with me. Not these people."

Savior held his gaze. Something about the shape of his eyes suggested he smiled beneath his mask.

"Les Fulbrook," he announced. "Littering."

A man in the scattering crowd screamed as he became a column of flame. He made it just a few feet before his legs gave way and he hit the ground as charcoal and ash.

Roaring, Kapitän Nazi raced at the murderer, gritting his teeth and throwing up a hand to shield himself from the heat.

A bolt of fire erupted from Savior's hand, but Nazi lurched to the left, narrowly dodging it.

Nazi pushed on, ignoring the heat and the pain. His t-shirt blackened, then disintegrated, the ashes fluttering away on the heat-breeze.

Another blast hurtled toward him. He zig-zagged, avoiding it and the one that immediately followed. His legs were still powering him on, but it was like moving through molasses now, every step requiring more and more effort.

"Well, well. You are a persistent one, aren't you?" Savior said.

He raised a hand to a news crew—a journalist and a cameraman—who'd stood their ground, capturing events for the world to see.

"Let's see where your priorities lie," Savior said.

He fired.

Kapitän Nazi jumped.

Sam had been slowly recovering and was watching when Kapitän Nazi threw himself in front of the reporters. He was watching when the former supervillain stood his ground, shielding them.

Watching as the blast struck him in the stomach, and as the agony contorted his face.

Nazi landed heavily on the asphalt and slid several feet to a stop. He was moving, but not in a way that suggested he was going to continue the fight any time soon.

Savior gave a little contented nod, then spent a few moments watching the last few of the crowd's stragglers flee.

Only the news crew he had just been targeting remained. He turned to the camera and stared straight down the lens.

"Demonstration complete," he announced. "Innocent citizens of planet Earth, rest easy. Your Savior is here. Crime—and those who commit it—will soon be a thing of the past."

There was a faint *whooshing* noise as he rose into the air on a shimmering column of heat. He looked down at Sam, Anna, and Randy, and there was that suggestion of a smile in his eyes again. "Nice outfits, guys," he said, and then he continued climbing until he was lost in a bank of gray cloud.

"Nazi's down," said Anna. "Sam, you OK?"

Sam nodded. "Go. Randy, help me up."

Randy, who had been watching the sky, turned to him. "Why can't you help yourself up?"

"Because the evil fire guy almost killed me," Sam wheezed.

"Oh. Yeah. Makes sense," said Randy, holding out a hand. Sam took it, and between them they managed to wrestle him up onto his feet.

Limping, Sam made his way over to where Anna was kneeling beside Kapitän Nazi. His face was twisted up in pain, both hands jammed over a nauseatingly horrible wound in his stomach. "How is he?"

"Not great," said Anna. "I mean, I'm no doctor, but..." She indicated the blackened, bloodied hole in his stomach. "That can't be good, can it?"

Nazi lifted a hand away from the wound for a moment and beckoned for Sam to come closer. Sam resisted at first, but a glare from Anna and a general feeling of weakness in his legs quickly brought him down to Nazi's level.

"I lied," the Kapitän wheezed. As he spoke, something *burbled* inside him. "I remember all of it. All of those things I did. And I am sorry, Sam. I am so... so very sorry."

Sirens wailed in the distance. Sam gave a shake of his

head. "It's... Let's not worry about it for now, OK? We'll get you fixed up. You're going to be OK."

"I doubt that, Sam," said Randy. "He's got a big hole in his guts."

"Randy, please."

"And his legs are on fire."

Anna jumped into action. "Oh, shit!"

A frantic few seconds passed as she slapped out the pockets of flame that had ignited near the bottom of Kapitän Nazi's jeans.

Sam looked down as something was pressed into his hands. It was a slim leather notebook.

"My burden," Nazi whispered, the effort of it etching itself across his face. His accent was becoming less American and more like his native German. "Please... take it for me. Put it... vhere it... belongs."

"Where it belongs? Where does it belong?" asked Sam.

"I leave you the book, but its content I take vith me," said Nazi, summoning his strength enough to strain his way through the whole sentence in one go. "Its burden follows me now."

"Jesus. Can we get an ambulance over here?" Anna yelled. "Randy, come help me find a damn paramedic."

They ran off, just as a series of wet coughs wracked Nazi's body. Unsure of what to do, Sam placed his hands on the Kapitän's shoulders, holding him down.

He should've been enjoying this. After everything the bastard did to him, after everything he put him through, Sam should be savoring every moment of his pain.

And yet...

"You saved those people," Sam told him. "You... you saved me."

Kapitän Nazi said nothing. His eyes swum vaguely as he gazed past Sam at the sky above. Sam looked around, but there was no sign of the ambulance yet. He drew in a deep breath, building up to saying something he never thought he'd say.

"I get it. It wasn't you," he said. "Back then, you weren't in your right mind. This... this is you."

Nazi's eyes focused a little. Pain whispered from his lips as he tilted his head to look at Sam.

"You saved those people, and you saved me, and... I guess..." Sam steeled himself. "I forgive you."

Kapitän Nazi's eyes widened in surprise. He gasped, but Sam couldn't tell if it was through surprise or pain. A tear cut through the ash marks on his face, rolling sideways across his temple, then plopping onto the black soot that covered the ground.

"*Thank you*," the Kapitän mumbled. "I think... Kapitän Nazi finally dies today."

Sam shook his head. "He died a long time ago."

Nazi managed to contort his mouth into something like a smile, and then his chest stopped heaving and his eyes became pebbles of glass.

"Nazi?" said Sam. He waited for a response, then gave him a shake. "Kapitän?"

Sam's throat felt dry. He forced the word out.

"John?"

But John was gone.

CHAPTER TWENTY-FOUR

IT WAS THREE HOURS LATER—AFTER the government agents had taken John's body away, and the black sedans had driven Sam and the others back to the underground base—when Sam found himself in Kapitän Nazi's room.

He'd peeled himself out of the remains of the suit and gotten changed into his training shorts and t-shirt. He hadn't seen Chuck yet, and thinking about doing so made his hands shake, so he tried not to. Now wasn't the time. There were more important matters to attend to.

First, the chalkboard. Sam found a chunk of chalk balancing on a ridge at the bottom of the board, and blew some of the loose dust off its tip.

He marked two lines beside each other, one for the cameraman, one for the journalist. The chalk *squeaked* lightly on the board's surface, two tiny screams of despair.

With those two marked off, he marked a line for himself, added another for Anna, then drew a diagonal through them all representing Randy. Sam didn't know for sure if John had saved all three of them from some grisly fate, but he was confident enough to mark them up.

He studied the board for a while, wondering who all the people marked on it were, and if they even knew that their lives had been saved, let alone by whom. He wondered how they'd feel if they knew. He wondered how he felt about it himself.

Returning the chalk to its slot, Sam walked to the book-cases and their countless notebooks. The notebook containing Nazi's list of names was in Sam's hand. He held it by the bottom edge, waving it up and down a little as he looked for somewhere to sit it. Kapitän Nazi had asked him to put it 'where it belongs,' but Sam had no idea where he was referring to. There was no space left in any of the bookcases, but Sam discovered that if he lay the smaller book flat on its back, he could slide it in on top of the other volumes.

He didn't know if this was what Nazi had meant, or if it qualified as where the list of names belonged, but it was close enough, he reckoned.

It was twenty-three minutes later when Sam threw the punch. It connected cleanly with Chuck's jaw and did quite a staggering amount of damage.

Unfortunately, almost all of that damage was to Sam's hand.

"Ow. Fuck!" Sam hissed, shoving his bruised fingers under the opposite armpit and trapping them there.

They were in a damp smelling meeting room for what Chuck had described as 'a debrief' but which had rapidly become apparent was actually 'a telling off'. He'd been halfway through trotting out some bullshit about responsi-bility when Sam had taken his swing.

Chuck frowned a little. It was the only indication that he'd even felt the punch.

"What was that for?" he asked.

"You know damn well what that was for!" Sam spat. "You set us up!"

Anna's eyebrows knotted. "Wait, what?"

"Tell them," Sam ordered. "Tell them what you did."

Chuck gave a confused sort of smile. "Sam, I don't know what you're talking about."

"The Beef Chief," Sam spat. "The footage of him killing those people. It wasn't real." He turned to the others. "He faked it, like he faked the Doc Mighty stuff on the news. It wasn't real."

Anna and Randy both shifted their gaze to Chuck.

"Oh... God," Anna muttered, closing her eyes and exhaling slowly through her nose.

"What's that? What's happening?" Randy asked, his head tick-tocking between them all. "What's the problem?"

"Chuck had Mari fake the footage of the Beef Chief killing those people at the bank. He knew if we saw it, we couldn't walk away. He used it to bring us back. To control us," Sam said. "To send us running off after an innocent man."

"I didn't send you anywhere. You snuck out! And like hell he was innocent," said Chuck. "The Beef Chief has arrest warrants in all fifty states, as well as from the Feds. He's stolen millions over the years."

"*But he wasn't a murderer!*" Sam roared. He looked taken aback by the ferocity of his own outburst and took a moment to compose himself. "He wasn't a murderer. He was an old man who just wanted to see his granddaughter."

"Oh, so we just forget everything he did?" Chuck barked back. "We just wave a magic wand, all is forgiven, enjoy your damn retirement?"

"Worked for Kapitän Nazi," Randy pointed out.

"That was different," Chuck said. "He was making amends."

"And maybe the Beef Chief would've too," Sam snapped. "But now he's dead. And it's our fault." He shook his head. "No. No, it's *your* fault. You signed his death warrant when you faked that footage. That Savior guy, he called him a murderer. That's why he killed him."

"I saw the news," Chuck said. "He burned a guy alive for littering. I reckon the Beef Chief would've gotten his no matter what."

"Maybe," Sam admitted. "But it wouldn't have been on us."

Chuck rocked on his heels. "Look, I get your point, and maybe you're right. Maybe I shouldn't have tricked you."

"Maybe?" Anna spluttered.

"But we got more pressing problems to deal with," Chuck continued. He beckoned to Mari, who came trundling out of the corner. A map of the city appeared in the air before her.

"This Savior guy has set himself up in Memetzo's cathedral," said Chuck. "Got a wall of fire around it to keep people out. Not that anyone's in any rush to get inside."

"Speak for yourself," Randy hissed.

"Why Memetzo's place?" Anna asked. "Why set up there?"

"We don't know," Chuck admitted. "We don't know much of anything."

"Guessing you don't know who he is, then?" asked Anna. "This 'Savior.'"

Chuck shook his head. "We're working on it," was the best he could offer.

Anna clicked her tongue against the back of her teeth. "There was something familiar about him. The helmet, I think. I'm sure I've seen it before."

Mari's voice piped up from somewhere inside her. "We are running searches of all available databases. If there's a match, we'll find it soon."

"What about those people he killed?" Randy growled. "Those crimes he'd said they'd committed. They check out?"

Chuck nodded. "We were able to corroborate a few of them, but not all."

"How did he know any of that stuff?" Anna wondered. "He had names, rap sheets... Where was that coming from?"

"We don't know that, either." Chuck admitted. "We also don't know what these things are, but we're getting reports of them from all over town."

The holographic map was replaced by something four-legged and horrifying.

"Jesus, what is that?" Anna asked. "It looks like Godzilla fucked a bear."

"Media's calling them 'Magma-Mutts,'" said Chuck, wincing in a way that suggested he didn't approve. "On account of their skin being all cracked and... well, magma-like. And how they kind of look like dogs, assuming you've never seen an actual dog before."

"Have they attacked anyone?" Anna asked. She gestured to the creature's spiked spine, deadly claws, and slavering jaws. "I mean, that's what they're for, right? Look at them."

Chuck shook his head. "Not that we know of. Not yet, anyway. But we think it's only a matter of time. The military is on standby but, well, you saw what he could do. That's why we need you guys to—"

"Jesus. Will you listen to yourself?" Sam said. "You need *us* because you don't know if the *entire US military* is capable of stopping this guy. Are you out of your mind? Look at us. We're nothing. We're nobody."

"Again, speak for yourself," Randy growled.

Sam rolled his eyes. "Oh, sorry, Randy. I forgot—you're the Butterfly King. You're *awesome*! You could probably beat this guy single-handed, right?"

"Damn straight!"

"And good job, too, because I notice your butterflies didn't show up. As usual." Sam snorted. "And, I mean... what if they had? What then? He turned those people to *ash*, Randy. He killed Kapitän Nazi by *pointing in his general direction*. You think a few butterflies are going to stop that?"

Randy narrowed his eyes, but said nothing. Sam wasn't letting him off that easily, though.

"And, I mean... why? Why all *this*?" He gestured to Randy's cape and goggles. "What's wrong with you? You're a joke. We're *all* jokes, even Doc Mighty and the others. Hell, especially them. You almost get yourself killed every time we step outside. Why do that to yourself?"

"Because I care about justice!" Randy snarled.

"Bullshit. That's not it!" Sam countered. "You could go be a cop, but you don't. You dress up. You play... fucking... pretend with a cape and a gravelly voice. Why? Why are you so into all this stuff?"

Randy took a few seconds to answer. His voice, when it came, was devoid of any growling, hissing, or snarling. It was just his voice. His real, actual voice.

"What else do I have?"

Sam opened his mouth to snap back, but no words came out. Randy was still much taller than Sam was, but he seemed to be shrinking before Sam's eyes.

Instead of arguing, Sam turned away. "Savior was right. I mean, not about the killing people, but the rest. The Justice Platoon didn't care about us. They could've kept the supervillains locked away, gotten some of them the help they needed, but they didn't. They needed the villains so they could keep playing at being heroes."

He sighed and looked to the ceiling for a moment, biting back the anger that he could feel building. "I can't do this anymore," he told Chuck. "I won't. I'm out."

"What? No. We need you, Sam," Chuck said. "We need all of you. Now, more than ever. You guys can make a difference."

"We've already made a difference," Sam said. "A man is

dead. All those people are dead. That was us. That was the difference we made."

He scowled. "Or is that all fake, too? Is Savior another trick to keep us doing what we're told?" He felt his throat tense, but managed to keep his voice from cracking. "I can't be a part of this. I never should've tried."

Chuck bristled. "You destroyed a multi-million dollar supersuit owned by the US government," he said. "You don't get to just walk away."

"Send me the bill," Sam said, calling his bluff. "I'll pay in installments."

He stepped past Chuck, only to find Mari blocking his path. Her digital face looked sternly at him. Sam forced himself to hold the robot's gaze. "Mari, get out of my way," he told her. He held a thumb and forefinger up, pinching them together so they were almost touching. "I am *this* close," he warned, and the shape in his head twitched into life.

Mari raised her eyes to Chuck, who must've given some sort of signal for her to step aside. Sam stormed past and marched out into the corridor in victorious triumph.

Ten seconds later, he stopped, and sheepishly made his way back. "Uh, can someone tell me where my regular clothes are?"

➤

Sam stood by the elevator, dressed in his work shirt and suit pants, his tie rammed into the pocket of his jacket beside the soft toy he'd bought for Corey. He rubbed the stuffed animal's fur with his thumb while he waited for the elevator to descend.

"Hey, wait up," said Anna, hurrying along the corridor to join him.

"I'm not staying, Anna," he said, not turning. "I can't."

"Huh? Oh, no. I know."

She appeared beside him, dressed in her green dress and holding one high-heeled shoe. "If you're getting out, I'm getting out."

"Oh. OK."

They stood together in silence. The elevator trundled to a stop, then the door slid open. Sam gestured for Anna to go first, before following her in. He pressed the button to take them up, then stood across from Anna, his back against the opposite wall, his gaze fixed on the floor.

"Can't believe he did that," Anna said. "The fake footage, I mean."

Sam nodded in agreement. "Makes you wonder what else they'd do."

It was Anna's turn to nod. "It does."

The elevator trundled upward.

"Randy OK?" Sam asked, raising his eyes from the floor.

"He'll live."

"Do you think I was too hard on him?"

Anna smirked. "What, when you told him he was a joke and then crushed all his hopes and dreams? Nah."

Sam winced and went back to looking at the floor.

"He'll be OK," Anna said. "Pretty sure he's been through a lot worse."

"Yeah," Sam agreed, although this didn't make him feel any better. He shuffled awkwardly. "Listen..." he began, but then the elevator stopped and the door slid open.

Anna looked at him expectantly. "I'm listening."

"Hmm? Oh, uh," Sam blushed, the moment passing him by. "Nothing. Doesn't matter."

He stepped out into the reception area of *Bland, Inc*. The reception lights were off, but the light streaming in from the windows was more than bright enough to see by.

The front door unlocked at their approach, *clicking* off the latch and swinging inward in time for Sam and Anna to pass through. It waited a few moments once they'd left, perhaps hoping they might change their mind, then swung closed with a mildly offended *clunk*.

The street outside was quieter than normal for this time of day. The acrid tang of smoke set up camp in Sam's nostrils in a way that suggested it had no intentions of moving on any time soon. They couldn't see Memetzo's cathedral from here, or the wall of fire that apparently surrounded it, but dark smoke clouds hung heavy and ominous in the air, suggesting the flames were still burning.

Helicopters buzzed around high overhead, out of sight behind the tall buildings. Sirens wailed in various directions, but other than that, the city seemed muted, like it was holding its breath and waiting to see what was going to happen next.

Anna puffed out her cheeks. "So... I guess we're ruled by a tyrant now."

"I guess so," Sam concurred.

"That sucks," Anna said. She jabbed a thumb vaguely along the street. "Want to go get a drink? Or several?"

Sam nodded and shook his head at the same time, a battle raging inside him. "I'd love to," he said. "But I can't. I should go check on my son, make sure he's OK."

"Oh. Yeah. Totally. I mean, of course," said Anna. "You should definitely do that."

She swept a strand of loose hair back over an ear and began to back away. "So, I guess I'll just..."

"Hmm? Oh, yeah. I guess that's... Bye."

Anna stopped, shuffled back, and they exchanged an awkward hug. "Listen, it's been... We should catch up again," she said. Sam glanced down as a business card was pressed into his hand. "Call me, OK?"

Sam nodded dumbly. "OK. I'll call you."

Anna's face brightened into a smile. She pecked him on the cheek. "Make sure you do," she said.

And with that, she turned and walked, barefoot, around the corner, and was gone.

Sam studied the card. It was a cheap, flimsy thing, probably printed at one of those machines at the Cityopolis airport. It had Anna's name, a phone number, and an address that was only five or six blocks from Sam's own place.

Emblazoned across the front in bold black type were the words: Homeopathic Allergist.

Sam looked in the direction she'd gone, half-hoping to find her there waiting. When he didn't, he slipped the card into a jacket pocket, patted the soft toy to make sure it was still there, and set off on the long walk to see his son.

CHAPTER TWENTY-FIVE

LAURA KEPT the door held against her shoulder like she was worried Sam might be about to force his way in.

"What are you doing here, Sam?" she demanded. "You're supposed to call first. You know that."

Sam sighed. "I came to see if Corey's OK," he said. "I just... After what happened the other night—"

"You mean when you almost got him shot and killed?"

"I didn't almost... That's not how... Look, is he there? Can I talk to him?"

The door didn't budge.

"Please, Laura. I've had a crazy couple of days, and I just... I need to see him. You know?"

Laura tutted. She stiffened, like she was preparing to slam the door, but then relented. "Fine. Five minutes. That's it."

"Thank you. Five minutes," Sam said, exhaling with relief.

They found Corey in front of the TV, the firelight from the screen flickering in his eyes. Memetzo's cathedral was right in the center of town. Sam had caught a glimpse of it between a couple of tower blocks on the walk here, but was only now seeing it in its full glorious horror.

The cathedral had stood for decades as one of the great architectural landmarks of Cityopolis, with its pointy bits, knobbly parts, and tall twisty things. Sam wasn't really clued up on the technical jargon, but that was a fairly accurate summary, all the same.

Now, the whole place, from the pointiest point to the twistiest twist, had been scorched and blackened. Even the great stained-glass window that took up a full third of the front had been tinted to shades of charcoal and gray.

Flames encircled the whole building like a moat, cutting the place off from the city around it. Eight or nine of those Magma-Mutt things padded around behind the wall of fire, like an extra line of defense protecting the murderer inside.

"I told you not to watch that, honey," Laura said, bustling with the remote until the screen went dark.

"Sorry, mom," Corey said in that automatic response way kids do, with no real sincerity behind it. He noticed Sam and jumped up from the couch. "Dad!"

Sam dropped to one knee in time to receive the flying hug. Wrapping his arms around his boy, he pulled him in tight, savoring those few moments where everything was right with the world.

"Hey, buddy," Sam said. "You OK?"

Corey nodded, his face rubbing up and down against Sam's. "I thought you were in jail," Corey said, his voice wobbling. "I didn't think they'd ever let you out. I didn't know if I'd ever see you again!"

"Hey!" Sam laughed. "You think I'd let anything stop us seeing each other? No way!"

Corey unhooked his arms and stepped back, but stayed close. "Why did they take you away, Dad? You didn't do anything wrong, did you?"

"No. No, of course not, son. It was a mistake, that's all," Sam assured him.

Corey bit his lip, his eyes wide and watery.

"What's the matter, buddy?" Sam asked.

"So... Savior isn't going to come for you?"

Sam frowned. "Savior? No. No, of course not. He's... Look, you shouldn't worry about that stuff. We're OK. We're all OK. You, me, your mom."

Corey sniffed. "Brian?"

Sam hesitated. He could feel Laura's eyes boring into the back of his head. "Yes. And Brian. We're all going to be just fine."

"OK, that's five minutes," Laura announced.

Sam and Corey both turned to her, wearing matching wounded expressions.

"Kidding," she said. She crossed her arms and slouched her weight onto one hip. "I'm making coffee. You want one?"

Sam couldn't keep the smile from his face. "Won't Brian mind?"

Laura motioned toward the door.

"Kidding," Sam said. "I'd love one. Thanks."

"OK." Laura headed for the kitchen. "You look like shit, by the way."

"Thanks again," Sam called after her.

Corey lowered his voice to a whisper, not wanting his mom to hear. "Are you sure everyone's going to be OK?" he asked.

"Of course, buddy. Why?" Sam whispered back.

There was some anxious shuffling. Corey's bottom lip wobbled. Sam put a hand on his shoulder. "What's wrong?"

Silent tears trickled down Corey's cheeks. His words, when they came, were a whispered babble. "It's just that Mom told me not to, but I saw the news, and that man who went on fire, and they said he had dropped litter and, well, I drop litter sometimes, too, even though I know I shouldn't, and now he might come and—"

"Hey. *Hey*," said Sam, pulling him in close. "That's not going to happen, OK? He's not going to come for you. They'll fix this, OK? They'll take care of this."

Corey sniffed and wiped his eyes on his sleeve. "Who?" he asked.

That caught Sam off guard. He swallowed, buying himself a moment. "The, you know, the army. Or the superheroes."

"The Justice Platoon is all dead," Corey said, his voice threatening to break again.

"But there are others. You know, less... But there are others. They'll fix all this, OK?"

"Promise?"

Sam promised, prayed and hoped, all at once.

The coffee arrived soon after. Sam took a seat on the couch, and had to hold the mug high off to the side to avoid spilling it as Corey jumped into the space beside him, snuggling up.

Laura remained standing in what seemed to be a deliberate indicator to Sam that he shouldn't get too comfortable.

"So, what happened to you, exactly?" she asked, sipping on her coffee. "Why did they arrest you?"

Sam puffed out his cheeks. "Just... mistaken identity. They got the wrong guy. We all laughed about it, in the end."

Laura frowned. "You laughed about it? The cops tackled you to the ground, locked you up for two days and you 'laughed about it'?"

"Well, not *laughed*, exactly," Sam said. "But there were no hard feelings. On either side, I mean. Not that... I didn't do anything wrong, obviously, so why would there be any...?"

He took a drink of his coffee to stop himself talking, then smacked his lips together and let out a long, satisfied, "Aaah!"

Laura's phone *bleeped*. The word was out of Sam's mouth before he could stop himself. "Brian?"

"No." Laura frowned as she studied the message. "Breaking news. Put on the TV."

Sam found the remote on the arm of the chair beside him. "What channel?"

Laura's hands shook as she stuffed the phone back into her pocket. "Any channel," she said. "Corey, honey, I want you to go to your room for a few minutes, OK?"

"But, Mom!"

"Corey, *please*," Laura urged. "For me, OK?"

Sam looked down to find the boy gazing imploringly up at him. "You, uh, you should do what Mom says, buddy," Sam said, his thumb hovering over the TV power button on the remote. "I'll come through in a minute. You can show me your room."

"Fine!" Corey huffed. He stood up, crossed his arms, and stomped off to his room. Sam waited until he heard Corey's bedroom door slam before thumbing the button.

The television blinked into life, and the room was filled with screaming and panic. When the picture fully appeared, it showed shaky handheld footage captured from a phone camera. It was hard to make out exactly what was happening, but a crowd of people seemed to be running from something.

A ticker tape at the bottom of the screen warned that 'Some viewers may find these images disturbing," but Sam was merely finding them confusing.

"What is it?" he asked, glancing from the screen to Laura. "What's happening?"

She shushed him and directed his attention back to the TV, just as the reason for the screaming made itself clear. One of the Magma-Mutts had brought down what looked to be a woman in a jogging suit. The footage had been blurred, but the monster was quite clearly tearing her to pieces with its eagle-like claws.

Sam felt the world grind into slow motion around him. He

watched as a photograph of a smiling woman—presumably the same one—was overlaid across the other footage. Sam felt confident that she wouldn't be smiling now. Smiling required a face.

A map of the city appeared, with several red dots denoting other Magma-Mutt attacks. The news anchor was talking, explaining the details, but Sam didn't hear them. Couldn't bring himself to hear them.

"Jesus. Jaywalking," Laura said.

Sam snapped out of his stupor. "Huh?"

"The woman. Jaywalking," Laura said. "And that's what happens."

She crossed her arms, but it wasn't the defensive blocking gesture it usually was. It was more like she was hugging herself in an attempt to feel better. "What's happening, Sam?" she asked, and there was a vulnerability to her voice he hadn't heard in years.

"The military will come in," Sam said. "Special Forces, or... someone. It'll be OK."

"Will it?" Laura wondered. "You saw the news, right? What he did to those people? And now these, these dog things. If what they're saying is true, if Doc Mighty's dead then... I don't know. Can anyone stop him?"

Sam looked at the screen again. It had gone back to showing helicopter footage of the blackened cathedral. The Magma-Mutts that had been padding around outside it were now gone. Sam didn't want to think about what they might have gone off to do.

"It'll be OK," he said, although it wasn't clear if he was addressing it to Laura or to himself. "It'll be fine."

He was still trying to convince himself when the front door flew open and a breathless Brian stumbled in. He slammed the door behind him, jammed his weight against it, then seemed to think better of this and came stumbling into the room.

His face was a ghostly white, his eyes two balls of anxiety that bounced around in his face.

Sam jumped to his feet, although wasn't entirely sure what to do when he got there, so he just sort of bounced anxiously from foot to foot, waiting to find out what was going on.

"Brian?" Laura asked. "What is it? What's wrong?"

Brian briefly recoiled at the sound of her voice, like he hadn't realized she was in the room until then. "Oh God, Laura," he whispered, grabbing her by the arms and pulling her in against him. "Oh God, it was horrible. It was horrible."

A flash of surprise crossed his face when he saw Sam standing there, making Sam feel even more conspicuous and awkward.

"What was?" Laura asked. "Calm down. What's wrong?"

Brian fought hard to get his breathing under control, although the results were mixed, at best. "I drove past it. The cathedral. I know, I know I shouldn't have, but I drove past it, just to see, you know? And, well, I was looking at it—it's crazy—and I was driving, and I only had my eyes off the road for a second..."

Sam took a step closer, feeling his stomach bunch into a knot. "What happened?"

"I ran a red light," Brian whispered.

Laura slapped him on the arm. "Jesus! Is that it? I thought you were going to say you'd run over a kid or something. You ran a stop light? Big deal."

The rictus of horror on Brian's face suggested that yes, actually, it was a big deal. "They saw me," he whispered. "The dog things. They saw me, and... and... they chased me. I floored it, but they kept coming, and coming, and I didn't know what to do, or where to go."

Shit.

Sam moved to the window. The apartment was first floor, ground level, and looked out onto a parking lot. A bright red muscle car had been abandoned across two bays, but there was no sign of anything moving near it.

"Did you lose it?" Sam asked.

"I... I think so."

"Don't think, *know*, Brian," Sam said, and the authority of his voice caught him off guard. "Did you lose it or didn't you? Is that thing coming here?"

"Here?" Laura gasped. "No. Why would it be coming here? Brian? Did you lose it?"

Brian gulped down a steadying breath. The color was coming back to his cheeks a little now, and his eyes weren't quite so frantic. "Yes. I'm pretty... I'm *sure* I did. The roads were clear. There wasn't a lot of traffic. Once I floored it out of there, there's no way it could've kept up. It's gone, trust—"

The rest of Brian's sentence was drowned out by a scream. It was loud, high-pitched, and over far too quickly.

Sam's guts twisted sickeningly.

Corey!

CHAPTER TWENTY-SIX

SAM DIDN'T THINK. There was no time for that. His body moved instinctively, vaulting him over the couch, his mug tumbling from his hand, coffee and all. He raced out into the hall and hit Corey's bedroom door with a flying charge that splintered it off the latch and threw it wide open.

The first thing he saw was Corey sitting up at the top end of his bed, his knees drawn up to his chest, his forearm jammed into his mouth to stop himself screaming any more.

The second thing he saw was the monster. It lurked just outside the window, its eyes like two hot coals burning in a bed of black embers, its breath fogging the glass. It twitched violently when Laura's voice screamed from the hall.

"Corey? Sam? What's happening?"

"Shh. Shut up," Sam hissed.

"Don't you tell me to—" Laura's voice snagged in her throat as she entered the room and saw the thing at the window. "Jesus. What is that? Is that one of those things from the TV?" She beckoned to her son. "Corey! Corey, come here, honey!"

Corey began to move. The eyes of the monster outside

narrowed and it drew back, preparing to leap. Sam urgently raised a hand. "Corey, stop. Wait!" he hissed.

The boy froze, his body still heaving with silent sobs. The Magma-Mutt relaxed a little, and Sam kept his hand raised, urging Corey to stay still.

"OK, nobody move," he whispered. He heard Brian stifle a gasp as he looked in through the open door. The Magma-Mutt's eyes narrowed further. "Brian, wait out in the hall," Sam hissed. "Don't let it see you."

The floorboards *creaked* as Brian backtracked out of the room. At the same time, Sam crept toward the window, making as few movements as possible. He could hear the monster breathing through the glass as he caught the corner of Corey's *Spongebob Squarepants* curtains and carefully pulled them closed.

Turning, he put a finger to his lips and silently motioned for Laura to get Corey. The boy wrapped his arms tightly around his mom as she picked him up from the bed and tiptoed toward the door. Sam shuffled away from the window, watching it closely. There was a thin gap where the curtains hadn't quite met, and he got the impression of movement through there.

At first, he thought the Magma-Mutt was preparing to come through, but when the glass failed to shatter and the monster failed to appear, he realized it was something worse.

Returning to the window, Sam pulled the curtains aside. He could see Brian's car out there in the parking lot, but the monster was nowhere to be seen.

Sam's pulse quickened. He spun to the door and shouted in panic. "Get down!" just as a different window pane came crashing into the house, and he heard his son scream for a second time.

Frantically, he searched for something he could use as a weapon, but everything at hand was either plush or plastic.

His eyes fell on the bedside lamp and he ripped its cable from the wall before launching himself out into the hallway.

What he saw there surprised him. The tiger-sized fire-dog was the biggest shock, of course. The glimpses he'd had of them up until now had been horrifying, but there was nothing quite like seeing one up close to make the blood run cold.

It was easy to see why the press had dubbed them 'Magma-Mutts.' This one's flesh was black and rock-like, with fiery seams of orange visible through a series of irregular cracks in its hide. Add in the burning eyes and the myriad of pointy bits, and you had a hound right from the depths of Hell itself.

And it was standing right there in the hall.

The most surprising thing was that Brian was standing in front of Corey and Laura, one hand held out as if to hold the monster back, the other stretching back protectively like he could somehow shield them with his body.

Sam hadn't expected that. He wasn't sure why, exactly. Maybe he'd hoped Brian would be revealed as a sniveling coward, and Laura would never want to see him again. But, no. He wasn't running from the thing, trying to hide, or throwing himself around in pitiful sobs. He was standing up to it. Standing up for *them*. Sam wasn't sure whether to be pleased or disappointed.

He'd decide later. Right now, he had to do something about the monster in the hallway, which was dropping back onto its haunches, preparing to leap. It might have been coming for Brian, but Corey and Laura were at risk, too, and Sam couldn't just stand back.

He threw himself onto the Magma-Mutt's broad back and looped the lamp's cable over its head and across its throat. His plan—which was a generous way of describing it—had been to throttle it from behind, strangling it with the cable until it passed out.

Sadly, he hadn't planned for the heat. His pants caught fire immediately. Screaming, he released his grip on the cable, then was sent flying through the air when the Magma-Mutt bucked its rear end. He landed on the floor in front of Brian, slapped in frantic, wide-eyed terror at his crotch until it stopped smoking, then shuffled back on his hands.

OK, so that didn't work.

"What do we do?" Laura sobbed. She had Corey clutched against her, one hand on the back of his head as she pulled him in close. "Brian, what do we do?"

Sam tried not to take that to heart. On the face of it, Brian definitely looked the more capable of them both, and she'd just watched Sam inadvertently set his own testicles on fire, so her lack of faith in him was understandable.

It stung, though. Sure, not as much as his balls did, but it still stung.

"It's me it wants," Brian said, his voice hoarse. "Sam, you OK down there?"

"Fine," Sam replied.

"I'm going to need you to get Laura and Corey out of here," Brian said.

Sam felt that twist like a knife. How dare he? How *dare he*? They weren't Brian's to protect, they were *his*. His son, his wife.

OK, ex-wife, but the point still stood.

"No. Get clear," Sam instructed, standing. He planted his feet and squared his shoulders in a pose that would've made Randy proud. "Laura, get Corey out of here. Brian, too. I'll deal with this thing."

Had the situation not been so dire, Laura would've laughed. "You?" she said, more witheringly than she'd probably intended. The high-pitched inflection in her voice drew a guttural growl from the Magma-Mutt. "What are you going to do?"

"Trust me," said Sam. "I'm going to deal with this."

"OK, but how?" Laura persisted.

Sam opened his mouth to reply, then closed it again.

Shit. How *was* he going to deal with this thing? Maybe he should've left it to Brian, after all. If it had eaten him, that would've solved a lot of problems.

Randy's voice came to him, as if from a dream.

Confidence is a superpower.

He'd dismissed it as nonsense at the time—because it was —but Sam didn't exactly have a lot of other options left at this stage. And who knew, maybe there was something in it?

Drawing himself up to his full height, Sam wagged a finger at the Magma-Mutt and spoke in his most commanding voice. "Sit!"

The monster cocked its head a little.

"Sam, what the hell are you doing?" Laura hissed.

"Trust me," Sam replied. He gave the Magma-Mutt his most reproachful look. "You heard me. *Sit!*"

The monster lunged, teeth bared, claws swiping. Sam yelped and staggered back into Brian, the heat from the Magma-Mutt's paw prickling the skin of his face.

"Shit, no, that didn't work. Run!" he cried, shoving Brian and sending everyone staggering along the narrow hallway.

The door to the kitchen was dead ahead, standing open. Everyone bundled through as the Magma-Mutt readied itself for another lunge. Brian grabbed a couple of large knives from a wooden block.

"Sam. Here."

Sam took the offered knife. He managed an awkward, "Thanks," before the monster appeared in the doorway, the smell of sulfur swirling around the room.

"Laura, get in the corner by the window," Sam urged. "Brian, help them get it open. Get out. Keep them safe."

"What? No, Sam. This is my fault. It's my problem," Brian

said. He had grabbed another knife and held one in each hand, blade down, ready to start stabbing.

Sam shook his head. He wanted to believe that. He wanted to be able to shift the blame onto Brian, but that would have been a lie.

"No. It's mine. I should've done something. It's my fault this thing's here. It's my fault they're everywhere."

He raised the knife. "But I'm going to stop it. I'm going to—"

The next few words were knocked out of him by the Magma-Mutt landing on top of him and slamming him to the ground. All four human occupants of the kitchen screamed, but Sam narrowly took the prizes for both volume and pitch.

The thing's two front paws were on his chest, its immense weight pressing down on him, its heat suffocating him like a blanket. He stabbed frantically at its side, the blade *chinking* off its rock-like hide a few times, before finally finding a crack.

The Magma-Mutt roared. Pained. Angry. Sizzling saliva rained down on Sam's face. Its breath was like a blast furnace that dried out his eyeballs and stole all his breath.

Sam dragged the knife along the line of the crack and the hellhound twisted in pain. He got the impression of movement, then heard a *shnick* and a triumphant cry from Brian as another blade was buried in the monster up to the hilt.

More roaring. More twisting. Sam was able to scramble out from beneath the monster as it twisted its head and pawed at the knife handles.

The doorway was clear. Laura saw it before Sam did and made a dash with Corey, dodging past the thrashing Magma-Mutt and out into the hallway. She raced along it to the front door, then out into the apartment's communal lobby beyond.

"Sam, come on, let's go!" Brian hissed, beckoning Sam over to the kitchen door.

With a final glance at the beast, Sam ran to the door. He had barely made it out into the hall when the door slammed behind him, trapping Brian inside.

"Brian? Brian, what the hell are you doing?" Sam demanded. He pushed down on the handle, but Brian had already wedged it closed. "Brian!"

"It's me it wants," Brian said, his voice cracking around the edges. "Get Laura and Corey out of here. Tell them... Tell them I..."

"Don't be an idiot, Brian!" Sam shouted, banging a fist on the wood. He didn't really want to hear the rest of that sentence, but—damn it—he could see why Laura liked the guy. "Get out of there before—"

A roar from the Magma-Mutt drowned him out. He heard Brian scream—more battle-cry than panicky squeal, but there was definitely an element of both in there.

The idiot! He was going to get himself killed.

As if to confirm this concern, Brian's voice came as a hiss from the other side of the door. "Oh shiiiit!"

The shape in Sam's head flicked, just once. From beyond the door there came a thunderous crash, the sound of something heavy being hit by something heavier, then silence.

Sam held his breath, and the whole world seemed to join in.

After a while, he tapped on the door. "Brian?" he said.

"What was that?" demanded Laura, appearing around the corner with Corey in her arms. "What happened? Where's Brian?"

"He's, uh. He's in..."

"I'm OK," Brian said. There was a note of surprise in his voice, like he wasn't quite sure how or why this was the case, and a note of relief that suggested he was pretty damn happy about it.

From the other side of the door came the sound of a chair

being moved aside. Sam gestured for Laura to get back as the door creaked open, but there was no need. The Magma-Mutt lay dead on the floor.

More than dead, actually. Squashed. It was mangled like a swatted fly, its limbs all pointing in different directions, its innards spread out around it on the lino floor.

"What the hell did you do to it?" Laura asked, her sudden appearance right behind Sam making him jump in fright.

Brian shook his head. This went on for quite some time. "Um, no," he eventually said. "It wasn't me. I think... I think..."

He turned to them. There was a faintly confused look on his face, like he was trying to remember something he'd forgotten. "I think it was a hippo. Or, like, I don't know. An elephant, maybe?"

Laura stared at him, waiting for the punchline.

Sam's hand went to his jacket pocket. Empty.

Brian pointed to the kitchen table. All four legs had been broken.

"It, uh, it came from under there," Brian said. "It just sort of appeared, flattened the shit out of that thing, then..."

"Then what?" asked Laura.

"It, uh... It... uh..." Brian took a deep breath. "It ate itself."

Laura blinked. "Are you high? Is that what's happening right now?"

"No. God, no, I swear," said Brian. "It just sort of, I don't know. It ate itself. It opened its mouth, stuck one of its back feet in, and then just swallowed itself and vanished."

He frowned. "Jesus. *Am I* high?" He waved a hand in front of his face. "I don't think so, but... I mean... *Wow*, that was some trippy shit."

Brian picked his way through the mess of guts and hugged Laura. Sam looked away as Brian kissed her on the head and ran his hand down the back of Corey's head. "You guys OK?"

"We're fine," said Laura. She jiggled Corey. "Right, sport?"

Corey looked around, and Sam saw his red-ringed eyes and the parallel lines of snot on his top lip. The boy's eyes bulged as he saw the splattered monster, and Laura quickly angled him so it wasn't quite so in his face.

"Is it dead?" he asked in an anxious whisper.

"It is," Brian confirmed.

Corey's eyebrows raised in wonder. "Did you kill it?"

Sam stepped in. "What? No, he didn't do..." he began, but he stopped himself going any further. "Uh, yeah, buddy. Yeah, he did," Sam confirmed. "Brian's going to keep you safe, OK? He stopped that thing, and if any of them come back, he'll stop that, too."

"But they won't come back," said Laura. "Will they?"

She tightened her grip on their son when Sam shot her a look. "What are we going to do?" she mouthed.

"Is it coming back? Is it going to get me?" Corey whimpered.

Sam put a hand on the boy's back. "No. No, they're not going to get you, Corey. You don't have to worry, OK? You don't have to be afraid. We'll keep you safe."

Corey nodded, but it was uncertain, doubting. "What about everyone else?"

Sam blinked, confused. "Huh?"

"Everyone else. All the other people. Do they have someone to keep them safe, too?"

The look on his face was so concerned, so sincere, that Sam felt his throat tighten and his eyes prickle. Something stirred inside him, only not in his head this time, but in his chest.

"Let's not worry about anyone else right now, OK, sweetheart?" said Laura.

"But we have to look out for each other. Right, Dad?"

Sam stared blankly back at him. Not because he didn't know how to respond, but because he did. For the first time in a long time, he knew *exactly* what he should do.

"That's right, buddy," Sam said. He leaned in and kissed him on the top of his head. "Trust me. Everyone's going to be fine."

"You promise?"

Sam nodded. "Promise."

He turned to his ex-wife, suddenly all business. "Take Brian, get him to drive you out of town. Don't come back until all this is over."

"Over?" said Laura. "Will it ever be over? If the Justice Platoon is..." She flicked her eyes to Corey and lowered her voice. "...*gone*, then who's going to stop this guy?"

Sam exhaled slowly. "You wouldn't believe me if I told you," he said. He put his arms around Laura and Corey, and she didn't push him away.

"Sam?" she said, once he'd stepped back. Concern lined the creases of her face. "What's going on?"

"Long story," Sam said. "I have to go for a while."

"Go? Go where?" asked Laura. Her concern deepened, and Sam felt a pang of guilt that this made him happy. She cared. Jesus, she actually still cared.

"I'll explain later," Sam promised her. He ruffled Corey's hair, then turned to Brian. After just a moment's pause, he thrust out a hand for Brian to shake. "Look after them," he said.

"Uh, yeah. I mean, of course," said Brian. He looked at Laura, but she could only shrug in response. "Sure thing, Sam."

Sam nodded. He took a look around the kitchen and hallway, then brushed his fingertips lightly against the doorframe.

"OK, then," he said, in a way that suggested it was some sort of big announcement.

He'd barely made it halfway to the front door when he stopped and looked back. "Uh, I don't suppose I could borrow some money for a cab?"

CHAPTER TWENTY-SEVEN

ANNA STOOD IN HER HALLWAY, one hand leaning against the door, the other clutching an almost-empty glass of red wine.

"That was quick," she said.

"Uh, yeah. Yeah," said Sam. "I didn't know if you'd be here or..."

He glanced back over his shoulder, fearing he'd been followed. Black smoke hung over the city, blocking most of the early afternoon sun. A soundtrack of gunshots, screams, screeching brakes and monstrous growls came at him from every direction.

The cab ride here had been an eventful one. Police cars and ambulances had come hurtling past. Pedestrians had thrown themselves into the street, so desperate to escape whatever was chasing them that they didn't notice the traffic.

The taxi driver—a Russian—had seemed largely unperturbed by most of it, like this sort of thing happened every day. He'd helped pass the time by singing an old Russian song about potatoes, Sam thought, although the accent, and the fact that most of the words were in Russian, made it hard to be certain. Sam had wondered if the simple fact of being a cab driver in Cityopolis meant you became blasé about anything involving supervillains, world-troubling despots, or just bad guys in general. There was always some superhero around to help out, after all.

Or *usually* always.

A pile-up had clogged the road a few blocks away, and Sam had run the rest of the way to Anna's apartment. Her front door opened directly onto the street, and now that he was standing there, he wasn't quite sure what to say.

"What's the matter?" Anna asked, picking up on his uncertainty. "What happened?"

"My son. They... one of those dog things. It came for my son."

"What? Jesus!"

"Well, not for *him*, exactly, but... yeah." He blushed slightly, embarrassed by what he was about to say before he had said it. "I told him not be afraid. That someone was going to take care of it."

She crossed her fingers and pulled an exaggerated 'here's hoping!' face, then took a sip of her wine. When she realized that Sam was still staring at her, she snorted into the glass.

"Wait. Who? Us?"

Sam fumbled with the words. "Well, uh, I mean, I thought..."

Anna's smile seemed to push away the darkness. "I'm kidding. Relax. And sure. I'm in," she said.

"You are?! I mean... You are?"

With a nod, Anna drained the rest of her glass. "Fuck it. Why not? Not like I've got anything else going on."

"Uh, great! But should you be doing that?" Sam asked, pointing to the empty glass. "Doesn't it dampen your powers?"

"I knew you'd be coming back," Anna told him. "It's non-alcoholic."

She pulled a face that suggested she was disgusted by both the wine and herself, then stepped out onto the street and pulled the door closed behind her. "What about Randy?" she asked.

"Randy?" said Sam, raising an eyebrow.

"He still has a full charge in his suit. We should go find him."

"No need," said Sam. He looked back over his shoulder a little and raised his voice. "I can see you, Randy."

There was some shuffling and scuffing from over by a parked car. Sam rolled his eyes. "I can still see you."

"Impossible!" Randy spat. "I'm completely hidden."

"I can see your reflection in the car behind," Sam said.

There was some more scuffing, followed by a quietly hissed, "Damn it."

Randy stood up. "OK, since you asked so nicely," he growled, narrowing his eyes to slits. "I'm in."

Sam smiled. He couldn't help himself, despite the fact they were all, almost certainly, going to die.

"Sidekicks," he said. "Let's kick some side."

He paused dramatically for a moment, then sighed and shook his head.

"No. That still sounds fucking ridiculous," he said. "Let's just go beat this bad guy."

❧

"No," Chuck said. "Sorry."

"What do you mean? Why not?" asked Sam.

"Because you destroyed it," Chuck pointed out. "Because there's barely enough of the damn thing left to make a swimsuit out of, never mind a superhero costume."

Damn. Sam hadn't thought of that. Savior's heat had burned up most of the depowered outfit, and much of what was left had split and torn while Sam was removing it. He looked down at his crumpled shirt and pants. He couldn't wear those, but the training shorts and t-shirt, maybe? It wasn't ideal, but if he could make a mask it might afford him some sort of anonymity, if not protection.

"What about my suit? Is it OK?" Anna asked.

Chuck nodded. "Yeah. It isn't fully charged, but it's most of the way there."

Anna winked at Sam. "Well, looks like one of us is going to live through this."

"What about mine?" asked Randy.

Everyone turned to look at him. "You're wearing yours, Randy."

Randy looked down and reacted in surprise to his red costume.

"Oh. Yeah. Awesome!"

"I can't go like this," Sam protested. "What about the shorts and t-shirt I had?"

Mari rolled forward a little as she answered. "They're in the wash."

Sam looked from the robot to Chuck and back again. "Wait, what? A multi-billion dollar government program and I have one pair of shorts?"

"Like I said, budget cutbacks," Chuck explained. He stood up from the desk he'd been leaning against. "Look, I really appreciate you guys coming back. Things are getting crazy out there. There was a call to evacuate the city, but those damn dog monsters are blocking all the roads. The ones who aren't out hunting folks down, at least."

"What about Savior?" Anna asked. "Has he shown his face again?"

Chuck shook his head. "Not yet. But he sent a message to the governor. Told her that if every prisoner currently held in the state penitentiary isn't executed by midnight, he'll do it personally."

"He's tough on crime, tough on the causes of crime," said Randy.

"And he's a fucking psychopath," Anna added.

"OK, and that, yes," Randy agreed. He punched a fist into the opposite palm. "So, let's go bring him down!"

Chuck breathed out slowly. "I mean, don't get me wrong —I love this newfound enthusiasm, Sam. I'm all for it. But what do you plan to do, exactly? Even with the Magma-Mutts off, you know..."

"Killing people," said Anna.

Chuck winced. "Yeah. Even with that, Memetzo's cathedral is surrounded by a ring of fire. Anyone who tries to get near the damn thing is going up in flames. The suits might get you close, but it's going to deplete the charge pretty rapidly." He looked Sam up and down. "And I don't think a nylon shirt is going to fare much better."

"It's a polyester-cotton mix," Sam said, although he had no idea why he was choosing to argue that particular point. "But it's fine. He'll let us in."

All eyes turned to him.

"He will?" asked Anna. "What makes you so sure?"

"Trust me. He'll let us in," was all Sam had to say on the matter.

Mari interrupted before anyone could press the matter. Digital concern flickered across her features. "Pattern detected," she announced.

Sam darted his eyes between the robot and Chuck. "What does that mean?"

"No idea. What are you talking about, Mari?" he asked.

A map of the city appeared floating in the air in front of the blank screen that had been her face. It showed several dozen red dots. They were loosely scattered, but if Sam had to choose, he'd say they were more densely gathered around the southwest of the city.

"What are they?" Anna asked.

"The entities we are calling 'Magma-Mutts,'" Mari said. "At first, I thought they were moving randomly through the streets, however, I have since detected a pattern, and can project their eventual destination with a ninety-eight-point-nine-six degree of accuracy."

Chuck watched her expectantly. "So? Where are they going?"

The red dots converged on a spot near the city limits, beyond even the industrial estates that ringed that part of the suburbs.

"What's that?" Anna asked. "What's out there?"

"The Cityopolis Asylum," Sam gasped. "He's sending the dogs to wipe out the inmates."

"Tough on insanity, tough on the causes of insanity," Randy snarled.

"There are a hundred people in there," Sam said.

"One hundred and thirty-seven," Mari corrected. "Not including staff."

"So?" said Randy. "You said yourself, they're only going to escape, anyway."

"I didn't mean they should all be eaten by dog-monsters!" Sam yelped. "They're still people! We can't just let those things kill them. We have to do something."

"Doc Mighty, help!" Anna cried, in her best damsel-in-distress voice. She waited for a few moments, gazing up at the ceiling, then shrugged. "Fuck. Worth a try." She blew out her cheeks. "Looks like it's up to us."

"You know what'll happen if we stop his dogs, don't you?" said Sam.

"He'll give up quietly," said Randy.

"Well, no—"

"He'll send more dogs," Randy guessed. "Only bigger. Or bears. He'll send bears."

"No, not... I mean, I don't think..." Sam stammered.

"He'll come himself," said Anna. "Right?"

Sam nodded. "It's got to be a possibility."

"Yes!" cheered Randy, tightening his hands into fists. "It's like the saying goes, 'Kill some fire-dogs and a man with one stone!'"

"That's not the saying," Anna pointed out.

"It's kind of the saying," Randy countered. "It's like the saying."

Anna buried her face in her hands and groaned. "God, we're all going to die," she muttered, then she straightened, took a deep breath, and nodded her acceptance of this fact. "OK," she said. "I guess we'd better suit up."

Sam looked down at himself. "Easy for you to say. What am I supposed to wear?"

There was a *ding* and an image of a lightbulb illuminated on Mari's face-screen. "You know," she announced. "I think I may be able to help with that."

"Well, alright," said Anna. "But, bigger problem, the asylum is all the way across town, and I refuse to get the bus. Is there enough money left in the budget to stretch to a cab?"

A smile crept across Chuck's face. "Oh, I think we can do a little better than that."

CHAPTER TWENTY-EIGHT

PTCHOW!

A bullet ricocheted off the hide of one of the Magma-Mutts. A hundred feet behind it, a car window shattered and an alarm raised its voice in complaint.

"Shit! This isn't working!" barked Larry. He was one of two armed—if largely incompetent—guards who patrolled the asylum's grounds. Their job was primarily to watch for escaping inmates and, where necessary, to repeatedly shoot them in the head and torso until they were dead.

Sure, sometimes the occasional group of over-eager henchmen would try to break in, and there was that Egyptian Vengeance Demon that one time who came looking for Orangu-titan, but by and large it was people breaking *out* they had to worry about.

Not today.

The monsters had formed a tightening circle around the asylum grounds, and the wrought iron fence was beginning to buckle and bend from the heat that radiated from their blackened bodies. The tranq darts hadn't worked, and bullets were proving to be even less effective.

Larry was sure there was an old WWII hand-grenade paperweight on one of the doctors' desks, but even in the unlikely circumstances that it was live, there were too many of the monsters to blow up with a single eighty-year-old explosive.

He snapped off another couple of shots. *Ptchow-ptchew.* Both bullets ricocheted away, and the same car as before lost its windshield and gained a new air vent in the door.

"Wait!" yelped Glen, another guard. "That's my car!"

A voice crackled over Larry's radio, letting him know for the fourth time that police backup was on the way, and was only a minute out.

"It was a minute out five fucking minutes ago!" Larry spat back, but as he hadn't pressed the button, nobody but Glen heard him.

Part of the fence tore inward, *squealing* like the world's bluntest fork on the world's largest plate. The space where that part of the fence had been was filled by a Magma-Mutt head, its eyes blazing fire and hatred. Larry and Glen ducked lower behind the fountain they'd been using for cover, trying not to let the monster see them.

Too late. With a furious roar, it forced itself forward, buckling that section of fence with its sheer strength and weight. The metal glowed red-hot where it touched the monster, and both Larry and Glen knew, in that moment, that their company-issued snub-nosed pistols were going to do them no good whatsoever, except in the increasingly likely event that they decided to kill themselves rather than face their fates.

"How many of them do you make?" Larry asked.

"I been counting," said Glen. "I make eighteen."

Larry muttered something quite rude below his breath. "OK. Eighteen? Jesus. OK. I do have one bit of good news, though."

"What's that?" Glen asked.

"I can run a whole lot faster than you can."

Glen started to chuckle, then caught the deadly serious expression on Larry's face.

"You son of a bitch," he hissed.

"Survival of the fittest. And fastest," Larry said.

"You absolute *son of a bitch*! You're just going to leave me?"

Larry shook his head. "What? No! Of course not, Glen," he said. "I'm just going to run as fast as I can, and if you decide to fall behind, then that's on you."

"You son of a—"

Their argument was cut short by the sudden and unexpected arrival of a *Hot Wheels* armored car, and the splattering of Magma-Mutt guts as two of the vehicle's many caterpillar tracks plowed through several of them, tearing them to pieces.

It wasn't really a *Hot Wheels* car, of course, but it had come from the same school of design. It straddled the line between 'impossibly sleek' and 'implausibly clunky', with a rounded nose, a spoiler the size of a hang-glider, and so many exhausts its back end could pass for a pipe organ.

Its rear caterpillar tracks spun, raising the tank's nose into the air, then dropping it down on a Magma-Mutt that had moved to attack. The mutt exploded like a balloon filled with shaving foam, spraying soggy bits in all directions.

Larry watched on in amazement, his hand still gripping his gun. Behind him, Glen quietly backed away, neatly demonstrating that, while he may not have been the faster of the two, he was almost certainly the wiser.

A hatch on the roof of the tank opened. A woman with flame-red hair and a green mask sprang up like a Jack in the Box. Thrusting her arms above her head, she cheered: "Wooooh! Now *that* is a fucking Batmobile!"

She yelped in panic and ducked as another of the Magma-

Mutts bounded onto the vehicle with one twitch of its hind legs. A heavyset man in a dark suit and sunglasses rose up, a shotgun in his hands. He fired twice into the monster's open mouth, and its head became nothing but stone chips.

"Who the hell are these guys?" Larry wondered.

It took him a moment to realize Glen was nowhere to be seen. "Son of a bitch," he muttered, then a flurry of movement from over by the tank-thing caught his attention.

The woman in the green suit had clambered out and was now standing on the ground beside the vehicle, one arm leaning on a caterpillar track.

A tall, skinny man dressed all in red jumped down beside her, a small cape fluttering briefly as he fell. He landed in what Larry felt was an overly-dramatic way, and which must surely have been murder on his knees.

Another Magma-Mutt approached. The gunman in the hatch fired a couple of warning shots at it, and it drew back.

A fourth figure appeared. He clambered awkwardly out of the hatch, took a few tentative steps toward the point where the top of the tank became the side, then carefully sat and dangled his legs over the side, before cautiously sliding to the ground.

Larry barely noticed the fourth person's clumsy movements, transfixed, as he was, by the costume the guy wore.

It was mostly blue spandex, and was either a couple of sizes too small, or had recently shrunk in the wash. The pants stopped several inches above his ankles, leaving a gap of bare skin between where the leggings ended and the bright red boots began.

There was a similar gap around his midsection, and while Larry knew spandex was designed to be clingy, he didn't think it was ever intended to be quite *that* clingy. It accentuated the beginnings of the guy's middle-aged paunch, and cut into him in a range of unflattering ways. The red and yellow 'KR' emblem on his chest mercifully concealed the lines of his unimpressive chest, just as a red hood concealed the top sixty percent of his face. Despite the lower half of his face being uncovered, it was almost exactly the same shade of red as the top part.

"I can't believe I'm wearing this," he said.

"It looks great!" said the woman in green. "Well, I mean, no, not *great*, exactly. It's a long way from great, but—"

"Guys! We have company," growled the man in red, staring directly at Larry. "Superhero poses. Go!"

The man in red lowered himself into a half-squat, holding his hands out like a martial artist preparing to strike.

The woman in green looked unsure at first, then lowered herself into a pose that was similar in style, if not in enthusiasm.

"Oh, come on, is this reall...?" the guy in the blue spandex muttered. He sighed. "Fine, fine, OK," then turned side-on and lowered himself onto one knee. Clearly unsure of what to do with this hands, he tried a few different alternatives, then settled for holding them together, with the forefingers stretched out like a gun.

"What are you meant to be? Charlie's Angels?" asked the woman.

"Do it properly," growled the man in red.

"I am... what do you mean 'do it properly'? I have no idea what I'm supposed to be doing!"

"Fine. Then can this be it? Are we done? My legs are already killing me here," said the woman.

"Butterfly King welcomes the pain," the red-clad man snarled. He lowered himself deeper into his squat and let out just a hint of a high-pitched *eep*. "Oh... yeah."

Up in the tank, the man with the shotgun fired again. "Do you think we might get a move on?" he barked.

Sam stood up, adjusted his ill-fitting pants, then looked down at them in dismay. "Great. Now they've gone all baggy at the knees," he said, before looking up at Chuck. This made his hood go squint so he could only see out through one eyehole. He adjusted it as he spoke. "You OK with the Magma-Mutts?"

Chuck blasted another of the monsters that had tried clambering up onto the tank behind him. Its head, neck, and part of its chest exploded.

"Yeah. I got 'em. Go do what we're here for."

Sam nodded. "Right. Yeah. Right. Uh... let's go."

He led Anna and Randy through the wrecked fence, being careful not to get caught by any of the red-hot parts. The guard, Larry, had his gun lowered, but the way his grip tightened on it suggested he might yet start firing.

"Have no fear, uh, good citizen," Sam said, deepening his voice. "We're here to help. I'm..." He swore creatively inside his head. "...Kid Random."

"*Kid* Random?" said Larry. He pushed back his guard's cap with the barrel of his gun and looked Sam up and down. "Why *Kid* Random? Aren't you, like, forty?"

"*Forty?* No, I'm not forty!" Sam spluttered. He regained his composure again. "I mean, that's not important right now."

"Allergy Woman," said Anna, giving the guard a half-hearted wave.

"Girl," Randy corrected.

"Woman."

"It's Girl. Allergy *Girl*," Randy insisted.

Anna kept smiling at the guard as she *thumped* Randy hard on the hip. He gave a little grunt, then bit his lip for a moment. Behind them, Chuck opened fire with his shotgun.

"Butterfly King didn't even feel that punch," Randy whispered.

"Bullshit," Anna retorted.

Larry frowned. "What? *Butterfly* King?"

"Please. No autographs," said Randy. "Now's not the time."

Sam gave it a second for everyone to shut up, then continued. "We think Savior is coming here. You know, the guy off the TV?"

"He's coming *here?*" Larry spluttered. "Oh, God. Oh *shit!*"

"Don't worry, citizen, we'll protect you," Sam assured him. "That's why we're here. But we need access to the asylum. Can you help us with that?"

"Uh, yeah. Yeah! I can get you inside, no problem," said Larry. He scanned the skies. "You mean it? You can really keep me safe?"

Sam put a hand on his shoulder. "You have my word," he said, then Larry screamed as a Magma-Mutt pounced on him, and his guts exploded out through his back.

"Jesus *Christ!*" Anna yelped.

Sam stared in horror, his hand still raised where it had been resting on Larry's shoulder. For what felt like quite a long while, the only sound was that of tearing flesh and spurting blood, then two shotgun blasts rang out, and the Magma-Mutt fell on top of the mush that bad been Larry.

"Sorry," called Chuck. "Missed that one."

"It's fine," said Anna. "I'm sure no one noticed."

"How are we supposed to get inside now?" Sam groaned.

Randy raised his cape so it was covering half of his face. "Leave it to me," he said, in a dramatic whisper. Holding Sam's gaze, be began to back away mysteriously.

"Uh, it's that way," said Sam, jabbing a thumb over his shoulder.

Randy continued creeping backward, but turned in a wide arc so he was now backing in the direction of the asylum.

Sam and Anna exchanged looks of exasperation.

"Yeah, tell you what, we'll just meet you there," said Anna. They both marched past Randy, and he quickly turned in the right direction as he hurried to catch them up.

The front door was made of heavy wood, with even heavier iron straps and rivets that helped it fit neatly into the overall Gothic feel of the building. The only obvious anomaly was the shiny black glass screen fixed to the wall beside it.

"Biometric security," Randy growled. "Bypassing it won't be easy. Unless... wait. Did anyone bring that guard's thumb?"

"*Of course* we didn't bring his thumb!" Anna hissed. "Why would we bring his thumb?"

"For the biometric security," said Randy, like this should really have been obvious. "It's fine, doesn't matter. I can deal with it."

He dropped to his haunches and breathed on the pad. "Bingo," he said. He held a hand out to Anna, like a surgeon reaching for a tool. "Sticky tape."

Anna frowned. "What?"

"Sticky tape," Randy repeated. "Quickly."

"I don't have any sticky tape," Anna said.

"How can you be sure? You didn't even check," Randy growled, turning to look at her.

"I don't need to check. I know with one hundred percent certainty that I'm not carrying any sticky tape."

Randy tutted. "Fine. We'll just have to cut this thumb off." He held a hand out to Anna. "Scissors."

"I'm also not carrying scissors," Anna said.

"Have we checked if the door is even...?" Sam began, trying the handle. "It's open," he said. "They left it unlocked. Jesus, and they wonder why everyone keeps escaping."

The door *creaked* inward, revealing a dark and oppressive

entrance hall with a high ceiling, an abundance of shadow, and several grotesque gargoyles leering down from on high. A reception desk stood at the far end, bathed in a beam of light from one of the barred windows high up on the front wall. A mug of coffee sat on it, steaming gently, but there was nothing else to indicate the room had ever been occupied.

Sam tentatively led the others inside. Anna stuck close behind him, while Randy attempted—with limited success— to melt into one of the many available shadows.

"Hello?" Sam called.

Hello-hello-hello, said a low, whispering echo.

"Anyone here?"

Anyone here-here-here?

Fighting the urge to run screaming from the place, Sam shuffled on across the faded carpet. Its design was an endless spiral of twisting shapes in various shades of green. Had the inmates not been crazy when they arrived here, the carpet could well have been the thing that pushed them over the edge.

"Are we too late?" Anna whispered.

Too late-late-late.

Sam shook his head. "If Savior had already been here, the place wouldn't still be standing."

Be standing-standing-standing.

Anna tutted. "That is *really* fucking annoying."

...

All three sets of eyes crept to the ceiling, as if they might see the echo trapped there somewhere.

"Hello?" Sam called.

Hello—

Sam breathed a sigh of relief.

—yourself!

The echo became a hyena-like giggle that reverberated around the room. Shapes detached themselves from the shadows and emerged from behind pillars. Some whispered and mumbled, talking to themselves more than anyone else. Others sniggered, spat, and hissed. A few growled and grunted like animals.

One *squelched*, but the less said about him, the better.

"It's just like that phrase," Randy growled. "The inmates have taken over the Cityopolis Asylum!"

Anna nodded slowly. "I'm actually going to give you that one," she said. "It was close enough."

"Well, well, well, who do we have here?" brayed a voice from the darkness, gleefully enunciating every perfect syllable.

A tall man in a velvet jacket and a grinning mask sprang up onto the reception desk. He clutched a hand to his chest and held the other up to the window, basking in the glow of this naturally created spotlight.

His head spun on his shoulders. When it stopped, the face on the mask was contorted with sadness.

"Forsooth! You are not here to stop the show, are you?" he asked. His voice became a dramatic stage whisper. "Because that simply would not do *at all*. It must go on, you know? The show must always go on!"

"God, who's this asshole?" Anna asked.

The Tragedy mask spun, becoming the grinning Comedy version again.

"You wish to know who I am, dear girl? Behold, my name *in lights*!" the man on the desk announced. He thrust a hand up, indicating the wall above his head. "*Opening Knight*!"

Sam, Anna, and Randy regarded the wall in silence for a moment.

"You, uh, you know there's nothing there, right?" said Anna.

Opening Knight looked up. "Yes, there is," he insisted. "It's all lit up. See?"

He reached a finger out to touch something, then quickly pulled it back. "Ouch! Those bulbs are hot!" He spread his fingers wide and waved his hands in front of his face. His voice became an awestruck whisper. "Opening Knight!"

"Yep, he's totally bananas," Anna muttered. "We're in the right place."

His mask spun again, becoming the crying face. He pointed dramatically to the sidekicks. "Now, which of you wishes to audition for the role of my proscenium-arch-nemesis?"

Sam glanced at Anna and Randy, then at the circle of superpowered lunatics around them. "Your what?"

"*Proscenium-arch*-nemesis," said Opening Knight, with a smidgeon less conviction. "It's a theatre term, dear boy. 'Proscenium arch.' It's the frame through which events on stage are viewed by the attendant audience."

Sam nodded. Randy lurked. Anna scowled. "What the fuck does that have to do with anything?" she asked.

Opening Knight placed the back of a hand to his forehead, recoiling in horror at her words. Anna jumped in before he could start overacting again.

"Look, we don't have time for this," Sam said. "You guys are in trouble."

"Because we shook off our shackles?" sneered Opening Knight. "Because we imprisoned our wretched imprisoners, forcing them to suffer the same indignities that we ourselves were made to—"

He choked as his tongue swelled to three times its natural size, his eyes bulging as he clutched at his rapidly-bloating throat.

Anna lowered her hands, then nodded to Sam, indicating he should take over. "Continue."

Sam drew himself up to his full height, which really only made his costume look even more ludicrous. Looking around, he saw faces he knew from back in the day—the Smirker, Coldfingers, Johnny Racist—and several others he didn't recognize at all.

Most of them glowered hatred at him. A few dribbled. Another kept thumping the heel of his hand against his forehead and, unless Sam was very much mistaken, shitting himself. Sam groaned inwardly, but did his best not to show his concerns.

"Someone's coming here to kill you all," Sam told them. "Sorry to be so blunt, but he could be here any minute, so there isn't much time."

There was some general murmuring from the inmates. Opening Knight fell off the desk, still clutching his throat. Anna gave a dismissive wave of a hand and he gasped with relief from his spot on the floor.

"Who?" grunted a heavyset man with a badly scarred face. He'd torn the sleeves off his bright-green prison scrubs to reveal one arm made of smooth, polished wood and another that looked as if it had been hewn from a lump of granite.

"He calls himself Savior," Sam said. "He... He killed the Justice Platoon."

Silence fell. Even the inmates who had been muttering incomprehensibly to themselves stopped their incomprehensible mutterings.

"The Justice Platoon are dead?" asked a woman with piercing yellow eyes and scaly skin. Her hair moved as if alive, weaving and entwining atop her head like lovers at an orgy.

"They are," Sam confirmed.

"All of them?"

"All of them," Sam confirmed.

The woman's hair stopped moving for a moment. "Even Doc Mighty?"

"Especially Doc Mighty," Randy growled.

Sam smiled awkwardly. "Well, I mean, I wouldn't say *especially*. They're all equally as dead as each other."

"Not Su Man Chu?" said Johnny Racist. "I really liked her."

Sam shot Randy a meaningful look. "Yes, Su Man Chu, Doc Mighty, Absorbo, Brown Thunder, Memetzo—they're all dead. And the person who killed them, he's killing other people. Innocent people."

As one, the assembled inmates gave off a general air of indifference.

"And he's going to come here and kill you guys, too," said Anna. "Like, any minute now."

That got their attention. Sam had to shout to make himself heard over the sudden din. "Listen. Listen! We have a plan! We're here to help you guys!"

"Oh yes? And what might that be?" asked a woman whose face hung down like gloopy dollops of mud. Her voice was shrill and piercing, and cut through the racket better than Sam's could.

Sam took a deep breath, glanced at Anna for support, then began. "You're all in here because you've done bad things. You've hurt people. Killed people."

"Ate people," grunted a voice from the crowd.

"Jesus, really? I mean... and that, yes," said Sam. "The world sees you as villains, but someone recently made me realize that people are not black and white. That we are weighed both by the things we do, and the things we don't do. That even the worst of us can become the best of us."

He pointed to the ceiling. "The worst of us is out there. He's killing people all over the city. People whose only crimes are jaywalking, or littering or, God, just being human. He's burning them up from the inside. Or he's having dog monsters tear them apart in their own homes, in front of their families."

A number of the faces in the circle of inmates adopted concerned looks. A few feet shuffled uneasily.

"And he's coming here. The worst of us is coming here," Sam continued. He looked imploringly at the faces around him. "This is your chance. This is your chance to be the *best* of us. This is your chance to help us stand up against Savior. To fight back. You've all threatened Cityopolis in the past. Now we're asking you to help us save it. This is your chance to tip the scales."

He finished there. Anna gave him an encouraging nod and a down-low thumbs up nobody else noticed.

"Fuck that," announced a voice from the crowd.

A rising tide of agreement followed, which quickly became a stampede. Sam, Anna, and Randy bunched tightly together as dozens of clinically insane supervillains raced past them, fighting each other in their rush to pile out through the front doors.

"Exit!" proclaimed Opening Knight from the back of the mob. "Stage right!"

He bowed theatrically, wasted a moment giving them the finger, then slipped out through the front door.

Silence hung in the air for a few moments, broken eventually by the door clacking shut.

"Well, I thought it was a great speech," said Anna, patting Sam on the back. "I mean, if I'd been a mass-murdering superpowered cannibal, I know I'd have stuck around."

A voice crackled in Sam's ear. "Uh, I got a lot of supervillains running past me right now," Chuck said. "A *loooot* of supervillains. Tell me this is part of your plan."

"Yeah, it's... It's, uh..." Sam sighed. "No. No, it isn't part of the plan."

"So... what are you saying?" Chuck asked. "That you just let a whole asylum full of crazy-assed criminals escape?"

Anna touched her own earpiece and shrugged. "They were

probably already going to escape," she said. "At worst we just accelerated the process. On the other hand, maybe we slowed it down by a few seconds by keeping them talking. So, in a way, *go us!*"

"From where I'm standing, looks like they're the ones going," Chuck said.

Randy sighed. "Relax, Chuck. It's a few supervillains. I'll round them up personally when we're done here."

"Oh, that makes me feel *much* better," said Chuck, and Randy was the only one to miss the sarcasm.

"You're welcome."

"I cleared out the Magma-Mutts, best as I can tell," Chuck continued. "Not saying I got them all, but I don't see any more of—"

There was a roar of gunfire that made everyone grimace and clutch their ears.

"No, I tell a lie. Just got another one," said Chuck.

"Any word from Mari?" Sam asked. "Did her searches turn anything up?"

"Not that she's told me," Chuck said.

Anna scraped her top teeth lightly across her bottom lip, frowning. "I know I've seen that helmet somewhere before. She's seriously found nothing?"

"No. Says it looks like it's been deleted from the records or something. She's looking into it," Chuck said.

"Deleted? Why would it be deleted?" Sam wondered.

There was no response from Chuck.

"Chuck? You there?" Sam asked. He tapped his earpiece. "Hellooo?"

"Are you sulking?" Randy demanded. "Is this about the escaped villains? Because I'll go bring them back now, if it'll stop you panicking."

He looked back over his shoulder at the others as he set off walking. "Give me ten minutes, and I'll be—"

"Uh, guys!" Chuck's voice was fast and urgent, barely a hiss through the earpieces.

There was a *BOOM* from outside, and the entrance hall's single large window lit up in red and orange.

Sam and Anna both ducked. Randy stood his ground, fists clenched at his sides, cape billowing in the gust of hot air that blew open the front doors.

There was a whistling sound that started low, then grew louder.

The front of the asylum erupted as something large and heavy tumbled through it, spraying window and wood and chunks of masonry inward. Sam and Anna both grabbed Randy and dived behind the reception desk.

Deadly shards of glass *boinged* as they stabbed into the desktop. Pebbles rattled against the wood like high-velocity hailstones. Anna mouthed a series of expletives, but the din of the destruction drowned out the actual sound.

Eventually, an uneasy stillness returned, broken occasionally by the faint *plinks* made by small pieces of settling debris.

Sam, Anna, and Randy cautiously raised their heads above the edge of the desk. The tank they'd driven here in stood on its nose in the center of the ruined hallway. As they watched, the hatch *creaked* open, and Chuck slithered out. He landed on his shoulder on a pile of rubble, tumbled awkwardly over, then slid to a stop on the floor, grimacing and clutching his ribs.

"In case you haven't worked it out yet," he wheezed. "We have a problem."

CHAPTER TWENTY-NINE

HE DRIFTED in through the hole in the front of the building on a cushion of warm air, sparks igniting in the space around him.

Savior.

The collapsing wall had created swirling clouds of dust. They flashed briefly in his aura of heat, giving him a shimmering orange glow as he descended onto the melting debris.

His burgundy cape swished around him as he alighted with a *clank* that rattled his skull-motif shoulder pads. His eyes looked out through the holes in his helmet, taking in the room around him, before settling on the sidekicks.

"Where are they?" he asked. It wasn't a particularly menacing tone, and anyone listening in could be forgiven for thinking he was looking for his car keys, as opposed to several dozen mass-murdering super-psychos.

"They're, uh, they're gone," said Sam.

"Gone?" said Savior. "How can they be 'gone'?"

Randy punched his hand. "We set them free before you could kill them all. Because murder's a line we just don't cross!" he growled. "Except that one time."

Sparks crackled from Savior's fingers.

"Maybe twice," Randy added.

"You—"

"And all those other times, but they were technically accidents."

Anna shot him a sideways look. "Uh, Ran— Butterfly King?" she said. "Please stop talking."

Savior's conversational tone was rapidly evaporating, leaving his voice with a dark, heavy residue. "You let them go?" he said. "You destroyed my Heat-Hounds, and you *let them go?*"

"Heat-Hounds?" said Anna, unable to help herself. "And I thought 'Magma-Mutts' was bad."

A ball of heat struck Anna right between her artificial nipples. She spent a less than enjoyable few seconds hurtling backward, then slammed against the wall, her body imprinting itself in the plaster.

"Ow. Battle Mode," she said, somewhat belatedly. Her suit transformed around her, and she pulled herself free of the wall.

Randy clenched his fists. "Oh, you've done it now, scumbag," he snarled, leaping over the desk, before immediately being sent hurtling back over it by another heat blast.

Chuck found his gun in the rubble. Moving silently, he took aim at the back of Savior's head. The weapon's twin barrels melted before he could fire. He grimaced as his skin sizzled against the suddenly burning trigger.

Savior raised a hand toward him, but a yelp from Sam stopped him scorching a hole right through Chuck's chest.

"Jim, wait!"

The words hung in the air for what felt like an eternity.

Anna looked from Sam to Savior and back again. "Jim?"

"He's... He's Jim Flammable," Sam said. "Right, Jim?"

Savior lowered his arm and turned slowly to face Sam, saying nothing.

"It was your hands," Sam said, gesturing to Savior's crispy-fried fingers. "I knew when I saw your hands."

"Of course. It all makes perfect sense now!" Randy growled.

"Does it?" asked Anna.

"Probably," Randy replied. "I mean... Sure, why not?"

"You may call me Savior."

"OK, OK, sure," said Sam, nodding enthusiastically. "Savior. Absolutely."

He took a cautious step closer. "But you *are* Jim, right?"

"*Was*," Savior corrected. "Once. But that was a long time ago."

Anna hobbled over to stand beside Sam. The collision with the wall had taken it out of her, and she leaned on his shoulder for support. This did not go unnoticed by Savior.

"So... did you two finally get together?" he asked.

"Huh?" Anna removed her arm from Sam's shoulder. "No. We're not..."

"We just work together," said Sam.

"And what do you mean 'finally'?" Anna demanded.

Savior rolled his eyes. "Well, I mean, come on. It was obvious. You were both totally into each other."

"Right?" growled Randy. "Everyone could see it."

"Everyone," agreed Savior. "And Randy, what happened to your voice?"

"Nothing. My voice is naturally like this," Randy snarled.

"Is it? Jesus," said Savior. "Do you have throat cancer?"

"No!"

"Are you sure? Because you sound horrible," Savior continued.

"It's not throat cancer," Randy insisted. "It isn't."

"Well, OK. If you say so," said Savior. His mask tilted from side to side as he looked across the sidekick's faces. "So... how've you all been? Sam, you've switched back to your old costume, I see. It looks good. A little neat, maybe."

"You destroyed my other one," Sam said.

"Did I?" asked Savior, sounding genuinely pained. "I'm sorry. Ugh. I feel awful about that. I get so carried away by the mission sometimes."

"The mission?" said Sam.

"Yes. You know? The mission. Eradicating crime and those who profit from it," said Savior. "That's always been the mission, right?"

"Hell, maybe I should be on this guy's side," growled Randy. "I like his style."

He caught the looks from Sam and Anna.

"You know, except all the mass-murder stuff," Randy continued. "Obviously that's inappropriate."

"You've gone too far, Jim," Sam said.

"*Savior*. Please."

"You've gone too far, uh, Savior. You're killing innocent people. Or, like, *mostly* innocent people."

The air came alive around Savior for a moment, hissing and crackling. The sudden spike in temperature forced Sam back a step, his costume lacking the heat shielding afforded by Anna and Randy's.

"You know what happens to innocent people, Sam?" Savior asked. He held up his hands, displaying the blackened skin and gnarled fingers. "This is what happens. Sometimes, the innocent have to suffer so that justice can be done. Doc Mighty himself told me that, right before he forced me to set myself on fire to help stop Doctor Tinderbox."

He lowered his voice into what was quite a convincing Doc Mighty impersonation. "I'm sorry, Jim, but you have to give it all you've got!"

He doffed an imaginary cap and curtsied, adopting a snide, sniveling tone. "Yes, Doc Mighty. Of course, Doc Mighty!"

Savior jolted and looked around, suddenly remembering where he was. This time, when it came, his voice was flat and devoid of any emotion whatsoever. "I burned for six minutes. You can't imagine the pain. You know what I got for it?"

"The satisfaction of taking down Doctor Tinderbox," said Randy.

Savior shook his head. "Not really. The Justice Platoon did that. I was 'a distraction,' they said. That was how I contributed. All that screaming and thrashing made it difficult for Tinderbox to concentrate, apparently. The Justice Platoon could concentrate just fine, by the way. I'm not sure they even noticed."

He inhaled deeply through his nose. "No. I got an alternate cover on that month's comic. Lenticular. Look at it one way, and I'm normal. Tilt it a little, and I burst into flame."

Sam remembered that issue. It had been one of his favorites back in the day. He thought it probably best not to mention that, though.

"And all that for what?" Savior demanded, anger coloring his words. "Tinderbox escaped six weeks later. He killed three people, caused millions in property damage, and skinned a panda."

"Fuck," Anna ejected before she could stop herself. "Where did he get a panda?"

"Not the point. The point is, I knew then that it was all broken. That it wasn't sustainable. That the 'heroes' weren't in it for the little guy, they were in it for themselves." Savior gave a vague wave of a hand. "So, I decided to take matters into my own hands. By the time I'm finished, crime will no longer exist."

"But it's wrong. Surely, you must see that?" said Sam. "I

mean, what they did to you, it was terrible. Really. But what you're doing? It's not right. One of your dog things could've killed my son earlier."

Savior's eyes widened behind his mask. "You have a son? Holy shit, that's insane," he said, laughing a little. "Where does the time go? Ha! It feels like just a few weeks ago that we were all kids ourselves, and now... Wow. That's crazy."

"Speaking of crazy," said Anna. "You murder a guy for littering?"

Savior shook his head. "I stopped a criminal who had committed a crime."

"Yeah, but... *littering*? Seriously? That's a death sentence-worthy misdemeanor in your book?" Anna pressed. "And how did you even find out that stuff? What those people had done, I mean?"

Even through his mask, they could hear the smile in Savior's voice. "I had help," he said. "Remember Calcu-Lass? Sidekicked for Absorbo for a while?"

Sam nodded. "Yeah, I remember. She was pretty quiet. Had, like, supercomputer intelligence, didn't she?"

"She was hot," Randy growled. "And a nerd. Like a hot nerd. Which is great, because they don't know they're hot, since they're nerds. But, you know, take off the glasses, get them to shake their hair out a bit, and... *Bam*. Hot. I'd totally have tapped Calcu-Lass."

Burning embers danced in the air around Savior. "We're kind of together," he said.

"I didn't, obviously," said Randy. "Absolutely nothing went on. No way. My only lover was crime. Our bedroom? The filthy back alleys of downtown Cityopolis!"

There was a lengthy silence.

"What the hell does that—?" Savior began, but Anna held up a hand to stop him.

"Let's not even ask," she said. She put her hands on her

hips and flashed Savior a smile. "So, you and Calcu-Lass, huh? That's great. Good for you!"

"Thank you," said Savior. "I stuck electrodes in her brain and nailed her to a chair."

Anna's smile remained frozen in place, but her eyes stopped lending their support. "Huh! Well, that's, you know, *less* good. But still..." She clenched her fists and waved them beside her head. "Yay romance!"

"Oh! I know!" said Savior, jerking with excitement. "You guys should join me. We should do a team-up. It'd be like old times, except without those assholes bossing us around and trying to ruin our lives."

"They weren't trying to ruin our lives," Randy growled. "They were our trusted mentors. They helped make us who we are!"

Savior clicked his tongue against the roof of his mouth. He gestured around the group. "Yeah. Kind of my point," he said. "Besides, if they really had our best interests at heart, why does his logo look like a bullseye?"

Everyone looked at the emblem on Sam's chest. The letters 'KR' were positioned in the center of three concentric circles.

"Holy shit, it does! I never noticed that before," Sam muttered. He considered all those times when Doc Mighty had 'let' him stand in front during a supervillain takedown. "Man, that guy was a dick."

Savior laughed. It was a harsh scraping sound, like sandpaper on stone. "You know I'm right, Sam. They never cared about us. They made us their wards—adopted us, in some cases—but did you even once feel like they gave a damn? Like they actually gave the faintest shit if you lived or died? We were there to appeal to a younger audience demographic and to take the occasional bullet."

"Bullshit!" Randy snarled.

"He... He has a point," Sam said.

"You bet I do," Savior spat. "Remember Acrobattle? After the Golden Skull killed her, Brown Thunder went on his big dark revenge kick. You know how many comics he sold? Millions. That mini-series still stands as one of the biggest-selling runs of the Nineties. He got a publishing award for it. A *fucking award!*"

"No one's arguing that the Justice Platoon weren't a bunch of selfish dicks," said Anna.

Randy opened his mouth.

"Except Randy, obviously, but he's... We don't listen to him. The point is," she continued, "hating the Justice Platoon and killing a bunch of people for failing to properly dispose of their recycling, or whatever, is not the same thing."

Chuck, who had been trying with zero success to put his gun back together, limped around Savior and joined the others. He was clutching his side, and breathing was clearly proving more difficult than it should have been, but considering what he'd been through, he'd fared pretty well.

"So, you're Jim Flammable?" he grunted. "I've been looking for you."

Savior's eyes crept toward him. "Have you?"

Chuck nodded. "I thought we might work together. I hoped—"

The fireball struck him in the center of the chest, and the air was filled with the smell of sizzling flesh. Chuck tumbled backward like a ragdoll, his legs flopping over his head as he first flew, then rolled across the room.

"Chuck!" Anna turned to run to him, but a wall of heat blocked her path.

"Don't."

She turned back. Savior lowered the hand he had raised and tucked it behind his back. "When will people like that stop trying to tell us what to do?" he asked. Then, with a tilt of his head toward the ruined wall, he said, "So, are you guys coming, or what?"

CHAPTER THIRTY

Sam swallowed. He'd felt vulnerable enough in the super-suit, but standing there before Savior in his thin spandex, he felt practically naked. He might even have felt *less* exposed if he were naked. One gesture from Savior would kill him. One wave of his hand, that's all it would take.

Standing up to this guy like this was madness. It was *insane*.

Still, he'd made a promise. To his son.

Damn it.

"We can't go with you, Jim," Sam said. "I'm afraid we just can't do that."

Savior became impeccably still.

"And... Well, we can't let you do it, either," Sam continued. "You know, *ideally*. We'd like you to stop killing people, is what we're saying."

Anna gave him an encouraging bump on the shoulder. "That told him. Great work there, Sam."

Savior still hadn't moved, but the air above him rippled with rising heat.

"Stop?" he said. "You'd like me to 'stop'?"

Sam looked around at the others, then nodded. "Yes, please."

Savior fell silent again for a few moments, considering his response. When it came, it wasn't the one Sam had been hoping for.

"That's too bad," he said, then he raised an arm and Sam felt an inferno *whoosh* toward him.

Anna shouldered him aside, then hissed as the full force of Savior's fire blast hit her. The suit insulated her from the worst of the damage, but her eyes stung, her lungs burned and the worrying whiff of burning hair filled her nostrils.

She thrust both hands forward before Savior could get off another shot. His head jerked back as he sneezed, and he was forced to grab the dragon helmet to stop it falling off.

Seizing his chance, Randy raced in close and delivered a flurry of punches to Savior's ribcage, just as another sneeze wracked the villain's body.

"Float like a butterfly," growled Randy, driving a hook into Savior's right kidney. "Sting like another much larger butterfly."

Savior made a shrugging motion that knocked Randy backward off his feet with a blast of hot air. He sneezed again before he could follow up, and the inside of his mask filled with fire. Coughing, he held onto the helmet with one hand, then launched a fireball at the floor by his feet.

Sam's eyes went wide when he saw the explosion come racing toward him. "Oh shit," he squeaked in a small, quiet voice. The shape in his head thrashed, but then Anna was on him, her arms wrapping around his body, her back taking the brunt of the attack.

"Thanks," Sam wheezed.

"No problem," Anna said, her voice short and abrupt. "Now, you want to maybe stop this guy before he—?"

There was a *whoosh* as Savior took to the air. The cushion

of heat pushed down on the sidekicks, forcing Sam to cower beneath Anna as best he could.

"Now you've done it!" Savior roared from on high. "Now you've gone and done it! You were supposed to be my *friends!*"

Any traces of a booming supervillain voice were gone. Instead, his words came out as a petulant babble, like a five-year-old embarking on a tantrum.

"Well, I don't like you guys anymore!" he told them, raising a hand above his head. "This friendship is officially *over*! And thanks to you, this whole stupid city is going to pay!"

He snapped the hand down, igniting the air around it. The shape in Sam's head bloomed into life.

For a moment, Sam was cocooned in a cold, slightly damp, and vaguely smelly darkness that squirmed and moved on top of him. Then the fireball hit, and the darkness became a sudden sizzling brilliance that scorched Sam through his flimsy spandex suit.

And then, like that, it passed. Sam and Anna both stared at each other, their faces just inches apart in the dim light. The smell of barbecued meat snagged in their throat, but neither of them made any attempt to move quite yet.

"Are we alive?" Anna whispered.

Sam gave this due consideration, then nodded. "I think so."

They untangled themselves from each other, and their movements were accompanied by dozens of hollow-sounding *clacks* and *clatters*.

When they eventually stood, they found themselves in the center of a large pile of blackened bowls. After looking up and finding Savior gone, Anna picked up one of the several thousand bowls and turned it over in her hand. Chunks of crispy charred meat clung to the inside.

"This might sound like an odd question," she said. "But did you cover us in turtles?"

Sam looked around at all the smoking shells, remembering the sensation of movement he'd felt right before they'd first appeared. He also remembered the cold and wet crawling sensation he'd felt right after they'd appeared. "Possibly," he admitted.

"That is dark," Anna said. She dropped the shell, then rubbed her hands on her legs, cleaning them off. "And fucking weird. But, you know, good job, I guess. Guess you're getting better at the whole concentrating thing."

"No, it's not like that," Sam began. "It's actually—"

"SAVIOR!" roared Randy, erupting out from within another mound of turtle shells. He posed dramatically as he scanned the ceiling and the sky just beyond the hole. With a tut, he let his arms drop to his sides. "Damn. Is he gone? I was totally about to kick his ass."

"He's gone," Anna confirmed.

"What's all this?" Randy asked, wading through a pile of shells.

"Sam saved us from the fireball by covering us in live turtles," Anna said.

"Ah, yes!" said Randy. "Oldest trick in the book."

Anna laughed. "Yeah, it's a classic all—" Her face fell. "Oh, shit, Chuck!"

It took almost a full minute of kicking through turtle shells before they found him. He was folded up over by the back wall, his face pressed against the dirty linoleum floor.

Randy dropped to his haunches and pressed two fingers to Chuck's throat. He squatted there for several seconds, peering down through his steamed-up goggles.

"Well?" Sam asked.

Randy shook his head. "He's dead."

Chuck inhaled sharply, his eyes flicking open.

"Wait, no," said Randy, his fingers still on Chuck's pulse. "I'm getting something."

"Get out of the way," Anna snapped, catching him by the arm and pulling him aside. She kicked aside some turtle shells and knelt beside Chuck. "Hey. You still with us?"

Chuck coughed out a bloody wad, then managed a nod. With a groan of effort, he flopped over onto his back, *crunching* several shells beneath his weight. The buttons of his jacket and shirt both popped as he pulled on them, revealing a black rubber suit below.

"Prototype," he wheezed. "Still hurts like hell."

With Sam and Anna's help, he got himself up onto his elbows. The movement took a lot out of him, and he spent several seconds remembering how to breathe before he could speak again.

"Savior?" was all he said.

"Gone," said Sam.

Most of Chuck's eyebrows had been burned off. He raised what was left of them. "Dead?"

Sam shook his head. "He flew away. I think we scared him off."

Chuck's partial eyebrows remained raised. "You 'scared him off'? The guy who single-handedly murdered the Justice Platoon? You *scared him off?*"

"It's the helmet," said Sam. "I'm sure of it. When he sneezed, it almost fell off and he panicked."

Anna let out a sudden, "Oh!" that echoed through the empty turtle shells. "The helmet! I remember the helmet! Memetzo had it in his vault. He took it from..." She clicked her fingers. "Shit. Who was that guy with the alligators?"

"Mr. Alligators?" Sam said.

"Yes! Him! OK, so he was, like, a total Z-Lister in supervillain terms. Like, some of his own henchmen had a better name for themselves than he did," Anna said. "He had two baby alligators that he kept on leashes. That was his whole schtick."

"Right, I remember," said Sam. "What about him?"

"So, he's hopeless, but then one day he leads a whole army of alligators into the city and starts tearing the place up. There were thousands of them, remember?"

Sam shook his head. "No. I mean, yeah, I heard about it, but we were on Neptune, so I didn't see. I still don't see your point."

"His schtick got supercharged. That's my point," said Anna.

"Like Jim Flammable," growled Randy.

"And that's not the only thing they have in common," said Anna. She tapped herself on the side of the head. "Guess what Mr. Alligators was wearing."

"Crocodile pants!" Randy spat, punching his palm.

Anna side-eyed him. "Uh, no. The helmet. He was wearing the helmet. Also, why would Mr. *Alligators* be wearing... Forget it."

"It's boosting his power," Sam realized. "That's why he's so much stronger."

"We get the helmet off him, we stop him," Anna said. "But there was something else, too. Afterward, Mr. Alligators said the helmet had been controlling him. He'd said it had *told* him to attack the city."

"So, maybe Jim doesn't want to be doing this?" said Sam.

Anna sniffed and shrugged. "Well, Memetzo figured that was bullshit, so... I doubt it."

A shadow passed briefly across the hole in the roof, catching Randy's eye. He stood, slowly, and squinted through the opening.

Chuck grimaced as he tried to sit up further. "We should go catch him," he said.

"Uh, no. You're in no state to go anywhere," Sam said. "We'll do it."

Chuck seemed unsure. "Just you three? I don't know. Maybe we should wait. Regroup and take stock before you go running in."

Anna shifted awkwardly. "Uh, yeah. While you were unconscious, he kind of said he was going to go destroy the whole city. So... there's that."

Chuck stared blankly back at her for a while. Finally, he blinked.

"No, you're right. You three should go stop him."

"Guys," whispered Randy, his eyes glued to the hole in the ceiling. The light spilling in through the gap had dimmed, suggesting the sky had become overcast.

"Can we salvage the Sidekicksmobile?" Anna asked. She, Sam, and Chuck looked over to the up-ended tank, half-submerged in turtle shells and partially on fire.

"I doubt it," Sam said.

Chuck groaned. "God damn, I hope they don't take that out of my paycheck."

"Guys!" Randy hissed.

"Give us a minute, OK?" Anna sighed. "We're trying to figure out the transport situation here."

Randy turned to her, a grin splitting his face. "That's not going to be a problem," he said. "They're here. It took them a little longer than I expected, but they're finally here."

"Who's here?" Sam asked. "What are you...?"

His voice trailed off as a heaving rainbow of fluttering colors poured in through the hole in the asylum roof. The sound of a hundred million fluttering wings rippled like polite applause that reverberated around the entrance hallway and across the sea of turtle shells.

Anna's jaw dropped open. "Ho-lee shit, he isn't delusional."

Randy's grin was still fixed in place as he pressed his fingertips to his temples. The vast cloud of butterflies changed direction in a single undulating shift, moving like a single living organism. Sam and Anna both gasped as they were suddenly lost in a cloud of fluttering wings.

"You want transport?" Randy's voice called to them through the butterfly storm. The floor fell away as they were each lifted off their feet. "How's this for transport? Fly, my butterfly brethren. Fly!"

Chuck lay on his back, surrounded by burned out turtle shells, watching as the cloud of fluttering insects carried the sidekicks up, up and away.

With a grunt, he let his head fall back onto the floor. "Wow," he muttered, clutching his ribs to keep them in place. "What a day."

CHAPTER THIRTY-ONE

THE CITY SPREAD out like a map far below, visible in glimpses and snatches between the gaps in the three butterfly clouds.

It had been a mildly terrifying sensation to begin with, being hoisted aloft on millions of fragile wings. Now, though, hundreds of feet above the streets of Cityopolis—which, despite the distance, somehow seemed more solid and imposing than ever—it was *all the way* terrifying.

Seriously. What the hell were they doing?

"This is suicide," Sam croaked, his stomach lurching as the mass of insects pootled him along in an irregular bobbing motion through the air. "We're going to die."

"Relax," called Randy from inside another butterfly swarm just eight or nine feet ahead. "What could be safer than this?"

"Everything!" Sam yelped. "Birds! Bees! A big kite! *Anything* would be safer than butterflies!"

"You might want to keep your voice down there, Kid Random," Randy growled. "These guys have feelings, you know? Now's probably not the time to make them upset."

Sam promptly shut up. Anna's voice came from somewhere just behind him.

"Could they go a little faster, do you think?" she asked. She had deactivated the Battle Mode of her suit, despite Sam's insistence that this was a mistake. A bird passed her from behind, eyeing them quizzically as it drifted along on its wide-open wings. "It feels like we're going quite slowly."

"They're butterflies, not jet-engine-flies," Randy spat. "They're going as fast as they can."

Anna peered down through a gap in the fluttering cloud, ignoring the knot of panic that formed in her stomach. "Right. It's just... I can see people walking faster than this." She squinted. "Actually, I think I see people *standing* faster than this."

That wasn't all she could see, either. A hand emerged from her butterfly cloud as she pointed. "Wait. Look down there."

"*Fuck off!*" Sam spat. "I'm not looking down."

"Oh, don't be such a baby," Anna scolded.

"It's alright for you, you've both got supersuits. If we fall, you'll probably bounce," Sam pointed out.

Anna sighed. "*Such* a baby. Randy. You see it?"

"You're goddamn right I see it," Randy growled. "And it's incredible."

"What is?" asked Sam. "What is it?"

"I've never seen anything like it," Randy continued.

"What is it? What are you looking at?" Sam demanded.

"I can't... I don't really know how to describe it," said Anna. "You have to look."

Sam shook his head emphatically. "I'm not looking."

"Just look at the damn ground, Sam," Anna told him.

A series of sighs and groans emerged from the fluttering cloud, followed by some quite uncomplimentary remarks about butterflies.

Summoning what scant courage he had left, Sam looked in the direction Anna had pointed. "It's fire," he snapped. "How could you not describe fire? Look, I just did it then. 'It's fire,' see?"

"But it isn't just fire though, is it?" said Anna. "Look."

Begrudgingly, Sam looked again. At first, all he saw was the fire. It surrounded Memetzo's cathedral in the center of town. But, as he studied it more closely and his fear of plunging to the ground subsided enough to let him pay attention, Sam noticed the way the flames were moving. They moved like ripples in a pool of water, rolling outward from the cathedral and lapping against the buildings that lined the square.

"I mean... that's weird, right?" said Anna. "That's not normal?"

Sam shook his head. "No. I wonder what it means?"

Before anyone could speculate, a solid pillar of flame appeared in the sky, exploding from the cathedral's roof and stretching upward like the beam of a high-powered torch. Even from this height, Sam heard the screams of the people below.

"Uh-oh. That can't be good," said Anna.

"You think that's him?" asked Randy. "You think that's Savior?"

"It's a column of fire coming directly from the roof of his headquarters, Randy. Who else would it be?" asked Anna.

"We have to get down there. And fast," said Sam.

The butterflies surrounding him parted momentarily, and he dropped several feet in one sudden lurch.

"Jesus *Christ!*" Sam yelped, scrambling to grab hold of something, but finding nothing solid. The butterflies tightened around his top half, leaving his legs windmilling frantically in thin air. "Not that fast!"

Through the mass of flapping wings, Sam caught Randy's reproachful look. "Butterflies are very literal creatures, Kid

Random," he said. "You might want to be careful what you say around them."

More screams rose up from the streets below. Magma-Mutts were leaping from the fire column and bounding off into the city. Even from way up here, they could hear the growling and snarling.

"God, it's getting worse," Sam fretted. "We need to get there quickly. *Without* dropping me!" he added, for clarity.

"I have an idea," said Anna. "But it's dangerous."

"I'm in!" Randy snarled.

"Wait. How dangerous?" asked Sam. "More dangerous than *this*?"

Anna made a weighing motion. "Actually..." she said. "Yeah."

***

Sam dangled from the cloud of butterflies, his legs kicking frantically, his words coming as short, sudden sounds like, "Welp!" and "Unk!" and "Ohfuckfuckfuck."

Just a few feet below him, the roof of an Elevated Train *whizzed* past, the train's wheels clattering and clacking on the raised track.

"Ready?" Anna called, shouting to make herself heard above the din.

"No!" Sam cried.

"I was born ready," Randy growled. "Follow my lead!"

He dropped before anyone could stop him, pulling off a textbook landing on the roof of the train.

The train's momentum immediately whipped him off his feet and he screamed as he plunged over the side of the roof, before his cape snagged on a pointed overhang, jerking him to a stop.

"Totally meant that," he insisted, but the carriage he had

landed on had whooshed ahead, separating him from Sam, Anna, and his butterflies.

Several coaches back, Anna reached out from her own cloud and caught Sam by the arm. The slipstream of wind from the train was peeling butterflies away by the dozen, and both clouds were rapidly thinning. It was now or never.

"We're going in three, two..."

"No! Don't! Don't you dare!" Sam protested, but an increasing lack of butterflies took the decision out of their hands. Sam flailed wildly with his arms, legs, and—for reasons he'd later come to question—tongue as he plunged the few feet onto the roof and slammed hard against the fast-moving metal.

Both Anna and Sam bounced, tumbling together toward the back of the train, and the almost-certainly deadly gap between this coach and the one behind.

When they landed after the second bounce, the weight of the few thousand remaining butterflies pressed down on them, stopping them sliding any further. Sam felt like he should probably say, "Thanks," but there were so many of the insects sitting on his face he was terrified he might inadvertently inhale one.

Now that the immediate danger of sliding off the roof had passed, Sam and Anna were able to look ahead in the direction the train was going. Memetzo's cathedral was a mile ahead on the right, the column of flame still stretching up from within it.

The El Track passed pretty close, and while a human driver would almost certainly have stopped well before now, the AI steering these things obviously didn't share the same concerns about dying horribly in a big fire as their human counterparts did.

"Is Randy alive?" Sam asked.

"His cape is," Anna replied, squinting against the

oncoming wind. "It's pulled pretty tight, so hopefully he's still on the other end of it."

Holding onto one of the roof ridges, Sam risked a glimpse over the side. He regretted it at once. He'd been on the Elevated Train a handful of times in the past, but he'd never quite realized just *how* elevated it actually was. From where he lay the current situation went roof, train, tracks, a forty foot sheer drop, then the ground. Hitting anything after that first one spelled instant death if he was lucky, prolonged death if he wasn't.

"This was a great idea," said Anna. "Seriously, should've thought of it before."

"Was it?" Sam said, fighting the urge to sob.

"We're almost there. We'll be level with the place in a couple of minutes," Anna pointed out. "The butterflies would've taken hours." She smiled at the sea of colorful insects that covered her, Sam, and most of the carriage roof. "No offense, guys."

"What then?" Sam asked.

Anna raised an eyebrow. "Hmm?"

"When we get there, what then? How do we get off?"

Anna's other eyebrow raised. She inhaled slightly like she was about to speak, but nothing came out.

"You don't know, do you?" said Sam, his voice rising in panic. "You didn't think that far ahead."

Anna wrinkled her nose. "I'm kind of an act first, think later kind of person," she said. "Sometimes that's to my credit. Occasionally, it is not. This would be one of those occasions."

"Hey, guys."

Randy's guttural growl startled them both. They raised their heads to find him standing upright atop the train, his cape whipping around him.

"Where the...?" Anna peered along the train to where Randy had been. "How the fuck did you get here?"

Randy frowned and glanced back over his shoulder. "I walked. It's not far."

"We're on a moving train!" Sam yelped.

"Uh, yeah. Obviously," said Randy.

Sam looked him up and down. Mostly up, given that he was still lying flat on the roof. "I mean... But... Aren't you scared?"

"Of trains?" said Randy, appearing genuinely perplexed by the question.

"Of falling!"

"Oh. No," said Randy. "I mean, I used to be, but not anymore." He tapped the side of his head. "Brain damage. Everyone talks about it like it's a bad thing, but... I don't know. It has its perks."

"Brain damage made you stop being scared of falling?" asked Anna, genuinely intrigued despite the urgency of the situation.

Randy nodded. "Falling. Ghosts. Being stung in the eyes by wasps," he said, ticking them off on his fingers. "Oh, and dying alone in a filthy alleyway with a bullet in my gut."

Sam and Anna both stared up at him, saying nothing.

"But mostly falling," Randy concluded.

He turned away, checking how close they were to Memetzo's cathedral. Close. Very close.

"We should probably get off soon," he said, turning back.

"And how are we supposed to do that?" yelped Sam, his knuckles white from gripping the ridges of the roof. His heart leapt into his throat as Randy picked his way through the carpet of butterflies and stopped right at the edge.

"We jump," Randy said.

"We can't jump from up here!" Sam cried. "We'd be splattered."

"Not if we do the superhero landing," Randy countered.

"*Especially* if we do the superhero landing!"

Anna raised herself shakily onto her knees, keeping her gaze focused on the roof. "I hate to agree with Sam on this one—"

"Kid Random," Randy corrected.

"But if we jump off we'll *definitely* die."

Randy pressed his fingers to his temples. "Not if my butterflies help."

"Uh, hate to break it to you, pal, but we lost half of the butterflies. Maybe more," said Anna, jabbing a thumb back over her shoulder. "They're somewhere that way."

"Maybe they can't carry us, but they can slow our fall," said Randy. "Probably. I mean, they look pretty confident." He pointed to one of the insects. "Maybe not that guy."

Anna wobbled unsteadily on her feet, half-squatting against the wind. Reaching down, she tried to pull Sam up, but he clung to the roof like a limpet.

"Come on, it's the best plan we've got," said Anna.

"It's not a plan. It's not even an idea. It's... it's a *notion*. And it's also suicide!" Sam babbled.

Anna pointed to the column of fire that now loomed almost dead ahead. Screams and cries for help rose up from the streets below the speeding train. Overhead, the sky was filling with a layer of thick, black smoke clouds.

"You see that, Sam?"

"Kid Random," Randy grunted.

"You see what's happening? You hear those people?" Anna demanded. "Tell me something, Sam—"

"Kid Random."

"Why did you come back? Why did you come back and get me?"

Sam's mouth flapped open and closed a couple of times. "I didn't want my son to be in danger."

"Bullshit," Anna barked. "If that was it, you'd have stayed with him. You came back because you didn't want *anyone* in danger, and you knew—God help them—that we were the best shot at making that happen. We're the only ones who can stop this, Sam."

"Kid Random."

Anna twitched and Randy clutched at his throat, unable to draw in enough breath to contribute any more to the conversation.

Holding a hand out to Sam, Anna raised her eyebrows. "So, are you going to lie there and let everyone die? Or are we going to jump off this fucking train right now?"

For a moment, Sam just stared at the outstretched hand. He studied it, like he'd never seen one before, then finally slipped his own hand into hers.

"We're going to jump off this fucking train right now," he said, gritting his teeth, steeling his nerve, and girding his loins as he rose first onto one knee, then the other.

Some of the butterflies that had been on his back clambered up onto his shoulders as he got to his feet. He felt the spandex costume go tight as thousands of tiny legs gripped him, and thousands of fragile wings fluttered wildly in the wind.

The insects that had been on the roof climbed up onto Randy's back, taking up positions on his costume and cape. Anna turned to the half-dozen or so butterflies perching on one of her shoulders. "Good luck," she whispered.

The heat from the fire was intense now. Sam could feel it licking across the exposed part of his face, and the strip of belly visible between the costume's top and bottom halves. They were almost there. Time was running out.

"OK, we go on three," said Anna. "You guys ready?"

"I was—"

"Sorry, yes, you were born ready, I forgot." She took Sam's

hand and held it. "Ready?"

Sam squeezed her hand but didn't look at her. The track was a blur beneath them, the ground all-too-solid thirty feet below that.

"Sure," he croaked. "Why not?"

Anna drew in a deep breath. "OK. On three. One..."

Sam closed his eyes and said a quick prayer to anyone who might be listening.

"Two..."

"This is going to be awesome!" Randy growled. "Don't forget the superhero landing! It's totally worth it."

Anna's voice came out as a shrill yelp of panic.

"Thr—"

The train slowed rapidly as it pulled into a station. Sam and Anna both held their hands out, frantically trying to surf through the sudden change to the train's velocity. Randy, on the other hand, appeared completely unperturbed by the deceleration.

With a *hiss* and a *screech* of brakes, the train stopped at a platform.

"Shit. Yeah. Probably should've seen that coming," Anna muttered.

"Oh, thank God," Sam sobbed, then he and Anna both quickly slid over the edge and clambered clumsily down onto the platform.

A moment later, Randy superhero-landed between them, the butterflies fluttering crazily on his back.

"Boom. Nailed it," he announced, then he sprung to his feet and raced toward the railings at the station's edge. "Let's do this!" he roared, throwing himself over the railings and tumbling out of sight.

Sam and Anna exchanged shrugs.

"Stairs?" Anna suggested.

Sam nodded. "Yeah," he agreed. "Stairs."

CHAPTER THIRTY-TWO

"WHAT KEPT YOU?" growled Randy, when Sam and Anna reached the bottom of the stairs, both wheezing slightly, out of breath.

"Uh, we're not insane. That was the main hold-up," said Anna. Turning to Sam, she added: "You're right. He *is* alive. I owe you twenty bucks."

This close to the cathedral, and without the wind from the train to cool them, the heat was immense. Sam's spandex clung to him with sweat. Dark patches bloomed from beneath his armpits and dotted his front. The costume hadn't been a great look to start with, but it was rapidly going downhill.

He took a deep breath, but the air was tainted with smoke, and he coughed it back up again. "I guess we should go do this," he squawked, half-choking on the words.

Anna patted him on the shoulder. "Great pep-talk there, Sam. Really inspirational. Doc Mighty-esque, even."

Randy opened his mouth to complain about her use of Sam's real name, but she shot a warning look at his throat. "I wouldn't," she said, then she gestured in the direction of Memetzo's cathedral. "Now, let's go get ourselves killed."

Memetzo's cathedral had always been an imposing place, its dark towers and Gothic spires standing in stark contrast to the sleek and modern skyscrapers surrounding it. It stood almost at the heart of Cityopolis on a square of green-blue grass that shimmered with magic when the stars were properly aligned, and visitors to the city would flock there on a regular basis, hoping to catch a glimpse of some sorcery or another.

Now, the blue-green grass was gone, the earth below it scorched and blackened. Flames licked across the cathedral's walls. Their movements were like the bowing and scraping of worshippers before the great god of the fire column roaring up through the building's roof.

Sam, Anna, Randy, and several thousand butterflies took cover behind an abandoned delivery truck. It had tipped over onto its side, blasted away from the cathedral by a wave of heat that had blistered the metal.

"OK, what's the plan?" asked Anna.

"We run in there and kick his ass!" Randy spat. "Sidekick-style!"

"No! That's insane! We need to find out what he's doing," Sam whispered, even though they were still fifty feet or more away from the building. "We need to get eyes on the inside."

Randy nodded slowly. "Yeah. OK, that makes sense," he said, a little begrudgingly. "But how are we supposed to do that?"

Sam gestured to the butterflies covering every available surface. "Well, I mean..."

Randy frowned, not yet getting it.

"I think what he's trying to say is, maybe you could do that thing where you look through the eyes of a butterfly?" Anna suggested. "If, I don't know, if that's even a real thing."

"It's totally a real thing," Randy snarled. A smirk appeared somewhere in his beard as he placed his fingers to his temples. "But why look through the eyes of just one butterfly, when I can look through the eyes of *all* of them?"

He concentrated briefly, then his whole body was wracked with violent spasms. He dropped to the ground like a sack of potatoes, thrashing violently, foam bubbling from his lips.

"Jesus," Anna muttered, watching him twitch and convulse.

"Too... many," Randy wheezed, his limbs jerking. "Too... Oh God. Kill me. Too..."

He retched violently, shook his head a number of times, then shakily rose to his feet. "On second thought, it might be best if I stick to just one."

A single butterfly fluttered into the air and landed on Randy's outstretched finger. "It's all on you, Callum," he said. "Get in there, get yourself in position. You can do this!"

Anna leaned in closer to Sam. "Did he just call it 'Callum'? That's weird."

"Seriously? That?" Sam whispered. "That's *way* down my weird list for today."

"You don't think it's weird he has such a close relationship with them that he knows them *by name*?" Anna asked.

"I don't find that any more weird than the fact that he has *any* sort of relationship with them at all, no."

They all watched as Callum fluttered out from behind the truck. His wings flapped furiously in the heat-wind, and then he was off, powering his way toward the cathedral.

"We should probably give him a few minutes," Randy said.

"Sure," said Anna.

"God, I hope he does this," Randy said. "He has self-confidence issues. This'll really give him a boost."

Sam met Anna's eye. "OK, that just bumped it up a couple of places," he said.

"Believe in yourself, Callum," Randy called, as the butterfly fluttered toward an open window. "Like *I* believe in you!"

"Yes, fine, it's weird," Sam conceded.

"Thank you," said Anna.

Randy pressed his fingers to the sides of his forehead. "OK, let's tune in and see what Callum can... Oh. Wait. No, he's dead."

"What? Damn it!" Anna groaned.

"He totally just caught fire," said Randy. "We probably should've seen that coming."

"Shit," Anna spat. She clicked her tongue against her teeth a few times, then stood up. "Well, I guess we'll just have to go with Plan A. Charge in and hope for the best."

"Finally!" Randy growled.

"Wait, no, we can't," said Sam, stopping them before they could make their run. "I don't know if you noticed, but the whole building is cocooned by fire."

"We've got supersuits," Randy pointed out.

"No, *you've* got supersuits. I've got a spandex costume I first wore when I was twelve, and which—in the unlikely event that we survive—you'll probably have to cut me out of."

Anna peered around the edge of the truck. The heat stung at her eyes and forced her back into cover. "OK, fair point," she said. "Can you do anything? With your powers, I mean? Can you, I don't know, shut it off?"

"What? No. It doesn't work like that," Sam said.

"Then how does it work, Kid Random?" Randy demanded. "Chuck said you were the most powerful guy on the team. Obviously, that's wrong. We all know it's me."

"We don't know that," Anna countered.

"Well, who's the one with the army of butterflies?" Randy asked.

"That doesn't make you the most powerful one on the team," Anna said. "I mean, it's almost irrelevant."

"My point is, you and Butterfly King have done your share. Some of us more than others," Randy said, slipping effortlessly into referring to himself in third person. "But Kid Random? What has he done besides hold us back and kill a lot of turtles?"

"I made that bull disappear," Sam protested. "Or... I don't know. Go away somewhere."

"Oh, whoop-te-do," Randy spat. "Who *hasn't* made a bull disappear?"

Sam opened his mouth to question this, but an excited yelp from Anna stopped him.

"Shit! Wait! Of course!" she said. "The secret entrance."

"The what?" asked Sam.

"It's a superhero headquarters," Anna said. "It has a secret entrance. I know where it is."

Sam blinked in surprise. "Will it get us inside?"

"Well, that's generally what entrances are for, so yes," Anna said. Keeping low, she ran away from the cathedral, keeping the truck between her and the building. "Come on, it's this way," she urged. "But I should warn you, you're probably not going to like it."

Sam stood knee-deep in raw sewage, trying very hard not to vomit while Anna stood before what appeared at first glance to be a perfectly ordinary brick wall, albeit one dappled with human waste.

At second glance, it appeared to be the same thing, and

the past few minutes of watching Anna randomly jab at bricks had done nothing to convince Sam otherwise.

"I'm sure it's one of these," Anna said, prodding another of the stones. Her fingertip left an oval-shaped smear in the slick brown surface. "Or maybe you had to press a few in order. I think that was it."

She poked at a few others, with much the same lack-of-effect. "Maybe if I just sort of mash them all at once," she suggested, slamming the palms of her hands against the brickwork.

Sam wanted to voice his concerns that this was a big waste of time, but he knew that if he opened his mouth he'd immediately be sick down his front, and his costume was in a bad enough state as it was.

"Or two at once, maybe?" Anna guessed. She chose two apparently random bricks and pressed them.

Nothing happened.

"Are you sure it's the right wall?" Randy growled.

"Yes! Of course it's the right wall!" Anna snapped. "We used to come in this way a lot if Memetzo didn't want people knowing he was at home."

She shrugged. "Well, I mean, he could teleport straight to his chamber from anywhere in the world, but I came in this way a lot, and this is *definitely* the right wall." She pressed another couple of bricks and watched, hopefully, while nothing continued to happen.

"Shit!"

"Right," said Randy. "It's just this one has a load of magical symbols on it." He gestured to another apparent dead end beside him. "And it's in the shape of a door."

Anna frowned over at Randy's wall, then back to her own. She shot a quick look up at the ceiling, getting her bearings, then sloshed through the river of shit. "He must've moved it," she said.

The sight of the symbols stirred some dormant muscle-memory, and Anna's fingers prodded several of the bricks in quick succession. As she pressed each one, the magical symbol carved into the stone illuminated.

After she'd touched the final brick, the wall shifted aside, revealing a staircase lit in an eerie shade of blue. "Ta-daa!" Anna announced.

She stepped through the doorway, and the space around her seemed to ripple as she passed beneath the arch. The layer of greasy excrement that had been clinging to her costume evaporated.

"Great, that still works!" she said, beckoning the others through. Sam followed quickly, breathing with relief as his own costume instantly became sewage free. He was relieved to find that breathing with relief was a possibility here, as whatever had magically cleaned him up was also blocking the smell from the other side of the door.

Randy stepped through, laden down with butterflies. They sat on his head and shoulders, clung to his cape, and hung from his back, their movements making it look as if his whole costume had come to life.

The staircase was an old wrought-iron thing that twisted in a corkscrew shape to a platform above. Anna crept up it, leading the way.

A wooden door stood at the top. Anna reached for the handle, but Sam stopped her.

"Wait. We don't know what's through there," he said, pulling off one of his gloves. He tentatively touched the metal handle a couple of times, then gripped it more firmly. "It's cool," he whispered. "I think we're OK."

While Sam replaced his glove, Anna *creaked* the door open. The room beyond was dark, the light from the doorway illuminating only a few feet of flagstone flooring.

"You sure we're in the right place?" Sam whispered.

Anna nodded. "This is the crypt. Or, like, the basement," She gestured upward with her eyes. "That's where the action will be."

"Guys, listen," Randy growled. "Can you hear something?"

They listened. They could hear the crackling of distant fire, but that was all there was to...

Wait.

No.

There was another sound, too. A low, rasping hiss, like the dying wheeze of a set of burst bagpipes.

And below it, other sounds, still. A clicking. A soft regular *bleep*. It reminded Sam of a hospital.

"Lights," Anna whispered.

The darkness remained.

"Shit. No. Uh, Illuminus," she said. "Illuminai?"

Light seemed to explode from the molecules in the air itself, obliterating the darkness and revealing Sam's brand new, no-doubt-about-it, most disturbing thing he'd ever seen.

A frail, thin woman sat in a chair in the center of the room. Or maybe *was* the chair. It was hard to tell where it stopped and she began. She was surrounded by breathing apparatus and banks of machinery, most of which connected to her arms and legs, or fed via transparent hoses into her nose and mouth.

Wires—thousands of wires—had been plumbed directly into her skull. They rose straight up like the world's most ludicrously elaborate crown, tangling and entwining before vanishing into the ports of some flashing and blinking metal cabinet mounted to the ceiling.

Her eyes stared blankly ahead, and threads of saliva hung down from her chin. She groaned faintly in the sudden brightness, but otherwise did nothing to suggest she was conscious.

"Holy shit," Anna whispered. "Is that...?"

"Calcu-Lass," said Sam, the urge to throw-up returning. "It's Calcu-Lass."

"Is she OK?" Randy asked.

Anna tutted. "Does she *look* OK?"

Randy contemplated this. "Well, I mean, she's looked better," he said. "But she's still pretty hot. You know, for a nerd."

Anna threw him the dirtiest look she could muster, then crept past the banks of machinery and over to Calcu-Lass's side. Calcu-Lass's cheeks were gray and sunken. Much of her long dark hair had come out in clumps. What was left had a dry, straw-like texture and appeared as if it would crumble at the slightest touch.

"Hey," Anna whispered. "Hey, uh, Calcu-Lass? Can you hear me?"

The machinery *huffed* and pumped. Drool dribbled down her chin.

Anna turned to the others. "What was her name? Can you remember?"

"Calcu-Lass," said Randy.

"Her real name."

Sam's brow furrowed for a moment. "Tahira," he said. "I think... I'm pretty sure it was Tahira."

"Tahira? Can you hear me? It's Anna. It's... Allergy Wo—Girl. It's Allergy Girl. We're here to help."

Anna's phone buzzed in her utility belt. She ignored it.

"Can you talk?" Anna asked, then she shook her head. "You've got a fucking hosepipe down your throat, of course you can't talk."

Randy punched his palm. "Sign language! Can she do sign language?"

"I doubt it," said Anna, but as they didn't have much other option, she asked the question, anyway. "Can you do sign language?"

Anna's phone *bleeped* loudly. She glanced down at her belt, frowning. She was sure she'd turned it off.

Randy rapped on Tahira's forehead with his knuckles.

"Jesus! What are you doing?" Sam demanded, pulling his hand away.

"Standard vegetable test," Randy explained. "It's the first thing they teach you at medical school."

"I'm pretty sure it isn't," Sam said, but Randy dismissed it with a wave.

"She's basically a potato. Damn shame," Randy grimaced. He clenched his fists dramatically and spat out a snarl. "But mark my words, Calcu-Lass, you shall be avenged!"

"Uh, guys?" said Anna. She held up her phone. A message on the screen read:

Hey Anna! Long time no c. x

The name at the top of the message revealed it had been sent from 'CL'.

"I don't think she's a potato," Anna said. The phone bleeped immediately.

Lol. Def not!

Anna had barely finished reading that message when another one arrived.

In ridiculous agony tho.

This was followed by a sad smiley. Anna started to compose a, *Well that sucks* response when another message arrived.

U can talk. I can hear u.

"She says we can talk," Anna said. "She says she can hear us."

Randy's eyes widened. "Did she hear me say I thought she was hot?" he fretted.

There was a *bleep*.

Totally. :p

"She may have heard something along those lines, yeah," said Anna.

Sam stepped closer, being careful not to accidentally yank out any of the tubes and cables hooked up to her. "Did Jim do this to you?" he asked.

Savior. Yes, came the reply on Anna's phone. She held it up for the others to see.

There was a momentary pause, then:

He's a dick.

"You can say that again," said Anna.

He's nuts. He's going to destroy whole city. U need 2 stop him.

"How?" asked Anna.

I can help. I can distract him so u can get his helmet of him.

This message was followed a half-second later by one that just said:

*off not of. Sorry.

U need 2 b quick, the next message read. *He's powering up. He's going to kill every1.*

"Shit. OK," said Anna, glancing over to the corner where another door stood. "We'll go up the stairs and try to catch him off-guard. Everyone good with that plan?"

"Bring it on!" Randy barked.

"Uh, yeah. I mean, sure," said Sam.

Anna's phone bleeped.

Can some1 stay? the message read. *Don't want 2 b alone NE more. :(*

"Uh, sure. Yeah. I mean, of course," said Anna. She handed the phone to Randy. "Stay here, will you? Talk to her with this."

Randy turned the phone over in his hands a few times, then put it to his ear. "Hello?"

"No, I mean she'll text you," Anna said.

Randy frowned. "Text?"

Anna sighed. "Yes, you know, like... Shit."

"He can't read," Sam pointed out. He took the phone from Randy. "I'll stay."

"What? No. You're our big hitter. We need you up there. I'll stay."

Sam held onto the phone. "You said it yourself, I've contributed nothing," he told her. "You almost got Jim to sneeze his helmet off. If anyone can stop him, it's you. And now that Randy has his butterflies, he can help you."

"*She'll* be helping *me*," Randy said. "Just want to make that clear. I'll be the main one, and she'll be helping me."

Anna held Sam's gaze for a moment, weighing up his words. At last, she nodded. "OK, then. We have a plan. Calcu-Lass distracts him, you keep her company, we'll go kick the shit out of him when he isn't looking and take his helmet off. Sound good?"

"Sounds *awesome*," Randy snarled. He consulted the butterflies on his shoulders. "Right, guys?" he asked, then he grinned. "They're totally in."

Anna nodded, puffed out her cheeks, then nodded again. "OK, then. Let's do it," she said. "Battle Mode."

Her suit transformed. Her phone bleeped.

That's 2 cool!!!

"She's impressed," said Sam.

"Well, we'll see if she's still saying that three minutes from now when I'm on fire," said Anna. She smiled at the motionless Calcu-Lass. "But thanks."

Sam watched as Anna and Randy crossed to the door. His stomach twisted in fear and shame. He wanted to call out to them, to tell them not to go, but the words wouldn't come. Instead, he managed a strained, "Good luck," then the door clattered closed behind them, and they were gone.

He watched the door for almost a full minute, hoping it would open again and they'd come back. Mostly Anna. It'd be

OK to see Randy too, obviously, but Anna was his more pressing concern.

The door didn't open, though. Neither Anna nor Randy came back through.

Sam sighed and lowered himself onto a piece of equipment, taking a seat. It *buzzed* urgently and he jumped up again.

Please don't sit on that.

"Sorry!" Sam said. "I didn't... I wasn't thinking."

No worries

Sam shifted awkwardly on the spot. He clicked his fingers a few times, trying to think of what to say.

"So," he began, finally settling on something. "How've you been?"

Not great.

"No," said Sam. "No, I guess not."

I lied.

Sam gazed down at the message, confused.

"What do you mean?"

I don't need company. I'm in 300 chat rooms and I'm 40% of Facebook.

Sam looked from the screen to Tahira's lifeless face. "Then why did you want someone to stay with you?" he asked, the fine hairs prickling on the back of his neck.

Y? Simple, the next message read. *BCos U and me need 2 have a little cat.*

Sam blinked several times in surprise. The phone bleeped again. The next message was brief, but helpful.

*chat. Sorry.

CHAPTER THIRTY-THREE

THEY FOUND Savior standing on the Sanctuary, the raised platform at the head of the long aisle that ran almost the full length of the cathedral's interior. He was pretty difficult to miss, what with the column of flame that surrounded him and stretched up through the gaping hole in the roof high above.

Anna and Randy peeked out through a doorway, half-hidden by a set of purple velvet curtains. Savior had his back to them, which would've made him ripe for attack, had it not been for the whole pillar of fire thing.

"Now what?" Anna wondered, the question aimed more at herself than at Randy.

"We go over there and introduce him to Lefty and Righty," Randy growled, holding up his right fist, then his left.

"If we get out of this, we really need to work on your basic education," Anna whispered. She ran her tongue across her teeth, deep in thought. "I don't know if my powers can affect him through the fire," she said. "We need to get him out of there."

"I have an idea," Randy said. He brought his fists up again. Anna pushed them down.

"Let's leave Lefty and Righty for later," she said. "Calcu-Lass said she was going to distract him, so let's see what happens."

Randy nodded, although he didn't look happy about it.

They waited.

"Do you think she likes me?" Randy whispered.

Anna frowned. "Huh? Who? Calcu-Lass?"

Randy nodded.

"Uh, yeah. Sure. I mean... She wasn't giving a lot away body-language wise, but... sure. Why not?"

There was a loud *bee-beep* from the Sanctuary. Savior fumbled in his pocket for a moment, then brought out a phone and read the screen.

He spun suddenly, his cape twirling. Even from this distance, and through all that fire, Anna saw his eyes darken behind his mask.

"Alternatively," Anna groaned, "she may hate you, and want us both dead."

Sam studied the screen of Anna's phone, not quite sure how to respond.

I always liked u Sam. I watched u since u quit.

"Uh... OK," was the most articulate response Sam could muster.

U got married.

"I did."

:(:(:(

Sam glanced from the screen to Tahira's face.

She wasn't good enough 4 u.

"We, uh... She..." Sam said, fumbling for something to say, but coming up short.

No 1 is good enough 4 u.

U R special.

Sam's lips suddenly felt very dry. He licked them, but it did little to help.

"Well, *thank you*," he croaked. He edged toward the door. "So, anyway. I was thinking, if you don't need me here, maybe I should go see how Anna and Randy are..."

A rope of cables wrapped around his legs and snaked up around his waist. The phone buzzed insistently in his hand.

Don't go.

Don't leave me.

There was a gap between messages, then:

I won't let u.

———

Randy smashed through a row of pews, splintering the wood and tearing them from their metal fixings. He came to a stop flat on his back, his feet folded up over his head, a cloud of startled butterflies quivering in the air around him.

Over by the Sanctuary, Savior had emerged from within the fire column. Anna thrust out both hands, projecting a narrow beam of concentrated anaphylactic power toward him. He raised a hand and a circle of flame bloomed around it, blocking the attack.

"Yeah, I don't think we'll do that again," he told her, launching an attack of his own. Anna dived sideways, narrowly avoiding a scorching beam of heat that carved a trench along the aisle and sliced through another row of pews.

Anna's suit hummed faintly as she picked up a chunk of the heavy wood and launched it at Savior. He brought up both hands, turning the bench into ash mid-flight, but leaving himself open to an allergy attack. It caught him a glancing blow before he could protect himself, and a single sneeze echoed around the hall.

"Ha!" he said, his voice completely devoid of anything resembling mirth. "Sneaky." He tick-tocked an admonishing finger at her. "My turn."

He grinned as he clenched a fist and the floor on Anna's left burst into flame. She staggered clear, only for the floor on her right to ignite with another fist-clench.

"Dance for me, Anna," Savior said, giggling as the floor and pews flared in flaming jets around her. "Dance for me."

"How about a bench dance?" growled Randy. Savior's head snapped around right before half a church pew smashed into his back like a giant baseball bat, sending him staggering.

A cushion of hot air spun him around. With a flick of his wrist, he ignited the other half of the pew in Randy's hands, forcing him to drop it.

"'Bench dance?'" said Savior. "What the hell is a bench dance?"

"I was making a quip," Randy said.

"No, I know, but... *Bench dance?* That doesn't mean anything."

He made a gesture and a shield of fire wrapped around his back, burning up another of Anna's allergy attacks.

"You're wasting your time, you know?" Savior said. "You should be helping me, not getting in my way. Don't you see? This world is broken. It's rotten to the core. This is our chance to fix it. To start over fresh."

Anna shook her head. "God, it never changes, does it?" she said.

Savior blinked behind his mask. "What doesn't?"

"You. The bad guys. You just love the sound of your own voice. Blah, blah, blah, evil, evil, evil. We get it."

"Ha! 'Bad guys.' I'm not the bad guy, Anna," Savior said.

"Dude, you're totally the bad guy," Randy snarled. "I mean, have you looked in the mirror lately? You've got 'I'm totally the bad guy' written all over you."

Savior's sneer could be heard in his voice. "How would you know, Randy? Those mentors you care so much for never even taught you to read."

"Stop being a dick to Randy," Anna warned. She raised her fists. "And just accept it. You're the bad guy, and we're going to stop... you know, whatever crazy shit it is that you're doing."

"Stop it? Oh, *Anna*," said Savior. He gestured to the fire column behind him. "Don't you see? It's already begun. First the city, then the world will burn. And there's nothing you can do to stop it."

Two texts appeared on Anna's phone screen, one after the other.

Chances of Anna and Randy surviving without u: 3%

:O

Sam wrestled with the restraints around his legs. "Let me go, Tahira," he pleaded. "I can help them."

Chances of Anna and Randy surviving with u: 2.2%

This stopped Sam's struggle for a moment. "What? No, that's not true. I can help."

THIS u.

Sam stared at the screen. "What? What's that supposed to mean?"

What R U afraid of?

"Uh, maybe I'm afraid because you've got me tied up?" Sam said, adding the, 'you psycho-bitch,' part in his head.

4 UR own good.

And that's not it.

What R U afraid of?

"What do you mean?" Sam snapped. "I'm afraid of him! I'm afraid because that lunatic up there is going to kill everyone! I'm afraid because I don't know how to stop him!"

Not true.

Be honest.

Pls.

There was a gap of a few seconds before the next text arrived.

What R U afraid of, Sam?

"This is stupid!" Sam protested.

What R U afraid of?

"Stop asking that!"

What R U afraid of?

"I'm afraid of what'll happen!" Sam bellowed. "OK?! You want me to be honest? Fine, I'll be honest! No, I'm not scared of what I can't do, I'm scared of what I *can* do. What I *might* do! Everyone keeps telling me I just need to concentrate to make my powers work, but that's not true. That's not it."

The phone bleeped.

Tell me.

"I'm *always* concentrating," Sam said, his anger losing some of its edge. "Every minute of every day. I have to concentrate to stop this... this *thing* in my head doing anything. I don't concentrate to make my powers work, I concentrate to *stop* them working because I don't know what'll happen if I don't."

The phone bleeped again.

Chances of Anna and Randy surviving without u: 3%

Another bleep. Another message.

Chances of Anna and Randy surviving if u STOP concentrating:

The next text seemed to take an eternity to arrive. It

contained a single website address. Sam tapped it with his thumb and the phone's browser opened to reveal a website.

"Random number generator," Sam read.

Another text arrived, overlaying itself on the screen.

Worth a try, right?

The cables around Sam's legs went limp. The phone bleeped again.

Thanks for the cat. Hope it helped.

It bleeped again.

*chat. Sorry.

It bleeped one last time.

Now, go B a hero. x

Randy and Anna stood back to back, a tornado of flame spinning around them. They could see Savior watching them, his outline distorted through the twisted, dancing flames. Even through the suits, the heat was scorching, the temperature increasing as the eye of the tornado grew steadily smaller.

"You did your best. That's the main thing," Savior laughed. "I mean, it really isn't, but that's what people say, isn't it? 'Well done. Good try. Better luck next time.' Except there isn't going to be a next time in your case, obviously. On account of you both being dead."

Randy smirked back over his shoulder. "Don't worry. I have a plan."

Anna sighed. "I swear to God, Randy, if you say 'Lefty and Righty' again..."

Randy hesitated.

"That's what you were going to say, wasn't it?" said Anna.

"No," Randy said. "I mean, yes. But... I have another plan."

"OK. What is it?"

Randy clicked his tongue against this teeth. "It's, uh... Give me a minute."

They both jerked in surprise as the tornado of flame became a spinning storm of flat white rectangles that completed a couple more laps before spiraling off in different directions.

Anna peered down at the floor and found it covered with thousands upon thousands of playing cards. Even more inexplicably, every single one of them was the Eight of Diamonds.

"Was that your plan?" Anna whispered.

Randy blinked behind his goggles. "Uh, sure. Yeah. That was totally it."

"It's over, Jim."

Sam's voice echoed around the cavernous cathedral as he stepped out of the curtained doorway and into the aisle.

"OK, it wasn't me," Randy admitted.

"Sam. So you *did* come!" Savior hissed. "And here I thought you were just going to hide yourself away somewhere and let your friends die."

"I'm here to stop you, Jim," Sam said. "You killed all those people, you made me jump onto a moving train and—more importantly—you scared my son. This ends now."

Savior raised himself a few feet off the ground on a cushion of hot air. "You think you're a match for me, *Kid Random?*" he asked, spitting the name out. "You think your powers are greater than mine?"

Anna and Randy stepped apart, leaving space in the aisle for Sam to walk between them. "You can do this, Sam," Anna whispered. "Just, you know, focus. Concentrate."

Sam smiled at her. "Meh. I'm done concentrating," he said.

Squaring his shoulders, he adjusted his mask then ran a hand down the front of his costume, feeling the bumps of the 'KR' on his chest.

He flicked his eyes to Savior, flexed his fingers, and cricked his neck.

"Hey, Jim," he said. "Let's get random!"

Savior frowned behind his mask. "What's that supposed to mea—?" he began, then the end of the sentence became muffled when he found himself completely encased in several hundred gallons of wobbling lime Jell-O.

Randy whistled through his teeth. "Well, I did not see that coming," he said.

"No," Sam agreed. "Me neither."

A fireball exploded from inside the Jell-O and rocketed along the aisle. Anna caught Sam by the shoulder and all three of them ducked. The air above them was filled with heat and smoke and the distinctive aroma of burning hair.

"That, I saw coming," Randy growled.

"We've got to get his helmet off," Anna said, as Savior's lime-flavored prison melted into a puddle of liquid.

Another fireball screamed at them. The shape in Sam's head kicked, and he made no attempt to fight it. A life-sized bronze statue of the actor, Henry Winkler, appeared directly ahead of them. The fireball ricocheted off it, spinning the statue on its base and melting the right side of the former *Happy Days* star's face into a horrifying grimace.

"Did you do that one, or was it me?" Randy asked.

Sam side-eyed him. "It was me."

"OK, cool. Because I wasn't sure," said Randy.

"How are we going to reach him?" asked Anna, as another flaming sphere obliterated what remained of Henry Winkler's head.

Sam shrugged. "Didn't anyone ever tell you? If you can dodge a ball, you can dodge *anything*."

"Oh, great," Anna groaned. "Because that worked out so well for us last time."

Sam charged ahead. He made it a full three feet before a

wall of heat slammed into him on the left, launching him across the aisle. His power kicked, and a cocoon of toilet paper appeared around him, cushioning his landing enough to stop him from breaking anything vital.

A blast of hot air ignited the toilet paper, and Sam spent a frantic few seconds clawing it away before the shape in his head kicked again and a gaggle of geese appeared directly in front of Savior, all blinking in surprise.

"Geese," said Anna, because she wasn't entirely sure what else to say about this development.

"Now we're talking," Randy growled. "Those things are vicious bastards. Trust me, I know. Don't ask me how I know, but I know. Savior doesn't stand a—"

The geese exploded, showering the front few pews in burning feathers and smoldering bird guts.

"I retract that last statement," Randy said.

Savior raised both hands in Sam's direction, and Anna saw her chance. Running for the Sanctuary, she threw each hand forward in turn, pumping the air, her fingers spreading wide with every thrust. The air rippled with a succession of blasts, and Savior erupted in a sneezing fit that sent his heat blast wide.

Three rows of pews just a little behind Sam went up in flames, billowing up a cloud of black smoke. Coughing, Sam clambered over the pew in front, the smoke nipping at his eyes and snagging in his throat.

"I'll get the helmet!" Randy growled, racing past Anna, his cape billowing behind him. As Randy ran, another stray bolt of fire erupted upward from the sneezing Savior. Anna's eyes followed it, as if it were moving in slow motion, as it sailed up, up, up toward—

"Look out!" Anna cried, as the blast exploded against the ornate ceiling directly above Sam's head.

Sam raised his eyes in time to see several hundred pounds of wood, stone, and slate come tumbling toward him.

"Oh, shi—" he began, then the sound of the debris crashing down on him reverberated around the cavernous cathedral.

CHAPTER THIRTY-FOUR

THE *BOOM* of the falling debris made Randy hesitate. A fireball that was almost as large as he was struck him like a battering ram, twisting him into a backflip and sending him tumbling along the aisle.

Rage rewrote the lines of Anna's face. She advanced on Savior, flinging blast after blast in the villain's direction, only for them to be swallowed by the wall of fire he raised before him. He stared out at her from behind it, the dancing flames twisting his mask into something even more monstrous and demonic.

A blast of heat swiped her legs out from under her and she gasped as her head *cracked* against one of the remaining pews. The suit protected her from any real damage, but the combined effects of the fire and the impact started the battery icon flashing.

Groaning, Anna started to get to her feet, but a cushion of hot air pressed down on her, forcing her back to the floor.

"Well," said Savior, dropping his fire shield. "Hasn't this been fun? Just like old times. Except, you know, I didn't want to kill you all back then." He shot Randy the briefest of glares. "Well, maybe some of you."

He advanced down the steps, his feet leaving burning footprints on the carpet behind him. "You hear that?" he said, touching the side of his helmet. "I'd imagine your ears are still ringing, so you probably don't. It's the sound of a city on the brink of destruction. See that fire column there? How it goes up? Well, in a moment, once it's fully charged, it's going to start going *down*. It's going to drill right down into the city's foundations. There, I will make it spread to every corner of Cityopolis. The whole place will be consumed from below. I will do what the Justice Platoon never could. I will finally cleanse Cityopolis of all crime."

"By killing everyone," Anna wheezed.

Savior shrugged. "A necessary side-effect."

"I don't think so, *punk!*" spat Randy, hauling himself to his feet. "Say hello to Lefty and—"

A fireball hit him in the shoulder, spinning him to the floor. He lay motionless for a moment, then forced himself to rise.

"Righty. They're going to teach you that—"

A rectangular platform of flame battered down on him, swatting him to the ground again. He coughed, his body wracked with pain, tears seeping out from the gaps where his shattered flying goggles met his cheeks.

"Crime doesn't pay," Randy wheezed, dragging himself to his knees. He wobbled unsteadily there, gathering himself before pushing any further.

A fireball slammed into his chest, folding him backward. Savior hissed furiously as he struck the inert Butterfly King with a succession of blasts.

"Stop it!" Anna cried, struggling against the weight of the heat pressing down on her. "Leave him alone!"

Savior cackled as he struck Randy again with another ball

of fire, before turning his attention to Anna. "Very well. I don't think he'll be going anywhere anytime soon, anyway," the villain spat. "Looks like it's just you and me, Allergy Girl. And soon, it'll just be—"

"Seriously?" Randy spat, his voice slurred. Savior and Anna both watched in amazement as he struggled to his feet and wearily raised his fists. His head moved from Savior to a spot just a couple of feet on the villain's right, like Randy was seeing two of him and didn't know which one he should be addressing. "That the best you got?"

Through the mask, Anna saw Savior's eyes narrow in rage. Flames exploded in their dark centers as he drew back both hands and let out a banshee scream of raw fury.

His hands thrust forward. A teardrop-shaped mass of blue flame streaked toward the swaying Randy, flying far too fast for him to react.

As it flew, its color changed, going from gas-flame blue to a swirl of yellow and brown.

The 'fireball' splattered harmlessly across Randy's chest, showering him in cream, caramel, and pieces of sliced banana. Everyone watched in confused silence as the delicious-looking dessert mush flopped to the ground with a *sploot*.

The mountain of debris that had been covering Sam became several dozen inflatable penises. Sam exploded from within them, throwing air-filled giant dicks in all directions.

"You heard him, Jimbo," Sam said, as three-foot blow-up schlongs rained down around them. "Is that the best you got?"

RAAAAAARGH!

Savior's howl of anger shook what was left of the ceiling. He shoved his hands forward, throwing all his body weight behind them. The shimmering heatwave that had been surrounding him whipped around to his front as he channeled it into a single concentrated fire blast.

Sam brought up his own hands and an eight-foot thick wall of raw, quivering pork fat appeared in front of him. It sizzled and popped as the heat struck it, and Sam gritted his teeth as the side nearest to him began to bubble and melt.

With the heat now off her—literally—Anna got to her feet. The battery symbol in her visor gave a final farewell flash, then the suit's Battle Mode disengaged. Even shielded by the fat wall, the heat from Savior's attack was intense. He had to be putting everything he had into this one.

Which meant...

"Randy! The helmet!" she hissed.

Randy turned slowly toward her, smoke rising from his beard, banana-based dessert dribbling down his front.

"Huh?" he said.

Savior roared, doubling down on his frontal attack. The heat forced Sam back a step, the edges of the fat-shield blackening.

"We need you for this, Randy," Anna yelled, shaking him by the shoulders. "You're the only one who can do this."

Randy's lips moved as he repeated the words silently, trying to figure out their meaning. At last, something seemed to click.

"Because... because I'm the leader," he slurred.

Anna gripped his shoulders tightly. "You're goddamn right you are," she said. "In a way. Now do your thing, Butterfly King. The good citizens of Cityopolis are depending on it."

That did it. Randy inhaled sharply through his nose. "I won't let them down," he said, his voice descending into its usual guttural growl.

Pressing two fingers to the side of his head, Randy raised the other hand and made a series of theatrical twisting motions in the air.

"Can we get a move on?" Sam yelped, bracing himself against the heat.

"Do my bidding, my butterfly brethren!" Randy cried, and the air was filled with the sound of flapping wings. Assuming you had exceptionally good hearing and were listening *very* closely.

The butterflies emerged from the shadows around the cathedral, then pootled around behind Savior until they formed a single colorful cloud. With a gesture from Randy, they forced their way inside Savior's helmet, wedging themselves up there in their hundreds, just as Sam's fat-shield bubbled away into nothing.

Savior twisted, grabbing for his helmet as more and more butterflies flooded inside. He tried to scream, but a particularly large and impressive Compton tortoiseshell jumped down his throat, making the ultimate sacrifice.

The helmet shifted upward. Savior scrambled to hold onto it with both hands, but was forced to bring one down again to heat-push Sam and Anna back when they started to run at him.

More butterflies forced their way inside the helmet, tickling his nose and covering his eyes. The helmet inched upward again, but he held tight, blindly sweeping arcs of fire out in front of him.

"It's not working!" Anna yelped. "There aren't enough of them! We need more butterflies!"

"I don't have more butterflies!" Randy spat.

With a *bang*, the front doors of the cathedral were thrown wide. Sam, Ann and Randy all turned in time to see a single butterfly come fluttering through the doorway.

"Callum!" Randy whispered, his voice cracking with emotion. "You son-of-a-bitch!"

They all watched, awestruck, as Callum bobbed gently along the aisle, his colorful wings flapping as fast as they could. Which, admittedly, wasn't that fast.

They watched for a while longer.

And a while longer.

Randy hummed the theme to *Superman* for a while, egging the butterfly on.

"Go, Callum!" he cheered, once he'd made it all the way to the end of the main overture. "You can do this!"

One of Savior's random blasts scorched the air ahead of the butterfly. Callum rose above it, drifted lazily on the cushion of heat for a few seconds, then resumed his slow and steady assault.

"OK, fuck this, this is taking all day," said Anna, turning and beginning another charge at Savior. A fireball exploded at her feet, cutting short her run before it had even started.

She was just preparing to try again when Callum fluttered past her, swooping and dodging to avoid another erratic volley of fire.

Banking around, Callum lined himself up for his final attack run, then stopped in mid-air.

Randy nodded, just once. "Go get him, big guy."

And with that, Callum fluttered up inside Savior's helmet.

There was a muffled shout from behind the mask.

There was a *pop*.

And, like a cork escaping a bottle, the helmet shot up into the air, then clanked to the floor and bounced down the Sanctuary steps.

For a moment, it seemed as if Savior's face was all the colors of the rainbow, but then the butterflies took flight and the true horror of his appearance was revealed. His skin was shriveled and blackened, his lips burned away to reveal all his teeth. He had no hair to speak of, just a shrunken raisin of a skull crusted over with scabs and burns.

"M-my h-h-helmet," he wheezed, collapsing to his knees. He stretched a hand out for the metal mask, but the movement was slow and creaking, and twisted him up with pain.

"Oh my God," Anna said, her hand going to her mouth. "What did they do to him?"

The air in the cathedral suddenly cooled, as the column of fire fizzled out. Sam leaned against one of the few remaining pews, his body sagging with exhaustion.

"We did it," he said. "We actually stopped him."

Anna's phone buzzed in his utility belt. Sam fished it out and read the message on the screen.

HELP!!!!!

Savior's laugh started as a wheeze, rose to a hiss, then struggled all the way up to a rattle. "You... idiots," he spat. "Y-you haven't sssstopped m-me."

The ground beneath their feet rumbled ominously.

"It has only j-just beg-gun!"

CHAPTER THIRTY-FIVE

Heat rose up from beneath the cathedral, sending cracks racing up the ancient stone walls. The whole building—no, the whole *city*—seemed to shake, as Savior's column of flame exploded through the foundations.

NOW WOOD B NICE!!! flashed up on Anna's phone, then:

*WOULD.

Sam snapped into action.

"You two go and help Calcu-Lass!" he urged, shoving the phone into Anna's hands. "Try to get her out of here."

"What about you?" asked Anna. "The whole place is about to come down."

"There has to be a way to stop this," Sam replied. "I'll find it. Now go."

Their eyes locked for a moment. Hopeless. Desperate. But then Randy caught Anna by the arm and they both raced off for the curtained doorway that led down to the crypt below.

Sam turned on the fallen Savior. The laughter still hissed

out of him, although the lack of lips made it difficult to tell if he was smiling or not.

"How do I stop this, Jim?" Sam demanded. "What do I do?"

"N-nothing," Savior sniggered. "There's nothing you c-can do, Sam. You... l-lost. Only G-God could sssstop it now."

He coughed and choked on what might have been more laughter, but might equally have been sobbing. He had no eyelids, and presumably no tear ducts, so actual tears were out of the question.

"Only God could stop it now," Sam whispered.

He reeled back a step as Kapitän Nazi's voice rumbled around in his head.

He is... How can I put this? He is a god. Properly focused, there is nothing he cannot do.

The ground trembled. Outside, building alarms wailed. Sam's eyes fell on the helmet lying at the bottom of the steps, the metal *pinging* as it cooled.

It was in his hands before he realized he'd picked it up. The empty eye sockets stared up at him as if daring him to put it on.

"N-no!" Savior spat. "It's mine. *Mine.*"

Sam shook the helmet a few times, dislodging a few mangled butterflies that had been stuck to the inside. It seemed to hum in his hands as he raised it above his head, then sighed with contentment as he slipped it on.

He wasn't sure what he'd been expecting, exactly, but it was more than the absolutely nothing that happened. The floor continued to rumble and the walls carried on shaking. Sam looked down at his hands like he might find instructions written there, then rapped his knuckles against the side of the helmet.

"Uh, hello?" he said. "Is this thing on?"

The shape in his head wriggled briefly, then exploded.

Sam screamed as his consciousness rushed outward and inward at the same time, collapsing his mind in on itself, then spitting it back out again.

Random bubbles of power appeared around him. A new lifeform burst into existence at his feet, before somehow becoming extinct again three seconds earlier. Air solidified. Smoke melted. Sam felt every part of himself become every part of everything else.

He saw himself standing in the cathedral, reality bending around him. He saw Anna and Randy dragging Calcu-Lass's chair away from the column of fire that tore down through the crypt.

And farther out he went. He saw the cathedral from above, manhole lids flipping out of the ground around it on jets of steam. He saw the legs of the Elevated Train track wobble and shake, and the streets of Cityopolis crack.

He saw the fire, too, and recoiled from its heat. It was everywhere at once, devouring the underside of the city, chewing up through the buildings above. There was so much of it. So much.

Too much.

Kapitän Nazi's voice came at him again.

His power borders on being unlimited. Truly unlimited. He can manipulate matter with a thought. He can create physical objects from thin air, turn people into memories, alter the very fabric of reality itself. Properly focused, there is nothing he cannot do.

Sam tried to clench his fists, but he wasn't in his body anymore. Or rather, he *was* in his body, but he was simultaneously everywhere else, too, and his fists were just two of countless billions.

"Focus, Sam," he whispered.

He saw buildings catch fire. He heard screams of panic and pain, felt the city shaking itself apart.

And then he saw the inside of a small apartment on the

other side of town, and the look of terror on the face of a five-year-old boy.

His boy.

Sam felt the flames licking through the city, gobbling it up, threatening to consume everything. Every*one*.

"Stop," he said, in a voice that was felt around the world.

The flames froze, not in ice, but in time itself. With a gesture, Sam rewound them, drawing them back through the tunnels and sewers of Cityopolis, back toward the cathedral, and back up through the hole in the floor.

The column of fire returned for a moment, stretching high up into the sky. Then, with a thought from Sam, it condensed down, briefly becoming a wide round pancake of flame, then simply a wide round pancake of pancake that landed on the floor with a *flomp*.

"I... I did it," Sam whispered. He saw the words emerge from his mouth as colors and shapes, and decided the time had probably come to take the helmet off.

But wait.

The voice whispered to him. Not Kapitän Nazi's this time, but another voice, much closer in his ear.

Think what you can do, it told him. *Think what we can achieve.*

"W-we?" Sam stammered. The helmet felt tight against his head. He reached up to pull it off, but his arms were suddenly too heavy to move.

All this power. Sooo much power, the voice whispered. *We can fix this broken world. We can put things right.*

An image flashed up in Sam's mind, unbidden. It showed Corey laughing and giggling on a swing, the chains *creaking* as he swung back and forth. Sam's heart fluttered like one of Randy's butterflies, then stopped when he saw Brian standing behind Corey, grinning as he pushed him.

Pushed *his* son.

That's your boy, the voice hissed. *Not his. Never his. Fix it, Sam. Fix this, then we can fix everything.*

"Fix... it," Sam said, his voice coming as a low growl. He could do it, too. He could blink Brian out of existence. Make it so he'd never existed in the first place. He could feel the power bubbling around inside him.

He could do it.

He could *fix* it.

He thought of all those things Brian and Corey would do together.

He thought of all those times Brian would be the one there cheering him on, not Sam.

He thought of Corey cowering in the hallway, Brian standing between him and the Magma-Mutt. Powerless, but refusing to back down. Keeping Corey safe.

"N-no," Sam spat.

Yesssss!

With a roar, Sam jammed his hands against the underside of the helmet and pushed. It screamed inside his head as he forced it off, and as it clattered to the ground Sam's consciousness snapped back into him like an elastic band.

The force of it knocked him off his feet and slammed him into a pew, knocking the air from his body. He recovered in time to see Savior's fingers tighten around the helmet. The villain's skin cracked and split as he grinned with glee.

"You f-fool!" he hissed, pulling on the mask. His eyes flared and the strength returned to his voice. "Now, you'll pay for—"

A hole opened in the sky directly above him. A three-thousand-pound mutant bull plummeted from within it. It landed with a *crunch*, a *splat*, and a brief, agonizing scream.

For a moment, all became still. The bull's eyes were wide and staring in a way that suggested it had seen things no bull should ever see, mutant or otherwise.

Then, a flattened black helmet rolled out from beneath the bull's immense torso, spun a few times like a coin, and *clunked* onto the floor.

The bull looked at Sam.

Sam looked at the bull.

It snorted, then let out a low, slightly quizzical *moo*.

"Yeah, pal," Sam wheezed. "You and me both."

✂

Sam, Anna, and Randy blinked in the glow of the spotlight from the helicopter hovering above the square. A thick layer of black smoke hung in the sky, blocking out the sun and turning day into near-night.

Behind them, Calcu-Lass sat astride the Beef Chief's giant bull, wires coiling from her head like Medusa's snakes.

"I reckon we're going to have a lot of explaining to do," said Anna, struggling to hold onto the giant inflatable penis she carried beneath one arm.

"You two, maybe," Randy growled. "I'll slip into the shadows like the night's phantom."

"Yeah, good luck with that," Anna told him. She squinted up at the chopper. "What do we think? Police or press?"

"Press," said Sam. "No way the cops would be getting this close."

"Fair point," Anna conceded. She looked back over her shoulder. "You OK back there, Tahira?"

Her phone bleeped.

I'm on a big bull.

Anna frowned. "I don't know if you're saying that like it's a good thing or a bad thing."

The phone bleeped again. This time, instead of text, it showed an animated GIF of a man dancing. Anna vaguely recognized it as the actor, Tobey Maguire, in one of the *Spider-Man* movies.

"I'll take it as a good thing," she said, slipping the phone back into her pocket.

A voice crackled from the helicopter. "Well, well, well. You actually did it."

"Chuck!" cried Sam. "That's Chuck!"

"Yay!" said Anna. "Wait. Hold on." She cupped her hands around her mouth. "Have we had a helicopter this whole fucking time?"

"We can talk about that later," Chuck replied. "But first..."

The spotlight swept across the blackened grass until it found a small but growing crowd of people. Men. Women. Even some children. Sam didn't recognize them individually, but as a group, there was no mistaking them.

"The good citizens of Cityopolis," he said.

A cheer rang out. Just one at first, but it was followed quickly by another. One by one, the citizens began to applaud and stamp their feet in celebration.

"Superhero poses, guys," Randy instructed, lowering himself into a dramatic squat. "Come on. Let's give them what they want."

Sam and Anna exchanged looks. Even the bull got in on it, ejecting a derisory snort through both nostrils.

"Yeah, we're not going to do that," Anna said. She waved and smiled at the crowd. "Thank you! Thanks! Appreciate it," she called. "Much obliged. Donations of alcohol gladly accepted."

Sam laughed at that, then slapped himself on the forehead. "Aw... no," he said.

"What?" Anna asked. "What's wrong?"

"We forgot the witty quip."

"*Damn it!*" Anna spat. "I had one prepared, and everything. I was going to say, 'Feel *this* burn, bitch!' then probably kick him in the dick."

"That's good," said Sam. He began to walk, and the others followed. "That's really strong. I was working on something about feeling the heat, maybe. Or, like, just... 'Savior. You're *fired*.'"

"God, I'd have loved to have seen that," Anna said. "Imagine his face."

"Fire burning," said Randy. "Wait, no. Burning fire guy. Guy fire. *Guy on fire*."

Anna sighed and put her arm around the Butterfly King's shoulder. "Randy, my friend," she said. "We have a *lot* of work to do."

"Hot man!" Randy said.

Sore, tired, and with a three-thousand-pound mutant bull called Russel plodding along behind them, the sidekicks limped on into Cityopolis, and into the welcoming cheers of its good citizens.

THE END

EXTRACT FROM THE DEATH RECORDS OF JOHN HITLER (AKA KAPITÄN NAZI)

INCLUDED HERE IS an abbreviated extract from the death records of John Hitler, detailing the names and causes of death of just some of those killed by his 'Kapitän Nazi' persona.

NAME AND CAUSE OF DEATH

Tim Blagbrough - Hit by flying baby
James Linehan - Aggressively ruptured
Ted Thompson - Dissolved in vinegar
Diane Carr - Force-fed frogs
John Carswell - Crushed by falling tank
Bobby Kennedy - Impaled on rusty spike
Jason Phillips - Impaled on rusty spikes (multiple)
AnnMarie Phillips - Eaten by Nazi wolves
Shane Phillips - Molested by Nazi wolves. Then eaten
Harrison Kyng - Steamroller
Chuck Daniel - Parasite (facial)
Tommy Donbavand - Parasite (rectal)

Brian Nimmo - Aggressive rash
Alan Donoghue - Exploding duck
James Farler - Sandpapered
Jessica Farler - Beheaded (twice)
Bryce Crux - Punched through hedge
Eli Picker - Choked on own feet
Danny Peters - Launched into space
David Whitworth - Catapulted into wall
Dan Williams - Force-fed until exploded
Stephanie Fraser - Erased from time
John 'Mojo' Morrison - Cut down by arrows
Andrew Dobell - Drowned in paint
Dan Robinson - Cleaved into eighths
Roibeard Padraig Gelms - Choked on own name
Chris Treise - Trapped in slowly contracting cube
Izzy Treise - Trapped in slowly contracting cube
Maisie Treise - Trapped in slowly contracting cube
Bob Brews - Locked in freezer
Christopher Smith - Vaporized
Robbie Smith - Vaporized
Martin Carter - Speared up the anus
Richard McAllister - Lava in eyes
Jackie Skidmore - Head swapped with dog
Boo Skidmore (dog) - Head swapped with owner
Chris Picken - Head twisted off
Lucy Martin - Ants. Lots of ants
Jeff Mychalchyk - Cleaved in half
Angela Crossley - Pickled in vinegar
Luke Brook - Buried alive
Lindy Pinckney Felder - Nazi wasps
Akbar Esfahani - Nazi bears
Austin Larocque - Nazi octopus
Claire Christie - "Nundroid" robot nun
Chris Hurden - Heavily sat on

Jeremy Stokely - Head imploded

Andrew Nicholls - Suffocated in Outer Space

Antony Evans - Gremlin things

Ian Turner - Hitler clones

John Thurmond - More Hitler clones

Emma Porter - 13th Century German Wizard

Iain Sutherland - A big fright

Claire Oxborough - Fired out of cannon

Ben William - Hit by Claire Oxborough

Caz Stanford - Partially inflated

Chris Green - Suffocated in Outer Space

April Wilcox - Turned to dough

Jeff Hollingsworth - Lost in time

Jason McMarrow - Covered in bees

Ken Hulme - Explosive diarrhea

Paul Smith - Vaporized

Nancy Lynch Gibson - Acid bath

Ben Miller - Diced by metal net

Graeme Simpson - German sausage

Kathryn Simpson - Drowned in own urine

Anna Beack - Violently folded

Justin Freeman - Tickled

Antony Garlick - Spit-roasted

Mark Blackburn - Disemboweled

James Taylor - Brain inverted

Michael Godwin - Nazi geese

Hunter Harbert - Loneliness

John Blair - A scary witch

Warren Whitley - Punched repeatedly in balls

Bryan T. Taureck - Consumed

Les Fulbrook - Axes. A lot of axes

Tami Yee - Nazi dinosaur

Ben Lea - Regular dinosaur

Esther Lea - Sandwiched between glass

Marcus Madden - Swatted
John Trewick - Blotted
Andrew Dyer - Drowned in quicksand
James Grey - Carried off by birds
Pete Nicholls - Chained to rocket
Natalie Nicholls - Chained to different rocket
Scott Sherman - Nazi sheep
Dawn Ward - Crucifixion
William Ward - Assorted bread products
Bill Beyer - Glockenspiel
Colin Mclay - Bludgeoned by pretzel
Lee Milnes - A big fire
Sarah Kernan - Nazi penguins
Adalee Schuster - Hit by clock
Brett Bushman - Nipple twister
Grayson Daniel - Weird smell
Trevor Sexton - Sexed on
Chris Tedder - Turned inside-out
Marty Elliott - Lightly poached
Paddy Healey - Rope burns
Stu Rusk - General neglect
Andy Mac - Lost in maze
Lora Hannigan McLaughlin - Nazi chickens
Eve Nixon - A big monster
Marcus Rayner - Mutated by slime
Stephen Waldram - You don't want to know
Alan Mascall - Head-swapped
Tracy Mascall - Head-swapped
Brenda Gregory - Laughed to death
Kelly Seeley - Chronic embarrassment
Devin Seeley - Licked out of existence
Mac Waygood - Space kittens
Hudson Mack Cagle - Nazi space kittens
Scuba Steve Conant - Fired into the sun

Joseph Kawalec - Covered in butter
Mark Denson - Ignored
Julian Cheal - Suffocated in Outer Space
Hanna Elizabeth - Stray apostrophe
Debbie Durr - Unraveled
Danielle Knight - Just plain murdered
James Richard Tyrrell - Organs harvested
Scott Evans - Trapped at Earth's core
Geoff Evans - Prolonged crucifixion
Stuart Walker - Spiralized
Cindy Watkins - Angry robots
Lynnette Buhrman - A big brute of a man
Mike Barry - Sentient mustache
Karl Binder - Demonic possession
Tina Stowe - Pitchfork somewhere unpleasant
Shawn Dvorak - Crushed by accordion
J. Barrett Kane - Tom Selleck
Chris Kane - Organs harvested
Jesse Kane - Brain sucked out
Benjamin Kane - Buried in laundry
Jake Kane - Steam-ironed
Kelly O'Donnell - Gored by rhino
Marcus Alexander Hart - Molested by rhino (not the
same rhino)
Kathleen Guilbeault - Nazi swan
Donny Oswald - Encased in concrete
Paul Agnew - Nuclear hat
The GeriTones - The hottest fire known to man
Joey Fatone - Nazi puppets
Connor Radtke - Deveined
Bob Cotter - Thumbs through eye sockets
Jackie Phipps - Dropped from a tremendous height
Tony Diperna - Dropped from an equally tremendous height
Tracey Weatherilt - Angry birds (not the game)

Jim Fleming - Evil dance-off
Deb Perkins - Horny pterodactyl
Mark Telford - Kicked by multiple horses
Rigel Meketa - Boiled in jelly
Bob Smith - Nazi mongoose
Charlie Dickie - Roughly manhandled
Mickey Lasky - Poorly treated
Lord Walter Lenz III - Vomited inside-out
Thomas Hernandez - Strangled with own entrails
Paul Danher - Shot 700 times
Dean Clark - Stage fright
Kim Worley - Punched through a wall
Heather Elizabeth Stone - Shoved off a roof
Sharon Bye - Crushed by giant pen
Keven Bye - Drowned in giant ink bottle
Mike Stone - Nazi marmot
Ozzie Lane - The Brown Death
Tom Tennille - Erratic dissection
Steven Slutsky - Covered in wax
Ross Slutsky - Shaved to the bone
Tom Blackerby - Meat grinder
Jeff Rosati - Gradually lowered into tar
Syed Shahrukh Hasan - Ruined by ducks
George McConnon - So much fire
Rob Olson - Several lasers
Nick Schult - Shat on by monsters
Jennifer Schult - Something unpleasant
Isaac Cowell - Sentient bread
Greg Parlmer - Cyborgs (not robots)
Victoria Bailey - Forced alcohol poisoning
Caleb Richardson - Thinly sliced
Peter Kingsbury - Slowly beheaded
Nathaniel West - Repeatedly twisted
Don Berry - Smeared liberally

Steven Berry - Nazi mice

David Wilkinson - Rectal insertions

Corey Lindsey - Tied to train tracks

Susan A Wallace - Tied to train

Mike W. Duncan - Whittled away

Glen Blagg - Long overlooked

Linda Frydl - Brain-smashed

Mike Frydl - Gut-munched

Rick Moore - The French

Patrick Giallombardo - Run up a flagpole

Jonathan Mack - Robo-Hitler

Michelle Bird - Ghost Hitler

Alex Sime - Alien Hitler

Scott Schoba - Alternate Reality Hitler

Simon Nichols - Hitler tribute act

Angela Nichols - Actual Hitler

Gordon Keller - High speed spin cycle

Vicki Sue Jones - Nazi sparrows

Desmond Armstrong - Implosion

Leela Armstrong - Teeny tiny men

Scott Jenner - Eaten by giant

Digby Reardon - Buttons

Buck Rogers - Sent to the distant future

Jenny Stoker - Died on a poker

Megs Long - Substantially shortened

Jamie Moriarty Thomson - A huge fucking snake

Gloria Jean Minnick - Miniaturized

Darcey Adamson - Large Hadron Collider

Sharon Roop - Distilled in vinegar

Rupert Doggsbottom - Thigh-slapped

Steve Dias - Disassembled

Leslie Vorhees - Aged prematurely

Alison Dishinger - Crocodile infested swamp

Jacob Brotbeck - An assortment of power tools

Jeff Goddard - One particular power tool
Andy Quickel - Deatomized
Colonel (Rtd) Jon Byrom - Buried in desert
Chris Henderson - Violently exfoliated
BioBob Henderson - Choked on cat
Roy Smith - Vaporized
Angela Weiner - Nazi woodlouse
Allen Lee - Mutant scorpions
Mary Margaret Devine - Nibbled by fish
Leslie Devine - A *lot* of frogs
Joe Bew - Hung, drawn, and quartered
Michelle Bew - Hung, drawn, quartered, and eighthed
Brandon Lam - Struck by lightning
Amy Clawson - Vending machine incident
Allen Molthan - Molthan Lava (see what I did there?)
Gary Turner - Halved by window
Francesca Knibbs - Firmly compressed
James Lee - Filled with sauerkraut
Ewan Lind - Sandblasted
Valerie Granger - Grabbed by a stranger
Deb & Stu Aitken - Toxic confetti
Rick Barrett - Nazi squirrel
Jack Barrett - Choked on nuts
Diana Giles - Sea serpent
Andy Seaton - Electric tornado
Vince Erceg - Leeches. So many leeches
Fabian J Valdes - Head-popping ray gun
Mark Sidanycz - A giant whisk
Adam Goldstein - A well-timed kick
Perry G. Fergin - Peregrine Falcon
Carol Gleeson - Parasite bugs
Malcolm Winn - Spider-dragon
Tom Hall - A bouncy ball
Christina Heine - Furious demi-god

Mojo Flucke, PhD - Hammond Organ
Rick Lambright - Nazi slugs
John Berryman - Rolling stones (not the band)
Joe Mulini - Glued to Washington Monument
Stacy Harper Watson - Sentient kitchen utensils
Quinn Watson - Sentient kitchen utensils
Jesse Watson - Sentient kitchen utensils
Olivia Watson - Tripped and fell. While fleeing sentient kitchen utensils.
Christopher Cicia - Sucked into television
Karen McAdam - Shoved in a fridge
Ryan Frazer - Multiple wormholes
Richard Womble - The Bulgarians
Don Sarginson - Forced strenuous exercise
U'i Lani Womble - Hypnotic suggestion
Jessica Smith - Torso removed
Graham Basden - Psychic dwarf
Richard Walpole - Magically induced constipation
Len Pearce - Overly effective love potion
Natalie Cleary - Evil shoes
David and Isobel Nurse - Smashed together
Mark Harwood - Pushed off bridge
James Mansell - Turned into ape
Estelle McNeill - Radioactive piercings
Garry Ferguson - Strangled by g-string (guitar)
Sherrill Neese - Strangled by g-string (not guitar)
Suzanne Ehrhardt - Chemical weapon disguised as adorable puppy
Rowan Kerwin - Adorable puppy
Ann Jackson - Several whales
Simon Bennett - Expertly aimed cucumber
Dave Rowlinson - Giant darts
Sharon Peters - Nazi goldfish
Tony Danza - Baked in foil

Hans Heussler - Too many sausages
Andrew Edmonds - A scary clown
Marge Pala - Whipped by lederhosen
Dave Fosbinder - Danced to death
Ashleigh Fosbinder - Embarrassment at above
Avery Fosbinder - Shame
Noah Fosbinder - Laughter
Broadus D. Weatherall - Turned to cheese
Charlene Lock P. - Soul torn asunder by folklore demons
Jacqui Ball Licht - Fell over
David L. Crooks, Jr. - Floated away
David L. Crooks, III - Cut into thirds
Lexa CrooksA - huge sheep
Barbara Crooks - A slightly less huge, albeit still massive
sheep
Steve Collins - Vomited himself up
Ann Duff - Cheese grater
Samatha Cooper - Stretched
Athena Crooks - Compressed
Persephone Crooks - Innards made into balloon animals
Sasha Smith - Neck removed
Mark Bright - Brains removed through rectum
Steve Bright - Force-fed great literature

AUTHOR'S NOTES

Hey there, you! So, you've made it to the end of my longest novel to date. Well done. I hope it wasn't too hard-going for you, and that you can now tell your Beef Chief from your Captain Handstand.

As well as being my longest novel so far, this was also my first book for adults that isn't directly connected to *Space Team*, or set within the Space Team Universe. If you haven't checked that series out yet, by the way, you definitely should. It's a lot like the nonsense you just read, but in space. Space nonsense.

Since I had your attention, I thought I'd explain why I decided to write about superheroes. To do that, I have to jump back a bit to when I was around six or seven years old, and had zero interest in books. Seriously, I couldn't stand 'em. All those words? No thanks.

What I *did* love, though, was comics. I couldn't get enough of those. Living in a remote part of the UK, there wasn't a lot of choice, comic-wise, but every week I'd devour as many of the British titles as I could – The Beano, The

Dandy, Whizzer & Chips — to name but a few you've probably never heard of.

I didn't literally devour them, incidentally. That would've been madness.

Anyway, each issue was made up of maybe a dozen different stories featuring that comic's regular characters. They were all short, funny, set-up and punchline type strips, running one or two pages long.

And I couldn't get enough of them.

Someone who didn't approve of comics, though? My teacher. She hated them. And, as a result, she didn't particularly like me, either.

One day, when I was around 7, my class was taken to the small local village library, where we met the new librarian. She'd be in the job a few months, but this was the first time we'd properly met her. She was keen to know what we liked to read, so our teacher made us stand up one by one to talk about the books we most enjoyed.

She left me for last. Once everyone else had said the type of books they liked, they were directed to the relevant section, so by the end it was just me, my teacher, and the librarian, Mrs Macallister.

"Tell Mrs Macallister what *you* like to read, Barry," my teacher said, practically sneering at me.

I stood up, feeling the weight of their gazes on me. I shuffled awkwardly, my head down.

"Comics," I mumbled.

"Louder."

"Comics," I said. "I... I like comics."

My teacher rolled her eyes and tutted. Mrs Macallister clicked her tongue against the roof of her mouth a few times. "Comics?"

"I know!" shrieked my teacher. "Comics."

Mrs Macallister raised a finger. "Wait there," she said, then she vanished into the back store.

My heart began to race. What was she looking for? Was she off to fetch some sort of horrible torture device with which to punish me? Was she going to bring some other librarians out of hiding so they could all point and laugh at me?

She emerged a minute later, staggering under the weight of a cardboard box. With some effort, she deposited it at my feet.

"There you go," she said.

Cautiously, I opened the lid, still expecting some horrible trauma to befall me.

Instead, I came face to face with Spider-Man.

I'd heard about Spider-Man, of course, but I'd never seen one of his actual comics before. US comics never really made it as far of the Highlands of Scotland at that time, as far as I knew, and yet here one was, sitting in front of me.

I remember the feeling vividly, like an electric shock, as I saw that comic. It imprinted itself so vividly that when I spotted the exact issue for sale in a comic shop almost thirty years later – *The Amazing Spider-Man #245*, in case you were wondering – I recognized it immediately, and bought it for my collection. The comic that started it all.

There were over 200 comics in that box, and Mrs Macallister let me come to the library every day to read them. Through the box I lived adventures alongside Superman, Batman, the Hulk, Captain America and, of course, Spidey himself.

By the time I'd read them all, Mrs Macallister had single-handedly also managed to convert me into a reader of books. She was responsible for the first book I ever wrote, aged 9, too. But those are stories for another time.

Nowadays, I'm lucky enough to write comics, and have

written for everything from The Beano, the comic that first hooked me even before that fateful library trip, to *SuperMansion*, based on the Bryan Cranston and Chris Pine-starring animated series. I'm even working on a *Space Team* comic series, which I plan to bring out at the tail end of 2018.

The Sidekicks Initiative is, I suppose, my love letter to comics, celebrating the lunacy and absurdity of the various comic book characters and the universes they inhabit. If you had half as much fun reading it as I had writing it, then I'll be happy.

If you enjoyed it, I'd really appreciate you leaving the book a review. If you *really* enjoyed it, you might want to consider telling your friends about it, getting the logo tattooed on your face or supporting me on Patreon in return for various goodies.

If you hated it, then sorry for wasting your time, but respect for sticking it out all the way to the end. You're made of stern stuff. I'm proud of you.

Until next time.

Best space wishes,

Barry J. Hutchison